BAHAMA MAMA

BOOK 2 OF THE KEY WEST ESCAPE SERIES

TRICIA LEEDOM

fhp
FIREFLY HILL PRESS

Printed in the United States of America

Firefly Hill Press, LLC

4387 W. Swamp Rd #565

Doylestown, PA 18902

www.fireflyhillpress.com

info@fireflyhillpress.com

Print ISBN: 9781945495021

E-Book ISBN: 9781943858125

BOOKS IN THE KEY WEST ESCAPE SERIES BY TRICIA LEEDOM

Rum Runner - Book 1

Bahama Mama - Book 2

Passion Punch - Book 3 - Coming 2019

Bahama Mama is dedicated to my mama, Joyce, and my godson, Steven, with love.

CHAPTER ONE

R ed Rocks Canyon, Mojave Desert, Nevada
Anders Ostergaard would be the first to admit he'd lived a golden life. From his high school years as star quarterback to his first hit country record at the age of 21 to multiple CMA and Grammy awards. Nothing seemed out of his reach—except for the piece of limestone protruding from the cliff above his head.

He had the long arms to match his 6'2" frame, but the smooth, rounded handhold jutting from the overhang was four feet beyond his reach. He'd dealt with this boulder problem plenty of times in the gym with a plush mat beneath him ready to break his fall. He needed to launch himself toward the handhold and grab on, but out in the open, with nothing but a rope, a few well-used bolts, and the Lord on his side, the risk to his life was significantly greater.

"Come on. You got this!" The words of encouragement shouted from some distance away echoed his own thoughts. His friend and trainer, pro mountain climber Jack Moser, stood on the cliff's ledge 100 feet below, belaying the rope and ready to brace himself in the event Anders made a dumbass mistake and fell.

They'd started early this morning when there was still a nip in the desert air, but it was approaching noon and the sun was on his back, baking him through his thin cotton T-shirt. He'd gotten cocky and hadn't bothered to clip the last carabiner when he had the chance. Now, eight feet above that safety point, he was wedged into the crease where the overhang started, his left hand jammed into a crack and the fingertips of his right crimping a one-inch ledge. His left foot was braced securely while his right sought purchase on a pucker in the sheer wall.

"Shake it out!" Jack called up to him.

Anders shifted his weight to the left so he could remove his right hand from the ledge. His tense arm dangled by his side and his muscles sighed with relief as he shook them out. The lyrics to one of his hit songs ran through his head. *You break my chops. You strike a nerve. You drive me up a wall 'til I'm hanging off a ledge, trying not to fall...*

He'd written it about his ex-wife but it applied to his current situation just fine.

The view sure was pretty. Jutting rust-colored peaks and dusty valleys patched with green spread out beneath an endless blue sky. A man could breathe out here. He took a deep breath to illustrate the thought and smiled.

He reached back and crimped the ledge again, then let his weight settle into his lower body. His core muscles locked and he crouched a bit, coiling his leg muscles tightly and making ready to spring. "Gimme some tension," he shouted to Jack.

The rope pulled tauter but still gave him enough slack for the big move he was about to attempt.

"You got this," Jack shouted up to him. "You can stick it."

"If I don't, give my love to my fans." Anders meant it as a joke, but a sudden tightening in his gut made him add a little hoarsely, "And my son."

He lunged for the handhold, cleared the four feet, and caught the rounded protrusion cleanly. There wasn't much to grip, but his hands were strong and the chalk on his fingers reduced the slippage. Adrenaline shot through his body, making him feel weightless as he dangled more than one hundred and fifty feet above the canyon floor.

This was what he sought. This was why he climbed. He did it to feel alive. To feel free. To feel what it was like to be himself and nothing else.

He shifted his body from side to side, building momentum until he could swing out to the right and catch the nearest handhold. The heel of his right foot hooked a foothold. He pulled himself over and settled into a more secure spot where he could rest a moment and then let out a big whoop. "Did you see that?"

"Hell, yeah, I did! You should give up singing and do this full time."

"Become a climbing bum?" Anders laughed. "Hell, I reckon there's better money in singing."

"But the women are hotter in climbing. Nothing better than a tight ass and a firm grip."

"You got a point there."

Still chuckling, Anders raised the rope and reached out for the carabiner near his left shoulder. Before he could clip the rope through the gate, his left foot slipped and he started to slide down the cliff face. Tiny bits of dirt and rock came loose as sharp edges snared his clothes and scraped his skin. He scrambled to grab another handhold, but he was moving too fast. Then, suddenly, he was airborne.

His stomach dipped, threatening to expel the granola bar he'd snacked on twenty minutes ago, but he kept it down and steeled himself waiting for the rope to stop his fall. His teeth snapped together as he was jerked backward violently. Slivers of fear darted through his system when the world tilted upside down. His head slammed against something solid and pain blasted through his skull a moment before everything went black.

"What happened?" was the first thing Anders had asked when he came to in the medical helicopter. Jack was by his side, his round baby face filled with concern. He'd explained that the foothold had crumbled beneath Anders' weight. He'd fallen fifteen feet, flipped upside down, and slammed into the cliff wall. He had a nice lump on the back of his head along with a concussion.

By the end of the day, the tabloids had reported his death, distraught fans were holding vigils, and his record sales had skyrocketed. Despite a pounding headache and a bruised cut on his right cheekbone, Anders managed to take a half-decent selfie and Tweeted it with the words: I'm not dead yet. Or so they tell me.

A couple days recuperating in the hospital were more than he'd needed, but his record label had stuck their noses in. They'd never been crazy about his choice of recreational activities and they were less than thrilled to learn he hadn't been wearing a helmet. As punishment, they demanded he stay put for a full week. They also postponed the next two months of concert tour dates and ordered him to take a vacation. A relaxing one. No extreme sports allowed. So, he'd upgraded his Vegas hotel room to the presidential suite and settled in for an extended stay on their dime.

But one week into his convalescence, Anders was already growing itchy.

"Come with me to the club that's opening tonight." Casey Conway knelt on the bed in front of him in a pink camisole top and G-string, biting her cherry-red bottom lip. Five days ago, the young starlet had sought him out when she'd learned they were staying at the same hotel. She'd ditched her friends to party with him and the paparazzi had already snapped some pics and labeled them the next Hollywood "it" couple.

They were hardly an item. She was beautiful—the typical tight, blonde California girl—but she was at a different place in her life. Young and ambitious, Casey was hungry for the spotlight while he was more interested in keeping a low profile when he wasn't on tour. He'd been there once himself though, and he understood Casey's goals even if his were no longer the same. She was a fun person to be around and a pleasant distraction but nothing more.

The feeling was mutual. Casey was getting what she wanted —a career boost from all the free press generated just from being spotted with him.

Plucking his guitar, Anders lounged back against the leather headboard in nothing but his boxers and a pair of white cotton socks. It was mid-afternoon though it felt like midnight. Time was irrelevant in Vegas. He used to like that about the city, but now it just made him feel tired.

Bright-eyed and restless, Casey tugged on his knee. "C'mon. Let's have some fun."

"I thought that's what we've been doing."

Her earnest expression melted into a soft, sexy pout. "We don't have to stay long. We'll walk the red carpet, have one drink, and then bail." Her hand brushed his inner thigh and headed north. "I'd be *very* grateful."

"Yeah? How grateful?

"Well, I can give you a little preview now."

He stopped strumming when cool fingers dipped beneath the loose leg of his boxer shorts and cupped his partial erection. At thirty-seven, he didn't recover anywhere near as quickly as he did when he was twenty-two, but his body was trying. His heart wasn't in it though.

He rested a hand over the lump in the front of his cotton shorts to hold her hand still. "The downside to dating a man fifteen years your senior is longer breaks between tango sessions."

"Then you'll go with me?" She gave him a squeeze that made him gasp and not in a good way.

A knock at the door saved him from having to answer. She sat up. "Finally!"

"Are you expecting someone?"

"Room service. I called while you were napping earlier." She leaned forward for a kiss and he obliged. She had a nice mouth. "Sleepyhead."

"Can't help it. You tucker me out." He grinned.

"Mmm," she purred and then gave him a mischievous grin. Mocking his Alabamian accent, she said, "Come to the party with me and I'll tucker you out until the cows come home."

"I don't talk like that."

"Yes, you do, and I like it." She kissed him one more time before she climbed off the bed. Sliding on his abandoned T-shirt, she padded barefoot out of the bedroom.

Anders set his guitar aside and followed.

"Took you long enough," she said to the male server who was wheeling in a cart containing a covered plate and a bottle of champagne with two glasses.

The chubby guy was busting out of his uniform and staring at Casey in awe. Very unprofessional, but then again, Casey Conway was a total knockout. How could he blame the guy for looking? His name tag said "Kwame." An unusual name for a pasty-faced white kid, but what did Anders know? His friend's sweet baby daughter was named Jezebel.

When Kwame's gaze lingered a bit too long on the lady's bare thighs, Anders cleared his throat. The server's head snapped up and his eyes bugged out of his head as if he was surprised to see Anders there.

"I called almost an hour ago," Casey said as Kwame placed

the cart in front of the sofa and nervously struggled to uncork the champagne.

"I'm sorry it took so long, Miss Conway." He reached back to tuck an escaped shirttail into his pants.

Casey relented, treating him to the smile that was making her famous. "I know it's not your fault. The kitchen in this place is ridiculously slow."

Kwame paused over the still-uncorked bottle to stare at Casey again. He used the cloth napkin that was wrapped around the bottle to mop his forehead.

"I hope you don't mind." Casey turned her pretty grin on Anders. "I charged it to the room."

"I don't mind." He came forward, took the bottle away from the server, and uncorked it himself in two efficient moves. The poor guy was sweating like a pig in a smokehouse. Anders put a hand on Kwame's shoulder and escorted him to the door where he offered him a couple of twenties. "For your trouble, boss."

"No trouble at all, sir."

Anders winked as was his habit and closed the door. When he turned around, Casey was already sitting down to eat.

"You're too nice." She reached for the bottle of champagne. "He couldn't even do his job properly. Seriously. Where do they find these people?"

As Anders watched her fill a flute glass, he had a PTSD-style flashback to his honeymoon in Cabo. Greer's complaining drove him nuts. He'd ended up sleeping on the couch that week just so he could fall asleep without having to listen to her bitch about her day. That should have clued him in to how the rest of their marriage was gonna go, but he was too damn stubborn back then to admit he'd made a mistake. He shook off the memory and reminded himself that what he and Casey had was only temporary. "What did you order?"

"A burger. You want a bite?" When he made a face, she said, "What's wrong?"

"I'm a strict pescetarian."

"What's that one again? I forget."

"Like a vegetarian, but I eat fish."

"Oops. My bad." She snapped open her linen napkin and draped it across her lap before reaching for the mini ketchup bottle beside her plate.

"It's all right. I'll order something after I take a shower."

"It smells awesome. You don't know what you're missing."

He hadn't eaten meat since he was fourteen, and he wasn't about to start now. "I'll pass, but thanks for the offer."

"So, you're coming to the party with me?"

"I wasn't planning on it, but I guess it won't hurt to stop in for one drink."

Casey let out a little squeal of delight and clapped her hands. "I heart you, Anders Ostergaard." She blew him a kiss.

He caught himself mid-cringe. *Only temporary.* Snorting instead, he gave her a wink and ducked into the bathroom.

Reaching into the marble-walled stall, he turned on the water before slipping out of his socks and boxers. He took his time shaving in front of the mirror above the sink, wiping the glass down when it started to fog up. Dropping the hand towel, he studied his reflection in the glass. He looked tired. And old as shit. Well, maybe not that old. But he was getting up there. The crow's feet around his eyes could attest to that. His twenties were long behind him now and forty was staring at him from the other side, way too close for comfort.

Sitting around doing nothing was starting to get to him, but he wasn't growing restless for the limelight. He wasn't missing the road or the thrill of being on stage performing to 40,000 fans like he thought he would. Maybe it was time to start focusing on other goals. Touring was a little easier now that he owned his own plane and could fly everywhere he needed to be. If he cut back to two or three months a year on the road, he could focus on getting his indie label up and running and signing a few new artists. It was something to consider. It might take the edge off his boredom and fill the void that had started eating at him long before his accident.

His face was still covered with splotches of shaving cream when he finally stepped into the shower. As the steaming hot water hit his back, he closed his eyes and let his head fall forward. God that felt good. Maybe he just needed a vacation. A real one. Someplace remote and tropical where he could kick back with a frosty umbrella drink and a fishing pole and recharge his batteries. He'd received an email invitation to his brother's wedding in Key West. It had been sitting in his inbox for the past couple months but he hadn't bothered to respond. Mostly because he hadn't made up his mind whether or not to attend. He needed to decide soon because it was coming up in a week. A jaunt down to the Florida Keys would help clear his mind so he could figure things out. His brother Jimmy was an enthusiastic supporter of island therapy. Anders chuckled. It would be good to see his little brother again.

He still couldn't believe Jimmy of all people was getting married. Just the thought of being shackled to one woman again gave Anders hives. He scratched the imaginary itch on his collarbone and then lathered an armpit with soap. He'd thought he was ready for wedded bliss once, but the daily drama of trying to compromise with a demanding woman who was way too serious had been exhausting. The relationship with Greer had never come easy, and it only got harder with marriage. Part of him wished things had worked out differently for Obie's sake, but it was better to grow up with two happy divorced parents than two miserable married ones. He knew that better than anyone.

Stepping out of the shower, Anders wrapped a towel around his waist. He didn't bother with clothes because they wouldn't be on for very long if the little minx in the next room had anything to say about it.

The steam from the shower billowed out ahead of him as he

opened the door and came into the living room. Expecting to find Casey still nibbling on her meal, he was grinning with anticipation. Being with heart-stoppingly gorgeous women like Greer and Casey could be a real headache sometimes, but it sure was fun. His smile faded as he stopped short and looked down. Casey was sprawled on the floor in an unnatural position. Her long blonde hair flung forward over her face in a tangled mass. She was as still as the—

"Casey?"

She didn't move. Not a hair. Was this a joke? Or some kind of twisted sex fantasy?

"Come on now. Quit playing. If you want to tango again before we go out, you're wasting time."

Still nothing. He looked past her to the food cart. The champagne flute had turned over onto her plate. Bubbly liquid pooled around the hamburger, which was missing only one bite. He'd seen Casey eat. She wasn't shy about pounding down food and she'd been ravenous. She wouldn't have wasted the meal for a silly game.

As his mind wrapped itself around the other possibility, something sour curdled in his empty stomach.

Going to her, he dropped to his knees and pushed aside the wild tangle of hair that shrouded her face. White foam bubbled from her lips. Her eyes were wide and unfocused, staring unseeingly at nothing.

"Oh my God." Hands trembling, Anders gripped her head and shouted, "Casey!"

CPR. He knew how to do that. Rolling her onto her back, he tilted her chin up and stuck his fingers into her mouth to clear the air passage. Frothy bile leaked down the sides of her bruised face as he pinched her nose and bent to put his mouth to hers. He blew two deep breaths into her lungs and checked for a pulse. Finding none, he compressed her chest thirty times, being careful to press hard enough but not too hard. She was so small, so delicate. His big hand spanned the width of her torso.

After the second repetition, he realized he needed to call 911. Not because Casey needed medical attention, but because she was gone. The purple splotches on her face weren't bruises. it was blood from her brain settling into her face as the process of lividity began. Who knew binging on true crime shows would give him the knowledge to identify something like this in real life? *Shit*. Lividity meant she'd likely been dead for about 30 minutes when he found her.

Checking her pulse one more time and finding none, he sat up on his haunches. "Jesus Christ," he muttered and rubbed his face. Still naked as a baboon's ass, he stood up and went to the phone.

"Mr. Ostergaard, how may I help you?"

"Call 911."

"Are you unwell, sir?"

Oh, Jesus, how did he explain this? "Someone is dead. Might have been an allergic reaction to something she ate. I-I don't know." Anders looked back at Casey and a wave of intense sadness swept through him.

Self-preservation born of years of experience in the public eye had prevented him from making the call to 911 himself. The last thing he wanted was a recording of his voice reporting Casey's death to become fodder for the news media to sensationalize. If she'd had a chance, he would have risked it, but Casey was beyond help now.

When he hung up the phone, he sat heavily on the sofa and squeezed his eyes closed as he drove his fingers through his wet hair. It was hard to look at Casey like that. Her beauty and vivacity preserved in a queer state of suspended animation. His heart hurt for her, for her family and friends, and for her fans. He forced himself to open his eyes and look at her again.

"God. What happened to you, darlin'?"

CHAPTER TWO

"I t wasn't an allergic reaction or a drug overdose unless the drugs were laced with poison," the police detective said a short while later when he entered the vacant hotel room where Anders had been asked to wait. Soon after the police arrived, a uniformed officer had escorted Anders away from the scene and into the empty suite across the hall. He'd been sitting on the sofa, a duplicate of the one in his room, staring at the floor in shock when Guy Dougherty strolled in and introduced himself. He was a grizzled Colombo type who had seen it all and was surprised by nothing.

Anders pulled himself out of his daze and looked up in surprise. "Poison? How can you be so sure?"

"Someone likely tampered with the food," the detective said, ignoring the question.

"But how do you know it wasn't a food allergy?"

"Trust me, son. I've been in this business long enough to know the difference. I'd guess strychnine based on the way her body is contorted. Nasty stuff."

What the hell? Anders frowned. "Strychnine? Is it that common?"

"No, it isn't. But back in the early days when I was a fledgling detective, I investigated a case where a jealous wife offed her husband by slipping rat poison into his pot roast. The way that poor bastard looked when we found him—" The detective pressed his lips together and shook his head curtly. "It's not something you forget. I hadn't seen anything like it until today. Let's just say there are more humane ways of getting rid of someone."

Anders' gut burned as he wracked his brain trying to figure out how something like this could have happened. A mistake in the kitchen? Meat contaminated at the factory? Or intentional poisoning? He shook his head at the thought. "No. No one murdered Casey with rat poison. She wasn't a bad person. It had to be an accident."

Scratching his whiskered chin, the detective nodded. "You're right, it probably wasn't rat poison. Strychnine hasn't been used in rodenticides since the early nineties. The compound is more difficult to obtain now but not impossible thanks to the internet. Of course, there'll be no way of knowing for certain if it was strychnine poisoning until the medical examiner does his thing."

"This is crazy." Anders stood up. He was starting to get angry at the skeptical way the detective kept eyeballing him as if maybe Casey was murdered and he had something to do with it. "Casey Conway was not poisoned. At least not intentionally, like you're suggesting."

Dougherty ignored him, muttering to himself as he jotted down some notes in a little spiral notebook. "The poison was added somewhere between the kitchen and the penthouse. Did you happen to see the server who delivered the food, Mr. Ostergaard?"

Anders drove his fingers through his still-damp hair and glanced at the uniformed officer who had quietly entered the suite while the Dougherty was talking. "Yeah, I saw him. He was a chubby guy. About 5'6", brown hair and blue eyes. His uniform was way too tight."

"Doesn't sound like any of the employees we've questioned so far, Detective," the officer said. He was a young guy. Looked barely old enough to shave. Like a kid playing cop. His nametag said D. Ramirez. "They're all impeccably dressed. One of them mentioned having to pass a strict inspection before they're let out on the floor."

Anders was only half listening to the cop. He was wracking his brain for any other details that stood out to him about the server. Anything that seemed off. "His name was Kwame," Anders remembered suddenly.

The detective turned around.

"He didn't exactly look like a Kwame, but you never know. Still, it's possible he could have been impersonating a hotel employee."

"Anything is possible. We'll look into it." Dougherty tucked the notepad into the inside pocket of his faded corduroy sports jacket and turned to Ramirez. "I'd like to take a look at the surveillance cameras. Ask the security guys to cue up the time-frame of Miss Conway's death, and I'll be down to look at the tapes as soon as I finish up here with Mr. Ostergaard."

"I'll take care of it." The officer nodded, but hesitated, fidgeting as if there was something more he wanted to say.

"You got a personal problem there, Ramirez?"

Color reddened the kid's cheeks. He gestured toward Anders. "I just wanted to say, I'm a big fan, Mr. Ostergaard. I grew up listening to your music. My mama just adores you."

Too many years of fan encounters in odd and sometimes embarrassing places made Anders oblivious to Ramirez's inappropriate timing. Anders smiled automatically and thanked him for the compliment. "Would you like an autograph?"

Ramirez's face lit up, and he started to reach for the notepad in his utility belt.

"Put it away, officer." Dougherty groused. "You have work to do and Mr. Ostergaard is grieving." He said the latter as if he didn't really believe it, raising Anders' hackles again.

Waiting as the dejected Ramirez left the room, Anders crossed his arms and narrowed his eyes at the detective. "Mr. Dougherty, should I call my attorney?"

The detective looked mildly surprised. "Why? Do you have something to hide?" The two men stared for a moment sizing each other up. Finally, Dougherty relented. "You aren't under arrest here, Mr. Ostergaard. I just have a few more questions for you."

"Fine. Ask them." He dropped his arms and took a seat on the couch again.

"Is there any particular reason you didn't order anything, Mr. Ostergaard?"

Anders frowned and started to tell him to stick his questions up his ass, but the detective raised a hand, interrupting him. "Just a routine question. I'm trying to paint the scene."

Anders snorted and glared at him. The muscles in his shoulder blades were tight as rocks, and he was losing his legendary cool. He took a deep breath through his nose and exhaled before answering. "Casey ordered room service without my knowledge and didn't order anything for me. She offered me half her burger, but I turned it down."

"And why was that? Not hungry?"

Anders shrugged. "I don't eat red meat."

"Do you have any enemies, Mr. Ostergaard?"

"Me?" His head snapped up in surprise. His momma always used to say you get more bees with honey, so he'd adapted that belief to his career and that was one of the reasons he'd made it as far as he did. People liked him. Some said it was his charisma. Some said he had star quality. Some credited his talent. But his success all came down to him being a hell of a nice guy to everyone. Even the people who didn't deserve it. "I don't have any enemies that I'm aware of."

Dougherty tilted his head to the side and cocked a thick gray eyebrow. "The food was delivered to your hotel suite. It's logical to suspect you may have been the intended target."

Anders shook his head. "No, it's a widely known fact I'm pescetarian."

"What's that?"

"Like a vegetarian, but I eat fish."

"Yet, Miss Conway didn't know this?"

Anders' eyes narrowed in irritation. "She forgot."

"Any business deals go south recently? Any jealous ex-girl-friends?"

He was friends with his ex-girlfriends. He always ended things amicably. *Except for Greer*, a little voice in the back of his mind whispered. Greer was a lot of things. Ambitious. Ruthless. A heartless bitch. But she wasn't a killer. "No. I can't think of anyone who would want to do me harm."

Dougherty nodded once. "Where were you when the death occurred?"

"In the shower." Anders had managed to throw on clothes before the police had arrived.

"That's why your hair is wet?"

He was tempted to compliment the detective on his excellent deduction skills but checked the sarcasm. He just wanted to get this over with. He had calls to make. And he needed more time alone to process what had happened.

"How about Miss Conway? Did she have any enemies? Anyone have it out for her?"

"I honestly don't know her all that well." The words left a guilty aftertaste in his mouth, but they were the truth. For the first time in a long time, he regretted the philandering lifestyle he'd chosen.

A smirk tugged at the corner of Dougherty's mouth. "The rumpled sheets on the bed in the next room suggest otherwise."

As if he'd never heard of two strangers sleeping together in

Vegas. Anders didn't like the salacious gleam in the detective's eyes, but he ignored it and pressed on. Exhaling, he laced his fingers and leaned forward resting his arms on his thighs. "We were just having some fun. I met her in the hotel lobby five days ago. She came here with friends. Two women. We met up with them for drinks last night."

Dougherty scratched his whisker-covered jaw. "The women. Did they join you in your hotel suite last night for the, uh, fun?"

Anders gritted his teeth but spoke calmly. "No."

"That'll be all for now, Mr. Ostergaard. You'll need to move to another room. The other is a crime scene and is closed pending the investigation. Oh, and don't leave town."

Anders' head snapped up. "For how long? I thought I wasn't a suspect."

Dougherty paused by the door. "In a homicide investigation, everyone is a suspect." His wiry brows furrowed over shrewd brown eyes that missed nothing. "You were the last person to see Casey Conway alive and for that reason alone you're a key factor in solving her murder. Don't go anywhere until we tell you you're free to go."

Anders' jaw tightened as he maintained eye contact with Dougherty. "You have my full cooperation, Detective."

Anders had just settled into his new room, a regular suite on an upper floor, when his publicist called. He wasn't going to answer, but he knew Selena Fry wouldn't quit calling until he picked up the phone. He wasn't ready to make a statement to the press. Not yet. It was too soon. Only two hours had passed since he'd discovered Casey Conway's lifeless body. They should have been getting spruced up for the red carpet at that club Casey was so hot to make an appearance at. He'd agreed to go because he had nothing better to do with his time and had difficulty saying no to beautiful women. And Casey was one of the prettiest he'd ever seen.

What a waste.

He sat heavily on the edge of the bed and put the phone to his ear. The only person he'd spoken to in the outside world so far had been his manager. Apparently, Tuck had wasted no time passing the news along "Yeah?"

"Did she OD?"

"Hello to you too, Fry."

"If there were drugs involved, I need to know so I can be ready for questions from the media. How did she acquire them?"

"Slow down. There were no drugs." He ran his fingers through his hair. "The police think she was poisoned."

"The police know the cause of death already?"

"The detective was just guessing, but he said he'd seen deaths by poison before. He thinks I was the intended target." That still rattled him. If he was the intended target, did that mean he was still in danger? He shook off the chilling thought. He really didn't want to hire a bodyguard. He only used them when he was out on tour. But maybe if he had employed one— He didn't finish the thought. He could still see Casey's beautiful, twisted body on the floor as clear as if she was right there in front of him. The sorrow and regret were still too raw for him to travel down the road of what-ifs.

"That's ridiculous." Fry snorted in his ear. "Wait. Do you think someone is trying to kill you?"

Anders shook his head and stared at the wall. The gaudy gold and black brocade wallpaper came into focus and the sight of it made him nauseous. He stood up quickly, suddenly feeling trapped and anxious to be anywhere but Vegas. "I have to get out of here."

"Where are you? Are you in danger?"

Anders paced the floor, traveling to the window and back

again. "No. I'm fine. I mean the hotel. I just need some air, but the damn press is already flooding the lobby."

"Stay where you are. I'm on my way." Rustling in the background made it sound as if she was already packing.

"You don't need to fly to Vegas, Fry."

"I insist. We're going to need a game plan, especially if the police make you their number one suspect. Bad press is good press, but bad press in relation to a murder charge is OJ territory. People are quick to be judge, jury, and executioner. When word of this spreads, there's going to be a full-on media frenzy."

A knock came at the door. Anders stood and headed toward it. "I'll be fine."

"Look. You've just been through a traumatic experience. You need someone to shield you from what's coming. I don't need to tell you there will be fallout. You know this has the potential to destroy your reputation and ruin your career."

Anders looked through the peephole and saw the last person he would have ever expected to find standing on the other side of the door. "Holy shit," he murmured as his shoulder blades tightened and started to itch.

"Exactly. I'm coming to Vegas." Fry hung up the phone.

Once she set her mind to something, there was no stopping her. That was one of the reasons he liked her so much.

But Anders had bigger problems at the moment. Stuffing the cell phone into the back pocket of his jeans, he opened the door and stared at the deceptively frail woman standing in the hall. She looked exactly as she had the last time he'd accidentally crossed paths with her in Santa Monica nearly four years ago, with a tight, smooth face courtesy of Botox, silver-blonde hair swept up in a fancy bun, and expressive deep-set blue eyes that seemed to glare perpetually with disdain. At least at him anyhow.

"Martha Mell. This is a surprise."

That was the understatement of the year. *What the hell was his ex-mother-in-law doing in Vegas?*

"I was directed to your penthouse suite by mistake. Can't say I was all that surprised to find two strapping young gentlemen from the coroner's office zipping up a body bag containing a dead stripper."

Anders' grip on the doorframe tightened, but he forced himself to maintain his composure. "She wasn't a stripper. Casey's death is a terrible tragedy."

"Casey? Casey Conway?" Martha's manicured silver eyebrows shot up. "That young actress you've been photographed with recently?"

"How do you know about Casey?"

"The two of you made the cover of Celeb Magazine's 'Most Intriguing Couples of the Year' issue. It came out yesterday. Greer was livid. She lost a role to Casey recently because the casting director said she was too long in the tooth to play the ingénue. It really got her goat."

Casey had mentioned something about the movie and how Greer was offered the part of her mother. He'd be lying if he didn't admit he enjoyed seeing her pretentious feathers ruffled once in a while. The smile that tugged at the corners of his mouth faded when he realized Casey would never get the chance to fulfill her dream of staring in her first major motion picture.

A damn waste.

Realizing he was being observed by a hawkeyed senior citizen with a taste for preying on people's weaknesses, he pulled himself together. "What do you want, Martha?"

"Theodore and I are moving to Scottsdale. We've found a darling little community for retirees, but unfortunately, they have a strict policy about children. No overnight visits."

"Good for you. So?"

"When Oberon isn't away at school, he lives with Theodore and I in Sacramento."

"Where the hell is his mother?" Anders leaned forward,

scowling. Like her daughter, Martha always managed to bring out the worst in him.

The prickly little woman didn't appear the least bit cowed. "Greer is working. She's been very busy lately despite losing a role to that twit. She has three movies coming out this year and two more already scheduled for next."

Gripping the doorframe like he intended to tear it off the wall, he growled, "She sued me for full custody of my son and you're telling me she doesn't even bother with him? That's just like her."

"Don't suddenly play the concerned father, it looks ridiculous on you. I do recall you signed your rights away before the case even went to court."

"Look—"

She put up a hand to stop him. "I didn't come here to argue with you. I'm actually glad you're showing an interest in your son. It gives me hope my trip here wasn't in vain."

"What are you talking about?"

"As I explained, Theodore and I can't take Oberon with us to Scottsdale. And his mother is booked for the summer. That would leave Oberon at home with only the staff and a live-in nanny to look after him. I believe he'd be better off with family."

"I agree."

"Good. Then you can take him for the summer."

"Wait, I never said that." Panic fluttered in Anders' chest. A Vegas hotel was not the ideal place for a kid. What the hell would he do with him? And after what happened with Casey, he didn't want to risk putting Obie in the same situation. If he'd been the one to eat that tainted hamburger... Anders didn't want to think about that.

"Why can't you take him?" Martha frowned. "Your summer tour has been canceled and the record company is forcing you to take a sabbatical. That story was all over the internet too. It's what gave me the idea to bring Oberon to you."

"Wait, Obie is here?"

She reached over and pulled a small boy into the frame of the doorway. As she did, time slowed down like a dramatic sequence in a music video. Oberon had been standing just out of view. Now he was standing in front of Anders, staring at the ground.

"Obie," Anders murmured and started to reach for him, but stopped when the boy flinched. It had been a very long time. Anders was practically a stranger. A lot could happen in two years, six months, and nine days. The little guy hadn't changed much though. His platinum blond hair was still trimmed into a neat bowl cut. He was small for his age and way too thin. Too pale, too, for a kid who'd been born and raised in California.

When Anders said his name, Oberon's head tilted back as his gaze traveled up the length of Anders. Slanted blue Ostergaard eyes blinked at him through bottle-thick, black, horn-rimmed glasses, and Anders' heart did a funny little flip. Despite his diminutive size, his son had the look of an Ostergaard.

Anders cleared the thickness from his throat. "Hi there."

When Oberon didn't answer, Martha said, "Don't bother expecting a response from him. He doesn't talk much. And he's particularly shy around strangers."

But I'm his father. Anders swallowed the words he wanted to say and stuck his hands in his pockets because he didn't know what else to do with them. He had trouble meeting the boy's unnervingly steady gaze.

"So, you'll take him for the summer?" Martha put her hand on the boy's back and guided him forward a step.

Anders gaped at her. His lifestyle wasn't conducive to children. He might have some time off right now, but he intended to get back to work and on the road as soon as possible. He couldn't take the boy on tour. He shouldn't take him at all. It wouldn't be fair to Oberon. Anders didn't know the first thing about being a father. His old man certainly hadn't been a good role model. Part of the reason Anders had kept his distance was so he wouldn't screw the kid up.

"Well?" Martha demanded.

An emotion flickered behind Oberon's magnified blue eyes. It was so subtle, if Anders had blinked, he would have missed it. Not fear, as he would have expected, but something more like hope. Or so he told himself.

The painful cramping in his chest was back. A thin sheen of sweat broke out on his forehead. He was pretty certain he was having a heart attack. It sure as hell felt like he was. He could think of a thousand reasons to ignore that flicker of emotion in his son's eyes and say no to Martha Mell. The dead body in his former hotel suite being reason numero uno. But those weren't the words that came out of his mouth.

"Yeah. He can stay."

CHAPTER THREE

ey West, Florida

Molly MacBain twisted her straw wrapper into a tight little rope. Sitting across from her in the two-person booth, her date stared at his utensils and fidgeted on the padded faux leather. Piped-in top-forty music filled the Grand-Canyon-sized gaps in their conversation.

"So," she dragged the word out slightly longer than intended, but talking to this man was like listening to a folk song that was six minutes too long. It was going nowhere and she just wanted it to end. "How long have you been on Couples.com?"

"A month."

Molly had been a member for five months but was a little embarrassed to admit it. It wasn't because she wasn't getting asked out on dates. She was. Just none of those first dates had led to a second one. "And what do you think of online dating so far?"

"It's okay."

When he didn't elaborate, Molly cleared her throat. "I've met a few nice men, but I just haven't clicked with anyone yet. My daughter says to give it a chance, so I'm trying."

She'd had four first dates prior to this one. All duds. Bachelor

Number One had shaken her hand when they met for lunch and then refused to let it go because he claimed he liked holding hands when he talked to people. *Just weird.* Bachelor Number Two was still mooning over his wife who'd left him for a woman. He was certain she'd grow bored and come back to him eventually. *Delusional.* Bachelor Number Three spent dinner ranting about how he longed to break his ex-girlfriend's neck for dumping him. *Psycho.* Bachelor Number Four provided a misleading picture on his profile. Molly had expected a man ten years younger and two-hundred pounds lighter. She might have gotten past his weight problem and thinning hair if he'd had a super personality. He hadn't, and she couldn't get past the food stains on his shirt or the fact he smelled like a cigar factory. *Gross!*

Bachelor Number Five sat before her now. Jeff Worth, an IT Specialist at Key West General Hospital and recent transplant from Canton, Ohio. He wouldn't be so bad if he would just relax.

At the mention of her daughter, life finally sprang into Jeff's dull brown eyes and his brow furrowed. "Wait, you have a daughter?"

Was he serious? "Um. Yeah. I talked about her in my profile. There's a picture of us in my photos."

"I thought that was your little sister."

Molly moistened her dry lips and looked down at her lap, gathering her patience before she pasted on a smile and looked at him again. "Didn't you read my profile summary? I explained I had a teenage daughter named Cheyenne. She'll be fifteen this month. That was a recent photo of us."

"Wow, you must have been really young when you had her. Did you get knocked up in high school?"

Molly bristled at the false assumption. "Excuse me?"

"It's cool. I meant it as a compliment."

She wiped the edges of her mouth with her napkin and returned it to her lap before she took a deep breath. "My ex and I started dating when I was sixteen. Trevor was older, but my parents really liked him. I married him right out of high school and had Cheyenne when I was nineteen."

"Are you divorced?"

"Yes." She smiled past gritted teeth. "That was in my profile as well."

"Oh," he said in a tone that sounded like *well, that changes things.*

Molly was going to ask him about it when the waitress popped up, her brassy voice interrupting the awkward conversation.

"How you doing tonight, folks? My name's Bea. Easy to remember, 'cause I'll *Bea* your server, get it?" She took a seat beside Molly, scooting into the tiny booth as if she was planning to join them for dinner. "Have you decided on your order?"

Moving over as far as she could to give the hippy, middle-aged woman more room, Molly looked at her sideways. "I'll have the petite filet and a baked potato, please."

"Sounds great. You want that spud loaded?"

"Sure."

"Butter. Sour cream. How about some bacon? I love the bacon here. It's thin and crispy just like bacon should be. I like to take it to go and munch on it in the car on the way home."

Molly wanted to smile at the absurdity of the situation. She glanced at Jeff to see if he shared her amusement, but his face was stoic and his deep-set eyes were dull and lifeless again. *Michigan J. Frog* came to mind.

"The bacon must be good then." Molly smiled at the waitress. "I'll try it. Thanks, Bea."

"You betcha. And for you, honey pie? What'll you have?"

"T-bone steak. Baked potato. Dry."

"You sure I can't get you an appetizer? Maybe a Bloomin' Onion?"

Molly shook her head. "No, thank you." She didn't want the date to last any longer than it had to. The only reason she'd stuck it out this far was because she was hoping to avoid another lecture from her precocious teenage daughter.

"Your dinner will be right up then. You kids have fun."

Molly watched the waitress go. She hated chain restaurants. Give her a local diner or dive any day. On an island filled with dozens of quirky, one-of-a-kind restaurants, Jeff had insisted on meeting at the Aussie steakhouse.

"So," she began again, gearing up for the fifth chorus. Or was this the sixth? It was always hard to tell with a run-on song. She leaned forward a little in the booth and smiled gently at her date, prepared to give him another chance. "What kind of music do you like?"

Jeff shrugged. "Anything but rap or country. I *hate* country."

Narrowing her eyes, Molly tilted her head to the side. "You do realize I'm a country music singer?"

His gaze lifted to hers. "I thought you said you owned a bookstore in town."

"I do. For almost a year now. But before that, I supported myself as a country singer for twelve years. I traveled all over the country singing in honkytonks, performing at state fairs… I even opened for Carrie Underwood once."

"Who?"

"She's a multi-Grammy-award-winning country music artist."

"Did you ever record an album?"

Pressing her lips together, Molly sat straighter in the booth. That was a touchy subject. "I had a little mouth to feed. Touring provided a regular income where knocking on doors and schmoozing record label executives in Nashville did not."

"And now you own a bookstore?"

"Yes."

"That's smart."

"How so?"

He lifted one shoulder in a partial shrug. "Not everyone knows when to give up on a lost cause."

Was he intentionally trying to be a jerk? She couldn't tell. Crossing her arms, she sat back in the booth and did her best to bite her tongue.

Nope, she couldn't leave it alone.

"I'm still a singer and musician. I headline at Dixie's Bar and Grille here in town two nights a week."

"Oh."

No apology? No sheepishness? She fought the urge to get up and storm out. The song was definitely over.

A server who wasn't their waitress Bea arrived with their food.

"That was quick." Molly gave the server a tight smile. She could hear Cheyenne's voice in her head saying: *Give the guy a chance, mom. Maybe he's just as nervous as you are.*

Molly forced herself to calm down and focused on her meal. She was on the second bite of her steak when a foul odor drifted toward her. For a moment, she thought it was her filet, but the sour, musky smell had the distinct scent of BO. She glanced across the table at Jeff and saw the telling stain spreading in a ring beneath his armpits. The guy was sweating like a glass of iced tea at a Labor Day picnic.

Molly put her fork down and the remnants of her anger dissipated into pity. "How's your steak?"

"Good."

Getting the man to talk was like persuading a cow to play poker.

"How's everything?" Bea returned, scooting Molly over in the booth again. The waitress pointed at Molly's plate. "Your potato looks delish. Did they put enough bacon on top?"

"Yes. It's yummy."

"Didn't I tell you? You enjoy it. You doing okay over there, honey pie?"

Jeff nodded.

"Good deal. You'll let me know if you need anything else. Okay?"

As Molly watched the waitress move off again, she grinned. "Gosh. That was weird. I thought she was going to offer to cut my meat."

Jeff just stared at her blankly, cartoon crickets chirping behind him. Strike three for having no sense of humor. Cheyenne was going to be so disappointed. She really didn't want Molly to be alone, but Molly didn't think that was such a terrible thing. As long as she had Cheyenne, a roof over her head, and a place to play music a couple of nights a week, life was good. She didn't need a man to make her happy.

When she got lonely, she had her celebrity crush to fantasize about. He never said the wrong thing, left the toilet seat up, or let her down. Her relationship with her music idol Anders Oster-gaard was the longest she'd ever had with a man. He was the most dependable type of boyfriend. A fictional one.

The remainder of the date passed in silence after Molly gave up trying. She took the rest of her meal to go and tried to decline Jeff's offer to walk her to her car. They stopped awkwardly beside the passenger side door. She had intended to put the white Styro-foam to-go container on the floor, but Jeff was in the way.

"So." He was the one to say it this time. "I had a really great time tonight."

He did?

"I'd like to see you again."

Now that was a pig in a pirate costume she wasn't expecting.

He stared at her with an overeager gleam in his dull brown eyes. Was he self-absorbed or just clueless when it came to reading body cues? She'd been edging away from him since they arrived at her car, clearly implying she wanted to leave. She felt sorry for him again. Maybe he was just really awkward around women, and she was being too hard on him. She didn't want to hurt his feelings, but she also didn't want to date him out of pity.

"Um," she said, fixing to take the chicken's way out. She wanted to tell him she would send him an email and then never send one, but her conscience wouldn't let her. So, she flat out lied instead. "Sure. I'd like that. Call me."

Dagnabit.

"Okay." He gave her an awkward hug.

"Okay. Goodnight." She smiled back a bit too brightly.

The teenage inquisition was waiting for Molly when she came through the door. Cheyenne was seated at the dinette table in the center of their kitchen-living room combo. Their modest two-bedroom apartment wasn't much, but it was home. It was a lot smaller than the ranch house they used to rent in Nashville, but they didn't have a lot of stuff. Most of the furniture and artwork had come with the rental. The two acoustic guitars on stands in the living room were Molly's as was the large painting hanging above the sofa. It was done by a good friend of hers from a photograph of Molly and her band on stage at the State Fair of Texas, the biggest exhibition of its kind in the USA. It was by far the largest audience she'd ever played for and one of the highlights of her career.

Her idol Anders Ostergaard was the headliner of the event, but he'd performed on the main stage and their paths never crossed.

"Well?" The teenager at the table looked up from her open laptop, one skeptical brown eyebrow raised in question. Her smooth mocha hair was tied back into a neat ponytail. She wore a conservative periwinkle blue top that brought out her freckles and matched her eyes. Cheyenne had inherited Molly's features, including her nose and dimpled smile, but that was where the comparisons ended. The demure teenager was a tall, lanky brunette, while Molly with her long, unruly red-gold curls was a curvy, 5'2".

As Molly dropped her purse by the door, she debated telling her daughter the truth but decided against it. "He was nice."

"But he had a lisp? Maybe a third eyeball on his forehead? Or wait, he wasn't tall enough?"

"Cheyenne Dallas MacBain, you can't force romance. You have no idea what it's like to connect with a man."

"Apparently, you don't either."

Molly paused in the process of kicking off her heels. One T.J. Maxx special dangled from her big toe. It landed on the floor with a clunk. Tears burned the back of her eyes. The jibe, which brushed too close to her deepest darkest fears, was even more hurtful coming from a naive and inexperienced fourteen-year-old girl. Molly blinked her eyes to clear them and took a deep breath. "I beg your pardon?"

The girl had the decency to look ashamed. "I'm sorry, it's just you always have an excuse why you didn't like this one or that one. I'm worried about you, Ma."

Placing the to-go container on the table, Molly pulled out the chair beside her daughter and sat. "There is nothing to be worried about, Cheyenne. I keep telling you that."

"I read an article recently that said ninety-three percent of women say being a mother is central to their identity and that's why many women sink into depression when their children leave the nest. I just don't want you to feel lost when I go away college."

"It's true you are my number one priority, but you're not central to my identity." At least, Molly didn't think so. Suddenly, she wasn't so sure. Did she identify herself as Cheyenne's mother first before Molly the country singer? Before Molly the bookstore owner? Before Molly the plucky redhead with a little too much junk in the trunk? She needed to go for a run. Her jeans had been starting to feel a bit too snug lately. She shifted uncomfortably in her seat. "Besides, you've only just finished your freshman year. We have three more years together before you go off to college. Don't worry about me, baby girl. I'll be fine."

"Ninety-one percent of the women surveyed said they don't have enough time for friends, hobbies, or their partners. I want you to have time for all that stuff."

"Well, they didn't survey me. Your statistics would have you believe real life fits into neat little boxes you can check off in a questionnaire, but it doesn't. Everyone's circumstances are different, and my priorities are unique to me. I do have time for myself. I have a regular gig at Dixie's and I meet my friends for lunch at least once a week. Having a man in my life would be nice, but it would take away from time I get to spend with you. Like you said, you'll be going off to college in a few years."

"I wouldn't mind." Cheyenne's gaze returned to the computer screen as she moved her finger around on the mouse pad.

Molly reached across the table to cover her daughter's bony wrist. Squeezing it gently, she said, "I know you wouldn't. And I know you had your hopes set on Jeff, by he's not for me, baby girl. I'm sorry."

Cheyenne nodded but didn't glance away from the screen. "Oh, my goodness!"

"What?"

"You know how April and I have been trying to solve that riddle? The one that was written on that old map that belonged to Sophie's father?"

"You haven't given up on finding that old treasure yet?"

Cheyenne pulled her gaze away from the computer screen to look at Molly like she'd just said the moon is purple and frogs eat cheese. "It's buried treasure, Ma. Why would I give up on it?"

"Oh, I don't know. Maybe because there is no such thing as the Firefly Emerald, and even if there was, I doubt very much it's still hidden where that dusty old map says." Molly got up and carried her leftovers into the kitchen. Grabbing a clean dish and fork off of the drying rack, she scraped the steak and baked potato onto the plate and popped it in the microwave. She was starving.

"Maybe you don't believe in it, but I do," Cheyenne said. "And April does too. I can't wait to tell her what I found."

"What does April Linus want with treasure? She's one of the richest teenagers on the planet." Spotting Cheyenne's dirty dinner dishes soaking in the sink, Molly rinsed off the remnants of the spaghetti sauce before sticking the plate and fork in the dishwasher.

"Oh, she's not in it for the money. She's just helping me figure out the riddle. I offered to split it with her, but she said I can keep it for myself."

"You realize if you find the treasure on someone's property you won't be able to just take it?"

Cheyenne blinked at her as if she'd never given it a thought. She probably hadn't. She might be a brilliant, straight-A honor student, but she was naive to the ways of the world. The girl opened her mouth and closed it again. "But that's not fair. It should be finders' keepers."

"I'm sure people will be grateful to you, and your name may even appear in the paper, but beyond that, you shouldn't expect to get rich from this."

Cheyenne blinked at her again before returning to her computer screen. "I just found a lead that suggests the location of the emerald is in the Bahamas. Can we go?"

"Of course not."

"What if April and I went? She'll be nineteen next week."

"No."

"But I'm almost fifteen, Ma. I can handle it. I won't be alone or anything."

Molly came back to the table with her plate of food in one hand and a drink in the other. "No, you are not going to the Bahamas with April Linus, and you're not going to Miami for the science fiction convention either, so get that out of your head too." Taking a bite of the tender, savory steak, Molly was happy to discover she hadn't over-nuked it. "Mmm," she said out loud. "This is actually really good."

"When are you going to start trusting me?" Cheyenne closed the laptop and leaned back in the chair with her arms crossed.

"I trust you. It's other people I don't trust."

"But how am I going to learn how to deal with people on my own if you don't trust me?"

Molly stopped chewing.

"The bus from Key West will drop me off one block from the sci-fi/fantasy convention. I'll spend a few hours there and catch the evening bus home. It's so easy. Why won't you let me go?"

"Because you're only fourteen years old and Miami is three hours away."

"I'm almost fifteen."

"It's not just about your age. We don't have enough money for trips to the Bahamas and excursions to Miami. We're barely scraping by as it is. You know that."

"But Ma—"

Molly opened her mouth to say *you're not going and that's the end of it* but caught herself just in time. Since when did she start resorting to clichés to parent her child? Lowering her fork, she looked at her daughter. "I'm doing the best I can here, Cheyenne. Please don't make me out to be the bad guy. Some things in life are negotiable, but not when they risk your safety or wellbeing."

"Fine." Cheyenne got up from the table so quickly she knocked her chair over. The cheap wood made a loud clatter when it hit the tile floor, but she didn't look back as she headed for her bedroom.

"Fine," Molly said to the empty table. She pushed her plate away because she suddenly wasn't hungry anymore. She hated having to play the part of the mean mom and putting a damper on her daughter's plans, but Molly was the adult in their relationship and that meant it was her job to say no whether she enjoyed it or not. Sometimes being a single parent sucked.

Cheyenne wasn't a bad kid. She was an excellent student, respectful to her teachers, honest, good-hearted, always punctual, and usually cleaned up after herself, but she was also shy and a bit socially awkward, and far too trusting. She didn't understand what might happen to them if Molly didn't come up with the rent each month. She'd always managed to keep a roof over their heads, even if it meant paying an extended visit to one of her many siblings or calling her mom and dad for money. Asking for help hurt her pride, but she'd always done what she needed to do to keep her daughter safe and happy.

Molly was fortunate that her big, loving, generous family was always willing to help, but it had been several years since she'd had to call her siblings for anything other than a hello, and Mom and Dad were retired now and living on a fixed income. Molly had to be even more careful with cash and that meant saying no to their wants and picking and choosing their needs.

It was tough saying no when what she really wanted was to give her daughter the world.

CHAPTER FOUR

S ummer in Florida was a lousy time of year to take up jogging again. Molly shoved her soggy hair out of her eyes and sprinted across a crosswalk as if she could outrun the rain. The cute, curly red-gold ponytail she'd tied on top of her head now shrouded her face like a medieval helmet. When she'd made the decision to go for a run this morning, she hadn't thought it through. She'd just been thinking how she was only fitting into her fat pants these days. Fat being a relative word. She was only a size eight, but she'd be into a ten soon if she wasn't careful. The morning had been a balmy eighty degrees and sunny when she left her apartment, but she'd forgotten she lived in the Keys where the only predictable thing about the weather was that it wasn't. She was paying the price for her mistake, dashing over a puddle on the sidewalk as another boom of thunder made the ground tremble beneath her feet.

Fat raindrops pummeled her face, her body, and the pavement, and everything else in their way. Her squeaking sneakers made her increasingly aware of her appearance. Her purple terrycloth jogger capris had taken on water, causing her ass to sag like a baby with a loaded diaper. She was self-conscious of the *squish, squish, squishing* sound she made as she extended her stride and hustled up the street.

She'd set off for Old Town that morning with the intention of challenging herself to a three-mile loop. Though her pace was slow and she was huffing and puffing, she wasn't as out of shape as she'd assumed and managed to find her groove. She'd just made it to Duval when the storm came out of nowhere. Running all the way home in an electrical storm wasn't the smartest idea and she didn't have keys to the bookstore. Or cash for a cab. Most businesses weren't open at this hour of the morning, but she knew Sue would be at Dixie's. She and her husband Oscar were early risers. They'd likely already be at work prepping for the lunch crowd.

Dixie's had been closed for renovations since the end of May, but the place had reopened a few days ago in time for Sophie and Jimmy's wedding. The bar and grille wasn't as flashy as the other buildings in the neighborhood. Like the pastel pink house on the next block with its peaked roof and gingerbread shutters, or the yellow Victorian B&B up the street with its twin whitewashed porches. Dixie's was a squat, white stucco building with a flattop roof and a red neon sign that stretched across the front windows.

The owner, Jimmy Panama, used to say customers didn't come to Dixie's for the atmosphere. They came for the food. But since becoming engaged to Sophie, an English socialite, the good ol' boy from Alabama had started sprucing up the place.

Molly spotted the lights inside the building as she came around the corner. Grinning, she paused to let a car pass. A bolt of lightning streaked through the sky above her head and struck something on the next street. She instinctively ducked, as if that was going to save her from a strike. The static electricity in the air raised the tiny hairs on her arms and gave her goose bumps. Smelling something burning, she shivered and dashed across the street. When she shoved open the brand-new glass front door, which didn't stick like the old one had, a roiling squall of water, wind, and leaves followed her inside.

"Dagnabit, that's a hootenanny of a storm. My goodness gracious."

"What are you doing here?" Sue stopped short just outside the kitchen door holding a steaming pot of coffee in her hand. The Alaskan native wore her long, silver-streaked brown hair in a single braid that skimmed her lower back. Her wardrobe consisted of tank tops and long floral skirts, and a well-worn pair of steel-toed combat boots she'd brought with her from her home state. She was a direct, no-nonsense kind of person and Molly usually appreciated her brutal honesty—except in moments like these. "You look like hell."

Molly shoved her hair helmet away from her eyes to see her friend better. "I was out for a run and got caught in the storm. Why are you looking at me like that? I know I look scary but—"

"You've got to go."

"Pardon me?"

Shooting a nervous look in the direction of Jimmy's office, Sue set down the pot and came around the mahogany bar that ran most of the length of the back wall.

"I mean it. You've got to go." She put her hand on Molly's shoulder and turned her around. "You can't be here right now."

Molly faced the door but dug in her heels. Her soggy sneakers emitted a sad squish. "Oh, my God, why not? It's not like you to toss a person in need out on the street. What's going on, Sue?"

Sue pressed her lips together tightly and shot another glance toward the office. "Sophie hasn't had the chance to tell you yet. She was going to talk to you tonight." She put her arms around Molly's shoulders and tried to guide her toward the door again. "I'll give you a ride home, but you have to wait outside while I get my keys."

A crack of thunder loud enough to rattle the windows made the suggestion even more ludicrous and out of character for Sue.

"What? No!" Molly dug in her rubber soles again. "Stop it. That's crazy. What's Sophie going to tell me? Am I fired or something? Is that it?"

"Molly, please—"

"It's okay, Sue." The deep velvety voice came from the direction of the office. The voice had an odd familiarity to it. Not a voice Molly had ever heard in person, but one her subconscious knew as well as it knew her own name and had identified before her conscious brain could put two and two together. Goose bumps traveled up her arms as the voice continued. "She the one Sophie was telling me about at dinner last night?"

Three things dawned on Molly in quick succession. One. Her musical ear was too good *not* to recognize that voice. Two. Her friends had been keeping something very important from her because apparently, they felt she couldn't handle the truth. And three. She was standing in front of Anders Ostergaard with a uniboob and a gallon of water in the ass of her pants.

"Dagnabit," she murmured as she turned around to face the man who was standing within spitting distance. Six-feet-two-inches of long, lean muscle packed into faded blue jeans and a form-fitting baby blue T-shirt. Artfully messy dirty blond hair and a ruggedly handsome, chiseled face that had helped him win the title of "Sexiest Man Alive" more than once. There was a healing cut on his right cheekbone that was from his recent accident, but otherwise, he was perfect. Seen in this setting, the family resemblance to Jimmy Panama was unmistakable. "You're related to Jimmy."

At least that's what she thought she said.

What came out of her mouth must have been gibberish because Anders sent a questioning look to Sue who shrugged. "I could be wrong but I think she said 'You're late, mini.'"

Molly shook her head and tried again, but she couldn't seem

to make her mouth work. She'd seen Anders Ostergaard in concert more than once, but she'd never been this close to him before. Looking at him was like looking into the sun. Her eyeballs hurt and she was pretty sure she was going to go blind or pass out before she was done, but she couldn't look away.

She knew that face so well. Knew it with the familiarity of someone who had studied hundreds of photographs of it over a decade and a half. She knew the bump in his slightly bent nose and the faint cleft in his chin. She knew how many laugh lines creased the corners of his slanted blue eyes. She knew the shape of his lips. The angle of his square jaw and the light dusting of dark blond stubble that covered it.

As impossible as it sounded, he was even more attractive in person. It had to be the natural charisma that oozed off of him, and the confident, relaxed vibe he radiated in waves that quietly commanded people's attention. It was that special, indefinable quality really famous people had that made them a star. And he had it in spades.

When he grinned at her, it had the equivalent effect on her insides as a solar flare on the sun's surface. Red blobs outlined in shades of yellow and orange flashed behind her eyelids.

"Hi, there," he said. "I'm Anders." The words were spoken through a tunnel, far away and too close at the same time.

What did you do when the man you've idolized for most of your adult life suddenly stood before you? She'd fantasized about this moment so many times, but she was supposed to be fifteen pounds thinner and four inches taller, looking like a bombshell in stiletto heels and a killer dress. She'd say something smart and sassy, and he'd chuckle and fall madly in love with her. Instead, she was standing there slack-jawed feeling like she'd been eaten by a shark and shit out in the ocean.

The toaster waffles she'd eaten for breakfast made a jump shot for her throat.

"Oh no." She covered her mouth and spun away. Shoving

through the glass door, she plunged out into the rain and just made it past the car parked in front of the building before she leaned on the hood and coughed up the contents of her stomach in the street.

A passing cab driver honked his horn. Molly gave him the finger.

Oh, God. The rain wasn't helping. It struck her face and stung her skin. She was pretty sure she was going to be sick again. Trembling, she bent at the waist and choked up bile.

"Are you all right, hun?" Sue called from the open doorway.

Breathless and weak, Molly forced herself to straighten up. Her eyes watered from the exertion of vomiting, but the rain streaming down her face washed the tears away. Gaping at her friend, she couldn't keep her voice from wavering. "You knew. Why didn't you tell me?"

"No one else was allowed to know. Boss' rules."

"But why didn't *they* tell me?" By 'they' she meant Sophie and Jimmy. Jimmy might be the boss, but Sophie was her best friend. If anyone knew how crazy she was over Anders Ostergaard, it was Sophie.

Maybe that was why.

Were they afraid Molly wouldn't be cool? They probably just assumed she'd start babbling like an idiot and throw up in the street. Okay, maybe they'd had good reason not to tell her, but it still hurt.

"Come back inside, Molly. I'll find you some dry clothes and take you home."

"I can't." She was shivering now. Standing in the street ankle deep in a puddle during an electrical storm, shivering.

"Don't be silly."

Anders appeared in the doorway behind Sue. He nudged her aside and stepped out into the rain.

"What are you doing?" Molly said to him when he reached the curb.

"Rescuing my car before you puke all over it."

Molly looked down at the two-tone black and silver machine with its rounded curves and sleek design and belatedly realized it was a Bugatti. She'd just vomited on Anders Ostergaard's million-dollar sports car.

"I only got a little bit on the wheel," she said lamely.

A boom of thunder reminded Molly where they were. Electrical storms in Florida were no joke. She wiped her mouth in case there was something stuck to it before she made up her mind and hurried past Anders and then Sue to reenter the building. She headed straight for Jimmy's office, which she knew contained a bathroom and shower stall. Both Sue and Jimmy always kept a change of clothes in the closet and stocked it with other necessities.

Peeling off her wet clothes, she stepped into the hot shower and relished the water warming her goose-pimpled flesh. She'd needed to hit pause just long enough to process what had happened out there, but her brain kept replaying the last five minutes of the whole humiliating scene. *I threw up on his car!* If Sophie had told her sooner, she would've had time to prepare herself. It wouldn't have been such a shock.

How was he related to Jimmy, she wondered? Were they cousins? Brothers? No, Jimmy's last name was Panama. *Panama.* A fake name if she ever heard one. *Oh, my God, they are brothers!*

When she was through with the shower, Molly found a toothbrush and a comb and made use of both before she dug some clothes out of the closet. She put on a white tank top belonging to Sue but had to forgo the bra. Sue was an A cup and Molly was a solid C. The floral floor-length skirt was way too long, but she solved that problem by rolling up the waist until she wasn't tripping over the hem.

Checking her appearance one last time in the mirror, she lamented the freckles sprinkled across the bridge of her nose and cheeks, made starker by the lack of makeup. She looked fresh-faced and much younger than her thirty-four years, but maybe that wasn't such a bad thing.

What did it matter what she looked like? It wasn't as if she had a chance with Anders Ostergaard anyhow. Even if she did, she didn't want one. Unattainable crushes, or UCs, as she and her drummer used to call them, were not supposed to be attainable. Ever. That was the whole point of them and what made them harmless fun. There might be an opportunity for a selfie though, and—

Ugh! What was she thinking? This was *not* the time to fangirl. She'd embarrassed herself enough already. Padding to the door barefoot, she took a deep breath and told herself to be cool before she cracked it open.

Anders sat on a barstool talking on his cell phone. He was alone in the room.

"I'm confused," he said. "The suspect had an accomplice?" Anders paused to listen. "I see. Well, I appreciate the warning, Detective."

Outside, the rain had stopped. The lingering drops on the window glistened like diamonds in the bright sunlight. Molly felt less rattled now. Still nervous, but less likely to lose her shit again if he happened to smile at her or, God forbid, say hello.

She walked past him and made her way around to the back of the bar where she helped herself to a cup of coffee.

When Anders glanced at her, she gave him a shaky smile and finished pouring the coffee.

"I don't reckon a bodyguard will be necessary considering you believe I wasn't the intended target after all, but I'll take the suggestion under advisement."

Molly thought maybe she should leave. It sounded as if the conversation was none of her business. She didn't leave, though, because they were in a public place. If he wanted the call to be private, he could have gotten up and gone into the office as soon as she'd vacated it. She sipped the piping hot coffee and closed her eyes for a moment, savoring the taste of the deep, rich flavor. When she opened her eyes again, Anders was watching her with a wry twist to his gorgeous lips.

Had she made a noise? She did that sometimes when she ate or drank. She touched her mouth and turned away from him so he wouldn't see the heat rising in her face.

"Keep in touch, sir. And thanks again." Anders set the phone down on the bar with a soft thump. A half-empty cup of coffee sat cooling on the bar in front of him. His big hands engulfed the ceramic mug as he cradled it between his palms. He let out a deep breath and then looked at her sideways. "Want to start over? I'm Anders."

The sexy timbre of his voice sent shivers through her body. She sucked air through her nose and bit her bottom lip. *Play it cool, Molly. Play it cool.* "I know who you are." She turned around to fully face him. "I've been a fan of yours for a very long time, but you know that already, don't you?"

"How long is long?"

"Fifteen years."

"Shoot, were you listening to me in the crib?"

"Hardly." She smiled and blew on the coffee before taking another sip. It was almost too hot to drink.

"My brother mentioned you last night. You're Marley—"

"Molly," she corrected. "Molly MacBain. So, Jimmy is your brother?

"Yeah."

She knew it. "I'm sorry for your loss."

"Loss?" His left eyebrow quirked.

"Your girlfriend? Casey Conway? I was shocked to hear about her murder."

Pursing his lips, he glanced away for a moment. "She wasn't my girlfriend, but thank you anyway."

"But the newspaper said—"

"The newspaper got it wrong." He lifted his cup and knocked back the remnants of his coffee.

Okay, then. Casey Conway wasn't his girlfriend. The revelation made Molly feel a little lighter, but she immediately felt guilty about it. She was a horrible person. Whatever Casey's faults were, the poor girl was dead. It no longer mattered that she had a reputation for being a fame-grubber who'd dated a string of B-list actors and reality show stars on her way to her first big film role. Or that Anders Ostergaard was probably just another famous name she was planning to add to her list of celebrity ex-boyfriends. Molly hadn't wanted to believe the dating rumors were true, but they were hard to ignore when photographic evidence of the gorgeous couple stared back at her from the grocery checkout line. She didn't really know Casey though. Maybe the young actress was just misunderstood. Molly didn't want to believe Anders was shallow or stupid enough to be duped like that, but then, she didn't really know him either.

Molly nibbled on the inside of her cheek. The newspapers had reported that Anders and Casey were on the verge of getting engaged when she was tragically murdered in their hotel suite in Vegas. Anders was initially a suspect, but he'd been cleared when evidence led to the arrest of a stalker who'd followed Casey from Los Angeles. Albert Everett Mooney, an unemployed, 24-year-old man with no prior arrest record, ended up confessing to the whole thing. Somehow, he'd gotten access to the room service cart and tampered with the food before delivering it to her room.

Okay, was it weird she knew so much about all of this? Molly blew on the hot coffee again as heat flushed her face. She couldn't help it. When your idol gets accused of murder, you pay attention to the news. She took another sip of coffee while she thought of something to say. "I'm really sorry about earlier. I'm not usually such a spaz."

"Glad to know I bring out the best in you."

"Funny." She scrunched her nose at him over the rim of her cup. She stared at him for a moment, hoping he'd pick up the conversation. She'd never been so tongue-tied in her life. When the awkward tension became too much, she let out a giddy giggle. "Spaz is probably too mild of a word to describe the hot mess I was, but you're probably used to women losing their minds over you."

"I don't reckon it's something you ever get used to." He leaned forward slightly and offered his hand. "It's nice to meet you, Molly MacBain."

Smiling, she started around the bar to accept the second chance he was offering. He turned on his stool to face her. She held her coffee cup with her left hand as she reached out with her right to shake his hand.

"It's nice to—"

She tripped on the dragging hem of her skirt. The piping hot coffee splashed over his chest as she tumbled into the juncture of his split thighs. She reached out to break her fall and grabbed his waist. He caught her by the upper arms as he hopped off the stool and set her back on her feet.

"Hang on a sec. Hot coffee. Damn it." He whipped the wet, steaming T-shirt over his head to stop the soaked fabric from burning his skin. Jerking back out of his way, Molly stepped on the hem of her skirt again and started to fall backward. He reached out and caught her. Hooking her waist with his right arm while his left missed her shoulder and landed squarely on her breast.

Molly gasped and tried to step back but his right arm was like a vice holding her in place. A flash fire tore through her body and she dissolved like a marshmallow in an incinerator. The glass entrance door swung open and a young man with professional camera shouted Anders' name. But that was all she saw because Anders tugged her close, smashing her face into his lean, ripped chest, turning her away from the flashing camera. He shouted at the photographer. "Get the hell out of here or I'll shove that camera so far up your ass you'll be taking pictures through your nose."

"Don't you think you're moving on from Casey Conway a little too quickly?" the reporter said. "Her corpse isn't even cold yet. Unless you had this piece on the side all along. Is she your mistress?"

"Get *OUT!*" Anders bellowed.

Molly's eyes snapped open as the force of his anger curdled her nerves.

The fine dark-blond hairs on his chest tickled her cheek as she turned her head to see the foolish man still snapping photos as he backed toward the door. Not much more than twenty-one, the kid wore a gray fedora that made her think of Jimmy Olsen from *Superman*. He laughed as if he was enjoying himself and tugged open the glass door.

Then he was gone and the room was silent. Outside, one of the famous Key West roosters crowed in the distance. Contrary to popular belief, roosters didn't give a fig what time of day it was, they cock-a-doodle-dooed whenever they felt like it.

Smashed between the bar and Anders' big, hard body, Molly got a nose full of his cologne. He smelled crisp and spicy, like an autumn day. Her favorite time of year back home in Oklahoma. The rise and fall of her chest made her all too aware of the fact that his hand was still firmly wrapped around her breast, which was free as a bird under the white tank top. Tendrils of smoke started to curl around that realization just before her body was engulfed in flames.

Sue came barreling out of the kitchen. "What happened?"

Anders released Molly and stepped back. He reached up and drove his fingers through his artfully mussed hair with the same hand that had clasped her breast with the tenacity of a chimp clutching a banana. "Paparazzo." He looked at Sue. "I know the guy. He's been following me around since my climbing accident, looking for anything he can exploit. He's relentless."

Molly's heart sank. Not only had she'd made a complete fool of herself in front of Anders again, but now she had to worry about the moment being immortalized in the tabloids. Could this day get any worse? "Dagnabit."

CHAPTER FIVE

M olly waited until she and Sue were alone in the car to explain what had happened because she was too embarrassed to rehash it in front of Anders. After the incident with the paparazzo, Anders had walked to the back of the bar—still shirtless and so buff it made her eyeballs fog up —to pour himself another cup of coffee. Molly had babbled an apology, which received no reply, and the rising tension in the room had made her nauseous all over again. When Sue dangled her car keys and said she was ready to go, Molly jumped at the chance to get out of there.

"Don't worry about it, hun. None of this would have happened if we'd been straight with you from the start." Sue reached over and squeezed Molly's knee. The car was idling in front of her apartment building. "It was only a matter of time until you found out Anders is co-owner of Dixie's."

"Come again?" Molly gaped at her friend.

"That's the other thing. Anders technically is your boss."

"Anders Ostergaard is the private investor who co-owns the bar with Jimmy?"

"Yeah. I'm sorry. We should have told you. *I* should have told you. Especially because he's one of Oscar's best friends."

"Wait." Molly put her hand up to slow Sue down. The bombshells kept coming and Molly needed a moment to process them. "Your husband is best friends with one of the most famous country music superstars of all time?" How did she wrap her mind around that one? Molly frowned and shook her head in exasperation. "How?"

"They met a few years back when Oscar catered an event for Reba McEntire. Anders asked Oscar to cater his world tour and they've been close ever since."

Bewildered by it all, Molly stared out the window at the elderly woman walking a Chihuahua on the sidewalk. Miss Barbara and her dog Mini. "You keep saying you should've told me. Why didn't you?" She shot Sue a sideways glance. "You didn't trust me not to hound you for an introduction?" Molly put up a hand to stop Sue from denying it. "I can assure you, I wouldn't have wanted to experience what just happened back there for anything in the world."

Sue's eyes narrowed with regret. "It had nothing to do with you personally. I wanted to tell you. Honestly, I did. Sophie did too, but Jimmy was against it. He said it wasn't our secret to tell. I disagreed, but Oscar made me swear I'd keep my mouth shut. It turned into a bear of an argument but I lost. I'm sorry, hun. I feel terrible about all of this. I truly do."

Sue's earnest expression deflated Molly's anger. Molly might have a temper but she could never stay mad at anyone for long, especially her friends.

She sighed heavily and then blew a stray red curl out of her face. "If I'd known Anders was coming to town, I probably would have hidden under a rock. If you haven't noticed, I kind of lose my mind around famous people. Not just Anders. Anyone famous. It's not pretty."

"You don't say." Sue quirked an eyebrow and they both let out a strained laugh.

Molly's head came up as she remembered something. "When we met, Anders said something about Sophie telling him about me last night. Is that what she wanted to talk to me about today? Did he give his permission to let me in on the secret?"

"Well, it wasn't going to be a secret for much longer, considering he's in town for Jimmy's wedding, but Sophie wanted to be the first one to tell you. None of us meant for you to find out like this. She told Anders about you over dinner last night and he said he was looking forward to meeting you."

This wasn't the first time someone had mentioned a dinner. Despite Molly's insistence that she would have laid low, it still hurt to know her closest friends had dined with her idol and she hadn't been invited. "Last night?" she said, probing for more information.

"Yeah. Anders got into town late yesterday afternoon and we had an impromptu get-together at Jimmy and Sophie's place."

That didn't include her. Molly nodded as tears filled her eyes. She turned away so Sue wouldn't see and looked out the window again. Miss Barbara and Mini had moved on.

"None of us thought Anders would ever come to Key West, even for his brother's wedding. He's usually way too busy. He hasn't been here in years. He didn't even come down when Jimmy bought the bar."

"So, you figured what I don't know won't hurt me."

"I knew it would come out eventually. That's what I told Oscar, but he wouldn't listen to me. I hate being right all the time."

Molly smiled through her tears. She blinked them away before turning to face Sue again. "Are there any other secrets you're keeping from me? You don't have to tell me what they are. I just want to know if there are any more surprises waiting for me down the road."

"No. No more secrets. None from me anyhow."

"Thank you." Molly reached to open the door but her hand hesitated on the handle. She wanted to ask more about the dinner party, but it really wasn't any of her business, was it? She wasn't part of Anders close circle of friends and never would be, so it was ridiculous for her to be jealous when Sue and Sophie got to hang out with him.

"Are you okay, hun?"

"Yeah. I'll be fine." The bright smile she gave Sue hurt her face. "Always am."

Inside her apartment, Molly changed into clothes that gave her self-confidence a much needed boost. A red pleated V-neck empire waist top that flattered the girls, white capris slacks that were a bit too snug in the trunk but would stretch as the day went on, and a pair of red patent leather high heels she adored. She wanted to feel sexy today. Needed to after that morning. She needed to prove to herself she wasn't the hot mess who spilled coffee on celebrities and puked on their million-dollar Bugattis.

Her hair was nearly dry by the time she added some mouse and fluffed it out with a pick comb. There wasn't much she could do with the thick, curly mass except tie it up or part it to the side and let it fall in a wild tumble to her elbows. She chose to leave it down and gave it one last fluff as she left the bathroom and headed for the kitchen to grab a snack before work. The bookstore opened at 10 a.m. every day except for Sundays when it opened at noon. It was Thursday though and that meant she had a good nine-hour day ahead of her. April Linus would be in at 4 p.m. to relieve her for a dinner break and then stay to close up the shop at nine.

Molly had just put two slices of toast in the toaster when the house phone rang. Picking up the cordless receiver, she glanced at the number but didn't recognize it. She answered anyway. "Hello?"

"Molly?"

"Who's calling?"

"It's Trevor."

Molly almost dropped the phone. She fumbled with it for a moment before she stopped and took a deep breath. "Wow. It's been awhile, Trev."

Thirteen years and six months to be exact.

Trevor Schaffer had walked out on Molly when Cheyenne was eighteen months old. He'd never paid a dime of child support, even when he'd finished law school and went on to become a hotshot entertainment attorney in Los Angeles. No surprise to Molly who'd supported him through his undergraduate program. When he entered Stanford law school, he decided having a baby around the house was too much of a distraction so he moved into a dorm on campus and abandoned them. Molly gave up her regular gig with a local house band, sold everything she owned including her car, and joined a touring band that took her away from LA and her husband. They divorced soon after and she hadn't heard from him since.

"Yeah, it has been awhile." His voice was both so familiar and so foreign.

She rubbed the burning spot in the center of her chest with the flat of her hand. "What do you want?"

"As you know, Cheyenne's birthday is coming up—"

"Wait right there. You haven't acknowledged your daughter in almost fourteen years and you have the balls to call this house and mention her name to me?"

"Molly. Please." His condescending tone singed the freckles on her cheekbones.

"Don't patronize me, Trevor Schaffer. I'm not your wife anymore and haven't been for a very long time." She paced between the kitchen island and the only window on the front wall. "I'm the woman who raised your daughter by herself and helped her to become the smart, beautiful, compassionate young woman she is today."

"I agree. Cheyenne is all those things and more, thanks to you."

Molly was about to tell him to go to hell, but his words derailed her. She stared at the linoleum floor as her brain processed what he said. Screwing up her face in confusion, she demanded, "How would you know?"

"She didn't tell you? We've been communicating on Facebook for several months now."

"Liar!"

"Come on, Molly. Why would I lie to you when you can simply ask Cheyenne for yourself?"

This entire day was turning out to be one big fat nightmare that just wouldn't quit. She needed to wake up and everything would be back to normal. Except the floor beneath her feet felt way too solid. Molly paced to her second-floor apartment window and gazed down at the parking lot below taking in the low-hanging power lines, the half-dead palm tree, and the crumbling pink stone wall that separated the complex from the thrift store/laundromat duplex next door. Her death grip on the telephone receiver tightened another notch as the air-conditioner kicked on and the vent above her head blasted her with cold air.

Trevor's voice was muffled as if it came from the other end of a very long tunnel. "I'd like for her to come to Los Angeles to spend a couple weeks with Michelle and me. Michelle's my wife. She's a family attorney. She's as eager as I am to meet Cheyenne."

Molly snapped out of it and forced herself to face facts. This was really happening. "You have to be lying. Cheyenne would've told me if you tried to contact her on Facebook."

"Actually, she contacted me."

Doubt bore down on Molly like a pile of boulders. Could he be telling the truth? What if Cheyenne had contacted him? It might explain her sudden interest in playing matchmaker. Maybe she was thinking about going to live with her father and felt guilty about leaving Molly alone. The possibility of this being true was unfathomable, and yet, Trevor was on the other end of the phone waiting for Molly's approval.

Like hell, she'd give it.

"Cheyenne is not flying to Los Angeles for her birthday. You can't believe for a second I'd be okay with that."

"Cheyenne was right. You are too overprotective."

"Excuse me?" Molly squeezed the phone, wishing it was Trevor's neck.

"She told me you won't let her go to a science fiction convention in Miami for the day. She's growing up. If you truly believe you raised her right, you should trust her judgment."

Molly's chest tightened and her head felt like it was about to pop off. Speaking was impossible for several seconds, but when the words did come, her voice was low and hoarse. "No. You don't get to tell me how to parent my daughter. You gave up your right to be her father a very long time ago."

"Actually, no papers were ever signed. I technically still have legal custody of Cheyenne. If we were to take this to court—"

"They would see what a deadbeat dad you are, you son of a bitch!" Molly gripped the back of the kitchen chair and squeezed her eyes closed, trembling in her effort to compose herself.

The calmness in Trevor's voice concerned her more than any outburst would have. It made her feel like an erratic, irrational, unfit mother. He was pushing her buttons on purpose.

"I've made mistakes," he said quietly. "I regret not being there for you and Cheyenne, but you've done all right without my financial support."

Molly looked at the threadbare carpet, the dated furniture that wasn't hers, and the lumpy white walls that had been spackled and painted over too many times. She could barely afford this place. Could barely make ends meet at the bookstore.

She performed two nights a week because it helped put food on the table. She wanted to hire a full-time employee so she could pick up a few more gigs in town and maybe go back to teaching acoustic guitar. Music paid a hell of a lot better than the small salary she gave herself out of the store budget. She kept the bookstore for Cheyenne's sake, to give her some stability while she was in high school. Everything Molly did, she did for Cheyenne.

Trevor had no idea what kind of struggle she'd been through or the things she'd had to sacrifice for her daughter, but then, he had no idea what those two words meant. Molly's life hadn't been easy, but she was damn sure she wouldn't have changed a thing if it meant having to be married to the self-centered bastard for another second longer.

"You know what." Molly pulled out a kitchen chair and flopped down on it. "I don't think any judge in this country would give you visitation rights after they find out you owe almost fourteen years of child support payments."

"Did you ever file for support?"

"You know I didn't."

"No judge will fault me for not being in my daughter's life when I didn't know where she was. You took her and disappeared. I looked everywhere for her for years and never gave up hope that one day I'd find her again."

Fear and frustration curdled Molly's stomach. She swiped at a tear. "God, you have no shame, do you?"

"Perhaps," he said matter-of-factly. "But it's your word against mine, and let's be honest here. Who's the judge going to believe?"

CHAPTER SIX

—————————————

Anders was reluctant to return to the penthouse condo he was renting in Old Town for no other reason than because his son was there. After spending the better part of a week trying to figure out how to be a dad to a kid who wouldn't even look at him, let alone answer a simple question, he needed a break and time to regroup. He'd changed into his workout clothes in the office at Dixie's after that unfortunate fan encounter and gone for a run in Old Town. He passed the Southernmost house, Hemingway's place, and the Key West lighthouse before pausing at a street vendor who was selling ice-cold coconuts. He'd drilled the hole for the straw while Anders waited. Fresh coconut water was so much better than the store-bought stuff, and he needed the electrolytes on a hot-as-hellfire afternoon.

He kept walking while he polished off his beverage.

Maybe he should just send Obie back to Greer's house in California. At least he'd be in a familiar environment. Guilt prickled the back of Anders' neck. What kind of life had the boy been living? Boarding school during the school year, handed off to nannies and servants or grandma's house during summer break and the holidays. Greer used to tell stories about how un-moth-erly Martha Mell was to her when she was growing up. It was one of the few things they'd had in common. Shitty parents. Before Obie was born, they'd both vowed they wouldn't make the same mistakes their parents had made. And they hadn't. They'd made new ones that were just as bad.

Anders stopped in front of a two-story Old-Key-West-style home. The yellow building was real pretty with its white trim and wrap-around porches on its upper and lower floors. It reminded him of the big house up the road from the trailer park where he grew up. His momma loved that house. She used to say it was a lot like the one she was raised in back in New Orleans. When Anders was about eleven, he made a vow to his momma that he would buy that house for her one day. She'd died a year later and the house was bulldozed two years after that. He could buy ten of those houses now. Funny how he didn't own a single home of his own.

The house in Old Town was for sale, but he had no need for it. He preferred to rent whenever he was in one place long enough. Otherwise, he lived in hotels. Still, he found himself reaching into the mailbox for a brochure. Out of curiosity, he told himself. But it was his dumb luck the real estate broker came out the front door and spotted him.

Rebecca Stein was very good at her job. She insisted he had to see the place because it was the perfect house for him. Before he knew it, he was getting the grand tour. Turned out, she was right. He liked what he saw, but he just wasn't in the market for real estate. He wasn't planning on staying in Key West any longer than he needed to.

Anders dropped his room key on the foyer table as he entered the air-conditioned condo. The blast of cool air that greeted him was so welcomed, he was almost glad to be home. Off to his right, Selena Fry, his publicist, was making herself at home in the galley kitchen. Wearing an apron she'd gotten from God-knows-where over a sleek black pantsuit, she was hand washing the dishes he'd left in the sink.

He quirked an eyebrow at her. "You realize the dishwasher works just fine."

She rinsed a glass under the running faucet and didn't glance over at him. "Washing dishes relaxes me."

Anders snorted, doubtful anything relaxed the woman.

She'd flown to Vegas as promised and had insisted on sticking close to him, especially when he announced his plans to fly to Key West for his brother's wedding. She'd wanted him to go to Casey's funeral and make himself as visible as possible, but she'd lost that battle. He'd had his son to consider and being in the limelight was the last thing the shy kid needed, so Anders had brought Obie here to live in a Parrot Head's idea of paradise.

The condo was furnished with rattan furniture and gaudy hibiscus prints. The view of the Gulf of Mexico from the lanai was a knockout though. There was a fully stocked kitchen and two bedrooms situated on opposite sides of the living space.

Through the sliding glass door, Anders spotted Obie curled up on a lounge chair on the lanai reading a comic book. How many did the kid have? Or was he reading the same one over and over again? That got him in the gut. Was the kid afraid to ask for another book to read? Hell, Obie was scared of him, period. Anders didn't know how to deal with that. Kids usually loved him. He never had to try too hard to coax a smile out of one of them. How ironic. His own son was the one kid who couldn't stand to look at him. A hollowness inside his chest ached at the thought, but he had nobody to blame for it but himself.

"Thought you'd be home sooner," Selena said, drawing his gaze away from Obie. The woman always reminded him of a tenacious pug with her turned-up nose and round, bulgy brown eyes. She'd cut her hair recently. Her dark brown locks used to hang limply to her elbows whenever she let her hair out of its bun. Now it was brushed back off of her face in a short, sleek bob. The style suited her better. She didn't smile or laugh very often, but that was just her way. She had a no-nonsense, businesslike demeanor that was as tidy and efficient as her whip slender figure and the conservative pantsuits she liked to wear. She worked hard though and was always there for him when he needed her.

"Sorry about that, I got sidetracked on my run. Thanks for watching him. I know it's not in your job description."

"Oh, I don't mind." Selena waved off his gratitude as she dried her hands with a hand towel and then reached into the drawer for a butter knife. "He's been out there reading since he got up."

Anders took his rental car keys and the house brochure out of his pockets and set them on the kitchen counter.

"What's that?" Selena gestured to the brochure with the knife.

"Nothing. Just something I picked up."

"Oh."

Anders studied the boy again. "He say anything to you?"

"No."

Obie hadn't spoken a word to him or to anyone else since his grandmother had shown up out of the blue and left him on Anders' doorstep four days ago. The kid ate like a bird, if he ate at all, and he'd rather be in his room than in the hotel pool or outside playing. Finding him on the lanai was an unexpected surprise—one Anders hoped was a step in the right direction.

It wasn't enough though. A kid needed exercise. A friend to toss a ball around with once in a while. At least, that was all he ever wanted when he was a kid. And he'd had it with his brother, Jimmy. Only a year younger, he was Anders' best friend and partner in crime. The only reason they'd survived their nightmare of a father was because they had each other. Obie needed someone like that. Someone who always had his back. A thought struck him. Maybe he did have someone back home in Sacramento. Maybe he was just missing his best friend.

"I gave him a bowl of cereal for breakfast but he didn't eat it. I thought maybe he'd want peanut butter and jelly for lunch." She cut the sandwich in half and then handed the plate to Anders.

He looked down at her pug face and smiled. "Thanks, Fry. That was very thoughtful of you."

She didn't smile nor did she release the plate when he tried to take it from her. "I still think coming here was a mistake. You should've gone to LA or even Nashville. Just because you've been cleared as a suspect in the murder doesn't mean the press is going to let this go. You were the last person to see Casey Conway alive. People are going to think you disappeared because you're hiding something."

"About that." He tugged a little harder and she released the plate.

"What? I don't like that look. What's happened?"

"The press. They found me. A paparazzo snapped a picture of me at Dixie's."

Selena sighed and went back into the kitchen to clean up. "Is that all? You had me worried for a moment."

"I was caught in a compromising position."

She dropped the knife she was about to wash off in the sink. Metal clattered against metal. "With who?"

"Nobody important. It was a misunderstanding. She tripped and I caught her. It was bad timing."

"Who was she, Anders?"

"It doesn't matter. It was an accident. She was very embarrassed by the whole thing."

Selena started pacing the length of the galley kitchen, finger and thumb tugging her bottom lip as the wheels turned in her brain. "She's probably out to sell her phony story about your secret romance to the highest bidder. We need to do some damage control. Was she ugly? If she was ugly, no one will believe you're dating her."

"She—" Anders stopped and took a moment to recall the woman he'd met at the bar. *Molly MacBain.* She'd looked like a drowned orange cat, but she'd cleaned up pretty well after her shower. She had an all-American, girl-next-door look to her. Freckled rosy skin, big blue eyes, and a heart-shaped face. He hadn't seen her smile, but he'd caught a glimpse of dimples. That long red-gold curly mane was something else. He didn't usually go for redheads, but he had to admit she had nice hair. The rest of her was nice too. His left hand suddenly tingled with the memory of the firm full breast planted against his palm. The nipple had peaked, responding to his touch despite all the craziness. She was way too short though. At 6' 2" his cutoff was 5'4". The redhead was five foot nothing in her bare feet. She was pretty but not in the same league as the company he usually kept. So, no, there was no chance anyone would believe he was dating her. "She's a fan," he finished his statement at last.

Selena stopped pacing. It was no secret he had a strict rule about dating fans and he didn't allow his bandmates to mix with them either. The blank stare she gave him melted into laughter. "Fans." She rolled her eyes. "Was she one of the batshit crazy ones hoping to be your best friend, or worse, your girlfriend? Do we need to file a restraining order?"

"Nah. Molly is harmless."

"Molly?" Selena raised her eyebrows skeptically. "What's her last name?" When Anders didn't immediately respond, Selena said, "For the press, if they contact us for a statement. The overzealous fan excuse is a perfect explanation. We'll say she threw herself at you for the benefit of the camera."

"No. We won't." Anders headed for the lanai with the sandwich. "No need to embarrass Molly like that. She didn't do it on purpose. She tripped. That's all. It was bad timing."

"Tripped." The muttered scoff made Anders pause by the sliding glass door.

Selena's thin eyebrows were raised with skepticism. She meant well, but sometimes she was a bit too intense.

"There's really no need for you to stick around Key West, Fry. I've got a call out to a local nanny service, so I'll have someone to look after Obie before the week is out. There's really nothing else for you to do here."

Selena stared at him unblinkingly. Her dark eyes hard and penetrating. He couldn't read her expression, but the tension coming off of her made it clear she wasn't happy with his suggestion.

The moment went on so long it turned awkward.

Anders shifted his weight from one foot to the other. "I'm just saying, I appreciate all that you do, but I know I'm not your only client."

"You're my biggest client."

"And you're the best at what you do. I just don't want to take you away from other folks who need your expertise." He turned away, sliding the door open so he could step out onto the screened balcony.

Obie didn't look up from his comic book. His little hand turned the page and then reached to push his glasses up the bridge of his nose. He was so small. So innocent. And so alone.

Suddenly, another boy was sitting in the chair. It was thirty years earlier and Anders was leaving for college. Jonas was six. Scrawny and quiet, he kept to himself and often had a book in his hands. He did that day. He didn't acknowledge Anders when he said goodbye and kissed him on the head. He'd hated bailing on the kid, but he had to get the hell out of there for his own sanity and a football scholarship had been his ticket out.

Jimmy used to say Jonas was born with an old soul, but truth was, he was forced to grow up real fast because he was on his own in the world pretty much from the day he was born. Jimmy and Anders had done what they could to make sure their brother was fed and changed and occasionally bathed, but they were kids themselves and didn't know anything about babies. Anders wished he could say Jonas turned out all right, but he was just as messed up as a man could be, having been raised with no mother and a drunken bastard of a father. All grown up now, he was an ex-con with a shady past and no connection to his family. Jonas hated Anders probably for the same reasons Obie hated him.

Anders' hand trembled as he sat the plate down on the small table beside the lounge chair. Blinking the moisture from his eyes, he said brightly, "Hey there."

Obie didn't look at him, but he glanced at the sandwich.

"PB&J. My favorite. Yum-my. If you don't eat it, I will."

The boy returned to his comic book, but after a moment, his gaze returned to the sandwich.

"Go on. Enjoy it. I would."

Anders closed the sliding glass door and took a seat on the second lounger. The two chairs were tilted toward each other but facing out at the pretty view. In the distance, the afternoon sun glinted off the sails of a boat gliding parallel to the horizon on water smooth as glass. He soaked in the scenery for a few minutes, purposely not making any sudden moves. When Obie started to nibble on his sandwich, Anders felt the rush of minor triumph.

He truly wanted to connect with the boy. Unlike the selfish teenager who'd abandoned his baby brother to pursue his own dreams. Or the stubborn new father who felt he had nothing to offer his toddler son. Anders was starting to realize that maybe just being there for the kid would be enough. The rest he'd have to make up as he went along.

That part terrified him the most.

He waited until Obie was about halfway through his sandwich before he spoke again. This time he modulated his tone to better reflect his sincerity. "What would you say about taking a walk with me later this afternoon after it cools down a bit? I reckon we can find a place on Duval that sells comic books."

The boy's face lit with surprise as he looked directly at Anders.

Houston, we have contact. He tried to clamp down on the emotions that made his chest swell like a balloon, but his damn eyes started watering again. "Sound like a plan?"

The kid nodded.

Anders grinned past the panic that flickered in his chest and nodded back.

CHAPTER SEVEN

The Ever After Book Shoppe was a tiny, freestanding building shrouded in tropical foliage. It was set back from Duval Street's bustling sidewalk, and Anders would have missed the place if he hadn't stopped to ask for directions. He'd given the street beggar some money for his trouble while Obie bent to pet his dog, a little dachshund wearing an Elvis costume.

"This must be it," Anders said unnecessarily, as the carved wooden sign above the door stated as much. Obie stood on tiptoe trying to peer through one of the bay windows. Anders smiled and tapped his arm. "Come on. I reckon we should see what they've got."

A little bell chimed over the door when they entered the shop. A refreshing blast of cool air swept over them as they were met with the warm scent of ink and paper. Obie tripped over a bump in the old carpet and Anders reached out to catch his shoulder, preventing him from going over.

"Are you okay?" The question came from someone else.

Anders looked around for the source of the voice. Two bookshelves ran the length of the deep but narrow shop, creating three neat aisles, all lined floor to ceiling with books.

"Over here."

Anders found the girl nestled in the alcove of the bay window. The young teenager sat curled on a bench seat, her eyeballs fastened to the book in her lap.

"He's fine." Anders turned toward the girl. "Do you work here?"

"No, my mom's the owner. She ran out for coffee. I'm just watching the store until she comes back." Her gaze lifted to his face. She sat up a little straighter and closed the book. For a moment, he thought she'd recognized him. If those pink cowboy boots she was wearing were any indication, she liked country music. She didn't say anything though, and her gaze dropped to Obie. "Can I help you find something?"

"Comic books," Anders answered for him. "Do you have any?"

"Sure. They're in the back of the store beside the cash register." The girl set her book aside and stood up. She was tall and slender. Her sleek dark hair rested against her narrow back in a single braid. There was something familiar about her face, but he was certain he'd never seen her before. Dropping to her knees in front of Obie, she reached for the comic book he was clutching. "Let's see what you've got."

She held out her hand, waiting patiently for Obie to give her the book. He stared at her for so long, Anders started to grow uncomfortable. He took a step toward them, intending to make an excuse for the boy and pull him back, but Obie released the comic book first.

The teenager took it gingerly and studied it like an expert. "This Scrooge McDuck is a classic. Take good care of it."

Something lit up behind Obie's eyes and he nodded earnestly.

"Have you read the Darkwing Duck series?"

Obie shook his head, indicating he hadn't.

"It was my favorite when I was your age. He's like Batman but a duck. It's pretty cool. Come on. I'll show you."

Obie followed the girl down the center aisle toward the back of the store. She looked back at the boy over her shoulder. "What's your name?"

Obie's head turned up. Anders didn't hear him respond even though he must have because the girl replied. "Oberon. That's an awesome name. I'm Cheyenne. Like the capital of Wyoming."

Cheyenne. Like the title of Anders' first hit single fifteen years ago.

He was passing it off as a coincidence when the bell above the door chimed and a short woman with long, curly, red-gold hair entered the shop carrying a venti-sized cup of coffee.

Molly MacBain.

She stopped short when she saw him. Her violet eyes flared wide and her pretty mouth went slack for a moment before she attempted to pull herself together. "Um, hello."

"Hi there." He grinned.

The color drained from her face, making the light dusting of freckles across the top of her cheekbones stand out in contrast. Her chin quivered as she attempted to smile back but failed miserably. He caught a glimpse of those intriguing dimples again before she darted a nervous glance toward the back of the store where Cheyenne and Obie knelt in front of the comic book rack.

She was kinda cute for a redhead.

Anders pursed his lips, fighting a smile and cocked an eyebrow. "We meet again."

She teetered on her high heels and took an awkward sidestep to catch herself.

"Easy now." Anders put his hands up in defense. He'd already worn one cup of coffee today.

She frowned, confusion evident on her face. "Can I help you with something?"

"Well, for starters, you can put that cup of Joe down nice and slow."

She looked at the cup she was holding as if she'd just realized it was in her hand. She shook her head in mild exasperation and walked past him, heading toward the back. "You took me by surprise is all. I'm pretty certain I'm not the first fan to lose my head over you."

"Nope. But I'm pretty sure you're the first to lose her lunch."

She *tsked* at the reminder, drawing a wider smile from him. She might be nervous as all get out, but she still had sass. He liked that.

As he followed her down the narrow aisle, his gaze was drawn to something else he liked. The small, full bottom nestled into a pair of snug white pants. Molly was about four inches taller thanks to the high heels that added a nice little sway to her strut. She glanced back at him and his eye caught the curve of her firm, full breast, which was accented by the tightness of her red top.

She quirked an auburn brow. "Is there something I can do for you?"

If the kids hadn't been in earshot, he might have responded with a flirty comment guaranteed to make her blush. He bit his tongue instead and averted his gaze from her shapely, compact, little body.

When she reached the counter, she sat her cup beside the cash register.

He glanced at Obie and the girl named Cheyenne. "My son was looking for some new comic books."

"Well, he's talking to the right person. Cheyenne was addicted to them when she was his age."

Obie was on his feet now, juggling at least a dozen comics.

Molly hurried to help him, catching the slipping stack before he dropped it. "Hey there, cowboy, looks like you found something you like. Whatcha got there?" Kneeling, she gave Obie a dazzling dimpled smile that made Anders' breath hitch. He only caught the periphery, but it was enough. Warmth buzzed in his belly and his libido quivered with interest.

Oberon stared at Molly with a startled, owl-eyed expression Anders had never seen on his face before. Once again, he felt compelled to rescue his son from an awkward situation, but the boy answered for himself in a barely audible voice. "I'm not a cowboy."

"Why aren't you?"

"I'm from California."

Molly let out a deep, unguarded chortle that was quite endearing. Obie must have thought so too because his face lit up with a giggle.

The sound coming from his son took Anders' breath away.

"You think they don't have cowboys in California?" Molly asked him. "Shoot, you bet they do. Ain't that right, Cheyenne?"

The girl nodded. "Cattle ranching is prevalent in California." She rested her hands on Obie's shoulders. "This is Oberon, Ma. Isn't that a cool name?"

"Sure is." She smiled at her daughter. "Is that from Greek mythology?"

Obie pushed his oversized glasses up the bridge of his nose while still trying to juggle the bundle in his arms. "It's from A Midsummer Night's Dream. My mom's favorite play. Oberon is the king of the fairies."

Cheyenne's mouth formed a neat little O. "That. Is. So. Awesome. Ma, why didn't you name me after something of sentimental significance?"

Molly stood up. She was still a couple inches shorter than her daughter even with the high heels. "I like your name just fine, Cheyenne Dallas MacBain."

"I have to agree." Anders watched Molly's face. "Cheyenne's a pretty name."

When Molly glanced at him, her eyes flared slightly before

she shied away again. "Do you know who this is, Cheyenne? I'm surprised you haven't said anything."

"Anders Ostergaard," the girl said matter-of-factly.

Molly's forehead knit with disbelief. "Okay. I just thought you'd be…" her voice trailed off as Cheyenne blinked at her with a calm, unimpressed expression. "Never mind. Why don't you take Oberon up to the front of the store where he can sort through the books and pick the ones he wants to take."

Obie hesitated, his steady gaze expectant as if he was waiting for something from Anders. Was he asking for permission? Shoving his hands into the front pockets of his jeans, Anders gestured with his chin. "Go on. I'll be right here."

Cheyenne guided Obie in front of her and then hesitated for a moment. "Ma?"

"Yeah?"

"Be cool."

Molly *tsked* again as the Cheyenne followed the boy down the center aisle.

"Be cool," Molly muttered as she moved behind the counter and sat on a stool. "Is there anything you're interested in, Mr. Ostergaard?"

He turned toward Molly. "Call me Anders. Please."

Her gaze met his for a second before slipping away. She was trembling almost imperceptibly. He hated making her so nervous, but he wasn't sure what he could do to put her at ease.

She took a sip of her coffee and set it down again. "Do you like to read? I can recommend a book for you if you'd like? We have a large selection of science fiction…" Her voice trailed off when their gazes collided. She didn't recoil this time, but the strain around her eyes suggested she was trying to work through her discomfort. She swallowed hard. "I read somewhere that you like science fiction movies so, um, I thought maybe that extended to your book preferences as well."

"I don't read a lot. Don't usually have time for it, but since I'm on a forced vacation maybe I should start."

"Well, what kind of science fiction do you like? First contact? Post-apocalyptic? Time travel? Space opera?"

He shrugged. "I don't have a preference." And he'd probably never get around to reading the book. He was just being polite.

"Okay." She slid off her stool and went to the shelf on the far wall opposite the counter. Three rows of forward-facing paperbacks were numbered one through ten. "These are our top fifteen best-selling sci-fi fantasy books right now. This one here is really popular. I can hardly keep it in stock." She brought the thick paperback novel to the counter and set it in front of him. "It's basically a teenage boy meets alien girl, alien girl's family wants to wipe out the earth kind of story."

"Sounds great. I'll take it."

"Super."

They stared at each other. When the awkward silence stretched between them like a widening sinkhole, Anders cleared his throat. He was usually better at chatting with fans. Or maybe they were better at launching questions at him. No, that wasn't true. He often got the star-struck ones who didn't say a word. He didn't reckon that was Miss Molly's problem. If anything, it felt like she was holding back, like a geyser suppressing its natural urge to let-her-rip.

He reached for his wallet, withdrew a gold card, and placed it on the counter. Obie appeared at his side with the entire stack of comic books, not one book lighter than before. He pushed them up on the high counter and then blinked at Anders.

Cheyenne came up behind him. "He couldn't decide which ones he wanted. It would have been a tough choice for me too."

A smile tugged at the corner of Anders' mouth. He held it back though and peered down at his son gravely. "Are you going to read all of these, cowboy?" he said, intentionally adding the nickname Molly used.

Obie nodded.

"Well, I don't see why we can't buy them all." Anders was a goner. He'd be broke within a year if the kid ever figured out his old man couldn't say no to him.

"What a good dad you have." Molly shot her thousand-watt smile at Obie again.

The boy nodded, staring at her mesmerized.

Obie's agreement struck Anders right between the ribcage. No matter the praise was coerced by a pair of fine dimples. Or that he didn't deserve it. Buying the kid a few comic books didn't make up for years of being absent from his son's life.

"Gentlemen always say thank you," Molly continued, pressing the issue. "Thank your father, young man." She spoke to Oberon sternly but with kindness, just the way Anders' mama used to speak to him whenever he behaved like an idiot.

Anders shook his head. "It's fine."

But Molly MacBain had cast some sort of spell over his son. The boy tilted his head back to stare up at him. His soft voice was barely louder than a whisper, but Anders heard it clear enough. "Thank you, sir." The words wrapped around Anders' heart and squeezed tightly.

He wanted to drop to his knees and hug the boy, but he didn't want to freak him out so he refrained and just enjoyed his son's smile as he admired his new comic books.

"Gentlemen also always say you're welcome."

Anders pulled his gaze away from Obie and blinked at the sassy redheaded woman who was waiting expectantly.

She shrugged. "Just saying." She graced him with her dazzling dimpled smile before she turned away to ring up his purchases.

"You're welcome, son," Anders said softly, resting his hand on top of Obie's head.

Cheyenne waved for Obie to follow her. "Let's go sit outside in the courtyard while they're finishing up."

Anders gestured for Obie to go on. The boy grabbed the

shopping bag full of comic books off the counter and ran after his new friend.

"It was nice meeting you again, Molly." He said as he signed the credit card receipt. As an afterthought, he held up the pen. "Did you want an autograph? Or a selfie or something?"

Rosy color bloomed in her cheeks again, but her mouth twisted wryly as she waved the receipt. "I've got your autograph. But I'll take a raincheck on the selfie." She gestured with her chin. "I've got customers waiting."

He glanced back to discover there were two people standing in line behind him and he was holding everybody up. Bemused at himself for not noticing other people had come into the shop, he grinned. "Some other time then. See you around, Miss Molly." He added a wink out of habit and scooped up his new book before he strolled out of the shop.

CHAPTER EIGHT

Molly dragged her gaze away from Anders Ostergaard's tall, broad form and smiled at the customer in front of her. A twenty-something hipster with trendy black glasses pushed his items, three horror novels, across the counter so she could ring them up.

The next person in line, a stout middle-aged woman, leaned around him. "Oh, my Lord, was that Anders Ostergaard, the famous country singer?"

The hipster shrugged. "Wasn't he arrested for murdering an actress or something?"

"He wasn't arrested," Molly said defensively as she totaled the sale. "He was questioned and released. That'll be twenty-four thirty-five. You can insert your card. Casey Conway had a stalker. He confessed to everything."

"Scary." The woman turned to peer out the front windows as if trying to catch another glimpse of Anders. "I guess that's the price of being famous."

"I'd take his millions any day." The hipster punched in his pin.

"Hallelujah," The woman murmured.

After the hipster left, Molly looked up a book for the next customer. They were just finishing up when Cheyenne came around to stand behind the counter.

Molly handed the woman the bag with her purchase. "You have a nice day now. Come back and see us."

"Thanks, I will."

Molly waited until the customer had departed before turning her attention to Cheyenne. Her daughter was leaning on the counter, chin in her hand, cupping a mouth that was spread into a giddy smile. "How come you're not totally freaking out, Ma?"

Molly sat on her stool and took a long swig of coffee before answering. "I did that this morning."

"You met him this morning? How? What happened? Why didn't you tell me the moment I walked through the door?"

Cheyenne had come straight from school like she did most days, grabbed a snack from the small kitchen in the back room, and curled up with a book on one of the window seats at the front of the store. Molly had been involved with putting a book order into the system, but that wasn't the reason she hadn't told Cheyenne the amazing news that Anders Ostergaard was in town and she'd puked on the tire of his Bugatti. She hadn't talked to Cheyenne because she was still far too upset about what she'd learned from her ex-husband.

Cheyenne contacted him on Facebook and had been talking to him for months, and she'd never mentioned a single word about it to Molly. If that wasn't bad enough, Trevor wanted Cheyenne to fly to LA alone to spend her birthday with him and his wife. Did Cheyenne really want to see her father? Molly was so incredibly hurt by all of it, her chest ached whenever she tried to open her mouth to ask Cheyenne if it were true. She was terrified of what her daughter might say.

Finding Anders Ostergaard in the shop had rattled Molly enough to make her forget about her ex-husband for the moment, but now that he was gone dread hung heavily in the air again. Molly cleared the tightness in her throat. "Anders and Jimmy are brothers."

Cheyenne's mouth dropped open in surprise. "Shut the front door. I thought they looked alike. When Anders walked through the door, I couldn't believe my eyes. I thought you were going to freak out when you saw him. His son Obie is a cute kid. He told me he's staying with his dad for the summer because his mom is busy making a movie. He said he hasn't seen his dad in a few years. He used to see him once a year on Christmas but that stopped when he was seven. I feel bad for him. A kid needs to see their dad once in a while."

Molly hopped off her stool so quickly it scraped against the floor. "He lost his right to see his child the moment he abandoned him. No wonder Obie looked scared of his own shadow. He's being forced to spend the summer with a man he barely knows."

Cheyenne was staring at her. "Are you okay, Ma?"

Molly paced past her, went to the farthest bookshelf where she started straightening books that didn't need to be straightened. "I'm fine," she snapped.

"It's just, you're talking about Anders Ostergaard, your idol. The man you worship, not just because of his music, but because of how kind and generous he is. You're always telling me that."

"He *is* kind and generous." Molly slammed a paperback onto the shelf too hard. It bounced and tumbled to the ground. "Dagnabit!"

"You're not making any sense."

She hadn't noticed the comparison. Was her idol a deadbeat dad just like Trevor? Anders was divorced and didn't have custody of his son, but she'd always assumed he was still in the boy's life in some way. Had he put his career first like Trevor Schaffer had? The thought made her ill. Suddenly, the man she'd put on a pedestal for fifteen years didn't look quite so perfect. That bummed her out as much as the conversation she knew she needed to have with her daughter.

After picking up the fallen book, she tucked the Clive Barker novel carefully back into place. She stared at the shelf, not really registering the creepy, ghoulish images on the horror novels. Cheyenne stood just a few feet away, a curious and confused expression on her face. Shoving the last book onto the shelf, Molly said, "I spoke to your father today."

No answer. The ticking wall clock above her head filled the silence. When Molly couldn't bear it any longer, she turned around. Cheyenne was staring at the ground, her face pinched with shame. Molly shook her head sadly. "Why didn't you tell me, Cheyenne? Why all the secrecy?"

"Because I knew you'd be mad."

"You're right. I would have been mad, but now I'm mad and hurt." She crossed her arms and asked the question burning brightest in her gut. "Do you want to know your father?"

"Yes. No! I don't know." The teenager brushed past Molly, heading toward her favorite alcove.

Molly stayed where she was because she was afraid if she moved an inch, she'd crumble into pieces. "I cannot allow you to see him." She used the parental tone she used whenever she meant business.

Cheyenne picked up the book she'd been reading earlier. "You can't stop me."

"Yes. I can." All of the fury Molly felt toward her ex-husband for suddenly appearing in their lives again bubbled up inside her. The anger held her together like glue as she marched toward her daughter. "I am the mother. You are the child. You do what I say. That man is not your father. That man was a sperm donor who gave up any rights he had to you the day he walked out on us."

"You don't trust me, Ma," Cheyenne said softly. "When are you going to start trusting me?"

The front door dinged and a blast of afternoon heat followed

April Linus into the shop. She gave them a big, sunny smile. "Hey, Chey! Hey, Molly. What's—" Noticing the tension in the room, she paused mid-question. "Up." The door banged closed.

"Hi," Cheyenne muttered.

"Is everything okay?"

Molly nodded curtly. "Fine."

Cheyenne turned to April. "Can I still sleep over tomorrow night?"

"Sure. I have some leads on our project I want to go over with you."

"Tomorrow night is Sophie and Jimmy's rehearsal dinner," Molly said. "And their wedding is the day after. I'd rather have you home Friday night so you're fresh for the wedding."

April interrupted before Cheyenne could protest. "Sorry, I forgot all about the rehearsal dinner! How about Saturday night after the wedding? Would that be okay?"

Molly nodded. "Yeah, Saturday night would be fine with me."

"Awesome. I'm going to the wedding too, so you can come home with me after. Okay?"

Cheyenne's furious, frustrated gaze bored into Molly, but Molly didn't back down. She was the parent here. She made the rules.

Turning back to her friend, Cheyenne nodded. "Sounds cool, April. I'll see you Saturday." Her book clutched to her chest, she pushed open the door and exited the shop.

April's head tilted with curiosity as she looked at Molly. "Is everything okay?"

"Yeah. It will be." But Molly wasn't so sure. Cheyenne was getting to the age where she could decide where she wanted to live, and with whom, and Molly wouldn't be able to do anything about it. But damned if she was just going to step aside and let her daughter spend the summer with that selfish rat bastard, Trevor Schaffer.

CHAPTER NINE

Cheyenne sat at the kitchen table staring at the words in the blue bubble on her computer screen:

Can't come to California for my birthday. Mom found out I've been talking to you and freaked out. Sorry. Really bummed.

Molly was still pissed. When she came home from work last night, she'd barely said two words to Cheyenne and she was even quieter this morning. Breakfast was tenser than final exams in her honors classes. Molly could be majorly stubborn sometimes, but she never stayed mad. And definitely not for this long.

It wasn't fair. Cheyenne pulled her braid over her shoulder and played with the end of it. She had a right to see her father if she wanted to. Trevor said Molly couldn't legally keep them apart.

Cheyenne hit ENTER on the keyboard. The second she did, a sick feeling crept into her stomach. Maybe she shouldn't have sent another private message to her father.

She didn't want Trevor to take her mother to court. That would just make this whole situation ten times worse. And she didn't want to hurt Molly any more than she had already, but it was too late to delete the PM.

Cheyenne slumped back in the chair and massaged her throbbing temples.

She didn't mean to complain to Trevor about Molly, but she could be so frustrating sometimes and Cheyenne didn't have anyone else to talk to. She couldn't talk to April because she'd lost her mom when she was twelve. It would be insensitive to complain when April didn't have a mother at all. She'd never understand when the one thing she wanted most in the world was to see her mother again. That left Cheyenne's father who'd turned out to be a great listener. He was smart, sympathetic, and kind, and he treated Cheyenne with respect.

Trevor wasn't all anti-Molly either. He tried to help Cheyenne see where her mother was coming from, but he also considered Cheyenne's feelings too. He'd invited her to visit him in California for her birthday, and Cheyenne was excited about the idea, but she was also torn. She and April had been planning their big shared birthday party for months and it was finally just over a week away. She didn't want to bail on her friend, but if staying home meant fighting with Molly, she didn't want that either. Her mother's anger was off the charts and completely unreasonable.

Cheyenne probably wasn't even going to get to make the decision anyhow and she hated that a tiny part of herself was actually relieved.

Resting her chin on the heel of her hand, Cheyenne leaned toward her computer screen. She moved the cursor over the page, intending to close Facebook when a message popped up at the bottom of the computer screen: *You received a new notification from Amanda Grace.* Cheyenne sat up straight. Her stomach turned into a block of ice as she stared at the name. *What now?*

Her heart beat slow and heavy like booted feet trudging through knee-deep mud as she forced herself to click on the notifications tab.

Amanda Grace tagged you in a photograph.

Cheyenne already knew what it was going to be. Amanda

Grace had a knack for being at the right place at the worst possible time. She hung out with April and her group of friends, but she never liked Cheyenne. She sneered at her clothes and poked fun at her accent when no one was around. Now that April was graduating and Amanda Grace was going to be a senior in the fall, she'd cornered Cheyenne twice to warn her that when she was queen bee, Cheyenne's days at Key West High School would be numbered. This was distressing because there were no educational alternatives on the island except for homeschooling, and no offense to Molly, but *that* wasn't going to happen.

There were only a few days left in the school year. The seniors were done. Getting the week off as a reward and to prep for graduation the coming Monday. So April wasn't around to stand in Amanda Grace's way. This morning, Cheyenne had found a dead lab frog in her backpack. When she didn't react and simply took the frog out, walked to the trashcan at the front of the classroom, and tossed it into the trash, Amanda Grace had come up behind her and bumped into her so hard Cheyenne tripped and fell. She'd managed to get her hands out just in time, but she'd landed with her butt pointed in the air.

The photo Amanda Grace tagged her in was a picture of Cheyenne in that humiliating position with the caption: *Downward Don't.*

Tears burned the back of Cheyenne's eyes as she crisply typed a reply in the comments of the post, banging out the words on her keyboard wishing she was typing on Amanda Grace's hateful face. *While I find the caption clever, the picture itself is the work of a childish, immature person whom I pity because the only way she can feel good about herself is by embarrassing other people.*

The cursor hovered over the send button. Cheyenne's chest burned as she reread what she'd written.

The door to their second-floor apartment flew open and Molly dashed inside carrying her oversized, overstuffed purse and a large T.J. Maxx bag. "You're not ready yet?" She dropped her purse by the wall just inside the door and kicked off her sandals. "We have to be at the bar by 5 p.m. for the rehearsal." She headed toward her bedroom. "That leaves us only thirty minutes to get dressed and get over there." She disappeared into her room.

The burning sensation inside Cheyenne's chest flared. She really didn't feel like going to the party. She selected the text and hit the delete button. Molly always said the best way to deal with a bully was to ignore them. Her mom might not be good at calculus and honors biology, but she knew people.

A glimmer of doubt flittered through Cheyenne's mind. *What if she was right about Trevor too?*

Cheyenne shoved the thought away and closed her computer. Following Molly into her room, Cheyenne found her on her knees half inside the small closet, digging for something. She didn't have a lot of clothes, but shoes were a different story. She was a total shoe hoarder.

"What are you looking for?" Cheyenne folded her arms across her chest as she stood behind her mother.

"The heels Sophie gave me. Have you seen them?"

"No."

The closet door, which had a tendency to swing shut, was propped open with a heavy bean bag door stopper shaped like a fat calico cat. They'd had a cat like that when Cheyenne was little. Her name was Smudge. Cheyenne missed that old cat. She missed her life in Tennessee too, even though they'd moved around a lot and she changed schools eleven times in nine years. The upside was that she was never in one place long enough to annoy anyone.

Above Smudge, a large poster of Anders Ostergaard was taped to the inside of the door. Cheyenne tilted her head to study the poster. Anders was leaning back against the door of a beat-up red pickup truck in a pair of equally worn out jeans. His legs were crossed at the ankles. His blue plaid flannel button down shirt hung open, revealing his naked chest. The expression on his stubbly face was squinty and brooding. The picture must've been taken seven or eight years ago. His shaggy, dirty blonde hair was longer than it was now, but he still looked pretty much the same. Molly practically drooled over the poster the first time she saw it. She said he looked like "sex on a stick," whatever that meant.

Molly hid the poster in the closet because she didn't want the maintenance guy to see it if he had to come into the apartment. She thought she was too old to fangirl over a celebrity, but she was a total fangirl. Cheyenne still couldn't believe Anders was here in Key West. Her mother was handling it surprisingly well.

"Are you going to get changed?" Molly tossed a pair of fuzzy slippers over her shoulder.

"I just have to put on my dress."

"Dagnabit!" Molly took a stack of shoe boxes out of the closet and set them aside. "Where did I put those shoes?"

Sophie had given Molly the very expensive pair of designer snakeskin stilettos last October as a thank-you gift for letting her spend the night at their apartment even though Cheyenne accidentally destroyed her designer dress. Okay, maybe it hadn't been an accident, but she didn't like Sophie when she first met her. She'd wrongly assumed Sophie was one of the rich, snobby types, like Amanda Grace, who thought they were better than everybody else. Turned out, Sophie wasn't like that at all. She was kind and caring and ended up becoming Molly's best friend. She was nice to Cheyenne too even though she didn't have to be.

Cheyenne frowned as a thought struck her. "Sophie didn't tell you she was going to be Anders Ostergaard's sister-in-law. Why aren't you mad at her?"

Molly stopped digging for a moment and sat up. "She apologized to me over the phone last night and swore she didn't keep the secret from me on purpose. She said she never meant to hurt me and she's relieved I know the truth. I forgave her."

Sure. She forgave her BFF for keeping a secret, but she couldn't forgive her own daughter. Disgusted, Cheyenne spun away from the closet and her gaze landed on a pair of jade green designer heels perched on top of the highboy dresser in the corner. She should just keep her mouth shut and go to her room. Maybe Molly would change her mind about going to the party or take so long they missed it all together. But Sophie would be really disappointed if they didn't come. Cheyenne sighed and grumbled, "Ma, I found your shoes."

Molly shimmied out of the closet and turned around. "Oh, thank goodness. I just bought a new dress to match them."

Still in no hurry to get changed, Cheyenne sat on the bed watching her mother wrestle with a price tag that refused to tear off. Molly was apparently speaking to her again, but Cheyenne was only half-listening. "I would've been home sooner, but Anders' publicist stopped into the bookstore and held me up. She was a little intense."

"Why do you say that?" Cheyenne laid back on the bed, her feet dangling over the side.

"Just the way she questioned me about what happened at the bar yesterday when that paparazzo snapped a picture of me falling into Anders' arms."

"Wait. What?" Cheyenne sat up.

Molly was struggling into a pair of Spanx now. "Ugh! I feel like a stuffed sausage in this thing." She tugged on the waistband and snapped it back into place.

Cheyenne growled with frustration. "When did you fall into Anders' arms?"

"You know how celebrities turn me into a spaz?"

"Yeah?"

"Well, as you can imagine, I was a wreck when I met Anders. I accidentally doused him in hot coffee and his shirt came off. And then I tripped and he caught me."

"Tripped?" Cheyenne arched an eyebrow, unsure if she was surprised or suspicious.

"Yes! It was all one big fat accident. You sound like that

publicist. She accused me of setting Anders up in a compromising position to further my career as a wannabe country singer."

"You *are* a country singer. One of the best. Who cares if you aren't famous? What does that woman know about anything?" It really ticked Cheyenne off when people criticized her mother's talent. She had a true gift from God. Molly always said success was part talent, part timing, and part luck, and she just wasn't one of the lucky ones. Cheyenne believed that was the only reason she wasn't famous. Dumb luck.

"Don't worry about it, Chey. I'm not." Molly slid the new dress over her head. The lacy jade green sheath and matching stilettos made her pretty, red-headed mama look like the country music superstar she was meant to be.

Moving to stand in front of the dresser mirror, Molly reached up to twist her hair into a bun. She caught Cheyenne's eye in the reflection. "Your dress. Go put it on. We've got to go."

Cheyenne had already re-braided her hair and brushed her teeth when she got home from school, so it didn't take her more than a minute to slide into the white and pink floral sundress. She sat on the edge of the bed to put on her pink cowgirl boots and hesitated. Amanda Grace's boyfriend Troy bussed tables at the Key West Beach Club. What if Cheyenne bumped into him and he saw the boots? Feeling suddenly nauseous, she put the boots back into her closet and pulled out a pair of boring black sandals instead.

When Cheyenne came out of her room, Molly was at the table, stuffing lipstick, cash, and an ID into a small white dress purse. She slid the silver chain strap over her head so it crossed her body and grabbed her keys from the hook beside the door. "All set?"

"Yeah."

"Hit the lights. And make sure you pull the door closed tight and double check the lock," Molly said over her shoulder as she went out the door and started down the stairs.

Cheyenne balked. *As if I don't know how to lock up the house.* When was Molly going to start trusting her? She wasn't a baby anymore. Cheyenne gave the door a hard pull, feeling it catch in place before twisting the knob to make sure it was locked.

Molly let out a shout as she slipped on a stair and pitched forward halfway to the bottom.

It all happened so fast. Cheyenne froze on the landing, stupidly watching her mother grab for the railing and land hard on her side against the metal steps. Her shoes flew off and the lacy fabric of her dress caught on a protruding bolt, which kept her from sliding farther.

"Ma!" Cheyenne dashed down the stairs after her. When she reached the step her mother had fallen from, she slipped too, but the scuffed soles of her sandals had better traction than her mother's heels. She merely fell backward and landed on her butt on a higher step. She sprang up, skipped the treacherous step, and carefully hurried down the rest of the way to reach her mother who had sat up in a daze.

"Oh my goodness. Are you okay?" Cheyenne was afraid to touch her, so she hovered close, waiting for her mother to say she was fine. Her hair had come out of its neat bun. Red-gold curls stuck out everywhere and spiraled down her back. She didn't appear to be bleeding, but her eyes were glazed and she seemed disoriented.

Molly squeezed her eyes shut for a moment and shook her head before she reached for the railing to pull herself up.

"No, don't try to stand yet."

Molly groaned and sat back down. "What happened?"

Cheyenne swallowed hard. "You fell."

"It's all right. I'm all right." She patted Cheyenne's knee and finally turned to look at her. The slight movement made her wince. "Just a little sore. I banged my hip."

There was a gaping tear in her clingy, form-fitting dress. Cheyenne's heart sank. "Oh no. Your dress is ruined."

Molly stared at the tear blankly for a moment and then her face crinkled up as she struggled not to cry. "Did I trip on something? What the heck happened?"

Cheyenne's throat thickened with emotion. She put an arm around her mother's shoulders and gave her a sideways hug. She hated seeing her mother hurt and upset. "No, the step is slippery. I don't remember it being like that before." *That's because the stair wasn't slippery before.* Not two hours ago when Cheyenne got home from school and not twenty minutes ago when Molly got home from work.

Amanda Grace. Was she to blame for this? Cheyenne stiffened as a surge of white-hot rage threatened to pop the top of her head off. Childish pranks were right up that witch's alley, but this one had almost killed someone. Molly could have broken her neck! When Amanda Grace talked about Cheyenne's "days being numbered" was she talking about something more sinister than just making her move to another school? Shaky and sick to her stomach, Cheyenne hugged Molly tighter. This was Cheyenne's fault for hiding behind April and not standing up to the bully months ago.

But did she have the nerve even now?

"I'm so sorry, Ma."

Molly touched her arm. "I'm all right baby girl. Where are my shoes?"

"I don't know." Cheyenne scanned the area and spotted one of the jade green stilettos several steps up. It lay on its side, the heel completely snapped off. The other shoe was missing. She spotted it below the metal steps bathing in a puddle of mud. "Oh, no, Ma. They're ruined!"

"It's all right. They can be fixed."

No, they couldn't. She was lying. She could see the disappointment hiding behind her mother's false smile. Cheyenne's bottom lip quivered as anger, guilt, and frustration bubbled over inside her and she started to cry.

Molly hugged her while she bawled her eyes out, but it only lasted about a minute because the image of Amanda Grace broadcasting her meltdown on Facebook Live crept into her mind. She pulled herself together and calmed the heck down.

"I'm sorry I scared you. All better now?" Molly gave her a tender smile that made her feel all warm and mushy inside, and the tears threatened to return.

Cheyenne blinked them back and wiped her nose. "Yeah. I'm okay."

"I need to change and text Sophie. We're going to be so late." Molly started to rise to her feet. When she hissed in pain, Cheyenne stood up and caught her under the arm.

"Here, lean on me."

They made their way up the stairs slowly, being extra careful when they came to the slippery step.

Once her mother was inside the apartment, Cheyenne turned around and scanned the parking lot. She couldn't shake the creepy sensation she was being watched, but the lot was empty except for a few parked cars. The rays from the shifting sun glinted off the surface of the slippery step. Cheyenne went to it and touched the shiny surface. Her finger came away coated with a thick, waxy substance. She put it to her nose and got a whiff of citrus and chemicals.

No, this definitely wasn't here before.

Someone had waxed the step on purpose.

A fresh surge of outrage heated her blood, but she tamped it down by focusing on something productive. She would scrub the step clean while her mother was changing. She didn't want Molly to have the chance to look at it too closely or she might start asking questions.

CHAPTER TEN

Molly felt like a freshly branded cow as she hobbled into the fancy beachfront restaurant, favoring her left leg. She'd changed into a simple black sleeveless dress with a rounded neckline and a straight hem that fell just below her knees. Long enough to cover the big red bruise that was already starting to turn blue in spots. She decided to forgo the heels she usually wore with this dress and settled on a pair of strappy sandals.

They were thirty minutes late for dinner and had completely missed the rehearsal. While changing clothes, Molly had texted Sophie an apology and an explanation. Her friend was more concerned about Molly's accident than her absence at the rehearsal and assured her they could go over what she needed to know when she arrived at the restaurant. But Molly was embarrassed for blowing one of her most important duties as maid of honor, especially when she stepped out onto the patio and the groom drew everyone's eyes to her.

"Hey, short stuff!" Jimmy Panama waved to Molly when he spotted her.

Normally, she would've brushed off the silly nickname, but there was nothing normal about this day. She was having dinner with Anders Ostergaard like it was no big thing. A blush warmed her face as she nodded hello to Jimmy and carefully avoided eye contact with Anders. She ushered Cheyenne into the two empty seats waiting for them at the round table.

Jimmy leaned forward. "Heard there was a scafuffle. You all right?"

"It's kerfuffle." Sophie bumped his arm with her elbow. "And she's just fine. Don't embarrass her."

"She's right. My ker was just fuffled is all. I'll be okay." Molly smiled at Jimmy and her gaze inadvertently strayed to Anders. She realized he was watching her over the rim of his glass, and a fresh surge of heat flushed her face.

Seated side by side, the brothers were framed in the red-orange glow of the sun setting over the Gulf of Mexico. The two men were shockingly similar. Both tall, broad-shouldered, and fit, they had the same slanted blue eyes and square jaw. Jimmy's face was slightly fuller than Anders' and his brow was broader. He was clean-shaven and his flaxen hair was cut short, while Anders' jaw was scruffy with a slight beard and his dirty blond hair scuffed the collar of his dress shirt. Jimmy wore a navy-blue button-down shirt open at the collar. Anders wore a white one with a bolo tie. Both men couldn't have been mistaken for anything but brothers. How had she not seen it before?

Because what were the odds?

Smiling too brightly at Sophie, Molly took in her friend's appearance. "You're absolutely glowing tonight." Tall, chic, and gorgeous, Sophie looked so much more relaxed than the first time they'd met just nine months ago. Had it been less than a year since they'd become friends? Molly felt as if she'd known Sophie her entire life and the feeling was mutual. Neither of them had ever had a best friend before and they'd become like a couple of teenagers latched onto each other at the hip. When Sophie wasn't with Jimmy, of course. Sophie's Alabama-born fiancé had a lot to do with the changes in her. He brought out her warmth and nurtured her adventurous spirit while she brought out the best in good ol' boy Jimmy, too. He'd shed his bad boy Casanova reputation on the island, and some people had started calling him a pillar of the community. Jimmy claimed he had more fun just being a pill.

Molly admired Sophie's slinky, sapphire blue slip dress. One of the many things they shared was their obsession with high fashion. But where Molly had the taste for filet mignon on a Big Mac budget, Sophie actually had the bank account and the supermodel body to wear it. "And, oh my goodness, that dress. It's new. Versace?"

"Yes. Seriously. How do you do that?"

"It's a skill."

"A talent. You look lovely as well."

Molly started to wave off the compliment but winced when the slight movement caused pain to dart up her leg.

Sophie's smile faded. "Are you still feeling poorly? I noticed your limp."

"My pride took the brunt of the fall. I'll be okay. Just a little bruised."

"Duchess, tell my brother here about the cha-cha lessons you've been making me take. He doesn't believe me."

The waiter appeared by Molly's side with a glass of champagne. She accepted it with gratitude and took a long sip.

Sophie's eyes twinkled as she smiled at Anders. "It's true. He's getting on quite well too, although he got off to a dodgy start."

"That's because he was born with two left feet." Anders lounged back in his chair, the light breeze from the ocean stirring his artfully messy locks. "It's the reason he sucked at football in high school." His devilish grin wasn't directed at Molly but it still made her stomach flutter.

Jimmy snorted with contempt. "That wasn't the reason."

Sophie put a hand on Jimmy's bicep and leaned forward to tell the story. "I made the mistake of employing a renowned dance instructor from Miami. He drove all the way to Key West to give us private lessons, but Jimmy didn't care for his teaching methods."

Crossing his arms, Jimmy grumbled, "That's because pygmy Patrick Swayze wouldn't let me lead."

"He was merely trying to show you the proper hold for the waltz."

Jimmy mimicked an upper-crust British accent. "'Point your toe, James. Point your toe.' I wanted to point it, all right. Straight up his can."

Sophie bit back a smile. "We ended up dismissing him after two lessons and instead hired Stella Marie, the resident dance instructor for the Key Breeze Retirement Home."

"Stella's a doll." Jimmy grinned. "She was a Rockette back in the sixties."

"For real?" Anders seemed genuinely impressed.

"Yeah. And she can still part her hair with the tip of her shoe."

Molly chuckled and glanced over at Cheyenne. She was engrossed in conversation with Sophie's father, Mitch Thompson.

"I know an old guy who lives in Bimini," Mitch was saying. "When he was a teenager, he and his father used to take Hemingway deep sea fishing. The guy wrote a book about it. Might be helpful."

Cheyenne had her phone out ready to look it up. "What's it called?"

"Can't recall the title exactly, but the guy's name is Emory Constantinople."

"Found it. *Old Hem: An Account of Hemingway's Life and Times in Bimini, Cuba, and Key West*, published in 1978. But, dang, it's out of print."

Molly smiled at Sophie's mother, Lillian Stone who sat on the other side of Mitch trying not to look bored.

It was hard to image two less likely people being together, but according to Sophie, Mitch and Lillian had once been very much in love. Sophie's American father looked like he just stepped out of the seventies, with his long brown hair, handlebar mustache, and bohemian rock star style, while Sophie's beautiful, sophisticated, fair-haired British mother could have been the poster girl for high society.

Next to Lillian, Sue Martin sat with her husband Oscar. Sue waved and mouthed, "You okay?"

Molly nodded and raised her glass of champagne to her friend in thanks before taking another deep sip.

Leaning toward Sophie, Molly spoke in her ear. "Where's your grandmother?"

"You know how Agnes feels about my mum. She passed on the rehearsal dinner but promised to be at the wedding."

"Without the shotgun, I hope."

"We hope."

When the waitress went around taking their orders, Molly noticed Anders ordered the surf without the turf, while everyone else ordered steak and lobster.

Sitting across the table from someone she knew so well but didn't really know at all was a disconcerting feeling. She knew his favorite ice cream flavor was mint chip. He preferred boxers over briefs. And he was a Taurus. Hell, she even knew he lost his virginity at sixteen. While she wasn't a hundred percent certain he remembered her first name.

"A toast." Oscar raised his glass and everyone followed his lead. Even Cheyenne lifted her Shirley Temple. "To two people who are such complete opposites, it's no wonder they complete each other so perfectly."

Anders put his hand on the back of Oscar's neck and pulled the stocky, goateed man closer. "Just like you and me."

Oscar laughed and shoved him away. "Exactly, now let me finish, boss. What I was trying to say is that not everyone is fortunate enough to find their soul mate. I think most people never do. I certainly never thought I would." He shot Sue a tender smile. "But when it happens... Pow, the chemistry is cosmic. Jimmy, Sophie, respect each other. Cherish the gift you've been given. And if you must fight, fight clean and naked. Salute!"

The table chuckled and drank to the toast.

Sophie looked at Jimmy and their eyes met in a private smile. He leaned closer and kissed her lips. Molly's heart constricted. The love in his eyes was undeniable. She couldn't help but wonder what it would it be like to have a man look at her the way Jimmy was looking at Sophie. Oscar was right. That kind of love didn't exist for everybody. What Sophie and Jimmy had was magical and kinda breathtaking.

"Where's Obie tonight?" Sue turned to Anders, who was laughing with Oscar about something Molly hadn't caught.

"With his new nanny. The agency sent her over. She was a lot younger than I expected, but she came highly recommended."

"You want me to run a background check on her?" Mitch offered. He wasn't a cop but he had his sources. If you wanted the skinny on someone, Mitch Thompson could have a whole dossier for you in about an hour. If you needed a fake ID or a place to lay low in Barbados, he could hook you up and then some. Sophie insisted he was only a treasure hunter, but Molly suspected he was a bit more than that.

Anders looked up from his cell phone. "Nah, that's all right."

Jimmy nudged his arm. "Come on. Based on the recent events in Vegas, you can't be too careful."

"Jimmy's right," Mitch said. "I'd be glad to launch my own investigation into that as well."

"The Vegas PD is on it, but you could check out the nanny if you'd like. Her name is Greenlee Fiori."

Molly winced and caught Cheyenne's eye. They shared an expression of mild horror.

Jimmy spit the beer he'd just swigged and sprayed the table, catching Anders on the downdraft.

"What the hell, bro!" Anders brushed off his arm.

Jimmy opened his mouth to respond, but then frowned at Sophie and said grumpily, "Go on, you tell it."

Sophie nodded and rubbed his shoulder. "Jimmy rescued Greenlee Fiori and her friend April from a bozo in Miami last autumn…"

As Molly took another sip of champagne, she smiled at Sophie's use of the term "bozo," one of Jimmy's favorite words. Realizing her glass was almost empty, she signaled to the waiter for a refill.

"…when they got back to Key West, Greenlee spitefully told the cops Jimmy was transporting an illegal case of rum on his boat and got him arrested for smuggling."

"And Sophie was arrested for prostitution," Jimmy added with a grumble.

Sophie poked him in the ribs. "My mum is here."

"Oh, sorry. My bad. Don't worry, Mrs. Stone, she only spent one night in jail."

When Lillian looked horrified, Mitch leaned toward her and whispered something in her ear. Whatever he said made a laugh bubble up her throat. She covered her mouth demurely and nodded an apology.

Jimmy shook his head. "I'd think twice about letting that bit—"

"Brat," Sophie interrupted, clutching his wrist as she leaned against his arm. "There's a young lady present."

"I'd think twice about letting that *brat* watch your kid."

Cheyenne shrugged. "It's all right, Jimmy. Greenlee Fiori is a bitch."

Molly almost spilled the fresh glass of Champagne she was leaning forward to sip. "Cheyenne Dallas MacBain!"

Anders laughed first before Jimmy and the rest of the table joined him. Sophie looked stunned and Molly didn't know what to think. Her baby girl didn't curse. Ever. Of course, she couldn't say the same about herself. Though she tried not to curse too much in front of Cheyenne. That was why she'd trained herself to say "dagnabit" when she really wanted to drop the F-bomb.

She didn't want to scold the girl for something she herself was thinking, so she said instead, "Now, Cheyenne, Greenlee is one of April's friends. You told me she's never been mean to you, and April says she's trying to turn over a new leaf."

"That's only because her sister is getting married and moving to Orlando. April says Greenlee's trying to prove how responsible she can be so her father will let her live at the house in Key West by herself."

Jimmy snorted with disdain, but Anders leaned back in his seat and took another swig of beer. He was drinking Sam Adams, Molly noted with approval. He had good taste.

"We were brats when we were teenagers too, brother." Putting a hand on Jimmy's shoulder, Anders shook him playfully. Molly stole a peek at him, all too conscious of the fact that she was probably never going to get an opportunity like this again. Anders was just sitting there across the table looking all gorgeous and relaxed like it was the most natural thing in the world to be hanging out with her group of friends. It was surreal. "I'm willing to give her a chance, but if I notice anything funny, I'll can her."

Molly wanted to say something to him, but she couldn't think of anything. The bruise on her leg was too distracting. It was throbbing like a kettledrum. Instead of relaxing her, the champagne was only making her more hyperaware. Her surroundings were a little brighter. The sounds of the sea and the chatter of conversation a little louder. The salty air a little brinier.

The mingled perfumes and colognes of her dinner partners a little headier. And Anders was less than five feet away, larger than life.

He was so stinkin' handsome, she couldn't keep her gaze from straying toward him. She was struck by his stark masculinity. The confident set of his broad shoulders. He was a man who was comfortable in his own skin. There was so much to like. His easy smile. His expressive eyes. Even the healing cut below his right eye was sexy. It was just deep enough it was probably going to leave a scar. And his voice, God, his voice. It was as rich and smoky as a fog-laden mountain valley. She followed his hand as it reached for the bottle of Sam Adams and tilted it to top off his glass. He had nice hands. The palms were broad. The fingers long and blunt. Talented hands that could play a guitar like nobody's business. They were strong but gentle hands. She could attest to that since her breast had unexpectedly had the privilege of being nestled firmly in his grip. The memory of his touch lingered on her skin. The warmth spread to her limbs and a pulse began to thrum, slow and lush, deep inside her.

She stood up quickly, startling herself and garnering strange looks from at least half the table. "I need some air," she announced in explanation. Heat flushed her face as she grabbed her purse and fled inside the building. She was halfway to the ladies' room before she realized the statement hadn't made a lick of sense considering they were sitting on a patio beside the sea. She'd felt too closed in though. Suffocated by the stress of trying to play it cool in front of Anders when down deep she was as jittery as a long-tailed cat in a room full of rocking chairs.

Molly was standing at the sink rooting through her purse when Sophie joined her in the ladies' room.

"Are you certain you're not feeling poorly?"

Molly shook her head. "No. It's not that. I can't do this. I can't be near him and be myself."

"You're talking about Anders? Why can't you?"

"Because…" Where to begin? How did she explain what she was feeling when she was feeling so many things? "He's my UC."

"Your what?"

"My unattainable crush. My fake celebrity boyfriend. He's fictional. He's not supposed to be sitting across the table from me drinking a beer with his brother. It's like frickin' Santa Claus decided to stay for Christmas dinner. Fantasy and reality are colliding in my world right now and it's messing with my head."

Sophie opened her clutch and looked through it. "He's a bit fitter than Father Christmas, isn't he though?"

That made Molly smile.

Finding the tube of Givenchy Le Rouge at the bottom of her purse, Sophie popped the cap off and bent closer to the mirror. "Anders Ostergaard is just a man." She paused to reapply the lipstick. "He swears, burps, and farts, just like the rest of us."

Molly laughed outright at that. Sophie was sounding more like Jimmy Panama every day, but that sounded a bit more like something Molly would say. "You don't fart, Sophie. I don't even think you poop. You're too proper for that."

When their giggles faded, Molly said, "My head is spinning."

"You can't be pickled. You barely drank two glasses of champagne. You just need to eat something. How's your leg?"

Molly touched her injured limb. "Kind of numb unless I bump it."

"It'll hurt worse tomorrow."

Not only was Sophie smart, witty, and generous, she was a great listener and she had excellent taste in shoes. Molly felt blessed to call her a friend. A surge of emotion welled up inside her chest and her eyes filled with tears.

"What's this, hon?"

"When I fell, I ruined the heels you gave me."

"Aww, I've got at least a dozen more just like them. You can have your pick. Even better, we'll go shopping when I get back from my honeymoon, and I'll treat you to a brand-new pair of your very own."

"I couldn't accept that kind of gift from you."

"I insist. Consider it a belated maid of honor gift."

"But you already gave me a spa day."

"I gave one to Sue as well. But you're my maid of honor." Sophie put her arm around Molly's shoulders and gave her a sideways hug. "I should've given you an extra special gift. A new pair of designer heels is perfect. Come on, let's tidy you up. Dinner should be arriving soon, yeah?"

Molly took a moment to powder her nose and fluff her hair. "It's the eve of your wedding, and I'm ruining the night for you. I'm sorry. I didn't mean to pull you away from your own party."

"You didn't pull me away. I needed some air too." Sophie winked mischievously and Molly couldn't help but smile.

When they exited the bathroom, they found Anders standing in the vestibule talking on his cell phone. The small room was cut off from the restaurant by another door that muted the outside world.

He cursed and said tersely, "Email it to me now." After tapping the screen to end the call, he started scrolling through the phone, searching for something. "Molly, can you hang back a minute?"

Startled by the request, Molly looked at Sophie for help. Her friend motioned for her to go talk to him before she slipped out the door.

Molly was trembling. He always made her tremble. Just a small vibration under the skin. Not enough to be physically noticeable unless you really looked for it but just enough to rattle her brain.

Anders seemed to find what he was looking for and stopped scrolling. "My publicist found this on the internet. I thought you should know." He turned the phone toward her so she could look at a picture and headline. It was an image of Molly and Anders.

She was in his arms. His hand was unmistakably grabbing her breast. The headline read: COUNTRY CROONER CAUGHT CHEATING ON RECENTLY MURDERED FIANCE.

"Three major trash mags are threatening to go with the story unless I give them something else. Selena is trying to squash it but says it's too late for the internet story. Best she can do is get the site to take it down and we'll have to ride the wave until the next big celebrity scandal comes along."

Molly felt queasy. She didn't know if she should be offended or embarrassed by the headline, but it didn't matter. This was going to hurt him more than it hurt her. She had nothing at stake while he had everything. "I'm so sorry."

He shrugged. "It's not your fault."

Molly snorted. "That picture wouldn't exist if I hadn't been so stinkin' clumsy. Your publicist thinks I set you up. How come you don't?"

"My publicist?"

Molly nodded. "Selena. I met her this afternoon when she came into the bookshop."

He shook his head. "What was she doing there?"

"Warning me away from you."

His eyebrows shot up in surprise, then he pursed his lips and nodded sagely. "Ah. Sorry about that. She means well, but when it comes to me sometimes she can be worse than a pit bull protecting a steak. I'm the steak in that scenario. Don't worry about her bothering you again though. She was on her way out of town."

"Do *you* think I set you up?"

The corner of his mouth quirked. "Nah. It was kinda obvious you didn't know I was in Key West. Besides, Jimmy says you're good people. He trusts you so I trust you, Molly."

Her heart did an odd little flip and warmth spread from her belly like a shot of whisky on a cold winter's night. He knew her name, and he trusted her. How amazing was that?

"Thank you," she said, smiling at him.

He sighed and looked away for a moment. Driving his fingers through his hair, he messed it up even more than it was and left it that way, which explained his perpetually tousled look. "People from the tabloids or media may try to contact you. Your best course of action is to say, 'no comment.' Anything else could possibly be misconstrued."

"Got it."

"Great."

He was such a nice man. A good man. So considerate and kind to his fans. And he was admired and respected by his peers. That was why she'd stayed loyal to him all these years—not just because he was incredibly talented and easy on the eyes. Though she admired him for those reasons too. In the fifteen years she'd been a fan, she'd never heard one negative thing about him from anybody. She knew he hadn't killed his girlfriend, or whatever she was to him, just as certainly as she knew the grass was green and the sky was blue.

The silence widened between them until she couldn't take it anymore. "Okay, then." She turned to go because standing there saying nothing was just getting weird.

"Molly?"

A small thrill spiraled through her at the sound of her name.

"Yeah?" Her hand was on the doorknob.

"I don't think you'll hear from Selena again, but if you do, will you let me know?"

"Sure."

He took out his wallet, flipped it open, and pulled out a business card. "Here." He offered it to her. "It's got my private cell number. Don't hesitate to call."

Her hand trembled as she took the card. It started to slip from her fingers, but she caught it. She was pretty certain he didn't notice because he was preoccupied opening the door for her.

With Anders's digits in her purse and his big hand on her back guiding her through the restaurant, Molly realized she was living one of her daydreams. She soaked in the moment, letting herself imagine a world where this was real. Where an average, red-headed nobody from a one-horse town in Oklahoma could actually be on date with her unattainable crush.

CHAPTER ELEVEN

Anders left the Bugatti in the hotel parking garage and opted to walk to Dixie's on that bright June morning. He wanted to see if there was anything he could help Sue and Oscar with while they were busy setting up the bar for the wedding and the reception afterward. Obie was beside him, his nose stuck in a comic book. The main reason Anders had suggested the walk was to give his son some fresh air and exercise.

It was a pretty day for a wedding. The vast sky was built of layers of powder blue, turquoise, azure, and pale indigo. The sun was already baking the sidewalk, and the light breeze carried the scent of the sea.

Obie still wasn't speaking to him, but he was acknowledging his questions with a nod or shake of the head. Just the fact he was no longer looking at him like he was a walking, talking grizzly bear was a step in the right direction.

Anders' phone chirped in the holster clipped to his belt. Assuming it was just another text from Selena about the photograph debacle, he ignored it. She hadn't been able to squash the story in the tabloids, and now the mainstream media was clamoring for a press conference. Anders wasn't interested. Casey

Conway's funeral was today, and her family needed privacy to grieve during this sad time. The press was bound to sensationalize anything Anders confirmed or denied, so it was better to say nothing at all. Selena didn't agree. She wanted Anders to skip his brother's wedding and hop on the next flight to Nashville. She thought coming out of hiding and talking to the press would curb the rumors that he had something to hide.

As they crossed the street to Dixie's, the sound of music floated toward them. The crisp twang of a banjo whined over the live band. Anders recognized the melody as soon as he heard it because he'd written it. The rip-roaring bluegrass-inspired country song was his first number one record. The voice singing the song that made him famous wasn't a baritone like himself. In fact, the voice wasn't even male. A woman with a rich alto was belting out the lyrics and doing a fine job of it.

He opened the glass door and motioned for Obie to go inside first. Anders wasn't sure who he was expecting to find on stage, but it definitely wasn't Molly MacBain. She was filling in for the lead singer of the cover band Jimmy had hired for the wedding. Molly sat on a stool looking as down-to-earth as a Southern girl could get, with her long, red-gold curls pulled back in a ponytail, a navy and white plaid shirt hanging open over a white tank top, and faded blue jeans tucked into an old pair of brown cowboy boots. She had a banjo on her knee and her mouth to the mic, pickin' and singin' the hell out of Anders' fast-tempo song:

"...*She was a fair, spare, raven-haired fun-lovin' lady*
    looking for a man. And, hell, it was payday
    A six-shooter on my hip, hip to let her rip
    Thirsting for some company, you bet I took a sip

Cheyenne, you're tearing me apart

Cheyenne, quit tryin' to steal my heart
Cheyenne, go easy on me now
Cheyenne, you're mine 'til our time runs out…"

Anders pointed to the table nearest the door and Obie slid into a seat. The stage was on the far side of the long room and Molly had the glare of Fresnel lamps in her eyes, but Anders didn't want to take a chance. He knew how nervous he made her feel. If he drew her notice, she might stop singing altogether and that would be a damn shame. Molly's tone was rich and effortless, but there was this underlying bluesy quality to it that came through when she dug into the lyrics:

"When the evening iron horse made the shingles shudder
I was at the mercy of a fancy frontier daughter
A six-shooter on my hip, hip to let her rip
She laid me down and went to town, yeah
it was a Wild West courtship. Ye hawww!"

The famous intermezzo was all banjo. Fast-paced and tricky, it took a skilled picker to do it justice, and Molly was killin' it and then some. The tempo sped up even faster. The lyrics in the next verse were meant to be sung double time as the song turned into a real barn burner. Molly stomped the heel of a dusty brown cowboy boot and kept on truckin'.

"She was a fair, spare, raven-haired fun-lovin' lady
who was having a fine time, while I was shouting mayday
A six-shooter on my hip, hip to let her rip
I was spent, spent the rent, and hell-bent

And Cheyenne, she left me heartsick

Cheyenne, you're tearing me apart
  Cheyenne, quit tryin' to steal my heart
  Cheyenne, go easy on me now
  Cheyenne, you're mine 'til our time runs out

Cheyenne, you're tearing me apart
  Cheyenne, don't you go stealin' my heart
  Cheyenne, think I'm fallin' in love
  Cheyenne, you just went and broke this stud"

Sue was seated at a table near the stage. When the song ended, she was the first to start clapping, but Anders and Obie joined in and Molly's head came up to look for the source of the applause. He knew the moment she spotted him because her face turned as red as a pepper. She nudged the guy who'd joined Molly in the center of the stage. Presumably the lead singer, the chubby, middle-aged dude did a double take at Anders before lifting his white, Texas-sized cowboy hat in greeting.

Anders projected his voice across the room. "Never heard a lady sing that song before."

She shot Tex a sideways smile before she leaned into the mic, "Who says that's changed?"

The drummer was quick with a rim shot. The *ba dum tsh* made Anders laugh out loud.

Glancing at Obie, whose nose was still planted in the comic book he'd brought with him, Anders got up and joined Sue at her table. "You play that banjo like Earl Scruggs."

"He was my grandpa."

"Seriously?"

She gave him a saucy grin and her eyes sparkled. "Nah, but my Uncle John was in a bluegrass band. He taught me to play when I was a kid."

"Music's in your blood then."

"You could say that."

Sue said to Anders. "That song 'Cheyenne' was one of your first big hits, wasn't it?"

"Yeah."

She turned a sly eye on Molly. "Is it just a coincidence or did you name your daughter after a song?"

Anders chuckled. "I sure hope not. The song's about a prostitute."

When the guys in the band chuckled, Molly flushed. "In my defense," she said into the microphone so it amplified her voice through the whole room. "The album is titled *Cheyenne* as well. I named my daughter after the album, not the song."

The guys in the band chuckled harder.

"What? If I'd waited a few more years to have Cheyenne, she might have been named *Devil Woman*, and that's definitely not in the top 100 most popular baby names."

The band roared and Anders chuckled too. *Devil Woman* was the name of his fourth album. He'd written the title track about his soon-to-be ex-wife. Molly might have been embarrassed by the revelation that she'd named her kid after his album, but she took it all in stride and even poked fun at herself. Pretty, talented, and humble. He liked that about her.

He was flattered too. He'd heard stories of fans tattooing his image on their bodies. He'd even heard of babies being named after him, but this was the first time he'd heard of anyone naming their child after one of his albums. It was a nice feeling, like she'd appreciated his work right from the beginning at a time when his record label's marketing department was banking on his looks and charm more than his talent. He'd let them because he was no fool and he worked out hard to look the way he did. He didn't mind posing shirtless and giving smoldering looks into the camera when he sang. But in his soul, he wanted to be admired for his music more than his pretty face. Peer recognition had come later, and he'd won numerous awards since, but it was the general consensus among critics that his first album wasn't his best despite the four number one hits that came off the record.

Molly slid off the stool and handed the banjo to the grizzled old guitar player. "Thanks for letting me play. I wish I still had one of my own. I'm getting rusty."

"You couldn't tell." The old man grinned and gave her a slight bow as he took his instrument back.

"He's right," Anders said as she stepped off the stage and came toward him. "You played that thing like you meant it."

"Maybe 'cause I did."

The flirty, dimpled smile she gave him made something in his chest flutter. Choosing to ignore the strange sensation, he leaned back in the wooden chair and crossed his arms. "You sitting in with the band tonight?"

She rocked back on her boot heels. "That's the plan. Only a couple songs though. I have maid of honor duties." Waving to the band, she said, "See y'all tonight."

Sue jumped up from the table. "Look at me sitting here like I've got nothing better to do. You sounded lovely, Molly. I'll see you later this afternoon."

"Do you need help with anything?"

"I've got it under control. You go on and enjoy your day off." Sue waved over her shoulder as she headed for the office.

Anders observed Molly's profile while she was turned away from him. She had a curvy compact body. Firm, small-but-full breasts, a trim waist, and a high round ass that was plump but not broad. A single wide rather than a double wide. She wasn't fat by any means but compared to the actresses and models he was used to dating, she had some meat on her petite bones.

When she turned back to face him, their gazes met. For a

split-second, he saw a nervous shudder roll through her, but she banked it. She was still jumpy around him, but she was getting it under control. That made him feel better. He hated making people uncomfortable.

Her eyes sparkled with mischief again. "If you're lucky, maybe I'll sing a duet with you tonight."

A smile tugged at the corner of his mouth as he watched her strut away from him, boot heels clicking on the concrete as she headed for the door. She stopped in front of Obie who was looking at her like she'd hung the moon. They exchanged words that Anders was too far away to hear before she caught his chin and bent to kiss him on the head. Then she continued toward the exit again, stopping for a second to wave at Obie before she disappeared through the glass door.

Anders stared after her, half jealous of Obie's obvious affection for the woman and half wishing Molly MacBain would fuss over him the way she fussed over his son.

CHAPTER TWELVE

"You don't need to fuss over me," Sophie said to Molly who was on her knees, her bridesmaid's dress hiked up to her thighs. She was searching for the source of the stray thread dragging from the hem of Sophie's gown, a gorgeous, white satin strapless number with a fitted bodice and a floor-length sheath skirt.

"I just want your wedding day to be perfect." Molly flipped another section of hem, still following the never-ending loose thread. "I wouldn't expect this kind of poor craftsmanship from a designer label. Are you certain you didn't step on the hem and tear it?"

"I'm positive. Do you have scissors? Just nip it off."

Molly raised her head to scan the room for Sue. The former hairdresser turned bar manager was styling Lillian's long silvery blonde hair into an elegant French twist. "Are there any scissors in the desk, Sue?"

They were in Jimmy's office, helping the bride and each other get dressed. In the next room, guests were already starting to arrive. They were gathering on the first floor of Dixie's until

Oscar, acting as the usher, could escort them upstairs to their seats.

Sue snorted. "You'd be lucky to find a pencil with a point in that desk. Jimmy doesn't keep up with his office supplies. There's a pair of scissors behind the bar in the little cubby under the phone."

"I'll get them." Molly climbed to her feet and tugged her skirt back down. She was wearing a coral-colored chiffon dress with a sweetheart neckline and a high-low skirt. Sue wore the same color, but her dress was floor length with cap sleeves and a scoop neckline. As far as bridesmaid's dresses went, they were very flattering, but then, Molly expected nothing less from Sophie when it came to fashion.

Molly was just closing the door behind her when Captain Tom walked into Dixie's.

Jimmy Panama yelled from the far end of the bar. "Captain Tom!"

"Panama." The old, crusty former fisherman hobbled toward the groom-to-be in a white button-down shirt and pair of avocado green trousers that were four decades outdated in style but still in like-new condition. "How come you're at the bar and not getting ready for your wedding?"

"Jitters," he said with a slow grin that suggested he was anything but nervous. Jimmy was dressed for a casual Key West wedding in a loose white linen dress shirt, khaki pants, and boat shoes.

"How's it going, Captain Tom?" Molly stopped to give him a quick peck on the cheek as she passed.

"Sweet Molly McB. Are you singing tonight, sweetheart?" He watched her make her way around to the back of the bar.

"A couple of songs. I wouldn't miss singing at my best friend's wedding."

"Aww, that's good to hear."

"Heyyyy, Captain Tom!" Anders came out of the kitchen. "Long time no see. How you been?"

At the sound of Anders' voice, Molly's heart skipped a beat. She looked up from the bin she was just starting to sort through.

The captain scratched the top of his head. "I must've went too heavy on the hooch 'cause I'll be damned, I'm seeing things."

"It ain't the hooch this time." Anders laughed as he gave the old man a hug.

Anders was dressed like Jimmy in the same casual, loose-fitting clothes. It was so different from his usual style, but he looked sexier and more relaxed than she'd ever seen him. His damp hair was swept back off his face in loose waves. He was freshly shaven and so gorgeous he made her eyes hurt.

"My God, ain't you a sight for sore eyes." The captain patted Anders' shoulder and then pointed at Jimmy. "You were holding out on me. When the hell did you get into town, kid? You owe me twenty bucks and a new fishing pole. I haven't forgotten."

Anders chuckled. "I'll square up with you. I promise."

Molly was so fascinated by the exchange between Anders and the captain, she almost forgot what she was looking for in the bin. She shouldn't have been surprised that Anders knew Captain Tom. He was an old childhood friend of Jimmy's, after all. It only made sense Anders would know him as well. The retired sea captain had taught Jimmy everything he knew about boats and had employed him as a deckhand on his shrimp boat when Jimmy was a teenager. He'd encouraged Jimmy to join the Navy to get away from his crummy home life.

A thought suddenly occurred to her. She didn't know much about Jimmy's childhood, but she knew his father had been abusive, forcing Jimmy to leave home at seventeen to get away from the violence. Anders was just a year older. He'd gone to college on a football scholarship, gotten a Bachelor of Science degree in Business, and had his first hit record not long after graduation. His career as a country music superstar had exploded from there.

Had Anders gone off to college leaving his younger brother home alone with that awful man? That would explain why Jimmy had sought a way out on his own. It would also explain why there was very little information available about Anders' childhood. Molly only knew that he was born and raised in Gulf Shores, Alabama, and his momma died when he was twelve.

"Molly?" Sue had opened the office door just wide enough to stick her head out. "Are you coming with those scissors?"

"Huh? Yeah. Found them." She grabbed the scissors and showed them to Sue.

"Hurry up."

Molly started back around the bar, keeping her eyes down so not to draw attention to herself. The men were involved in an animated conversation and didn't appear to notice her as she slipped between them and headed back to the office. Even so, it was hard not to feel Anders' presence when his charisma took up half the room. He couldn't possibly be watching her, but she felt his eyes on her back with the weight and heat of a caress.

Twenty minutes later, Molly was standing beside Anders in the stairway, waiting to walk down the aisle together to stand up for the bride and groom. Anders towered over Molly and crowded her in the confined space. His cologne drifted toward her and suddenly that was all she could smell. A crisp, spicy scent that brought to mind crushed leaves and wood smoke, apple cider, and the first signs of snow.

"Nervous?"

Molly's head snapped up and she stared into his gorgeous blue eyes for a moment, unable to speak. How she was going to sing in front of him again, she didn't know. "I need a drink."

A slow grin spread across his face. The cut below his right eye was just a white scar now. It made him look more ruggedly handsome than he already was. "Ditto. Weddings make me itchy." He scratched a spot on his arm to demonstrate.

A laugh escaped Molly's parched throat.

His smile widened as he laughed too.

"Hush, you two." Sue turned around and scolded them. "We're starting."

Molly nodded solemnly. She bit her bottom lip to keep herself from giggling when she looked at up at Anders and found him still smiling. She turned around to check on Sophie, who was waiting at the bottom of the stairs beside her father. "Are you ready? Do you want me to fluff your veil again?"

"No, it's perfect. And I've never been readier. As my fiancé would say, let's rock and roll."

Jimmy Panama and Sophie Davies-Stone were married on the rooftop of Dixie's in a gorgeous sunset ceremony overlooking the Gulf of Mexico. They stood in front of a simple bamboo altar draped with ivory linens that stirred in the summer breezes coming off the water. A touch of bright, tropical blooms accented the elegant backdrop. A long, narrow ivory carpet created a center aisle between the guests who sat in a dozen white folding chairs angled toward the altar and the beautiful view.

Holding the bride's bouquet, Molly stole peeks at Anders while the non-denominational minister spoke of the meaning of marriage. Anders was watching the ceremony with avid interest, love, and pride clearly in his eyes, despite his joke about not liking weddings. Molly tried to focus on the bride and groom too, but the top and bottom buttons of Anders' shirt were undone and the gentle breeze kept molding the linen fabric against his lean muscular torso. It was way too distracting.

Jimmy turned to Anders and put his hand out for the rings. Anders shrugged in a gesture that said he didn't have them. Molly's heart dropped. She'd watched Jimmy give the rings to Anders in the stairwell when they were waiting for the ceremony to start.

When Jimmy frowned, Anders grinned and pulled the rings out of his pants' pocket.

Relief and exasperation melted over Molly as Jimmy grabbed the rings and muttered "knucklehead," before turning back around to face his bride.

Taking her hands in his, he said, "Sophie, the moment I first saw you I thought to myself, now there's a woman who's so far out of my league she's in another stratosphere. But even though it meant I might never be able to come back down to earth, I was tempted to put on a space suit just so I could walk the stars by your side. Then you left your world and came into mine and decided you weren't leaving. I thank God every day for your stubbornness, Duchess." He paused when a few guests chuckled. "I vow to love you to the stars and beyond. To respect and cherish you and to always be faithful. This is my solemn vow."

Molly brushed a tear away as Jimmy slid the wedding band onto Sophie's finger.

The bride's eyes were glistening with love as she placed Jimmy's ring over the tip of his fourth finger and took a deep breath. "Jimmy, I believe with my whole heart I was destined to be yours. I promise to love, honor, and cherish you always with everything that I am. Wherever this new adventure takes us, I promise to be by your side, loving you for all the days of my life and beyond. This is my solemn vow." A tear leaked from the corner of her eye and dripped onto their joined hands. Jimmy reached up to brush the wetness from her cheeks. Cupping her face, he leaned forward and kissed her sweetly.

Molly's chest tightened and her heart overflowed with emotion. If she hadn't believed in soul mates before, and she wasn't sure that she had, she believed in them now. Jimmy and Sophie were perfect for each other. It gave Molly hope that her own perfect someone was out there somewhere. Her gaze strayed to Anders, but he wasn't looking back at her because this wasn't a Hollywood movie after all. This was real life. The wedding guests broke out in applause as the minister pronounced the bride and groom husband and wife. Molly smiled through her tears and clapped so hard her hands stung.

Oscar led the guests back down to the bar for the reception. The wedding party posed for photographs in front of the pretty sunset. After the bride and groom took several pictures by themselves, the rest of the party was invited in for group shots. Molly posed between Mitch and Sue while Anders stood on Jimmy's side of the line-up. Then the photographer shot the parents of the bride with Sophie's grandmother Agnes, but only managed to get one picture where the senior citizen wasn't shooting daggers at her ex-daughter-in-law.

"Best Man and Maid of Honor, you two stand in the center there by yourselves," the photographer instructed while setting up his camera for the next shot. He worked fast because he was racing the setting sun. At the moment, the oranges and purples in the sky were spectacular behind the pretty altar, but it would be dark soon.

Molly stepped into place, standing in front of the altar by herself.

"Best Man, where you'd go?" The photographer looked up from his camera.

Anders was talking to Mitch and didn't realize he was being summoned.

"Anders, hurry." Sophie tugged his arm. "We're losing light."

When he turned around and looked directly at Molly, her heart fluttered and she suddenly felt hot all over.

He joined her at the altar resting his big hand possessively on her hip as he pulled her close. "Sorry, about that." She barely registered the sexy half smile he gave her because she was too distracted by the searing heat of his palm cupping her hip like a football he was about to lob down the field.

"Maid of Honor, relax," the photographer said. "Smile. Best Man, whisper something shocking in her ear to loosen her up."

A sly smile spread across Anders' lips as if he was intrigued by the challenge. Bending down, he put his mouth to her ear. His warm breath tickled the tender skin, sending a thrill spiraling through her body. "If you were a vegetable, you'd be a cute-cumber."

What? She looked up at him confused, unsure she'd heard correctly. He met her gaze with a devilish twinkle in his eye and they both laughed.

"That's terrific," the photographer said, directing them as he snapped pictures. "Now look this way." He took several shots before he stopped to change his flashbulb. "Thanks, guys. Maid of honor, you've got a killer smile."

"Yeah, she does," Anders agreed.

It wasn't the first time in her life a man had complimented her on her smile, but it was the first time Anders Ostergaard had ever complimented her and for that reason alone she blushed so hotly the roots of her red hair flamed blue.

"Let's finish with the bridesmaid and groomsman..." The photographer moved on and Molly and Anders stepped to the side.

Molly hated feeling so flustered around him. She needed to push through her nerves just like she did when she stood up on stage in front of a large audience. Inhaling deeply, she blew out her breath forcing the jitters out of her system. Then, with determination, she turned and met his eyes.

Her heart skittered a little when she found him studying her with mild curiosity. She fought the urge to shrink away and studied him right back.

A smile rested on his lips. Beyond his dark blonde head, the sky was deep purple as the last remnants of the day were disappearing beyond the horizon. Dozens of globe string lights crisscrossed above the patio space, casting a soft golden glow over the rooftop. The breeze lifted the fine curls escaping from her loosely piled up-do and tickled the top of her shoulders. She shivered even though the air was warm. The scent of the sea mingled with the smell of the mouthwatering meal Oscar's team was preparing downstairs.

"That was the best line you've got?" Molly raised her eyebrows skeptically.

"What? You didn't like that one? Don't worry. I've got a million of 'em." He cleared his throat with all seriousness before his eyes took on a smoky cast. "Are you a baker? Because you've got nice buns, hun." His tone was an intimate rumble she felt deep in her abdomen, but as far as pickup lines went, it was ridiculous. "Are you a beaver? Because, dam, you look good in that dress." His gaze raked over her body as if he meant it and butterflies unfurled in her stomach.

If he'd been flirting with her for real, she would've melted like a stick of butter on a hot dashboard.

Molly waved at him to stop. "All right, I've had enough. Good thing you're famous or you'd probably never get a date with pathetic lines like those."

His eyebrows shot up as he pretended to be shocked by her declaration. "Pathetic? You're saying no woman would date me if I wasn't famous?"

Feeling buoyant and a little giddy, Molly gave him a flirty sideways glance. "Something like that."

His eyes glittered with mischief as he put his hand over his heart. "You wound me, Molly MacBain. Guess I better not quit my day job?"

"Guess you better not."

Confidence coiled in her belly and put a strut in her step as she headed for the stairs. She might still be vibrating like a hummingbird on the inside, but she'd managed to be more like herself with him and it had felt absolutely amazing.

Now she just had to sing in front of him again.

CHAPTER THIRTEEN

Molly was still soaring when she stopped at the bar for a shot of Scotch to loosen her pipes before she joined the band on stage. At the moment, they were rocking out to Lynyrd Skynyrd's 'Sweet Home Alabama' in honor of the groom. Billy, the bartender, set a glass in front of her when she slid onto a stool. He was a handsome guy in his late forties, tall and lanky with a goatee and a twinkle in his dark eyes. She liked him and liked to flirt with him, even though he had a long-time live-in girlfriend who was a waitress over at the Hog's Breath Saloon. Molly usually only had a one finger's width pour, but tonight, Billy gave her two.

"You sure know how to treat a lady right."

He grinned, sliding the glass of Glenlivet toward her. "Trained by the best. Nice wedding?"

"It was perfect. I'm so happy for Sophie and Jimmy."

"He's a lucky man."

Molly took a sip of the whisky. The woody taste coated her tongue and went down her throat in a smooth burn before it settled, warm and fuzzy, in her belly. She took another sip. "When are you going to get married, Billy?"

"Aw, hell, I've been with the same woman for fourteen years. I don't need a piece of paper to make it legit."

"No, I suppose you don't. Charlene's a lucky lady to have you."

He snorted. "Tell *her* that."

"I will. Next time I see her."

Billy tilted the bottle to top off her drink. "Oh, no. I couldn't. Are you trying to get me drunk?"

"It's a party." His dark eyes glittered. "Enjoy yourself."

The band was wrapping the last chorus of 'Sweet Home Alabama'. Molly's cue. She took another sip of whisky and nodded thanks to Billy before she headed to the stage. The restaurant's small four top tables were classed up for the night with white hibiscus floral centerpieces and linen tablecloths. Most of the wedding guests were drinking and nibbling on hors d'oeuvres in their assigned seats, but a few people were at the bar.

Big Roy Dodge, the bearded, pot-bellied lead singer of the band, leaned into the mic. "Here she is, straight from the bridal party. You can catch her here at Dixie's twice a week. Our own lovely, good golly Miss Molly MacBain."

Molly received an enthusiastic round of applause as she climbed the steps. She waved and set her whisky glass on a stool next to the microphone. The amber liquid sloshed around but thankfully didn't spill. She slid onto the stool Roy had vacated and accepted her acoustic guitar from a young, pimple-faced technician before he dashed away to adjust the lighting.

"Thanks, Roy. Thanks, everybody," she said into the mic, testing out the volume while she adjusted the stand.

Sue appeared at the bottom of the stairs. She waved at Molly indicating the bride and groom were almost ready to be announced. The tables closest to the stage had been removed to create a larger dance floor. The center table in the front row was reserved for the bride and groom and Sophie's parents who had just taken their seats.

"How y'all doing tonight?"

The chatter miraculously quieted. This was a different audience than the usual bar crowd. These people were friends, neighbors, and family who were actually interested in hearing her sing.

"It's almost time to announce the couple of the evening. Just waiting for the thumbs-up." Molly shielded her eyes to look for Sue who had disappeared back into the stairwell.

Anders appeared in the doorframe, looking tall and gorgeous as he scanned the dimly lit room before making his way to the bar. Billy's face lit up when he saw him. A big fan like Molly, Billy was still as freaked out as she was to learn Anders was his boss. The two men shook hands across the bar and then Billy poured Anders a three-finger glass of Jim Beam. *Good choice*, Molly thought with a private smile. She knew he was a whisky drinker like her, but he preferred good old American whisky over Scotch.

Anders turned on his stool and looked toward the stage. When Molly's stomach tightened and started to twist into a knot, she purposely looked away and focused on the faces in front of her. Cheyenne sat with April at Molly's table just to the left of the stage. Sophie's small, spitfire of a grandmother, Agnes, sat alone at the table on the right drinking gin and giving Lillian the stink-eye.

Then Molly could hardly see the audience because the spotlight popped on and heat kissed her face like the sun suddenly emerging from the clouds on a hazy day. She reveled in its warmth, which matched the warmth in her tummy courtesy of Mr. Glenlivet.

She leaned into the mic again. "Sophie came to me several weeks ago and asked me if I'd sing a song for her first dance with Jimmy as husband and wife. When I asked what she'd like me to sing, she said she'd leave the song choice up to Jimmy because she was planning everything else."

The audience chuckled.

The spotlight moved away scanning over the crowd until it landed on the empty opening to the stairwell.

Sue appeared in the doorframe and gave Molly a thumbs-up.

"All right then," Molly said a bit too far away from the mic and leaned closer before continuing. "It's with great honor I introduce to you my best friend and her handsome husband, Mr. and Mrs. James Arthur Panama. The guests broke into furious applause and whistles as Jimmy and Sophie entered the room and headed toward the stage. When they reached the center of the dance floor, Jimmy grabbed his beautiful bride by the waist, hauled her close, and spun her around in a half circle.

Roy played the opening notes of the song on the electric piano before Molly placed her hand on the mic and began singing about wise men as she crooned one of Elvis Presley's most famous songs, 'I Can't Help Falling in Love with You'. The rest of the band joined in on the second verse, putting a country-western twang on the pop ballad with a sweet whining steel guitar, a soft drum, and Molly on acoustic guitar.

Sophie really hadn't known what song Jimmy had picked for the dance and Molly had kept it a secret. You could tell by the way Sophie's eyes softened with adoration that he'd picked the right one. *Good call, Jimmy.* You could never go wrong with The King.

Jimmy bent his head to kiss Sophie and they swayed gently to the dulcet tune, celebrating their love with their closest friends and family looking on.

This. Molly thought to herself. *This is what I want.* Not some forced mediocre relationship because she was afraid of being alone. She wanted to marry the love of her life. A man who was her equal partner and best friend. When she married Cheyenne's father, she was so young. She hadn't known what she was doing and ended up with the wrong guy. She'd rather be single for the rest of her life than make that mistake again.

When the song ended, Anders led the applause. He slid off

his stool and let out a whistle between his fingers. He wasn't looking at the bride and groom though. He was looking at Molly.

"Mr. and Mrs. Panama, everybody." Molly rushed the announcement this time, trying to cover up the nerves that were threatening to take over her body. She took a deep breath and shoved them away on the exhale. Handing her guitar off to Big Roy, she reached for her glass of whisky and took a deep drink.

On the dance floor, Jimmy and Sophie bowed to their guests and kissed each other one more time before taking their seats at the center table.

Molly spoke into the mic. "I'm going to do one more number with the band before I resume my maid of honor duties, which means I'm gonna stuff my gut with Oscar's delicious food and enjoy getting drunk with the rest of y'all." Over the chuckles of amusement, she thanked everyone for listening and reminded them they could come see her two nights a week at Dixie's.

The band teased the next song by playing a long version of the intro while Big Roy returned to the front of the stage and adjusted the second mic stand to his height. Molly moved her stool aside and raised her own stand.

"The bride's father came to me a couple weeks ago and asked if he could request a song." She pointed to Mitch who grinned back at her through his handlebar mustache. "When he said he'd like me to sing one of his favorites, I thought for sure he was gonna ask for a Zeppelin tune. Or maybe some Aerosmith."

The audience laughed.

"Who knew you were a little bit country, Mitch?"

Mitch cupped his mouth to shout over the music but his words were drowned out. "Love me some Dolly."

"It's a duet, so Big Roy is gonna help me out—"

But Roy was stepping back from the mic so that Anders could take his place. Molly's stomach dipped. She frowned slightly in confusion as Anders grinned and winked at her.

The moment he stepped in front of the microphone, the audience went wild. They knew what was coming before Molly did.

Anders waited for the noise to die down. "I have to thank Roy for letting me sit in on this one. You see, Molly promised me I could sing with her tonight and I thought I better jump in here and grab my chance while I can."

Facing Molly, Anders trapped her with his mischievous blue gaze. His mouth quirked into a teasing smile. She was used to people dwarfing her, but Anders wasn't only a big, strapping man, he was larger than life. Her heart raced and her mouth went dry. She reached for the glass of whisky and knocked back the rest of it like a shot. This was happening. She was really about to sing with her idol. One more time, she took a deep, calming breath and thrust her nerves to the side. Then she pasted on a pretty smile for the benefit of the audience and concentrated on tapping her toe to the mid-tempo beat.

Anders gave the band a nod. They played one more round of the intro before he put his mouth to the mic and sang the opening lines of the iconic country duet, 'Islands in the Stream' by Dolly Parton and Kenny Rogers. Molly put on her mental suit and tie and went to work, trying her darnedest to be professional while trying to ignore the fact that Anders Ostergaard was singing about making love with her. When it was her turn to sing, she dug into the lyrics and used her full voice, taking her time with the song so she could savor the moment when his smooth, heady baritone joined her for the chorus.

When their voices met on the same note, it was almost orgasmic. At least, for her anyhow. Their harmonies blended so well, they sounded as if they'd been singing together for years. That was all Anders though. A seasoned professional, he adjusted his harmony to meet hers when they slipped off for a moment. She was a strong singer though and she knew it. She could hold her own with big guns like Anders Ostergaard and that gave her the confidence to stand beside him as his equal, if only for those three minutes and forty-seven seconds.

When they sang the last notes and the band struck the last chords, the audience burst into applause. Anders gave Molly a sideways hug.

Grinning like a fool, she tilted her head back to look up at him, intending to thank him for the duet, but he beat her to it.

"That was fun. Thanks for singing with me, Molly." Then he bent to kiss her cheek and she was totally enveloped in his scent and heat. The warm, gentle pressure of his lips on her cheek was brief, but it sparked a fire under her skin the made her go up in flames. Flushed and speechless, she stared after him as he left the stage.

Big Roy touched her shoulder, reminding her of where she was. She muttered one more thank you into the mic before passing it off to him.

Big Roy spoke to the crowd. "Molly MacBain and Anders Ostergaard, everybody. The band's taking a little break. We'll be back in a few."

Molly was still slightly dazed when she joined Cheyenne and April at their table.

"That was incredible, Molly." April clapped her hands. "You're amazing."

Cheyenne hopped up and down in her seat freaking out. "Oh, my goodness, you sang with Anders Ostergaard, Ma! That was incredible! I recorded it with your phone." She handed the phone back to Molly.

"Thank you. That was pretty darn awesome. Did you video the wedding too?"

"Yep."

Molly glanced down at the screen. The afterglow fogging her brain faded a little more when she saw there were three missed calls from an unidentified number. If the calls were from one of her brothers or sisters, they would have left a message or sent a text when she didn't pick up. Had to be a wrong number, she decided and planted the phone face down on the table. "I'll look at the video later. That was a lot of fun."

A waitress came to the table with a fresh tumbler of whisky and set it in front of Molly. "Billy is determined to get me drunk tonight."

"This one isn't from Billy." The waitress gestured toward the bar. "Mr. Ostergaard sent it over. Glenlivet. He asked Billy what you were drinking."

A thrill danced through Molly as she spotted Anders sitting on a stool talking to Mitch. She suppressed a giddy smile and played it cool. "Thank him for me."

"Sure thing."

As the waitress departed, Molly surreptitiously watched Anders while April and Cheyenne discussed their favorite moments from the wedding. Mitch was telling Anders an animated story he must have found amusing because his hearty guffaws broke through the clamor in the room. She smiled over the rim of her whisky glass and took a sip before turning back to the girls. "Are you still spending the night at April's house?"

Cheyenne nodded. "Yeah, I already put my bag in April's car. We're going to go soon."

"You really should stay at least until they cut the cake. It's the polite thing to do."

"But, Ma—"

Molly's cell started to vibrate. She flipped the phone over. The call was coming from the same 310 number as before. *Dagnabit.* "I'm gonna step outside and take this. It might be important."

She took her drink with her, because it would be rude to just leave it on the table, and headed for the door. The tech guy had put on some intermission music and Jimmy Buffet's 'Come Monday' played over the speakers beneath the hum of conversation. Molly answered the call as she walked. "Just a minute. Let me get somewhere I can hear you."

She pushed through the front door and stepped out onto the sidewalk into the warm June night. The noise was muffled as soon as the door shut behind her. She took a deep sip of whisky as she walked to the end of the building. "Sorry about that. Can I help you?"

"Molly?"

Molly gritted her teeth. "Hello, Trevor. What do you want?"

"We need to talk about Cheyenne."

"How did you get this number?"

"How do you think? Cheyenne gave it to me."

Of course she did. "This is a really bad time. I'm at a wedding."

"Yours?"

Molly rolled her eyes. "Remember when I used to tell you I loved your sense of humor? I lied. Make this fast, Trevor. I really can't do this right now." She took another sip of whisky and then wiped her mouth with the back of her hand.

"Cheyenne says you put your foot down about her coming to see me in California."

"You're damn right I did."

"You can't stop us from seeing each other."

"Yes. I can."

"For now, but a court may have something to say about it."

"Are you threatening me?"

"I'm just stating a fact."

"Take me to court then, because that's the only way you're going to see my daughter."

A car drove past Molly playing loud Latin music. The young man on the passenger side leaned out the window and complimented her ass. She raised her glass to him in thanks before she knocked back the rest of the whisky.

"You haven't lived the most steady, respectable life, Molly. It would be easy to make you look like a bad mother."

Her grip tightened on the phone. "You wouldn't dare."

"Look," Trevor said with a long-suffering sigh. "I was really hoping we could leave the courts out of this and come to a cordial agreement ourselves. It would be in the best interest for Cheyenne—"

"Don't you dare tell me what's best for my daughter. You turn up in her life when she's at a vulnerable, easily influenced age. You're confusing her. And we both know the moment she becomes an inconvenience, or you grow bored playing daddy, you'll disappear from her life faster than a fart in a windstorm."

Trevor was silent. Molly lifted the glass to take another drink, realized it was empty, and set it on the window ledge.

"You have every right to be upset with me," Trevor said quietly. "I made a terrible mistake, but what's done is done. I can only try to make amends now. I want to know Cheyenne. I want to be in her life and she wants to know me too. She's invited me to her birthday party. Michelle can't make it, but I'm coming. I've already booked my flight to Key West."

"What? No! You... No, you are not going to Cheyenne's birthday party."

"I'm arriving Friday afternoon and staying through Monday. I intend to spend some time with *our* daughter. Don't make me get a court order to make that happen because I will."

Molly tried to hurl a word at him that summed up her monumental dislike for the man, but instead, let out a frustrated grunt.

She hung up the phone because she needed to think. She absolutely couldn't afford a lawyer right now, but maybe she could take out a loan against the bookstore. Or maybe she could ask Sophie for a personal loan. Molly hated the idea of asking her friend for money, but this was for Cheyenne, and Molly would pay her back with interest. The fear and booze making her feel slightly dizzy, she turned toward the door and stopped short when it opened and Cheyenne and April stepped outside.

Molly frowned at them. "Where are you going?"

"They're having lobster." Cheyenne wrinkled her nose in disgust as she met Molly on the sidewalk. "You know how I feel about it." She hated how restaurants tortured the crustaceans by taping their claws together and putting them in cramped prisons before they boiled them alive.

Molly hadn't been planning to bring up Trevor, but she was still stewing like a tomato over her ex-husband and Cheyenne was ignoring her request to stay until dessert. "That was your father on the phone."

Cheyenne and April exchanged looks.

Molly shouldn't be surprised April knew about Cheyenne's father. Despite their four-year age difference, the girls had become very close friends over the past months which had led to their idea of sharing a birthday party. A thought suddenly occurred to Molly. "Can you give us a minute, April?"

April nodded and gestured with her jewel-bedazzled phone. "I'm parked around the corner. I'll go get the car."

Cheyenne watched her leave while Molly stared at the sidewalk listening to the *click, click, click* of April's backless high heels. When the girl finally disappeared around the corner, Molly looked at Cheyenne. "You and April cooked up this birthday party at her house just so you could invite your father."

"No! Ma…"

"I don't know what this is, Chey. Help me understand. Do you want to live with Trevor?"

"No!" She was quick with her answer, but she avoided Molly's gaze.

"Then what's all of this about?"

"I just… I just want to get to know him. He's my father. He went to Stanford. He's a lawyer. He's really smart like me and—"

"And I'm not?"

Cheyenne's eyes widened. Her gaze darted to Molly's face and then skirted away.

Molly crossed her arms and waited for her daughter to wipe the cow pie off her shoes.

"That's not what I meant. You're smart, Ma. Street smart. You always say that."

"Uh-huh. And?"

"I'm sorry."

Molly looked toward the street where a 57' Chevy in mint condition was cruising past, heading toward Duval. It was aqua and cream, just like the one her daddy used to own. Taking a deep breath, Molly decided to let her daughter off the hook. "It's all right. I know what you mean. I'm not a bookworm like you. You're at the top in your class and, yes, you got your book smarts from your father. But, Cheyenne, he has a lot of bad qualities too. He walked out on us."

"You, Ma. He walked out on you."

Molly drew back sharply and stared at her daughter, stung by the truth in her words. "You were just a baby."

"That's right. He didn't know me. Now he has the chance to. April and I didn't plan the party just so I could invite him, but he accepted my invitation, and you can't stop him from coming."

More truths Molly didn't want to hear. Heat climbed up her neck and flushed her face. She wanted to scold Cheyenne and send her straight to room. But what purpose would that serve? Apart from forbidding her to attend her own birthday party, there wasn't much Molly could do and that was the most frustrating part about the situation.

A silver Porsche turned the corner and rolled to a stop in front of the fire hydrant, the only open space on the busy street. April waited in the idling car.

Molly shook her head. "So that's how it's gonna be?"

Cheyenne's jaw tightened and she crossed her arms, unintentionally mimicking Molly's body language. They were alike in a lot of ways, but they were very different too. Cheyenne was right about that.

"Fine. You win." Molly waved her away. "But don't expect me to be at the party."

"That's fine because I don't want you there anyway!" Cheyenne stormed off, climbed into the passenger seat of April's car, and slammed the door shut.

Molly stood on the sidewalk watching the car drive away as doubt filled the empty hole her sinking heart left behind. She shouldn't have let their argument escalate like this. "I'm a terrible mother."

"Don't be so hard on yourself."

She whipped around in surprise.

Anders stood just outside the door to the bar. "Sue asked me to come get you. The meal's being served."

"Thanks." She shook her head. "I really screwed things up royally this time."

"Want to talk about it?"

Molly's throat tightened and tears stung the back of her eyes. She took in the width of Anders' shoulders, and the bit of bronze skin bared by the deep V of his linen shirt, and smiled ruefully. What she really wanted was a hug. She wanted to step into the shelter of his arms and let go of all her anger and frustration with a good cry. But since that fantasy was about as likely as tits on an alligator, Molly settled for talking.

She glanced in the direction her daughter had gone. "My ex. Cheyenne's dad turned up after being MIA for fourteen years. He suddenly wants to have a relationship with his daughter and it looks like Cheyenne wants that too."

Anders stuck his hands in his pockets. His brow crinkled over squinty, contemplative blue eyes. "But you aren't keen on the idea because he ran out on you once before."

"Yes."

"Is he still a loser?" Anders' left eyebrow lifted inquisitively.

"Trevor is an entertainment attorney. And he's married. His

wife is a family attorney. They don't have any children of their own."

Anders nodded as if he understood everything. "And now they want yours."

Molly's head snapped up. "Do you think that's it? Do you think they want Cheyenne as a substitute for the children they didn't have?"

He shrugged. "It's possible."

It was one thing for Trevor to want visitation, but would he take Cheyenne from her? Would she want to go? Was that why Cheyenne was being so secretive about this. Oh, God! She couldn't lose her baby girl.

Seeing her obvious distress, Anders moved closer and put his hands on her shoulders. She tilted her head back to look up at him.

"Look." He gave her shoulders a gentle squeeze. "The best thing to do is tell your daughter how you feel and the reasons you feel that way and then trust her to make the right decision."

"But what if she doesn't?"

"You raised her, didn't you? She'll make her decision based on everything you've taught her. If you push and tell her the way it's gonna be, she's only gonna push back and that won't turn out well for anybody."

Molly nodded. A tear escaped her eyes and she reached up to brush it away. "You're right. I have to trust Cheyenne to make the right decision. I just hope I can." She took a deep breath and tried to smile. "You're a good father."

Anders' hands dropped away and he shifted uncomfortably. He looked off into the distance before meeting her gaze again. "Hardly. Do you know my son hasn't spoken to me or his mother in two years?"

"But he talks. Not much, but he's able to speak."

Anders shook his head and for a brief moment, raw pain flashed in his eyes. "Not to me."

"I'm sorry." Without realizing what she was doing, she flattened her hand on his chest. "I think you're making progress though. Just the other day, he thanked you for the comic books."

Anders looked down at her hand.

"Sorry." Feeling sheepish, she started to move it away, but he stopped her.

Their eyes met. He covered her hand with his and held it in place against his heart. The strong beat pulsed against her palm, the hard flesh and heat making her fully aware of the fact that he was flesh and blood and not just some fangirl fantasy.

"That's because you made him talk to me." The vibration of his voice added another texture to the experience of touching him. "He likes you. But, I don't know, on his own, he—"

Across the street a car, a dark-colored four-door sedan with tinted windows suddenly pulled away from the curb, tires screeching. Belatedly turning on the headlights, the driver took the next corner too quickly. The back end of the car started to spin out, but the driver regained control sloppily and zoomed out of view.

"Come on," Anders said distractedly, staring after the car. "Let's get inside."

"Was that the paparazzi?"

"I sure as hell hope not."

An odd feeling crept over Molly. What if whoever was in that parked car had been watching her and snapping photos the entire time? She shivered, though the night was warm. The invasion of privacy was unsettling. How did celebrities ever get used to it?

Anders was still holding her hand. "Don't let it bother you. Nothing we can do about it now." He tugged her toward the door. "How about we continue our conversation over a drink?"

"Sure. I could use another whisky. Or three."

Anders chuckled as he opened the door and held it for her. He glanced back over his shoulder, scanning the street before he followed her inside.

CHAPTER FOURTEEN

Molly grabbed a couple glasses from behind the bar while Anders pilfered a fresh bottle of Glenlivet. They headed up to the roof to chat somewhere away from the noise of the party. They sat side by side on the low platform beneath the bamboo altar, their feet outstretched and the open bottle between them. The band was playing live again and the music drifted up to them. The white linens draped over the altar danced languidly in the warm evening breeze.

It didn't take them long to put a dent in the fifth of whisky. Molly sipped her second glass while she watched Anders pour his third. As she admired his profile, she paused to acknowledge the surreal situation. She'd daydreamed about this moment before. She and Anders alone on a rooftop or a beach or the top of a mountain. She didn't climb, but she knew he enjoyed it, so in her fantasy, she was athletic and wasn't afraid of heights. She'd imagined even minute details like what the buttons on his shirt looked like or what they were drinking. Funny, she'd always imagined bourbon instead of Scotch.

But her mind couldn't color in all the details, like the sensation of being in the moment. How it would feel to sit close to him, exchanging intimate details about their lives.

"How did you meet your ex?" Anders sat the bottle aside and turned back to Molly.

His avid interest was a bit unnerving, so she looked down at her glass. "A mutual friend introduced us. Trevor was four years older. I admired how ambitious he was and liked the idea of becoming his wife and moving to the big city."

"Where are you from?"

"Deerland, Oklahoma. It's a tiny town in Osage County."

"Near Tulsa?"

Molly looked at him, surprised. "Yeah. How'd you know?"

"I've heard of it."

She tucked a loose strand of hair behind her ear with slightly trembling fingers and focused on not spilling her glass. "Trevor promised to take me to Nashville. In the beginning, he supported my dream of pursuing a career in country music, but we never made it there. A week after we were married, he was accepted into UCLA Law School for his master's and decided to move there instead. I was disappointed about Nashville but still excited to get out of Deerland. And we were happy for a time."

"You put your dreams on hold for his. That says a lot about you."

"Does it?" Molly snorted softly. "It says I abandoned who I was and sold myself out for a man."

"No." He reached for a long red curl that had escaped from her up-do and toyed with it. "It says you're a selfless person who puts the people you care about first. That's a rare quality and one I greatly admire."

Molly met his slanted gaze and her insides turned to goo. Boneless and barely breathing, she couldn't move. Couldn't think of anything but a particular shade of blue that was as clear and pure as a tropical sky.

He tugged gently on the strand of hair. "What went wrong?"

Somehow, she managed to bring the glass of whisky to her lips and sip without choking. Moistening her dry mouth, she pulled her scattered brain together. "He was excited about becoming a father, but he wasn't prepared for the reality of it."

Anders' hand dropped away. She was close enough to smell him, his cologne mixed with his natural scent, and feel the heat pulsating off his big body. He was a truly beautiful man. All hard, flat planes and sharp angles. Tanned skin with the slightest hint of stubble. He'd shaved for the wedding, but his beard was already growing back.

She swallowed hard before continuing. "He started staying out later. Next thing I knew, he was renting a private dorm on campus so he could have a quiet place to study."

Anders' gaze narrowed. "You weren't worried he was cheating on you?"

"No. School came first for him. He barely had time for me let alone another woman."

As if suddenly noticing how close he'd drifted toward her, Anders' eyes flared slightly and he withdrew. Settling back against the low concrete wall, he took another sip from his glass. "Greer was a cheater."

"Really?" That was absurd. Who would cheat on *him*?

"Yeah." He took another sip. "She cheated every damn chance she got. Even before we were married. I knew it too, but I looked the other way." This time, he tilted the glass back and finished what was left of the whisky. Setting the glass aside, he looked over at Molly. "That's how I knew for certain I wasn't in love with her because I didn't care. Not really."

"You didn't care that your wife was cheating on you?"

"Nope."

There was a bleakness behind his eyes that hadn't been there before. It made her sad for him. She wanted to reach out and comfort him, but she stayed where she was and asked the question she was most afraid to ask because the answer might change her opinion of him. "Was that because you were cheating on her too?"

"No, ma'am." He was reaching for the bottle of whisky, but he stopped and turned toward her suddenly. Leaning closer, he looked into her eyes as if it was important she knew this about him. "I may be a lot of things, but I swear on my mama's grave, I'm not a cheater."

When Molly nodded, he turned away and finished refilling his glass. "I dealt with the bad marriage the best way I knew how. I threw myself into my work and went out on tour. It was a lot easier to feign ignorance that way. She was discreet. I'll give her that."

"We were very understanding spouses, weren't we?" Molly offered him a weak smile.

"Hell, we were saints." He reached over and tapped her glass with his in a toast. "To sainted spouses. May we both find someone who appreciates us."

"And isn't as worthless as a screen door on a submarine."

Anders laughed. "I'll drink to that." And he did. Wiping a dribble of whisky off his bottom lip with the back of his finger, Anders grinned at her. "You've got a way with words, Molly MacBain."

"I get it from my grandma. She's got an expression for everything. It's hard to keep up with her sometimes."

They both chuckled and then grew quiet. She felt him watching her and she gave him a sideways smile. He touched her cheek and gently turned her face toward him. Her senses were heightened by the booze and the magic of the night. She swayed closer to him and he bent his head.

And kissed her.

Her stomach dipped as warm, firm lips pressed against hers. Her nerve endings sizzled like sparklers at a Fourth of July picnic and she saw a full firework display behind her eyelids. When he changed the angle of the kiss, pushing his velvety tongue inside her mouth, Molly groaned and came up on her knees. Wrapping her arms around his neck, she plastered herself against his body and kissed him back with enthusiasm.

His hands settled on her ass and lifted her so she was sitting astride his hips. She dug her fingers into his hair and cupped his head, taking control of the kiss. The grunt of pleasure he made in the back of his throat made her heart leap. She never wanted to stop kissing him.

His hands found the hem of her skirt and slid underneath. Warm, slightly calloused fingers shoved under her panties and grabbed her bare ass cheeks. Only a thin scrap of fabric and his cotton-blend pants separated them as he pulled her down onto his erection.

Shocked by the contact, Molly's lust-fueled haze faded a bit and she pulled back. A pair of glittering blue slits gazed back at her above cheekbones that were tight and flushed with desire. The pulse beating between her thighs throbbed with the realization that Anders wanted her. She only had to unzip his fly and slide her panties to the side and— No, they shouldn't. Anyone could come up to the roof at any time.

Massaging her ass, Anders flexed his hips, deliberately grinding against her. A wave of pleasure careened through her body, and white stars burst in her brain. She gasped and clutched his shoulders to hold herself upright.

He cupped the side of her face and kissed her again, thoroughly owning her mouth before he said against her lips, "Want to get out of here?"

"Yeah." She nodded, half dazed. "Like a tail with its cat on fire. Wait, I got that one wrong." She giggled. "Maybe we should call an Uber."

"Good idea." Anders slid her off his lap and climbed to his feet. "Grab the bottle."

She picked up the Glenlivet and took his hand. Her head spun like a pinwheel when he pulled her to her feet, but she collected herself and followed him across the roof and down the narrow stairwell. She was still holding his hand when they made their discreet exit out the back door.

✶

Molly was drunk. Once they'd stepped out of their romantic bubble and headed for the street, it occurred to her just how drunk she was. She couldn't remember how they'd gotten to her apartment, but she recalled Anders calling an Uber on his cell and both of them cracking up over the silliness of word *Ooo-berrr*. Who came up with words like that?

Anders found the light switch on the wall and flicked it on. The glare of the recessed lighting above the dinette table hurt her eyes. She headed for the kitchen, kicking off her high-heeled sandals as she went and returned with a bottle of tequila and two glasses.

"This is all I've got." She set the glasses on the table and took a swig from the bottle.

Anders leaned against the lumpy wall looking very big, slightly mussed, and sexy as hell. When the corner of his gorgeous mouth lifted in a roguish smile, her stomach tightened and fluttered in anticipation. He pushed away from the wall and came toward her. She watched him, mesmerized by the fact that he was in her living room and they were about to get it on.

Anders accepted the bottle from her, took a deep swig, and set it on the table.

"I'm not a groupie," she blurted, wanting to make that clear. "For the record."

"Good. Because I don't mess around with groupies." He swayed a bit and caught himself on the back of the chair.

"You're drunk." She giggled.

"So are you. Want me to leave?"

"No." She shook her head slowly and then reached out and

touched his chest like she had earlier, her palm flat against a rock-solid pec. His body heat radiated through the thin fabric of his shirt.

How did they get to the apartment again? The roof. They were drinking on the roof of Dixie's. Talking about their kids and their exes and *Ooo-berrrs*.

"I'll stay then." He covered her hand with his and stepped closer so that he was looming over her.

"You're so tall." Her gaze took in his long, lean torso and broad shoulders before settling on his face.

He bent to pick her up and her legs slipped around his waist. Then his mouth came down on hers, hot, probing, and insistent. He carried her toward the bedroom, pulling back from the kiss just long enough to ask directions.

"To the left." She pointed and whacked the wall with her hand.

He was already ducking inside, shoving the door wider so its metal bumper bounced off the baseboard. He pressed her up against the wall and they unintentionally turned on the light and ceiling fan above her bed.

As Anders kissed his way down her throat, she stared at the spinning blades until her eyes lost focus. She shut them tightly and tugged on his shirt, urging him to remove it. He didn't. He was too busy touching her. His hands were everywhere. On her breasts, in her hair, on her ass. He pulled away from the wall, taking her with him, and they stumbled back against the open closet door.

He was nibbling a spot behind her ear when she opened her eyes and found his slanted blue gaze staring back at her from his poster. He looked like sex on a stick lounging back against the door of an old beat-up red pickup truck. If Anders were to turn around and see the poster on her bedroom wall... Her stomach tightened, dreading the thought. *Jiminy crickets!* How embarrassing would that be?

Trying to play it cool, she patted his shoulder. "Put me down. Put me down."

When he complied, she slid down his body until her bare feet hit the tile floor. Unbuckling his belt to distract him, she booted the cat-shaped doorstop aside with a silent apology to Smudge. Then she grabbed Anders by the waist of his pants and pulled him just far enough to kick the door shut.

The slam brought his head up and he looked at her funny.

"Messy closet." She shrugged and pulled his mouth back to hers.

He picked her up again, but this time he tossed her onto the bed and followed her down.

This was happening. She was actually going to do it with Anders Ostergaard. It was a shame she couldn't think straight nor would that damn fan stop spinning. Or was the room spinning? She wasn't sure of anything—only that she didn't do one-night stands. But this was no ordinary one-night stand. This was a once-in-a-lifetime event, like winning the lottery or being invited to ride the fucking space shuttle. Tonight, she was flying to the moon.

He was all over her and then inside her, pumping away, and she wished her brain wasn't so muddled. Wished the linen fabric of his shirt didn't separate her hands from his hot skin. Wished he'd removed his pants. And shoes. And her dress. The fan and room kept spinning. She closed her eyes, trying to concentrate on the lean, hard body working overtop of hers. He smelled so damn nice.

She felt the darkness tugging at her consciousness and desperately tried to hold on at least until he was finished. "Don't stop," she begged him as the booze won the battle and dragged her into oblivion.

CHAPTER FIFTEEN

"I'm back," April announced as she came through the gate and padded barefoot toward the pool. "Sorry about that. My very pregnant stepmom is about to pop. She dropped the TV remote and couldn't pick it up."

Cheyenne was already in the pool, shoulder deep in the heated water. A phone call from April's friend Greenlee had interrupted their conversation in the car, and then April was called away to help her stepmom just after they got to the house, so Cheyenne was busting to tell her what she'd discovered. But first, she wrinkled her nose. "That was the emergency she texted you about?"

"Yeah."

"No offense, but don't you have servants for that sort of thing?"

April shrugged. "They go home at night. My dad doesn't like anyone in the house after ten unless they're friends or we're having a party."

"Gotcha."

April stopped by the pool's edge to remove the T-shirt she wore over her swimsuit. Cheyenne tried not to compare herself to

April, but it was hard not to when April was wearing a skimpy white bikini that was practically see-through and Cheyenne was shaped like a twig. Of course, April's melon-sized boobs were fake, but she was still blonde, beautiful, and had a ridiculously tiny waist. Cheyenne used to be jealous of April, but now that she knew her better and had seen the way creepy old men ogled her, she almost felt sorry for her friend.

April waded into the pool and dove gracefully into the water before coming up in front of Cheyenne. "So, you really think the treasure is buried in the Bahamas?"

"I do because the name for the Bahamas comes from 'Baja Mar' meaning shallow sea. And the riddle mentions Alice, which is the name of a town in North Bimini where Hemingway spent some time in the 1930s. I think the Firefly Emerald could be buried near Alice Town."

Last October, when Sophie came to Key West to look for her father, Cheyenne discovered a map hidden inside the medallion he'd given to Sophie. On the surface, it was just a map to Ernest Hemingway's favorite fishing spot, but there was a riddle written around the edge of the paper that Cheyenne believed might be the real map to the mythical treasure called the Firefly Emerald.

"How does the riddle go again?" April dunked her head in the water to smooth her long hair back off her face. Cheyenne had shared the riddle out of frustration just a few days ago and was actually starting to get somewhere now that April was helping.

Riddles weren't Cheyenne's thing and she had no idea where to start. April suggested she think outside the box, break down each line, and make a list of all possible meanings and how they link together. When Cheyenne discovered the Alice Town/Baja Mar connection, she did some research and learned that Hemingway had spent some time there and, boom, she had her link. This was the discovery she couldn't wait to share with April.

"The riddle goes like this:

How I long for those halcyon days,
Alice basking upon my chaise.
Money came and money went,
But time with me was well spent.
The Devil's light so near and yet so far,
It rests beneath my baja mar."

"The Devil's light." April turned quickly in the water and accidentally splashed Cheyenne in the face. "Oops. Sorry. It's just that's what I wanted to tell *you*. I think it refers to the Firefly Emerald itself. I Googled the phrase and learned that 'Luciferins' is the term for the light-emitting compound found in fireflies. The word is derived from the fallen angel Lucifer and one of the many terms for fireflies is fire devils."

"I think you're on to something." Grinning, Cheyenne splashed her friend back.

"Hey. Uncool."

"You started it." Cheyenne giggled.

"That middle part is vague." April sank down in the water and floated backward. "It could mean anything. The 'me' could be talking about a person, place, or thing."

"You said the riddle's point of view usually comes from the answer itself, right?"

"Yep." April reached over to scoop up a drowning bug and carried it to safety. "So, we need to brainstorm how everything we know fits with that middle part. And it would help if we knew who exactly Alice was. It could be the town you mentioned or a person…"

"Sophie's father, Mitch, is a treasure hunter. He told me he knows a guy in Bimini who wrote a book about Hemingway, but it's out of print."

"Well, that stinks. Maybe Mitch can give you his phone number and you can call the guy and ask him some questions."

"Maybe." Cheyenne grew quiet as she contemplated the riddle.

April interrupted her thoughts. "Is everything okay with you and your mom?"

"Huh?" Cheyenne looked up in surprise and then shrugged it off. "Yeah. She's just pissed I invited my dad to our party."

"You mean, you actually did it? Oh, gosh, Chey. Why?"

Guilt crept up the back of her neck, but a flash of annoyance swept it away. "Because I want to see him. And my mom won't let me go to California on my own. She won't let me go to Miami either. She won't let me go anywhere because she doesn't trust me."

"She's probably just worried about you. That's what parents do. My mom used to worry about me all the time, even when she didn't need to."

It was difficult not to see reason when April explained something to you. She was just so kind and understanding. She was the big sister Cheyenne always wished she'd had. But Cheyenne wasn't ready to admit she was wrong. "I guess," she grumbled.

"Do you know what happened between your mom and dad?"

Cheyenne shook her head. "Just my mom's side of it. I'd like to hear what my dad has to say. Give him a chance, you know? But my mom thinks he's going to hurt me like he hurt her. And he might, but it's a chance I'm willing to take." Cheyenne raised her chin a notch, acting braver than she felt inside.

"Maybe she—"

A small plane appeared in the night sky, its growling engine growing louder as it came toward them, flying low. They both watched the plane circle the property before it dropped dangerously lower and skimmed the trees.

"Are they gonna crash?" Cheyenne's heart was in her throat as she watched the plane head for the wide canal behind April's house.

"No, it's a seaplane."

The aircraft started to fly away, but then it turned and came back, ducking beyond the forest of royal palms, inky black against the deep violet sky.

"It's landing," April said, stating the obvious.

"Do you know who it is?"

"No clue. That's our plane, but my dad's home." April headed for the steps, looking off in the direction of the canal. She climbed out of the pool, dried herself off with a plush white beach towel, and wrapped it around her waist.

Cheyenne followed her and stood dripping on the concrete as she patted her face dry. "Your family owns a seaplane? For real? Can I check it out?"

"Sure. Come on. Grab your stuff."

Cheyenne grabbed her small backpack, which contained the dress she'd changed out of, her PJs, and a change of clothes for tomorrow along with the book she was reading. She stopped to pull her waterproof beach shorts over her navy one piece and stepped into her Keds sneakers. Then she left her beach towel on the chair and followed April down the long, stone path that led to the dock.

As they walked along, Cheyenne admitted, "I feel bad about fighting with my mom."

"You should tell her that."

They walked in silence for a few moments. "Do you really think I was wrong to invite my father to my birthday party? My mom doesn't want to come now."

"It stinks that she's making you choose, but she has been the one who's been there for you since you were born."

Cheyenne's shoulders tightened with guilt. She lowered her head and nodded. "Yeah, she has."

The sound of men's voices made both girls stop and look toward the bend in the path. It was shrouded in darkness and bracketed by a hedgerow of sea grapes. The big round leaves of the plant blocked their view of the rest of the path and the dock beyond it.

Two men came around the bend. As they walked up the path, the tall, fit man dressed in black was calm and focused on their destination, while the much smaller man at his side was freaking out about something. The nervous guy was skinny and fair with big wire-rimmed glasses propped on his long nose. He kinda reminded Cheyenne of the cartoon dog, Mr. Peabody.

"Give me more time. I just need more time. I can fix this. Don't do this, Jonas. Please."

The man called Jonas didn't reply. He didn't even seem to be listening. He gave off a vibe that made Cheyenne think of a grumpy pit bull. The really muscly ones used for illegal dog fighting with ripped ears and a ferocious temper. She eyeballed the leather straps crisscrossing his chest and the pair of wicked looking knives protruding from the holsters attached to them, and a sliver of apprehension trickled down her spine. The gun on his left hip somehow seemed less daunting than those knives. She stepped back, deeper into the shadows.

April kept walking down the path and didn't stop until the man in black spotted her. He stopped then too and they stared at each other. Something as subtle as a lightning bolt traveled between them. The electricity in the air made Cheyenne shiver with goose bumps. April tilted her head and gave the tattooed gangster a flirty smile.

Oh my God, what is happening? Was her sweet, gentle friend actually interested in the guy? How'd April even know someone like him? He must work for her father. But, oh man, Mr. Linus would so *not* be cool with this.

With her wet blonde hair slicked back from her face, her skimpy white bikini top clinging to her curves, and the towel wrapped around her legs, April looked like an X-rated mermaid. Pale and kind of magical in the moonlight. Her hands fisted into the towel at her sides as she just stood there letting the hard, scary mercenary check her out.

"You have to understand; it wasn't my fault." Mr. Peabody

was oblivious to the drama unfolding right in front of him. "You know that. You have to help me."

The man in black turned his head sharply, threatening violence with just a look. "Shut it."

Mr. Peabody stopped talking.

"Jonas," April said brightly. "What are you doing here?"

"He's one of Linus' goons. That's what he's doing." The anxious little man didn't know when to quit. He was gonna eat Jonas' fist if he didn't stop talking. *Please stop talking.*

"I said shut it." Jonas' voice was gravelly and harsh, more frightening because of his soft tone.

Peabody shut his mouth, but the worried expression on his face deepened as he struggled to remain silent.

"You work for my father?"

Jonas's black gaze returned to April's face. He nodded curtly.

"I didn't know." April's chest rose and fell rapidly as if she'd just finished first in a swim meet. Her voice had a breathy quality to it. "Will you be staying long?"

Was that a note of hopefulness in her voice? Oh, geez, what was April thinking?

Jonas didn't respond, but Peabody started up again. "Your father is an impatient man. He wants me to work magic, but I'm not a wizard I'm a scientist. Cujo and his friend back there," he gestured in the direction of the plane, indicating they weren't alone, "they can't think for themselves. They just take orders like the dogs they are."

Jonas grabbed Peabody's arm and ushered him around April with very little effort.

April's face was pinched with worry as she watched them head for the house.

Cheyenne clutched her backpack to her chest. From the late-night seaplane landing to the appearance of the anxious Mr. Peabody and the Romeo/Juliet-esque forbidden lust thing going on between April and that tattooed mercenary, there was something very weird going on at Casa Linus. "Is, um, everything okay?"

"I don't know," April said distractedly. "Wait here."

"But…"

April started up the path.

"Can I still check out your seaplane?"

"Sure. Go ahead."

When April disappeared around the trees, Cheyenne turned in the opposite direction to head toward the plane. The sound of a man's voice coming toward her on the path stopped her in her tracks. She'd forgotten about the other man Peabody had mentioned. What if he was as scary as Jonas? She shivered at the thought. Heart thumping against her ribcage, she stepped into the shadows and bent to hide behind a shrub.

The man was talking on the phone. A dark shape on the shadowed path, he spoke with an accent. Jamaican maybe. "Jonas is bringing him up to the house as we speak. He still hasn't shared anything useful." A pause. "I understand. I'll take care of it myself."

The man proceeded up the path, disappearing into the darkness with the others. *More weirdness.* Maybe she was just letting her imagination run wild again. Ma always said she could daydream herself into a disaster. She emerged from her hiding spot and slid her backpack over her shoulders. April didn't seem frightened of those men because there was no reason to be. Jonas, at least, worked for Mr. Linus.

The seaplane sat alone in the water and was tied to the dock like a boat. Half red and white, it was bigger than she'd expected. It had two large front-facing propellers, a chunky body, and long floats bobbing gently in the water. It was the coolest thing Cheyenne had ever seen, but then, she'd known it would be. When she was ten, she discovered a book series called The Adventurers. It was about a girl and a boy who flew around the world with their pilot father in a seaplane just like this. Though she'd matured into reading more complex mystery and science fiction novels, that kids' series was still one of her all-time favorites. She'd have to share it with Obie. He'd probably love it just as much as she did.

The door hung open toward the dock. Cheyenne approached cautiously in case someone else was inside the dark plane.

"Hello?" she called into the open doorway.

When no response came back, she smiled as a little thrill spiraled through her stomach. She grabbed the handhold and stepped over the gap to reach the first step. The plane dipped slightly beneath her weight but not enough to deter her. She climbed into the fuselage and waited for her eyes to adjust to the darkness. The small door to the cockpit stood open, letting in a sliver of dusty moonlight. The space smelled of cherry Twizzlers and exhaust fumes.

Peeking into the cockpit, she saw all the knobs and dials on the dashboard and decided it was best she not go in there. Instead, she wandered down the center of the plane, taking in the plush seats—two on either side of the aisle. More moonlight crept in through the windows, illuminating her way. The sound of a motorboat in the distance made her pause to listen. There were other homes along the canal but they were spaced fairly far apart. The boat was just passing by.

She sat in the third row to test out the seat and something lumpy poked her bottom as the cellophane around it crunched. She rose up just high enough to pull it out from under her and discovered an open package of Twizzlers. After helping herself to one, she dropped her backpack and the candy package on the seat closest to the window.

This was nice. So much cozier and roomier than the seats on commercial airlines. Not that she was an expert. She'd only flown twice before, but she remembered it was tight. She could totally imagine Cassie and Steven Cavendish sitting in these seats, studying their old-fashioned paper maps as they planned their next adventure. If Cheyenne found the Firefly Emerald, she'd be able to buy Molly one of those historic houses in Old Town she loved so much and they could go on a vacation. A real one. Maybe to the Bahamas on a seaplane like this.

Cheyenne's ears prickled at the sound of voices. One voice, actually. Mr. Peabody. Was Jonas bringing him back? She peered through the small round window nearest her seat and her heart jumped. Mr. Peabody and the Jamaican were rushing down the stone path at a brisk pace. They'd already passed the hedgerow of sea grapes. Panic flickered in Cheyenne's chest. She backed away from the window and started for the door. Remembering her backpack, she went back for it and stopped again. She was being silly. She was doing nothing wrong. She was April's guest and had permission to check out the plane. She'd just explain that to—

"What are you doing, Wade? Wade, stop! No! Please!"

The fear in Mr. Peabody's voice made her stomach turn over sickly. The back of her ears prickled as she stood very still, listening. When she heard nothing, she stooped to peer out the window. The small, terrified man was standing on the dock, close to the edge, facing the Jamaican who was pointing a gun at him.

"Oh, my God," Cheyenne whispered beneath her breath as her mind tried to wrap itself around what she was seeing.

"You knew what would happen if you betrayed him." The Jamaican's light, lilting tone didn't match the animosity radiating from his body. He was ten times scarier than Jonas despite the fact that he was wearing a stuffy three-piece business suit.

"Please, Wade. I have an ex-wife and three children. They're expensive. I didn't have a choice."

"You always have a choice. You made the wrong one."

"No!"

Thwump. Thwump. The gun hardly made a sound as it discharged two bullets, plugging Mr. Peabody in the chest. He flew backward and landed in the water with a splash. Cheyenne slapped a hand over her mouth and reared back, a horrified scream caught in her throat. Looking for a place to hide, she ducked behind a row of seats. No, it was no good. She'd be seen if the man called Wade decided to walk down the aisle. She turned in a panicked circle and then spotted the two doors at the back of the plane. Movement outside the windows caught her eye. She ducked to peer out the window again, then realized if she could see him then he might be able to see her.

He was coming. Heading toward the plane at a brisk pace.

Grabbing her backpack and the Twizzlers, she headed for the back of the cabin.

She started to open the bathroom door but changed her mind. What if he needed to use the bathroom? The closet would be safer. She opened the door to the right of the bathroom and discovered a narrow, curving staircase that led to the belly of the plane.

Wade was just outside, doing something to the aircraft. It bobbed in the water and drifted slightly away from the dock. He was untying it from its moorings.

The plane dipped under Wade's weight. He was at the stairs. He was coming.

Cheyenne dove into the stairwell and carefully shut the door behind her. Plunged into darkness, her sense of hearing became more acute, but the only thing she could hear was the pounding of her heart and the harsh sound of her ragged breathing. She felt her way along the curved wall, being careful not to trip down the narrow, metal steps. Her instincts screamed at her to hurry, but she couldn't fall. If Wade found her, he'd kill her.

She was certain of it.

The smell of exhaust fumes was stronger in the cargo hold. Below was also cooler compared to the stuffy cabin. She took a few deep breaths and forced herself to calm down so she could listen.

Slow, heavy footsteps walked to the back of the cabin. She looked up, following the sound with her eyes. Had she closed the door all the way? She pressed her lips together and waited, her entire body vibrating with fear. If Wade came down here, where would she hide? She couldn't see anything.

A door opened somewhere, but it wasn't the door to the cargo hold because the light didn't change. Everything was still black as death. The sound of a long stream of liquid hitting water told her he was peeing. Opening her backpack, she fumbled around inside of it, searching for her phone. It wasn't there. *Dang it.* She'd left it somewhere. At home or maybe Molly's purse.

She needed to hide.

Now.

Reaching out in the darkness, she stepped cautiously away from the stairs. She had to duck because of the low ceiling. There was a square object just off to the right. A wooden crate. She followed the rough edge for about four feet until she reached the end. Finding a narrow space between this crate and the next one, she wedged herself in between them, backing up until she touched the wall. Curling her legs into her chest, she cradled her backpack on her lap and stayed very still.

The heavy footsteps left the bathroom, walked halfway down the aisle, and stopped just over her head. Wade stood there unmoving. Doing what, she didn't know. Tightening her grip on the backpack and Twizzlers, she had the sudden, heart-sinking feeling he was looking for his missing candy. Why had she grabbed the stupid candy?

Maybe he was listening for something. Realizing she was breathing heavy again, she forced herself to take long, deep breaths as quietly as she could. Her heart pounded in her ears but she knew he couldn't hear it. She held still, afraid to rock the plane in a way that would let him know he wasn't alone.

After what felt like forever, the heavy footsteps started moving toward the cockpit. The plane leaned to the left as he did something on that side of the cabin. She heard the whining creak of some bolts followed by a solid bang.

He'd shut the door.

Heart leaping, she started to get up from her hiding spot, struggling to squeeze herself out from between the two heavy crates. The engine rumbled to life. Four small lights came on above her head, dimly illuminating the four corners of the cargo hold.

A quick scan of the space revealed several smaller crates toward the front of the plane and a hatch big enough for the largest crates to fit through directly across from her. It appeared to open outward like a hatchback's upward-swinging rear door.

Kicking herself for not looking for an exit sooner, she scrambled across the floor and searched for a handle. There was a notch at the bottom of the outward-curving panel. If she opened the hatch, she could slip into the water and swim to the far side of the dock. The far side of the dock... Where poor Mr. Peabody floated dead in the water.

The gruesome image made her hesitate a split-second too long. The locks slid into place with a click. She grabbed for the handle, but nothing happened when she lifted it. She tugged again, more forcefully than the first time. Still nothing. It was no use. The aircraft was moving away from the dock. And she was trapped.

CHAPTER SIXTEEN

Molly had experienced her fair share of hangovers, but she couldn't recall the last time she'd been this torn up. It seemed like the older she got the harder it was to bounce back. This morning she felt about as bouncy as a medicine ball.

Lying in bed with her eyes closed, she could've counted the pulse beats pounding in her temples. She felt the room shifting behind her eyelids as she listened to the soft whirring of the ceiling fan. If she tried moving too quickly, she was pretty certain she'd throw up.

The phone beside her bed rang. Its shrill noise slashing her tender head to shreds. She sat up sharply and the world titled as her head spun. The strident sound filled the room again, and she dove for the receiver, desperate to make the punishment stop. She caught herself on the edge of the nightstand and croaked a hello into the phone.

"Molly? Are you all right?" It was Sue.

"Mm-hmm." She closed her eyes tightly and flopped back on the bed.

"Was that a yes?"

"Yeah."

"When you disappeared last night, I was worried about you, but then someone said they saw you leave with Anders—"

Molly's eyes flew open. "Oh no."

"What? Is something wrong?"

Ignoring her screaming head, she darted a look toward the other side of the bed, found it empty, and scanned the room. Her gaze dropped to the bridesmaid's dress she still wore. She reached up under the skirt, looking for her panties but came up with a handful of bare ass. Images from the night before came rushing back in a jumble of incoherent snapshots, flipping through her brain like a poorly edited music video. She and Anders drinking way too much on the rooftop of Dixie's, coming back to her apartment, kissing up against the wall, and—

"Oh, God!" She'd had drunk sex last night and not just with some schmoe she picked up in a bar. Nope. She'd done it with multi-Grammy-award-winning, three-time CMA Entertainer of the Year, two-time *People Magazine's* Sexiest Man Alive, Anders fricken' Ostergaard. *How did this happen?* Ordinary people like her did not hook up with megastars like him in real life.

But it had happened. The details were fuzzy and scattered in her brain, but she was certain of it.

"Shit."

"You're scaring me, Molly. What's going on?"

"It's nothing. I just—" Molly swung her legs over the side of the bed and immediately regretted it as the urge to puke rushed up her throat. "I'm going to be sick."

She made it to the toilet just in time. It wasn't pretty, but she felt better when it was over. Her poor stomach was a bit tender, but the spinning had stopped and the headache was just a dull thud. After rinsing her mouth out, she'd peeked into the main room of the house just to make certain Anders was truly gone, before she padded back to her room and picked up the phone she'd tossed on the bed. She didn't expect Sue to still be on the line.

"Molly, what happened last night?"

Molly pressed her lips together tightly, thinking it best not to talk about it, but the words just spilled out of her with a surge of shame and bemusement. "Anders stayed over."

"Oh no. Oh, God." Sue repeated Molly's exact words from earlier.

"I know!" Molly sat on the edge of the bed and stared at the floor.

"Is he still there?"

"No." Her gaze strayed to the white mesh wastebasket beside her bed. It was empty except for a lipstick-smeared tissue and a gooey, shriveled-up condom. "Oh God."

"All right, let's be calm."

"I am being calm," Molly snapped, sounding anything but. "What am I going to do?"

"You've had one-night stands before, haven't you?"

"No. Yes. Maybe one or two." Molly got up and started pacing the width of her room. "But I didn't work for those men. And I didn't have to see them the next day."

"You don't report to Anders. You report to Jimmy, so you're good there. And you don't have to see him if you don't want to. He'll be gone in a few days and—"

"He will?" Molly's heart dipped suddenly, and she hated herself for it. After last night, it would be better if she *didn't* see him ever again. "It was awful, Sue. *We* were awful."

"Drunk sex is never glamorous."

Molly snorted. "That's for damn sure." She gripped the phone tighter, trying to sound nonchalant. "You heard he's leaving town?"

Sue sighed. "Look. I don't need to tell you Anders is a big star. He doesn't have a significant other by choice. He likes to play the field. Oscar has told me stories about—"

"I don't need to hear the stories." Something caught on Molly's foot and she tripped. Catching herself on the dresser, she looked down and bent to pick up her discarded panties. The ones she'd worn to the wedding.

"But you catch my meaning?"

"Yeah, I'm just another notch on his Texas-sized bedpost."

Sue said nothing, letting the silence answer for her. It was like being dunked in a pool of ice water. She'd known it would be cold, but the reality of it was a shock to her system. In a daze, she paced to the corner of her room and tossed the panties into her wicker clothes hamper. "I'm so embarrassed."

"Don't be. He'll probably forget all about it in a few days."

That hurt. Sue wasn't the type to pull punches, but she was usually right. Molly paced back to her bed and sat down. "So, what do I do?"

"Avoid Dixie's, or if you can't avoid going there, then avoid him."

"And if I can't avoid him?"

"Pretend it didn't happen."

As if that was even possible. Molly swallowed the lump in her throat and nodded. "I'll try. Thanks, Sue."

"Glad I could help. Is there anything else I can do for you?"

"Actually, there is. I left my car on the side street behind Dixie's. Would you mind picking me up and bringing me over?"

"Only if there's breakfast in it for me."

"You bet, but I really need to take a shower first."

The bookstore was closed because Molly had known she was going to be tired after the wedding and figured missing one off-season Sunday wasn't going to break them. After showering, she changed into comfortable clothes, an old well-worn pair of jean shorts she called her Daisy Dukes even though they weren't quite as short as all that and a purple T-shirt with small white letters across her chest that said: *I'm not short, I'm fun size.* The shirt, given to her by her brother Marcus as a Christmas present two Decembers ago, was intended as a joke, but she happened to agree with the statement and liked the flattering cut of the V-neck. Hair tied back into a ponytail, Molly was slipping on a pair of white Keds when Sue rang the bell.

When Molly opened the door, the morning sun hit her square in the face. Pain darted through her head as she shielded her eyes with a groan.

"What's the matter? Too early for vampires?"

"You're funny. Hang on a sec." Molly snagged her sunglasses off the kitchen counter along with her purse and house keys. "I think I got everything. Let's go."

Following Sue down the stairs, Molly held on to the railing as an extra precaution. Cheyenne had scrubbed the slippery step, but Molly was still sore from her fall. The bruise on her outer thigh was fifty shades of purple now. It was healing, but she wasn't interested in a sequel.

As soon as she slid into the passenger seat of Sue's SUV, Molly dug her phone out of her bag and scanned it for text messages from her daughter. Chey was mad at her, but she always checked in, especially if she was sleeping overnight at someone's house. There were no messages from Chey or anyone else. Maybe she was madder than Molly realized.

When the SUV turned out of the parking lot, Molly regarded Sue. She showed no residual effects from the reception, which had wrapped up in the wee hours of the morning according to her. "What did you have in mind for breakfast? I'm starving."

"I was thinking The Pelican Cove Diner. They have great hangover food."

"Sounds perfect. Cheyenne must be pretty mad at me still. She didn't check in with me this morning." Molly typed out a text to her daughter. *What time will you be home? Need a ride?*

"She still bugging you about letting her take the bus to Miami for that convention?"

"It's not that. She invited her daddy to her birthday party. Apparently, she found him on Facebook and they've been talking to each other online for months."

"No!" Sue sounded scandalized.

"Yep." Molly hit send on the text. "She—"

Something beeped and buzzed in her purse.

Frowning, she opened the oversized bag and dug through all the junk she carried around, looking for the source of the noise. She had a feeling she already knew what had made that sound. Her hand settled on her daughter's cell phone. "Oh, Cheyenne."

"What she'd do?"

"She hates carrying a purse so whenever we go somewhere she sticks her things in my bag. Half the stuff in here is hers." Molly sifted through the bag some more. "Looks like she took her wallet though."

"You've got April Linus' number, don't you? Text her."

"I can't. Chey will think I'm checking up on her because I don't trust her. I suppose she'll call me if she needs me."

"You're a good mama, you know that?"

"Tell that to Chey."

Over breakfast, Molly filled Sue in on everything that had been happening with her ex-husband and daughter. Sue was of the opinion Molly needed to put her foot down and forbid Cheyenne to have contact with Trevor. Sue's wasn't taking Trevor's threats seriously, but Molly knew what he was capable of. The Schaffers were a powerful family out of Tulsa who were accustomed to having their own way, and now Trevor was a successful lawyer in his own right with lots of lawyer friends. Not to mention money. If he wanted a fight, Molly was certain she would lose.

And so would Cheyenne. Chey didn't need to be drawn into the middle of a custody battle. She was already angry at Molly. What if forbidding Chey to see her father drove her straight into the arms of Team Trevor? Nope. Molly had to tread carefully and wait it out until Trevor grew bored or Chey changed her mind about wanting a relationship with him.

Molly accomplished nothing at the diner but killing a delicious plate of pancakes and bacon and a half pot of coffee. It was just past 10 a.m. when Sue parked in a local lot close to Dixie's and they walked the two blocks to the bar. It was closed for lunch but would be opened for dinner later that night. Parting with Sue on the corner, Molly thanked her for the sympathetic ear and then turned down the side street where she'd left her car. Finding street parking in Old Town wasn't easy, but she'd gotten lucky and found a spot.

The four-door Kia Rio hatchback had seen better days. The twelve-year-old car's blue paint was fading and the body was dinged in spots, but it still got her where she needed to go. She'd left it parked in the shade beneath the gnarly, low-slung arm of an old gumbo-limbo tree.

Sticking her key in the lock, she leaned on one leg and winced as the muscle in her inner thigh screamed at her. She didn't want to think about how she'd pulled the muscle because it would only lead to thoughts about Anders and she definitely didn't want to think about him.

Opening the driver's side door, she tossed her heavy purse onto the passenger seat and gingerly bent to slide behind the wheel. It was hot as the Devil's sauna inside the vehicle, so she reached for the manual crank to roll down her window. Then she reached across the car to lower the passenger side window, but it was already down about three inches. She frowned. She never left her windows open, especially in summer when you never knew when a storm would blow in.

In fact, she distinctly recalled asking Cheyenne to roll up her window on the way to the wedding when the wind started to mess Molly's hair. Her daughter hadn't argued, probably because the air-conditioning had kicked in by then. The window had remained up for the duration. Molly was certain of it.

Maybe someone had forced the window down and broken into her car.

"Dagnabit," she muttered and opened the glove box. There were some old CDs inside along with her registration and insurance card. A car phone charger, pens, a few gas receipts, and even some loose change still littered the center console. Nothing appeared to be missing. She climbed onto her knees to peer into the back. A sweater and an ancient MP3 player lay across the backseat. A pile of something on the floor behind the passenger seat caught her eye. It was yellow, red, and black. A jacket maybe? It wasn't hers and she didn't think it was Cheyenne's either. Stretching to reach for the abandoned piece of clothing, her hand was six inches away from it when the pile moved.

The snake reared back in surprise, lifting its head even with Molly's dangling fingers. She gasped and yanked her hand away without considering that moving too quickly might provoke a strike. She climbed out of the car and slammed the door shut. Chills ran up and down her spine as she backed away from the vehicle and made her way around to the sidewalk. She continued backing up as if she was expecting the snake to slither through the open window and come after her. When she bumped into the fence, she stopped moving. Heart pounding in her chest, she opened her mouth to shout but choked on the word *help*.

CHAPTER SEVENTEEN

Molly grabbed Dixie's metal door handle and tugged on it, fully expecting it to open. It didn't. With hands still trembling from her encounter with the snake, she tugged on it again just to be sure.

"Today of all days," she muttered and then knocked frantically on the glass.

Shielding her eyes, she peered inside. The lights were still on, meaning Sue hadn't left the building. Something was wrong. Besides the fact that a very large, possibly deadly snake had taken over her car. She shivered again because the icy chill that had settled into her bones wouldn't quit.

In third grade, Cheyenne did a book report on venomous snakes. One of the reptiles she'd highlighted was the North American coral snake. Distinguished by its red, black, and yellow stripes, it was one of the deadliest snakes in the world. The powerful neurotoxins in its venom caused respiratory failure mere hours after a bite if not treated with antivenom. Molly's right hand tingled. It was just her imagination, but she checked her hand again, flipping it over just to be sure she hadn't been bitten.

She needed someone with a clear head to examine her hand.

Sue knew about this sort of thing. Where was Sue? She needed to call animal control. Her stupid phone was in her purse, trapped inside her car with the snake.

She pounded harder on the glass.

Oscar came through the kitchen door. He was reading something from a notepad. When Molly pounded again, he looked up, surprised.

"Oscar, please! I need help!"

"What's going on? Why is the door locked?" His voice was muffled as he came toward the door.

When he turned the lock and let her in, she threw herself into his arms and hugged him gratefully. "Oh, my goodness, thank you! This is crazy. There's a snake in my car. I think it's venomous."

"Were you bit?"

"I don't think so but I don't know."

"Let me see."

She held out her trembling hand to let Oscar examine it.

"I don't see any puncture wounds. Where's your car parked?"

"Around the corner on the west side of the building." Molly grabbed his arm when he started out the door. "But be careful. I think it's a coral snake."

"I got this." He winked at Molly, then grabbed the broom leaning against the wall and shoved open the glass door. "Call Animal Control. There's a Yellow Pages just under the counter below the phone."

"Where's Sue?"

"Upstairs."

Molly made the call before heading for the stairs. She wanted to check on Oscar, but she needed to find Sue first to let her know what was going on.

The wedding setup was gone, probably picked up by the supply company first thing that morning. Now the roof with its pretty view was being used for a photo shoot. Anders stood where the altar had been, posing for a professional photographer. Off to the left, Sue stood between Anders' publicist Selena Fry and another woman, a reporter possibly, if the notepad and small recording device she was holding were anything to go by. Her silver-blonde hair was styled in a neat, tidy bob that matched her conservative dress. Another man with purple hair and several tattoos stood off to the right behind a folding table covered with makeup and hair-care products.

When Molly's gaze met Anders', his expression stayed passively bland. Her heart sank. What had she been expecting? Him to drop to his knees and profess his undying love? She didn't even want that. She hated when guys got all clingy and possessive after sex.

Anders wore a black tank top tucked into a pair of tight, faded blue jeans and an old pair of sneakers. The bucking Bronco on his silver buckle glimmered in the sunlight. His head was bare. He'd never been one for cowboy hats, but he had an impressive collection of western belt buckles.

He was probably posing for a magazine—one she would've run right out and bought as soon as it hit the newsstand if the last twenty-four hours had never happened. She would've ogled the pictures, read the article, and then ogled the pictures some more, but now the thought of doing that just felt weird. She'd gone and robbed herself of a small but vital pleasure that helped her get through her mundane work days. Because of a stupid decision to get drunk with Anders, she'd never be able to look at him the same way again.

As she stood there watching him pose for the photographer, heat crept up her neck. She took a step back, wishing she had the ability to disappear into the background like a squid.

He continued to gaze in her direction without even a hint of acknowledgement on his face, which made her feel even worse. Had he already forgotten about what happened last night? When he missed a cue from the photographer and everyone stopped what they were doing to look Molly's way, she realized that maybe he hadn't forgotten everything. He was just better at hiding his thoughts. She was pretty sure her feelings were written all over her face: mortification, regret, and the distress from having found a venomous snake in her car.

"Molly!" Sue exclaimed, hurrying over to her. "You're shaking. What happened?"

"I'm sorry for interrupting."

"I thought you went home."

"This is a private shoot," Selena Fry said, scowling from the sidelines of the photoshoot. "I'm going to have to ask you to leave."

Molly ignored her and focused on Sue. "There was a snake in my car and Oscar—"

"A snake?" Selena scoffed. "Really? The groupies in Nashville come up with more interesting excuses to talk to Anders." She nudged the reporter who didn't share in the joke but instead seemed very curious about the drama unfolding in front of her.

Molly winced at the word "groupie." Selena might be an overprotective guard dog, but she wasn't blind or dumb. Molly felt so guilty she might as well have had a scarlet letter G sewn on the front of her T-shirt.

But she wasn't lying about the damn snake.

To Sue, she said, "Oscar's checking it out right now and Animal Control are on their way."

"Oh my!"

"Is everything all right?" the blonde reporter asked them.

Selena waved her off. "Everything is fine. Please continue with the shoot. They can take this downstairs."

"Hey, aren't you that woman from the tabloids?" The reporter's face lit with recognition as she left Selena behind and moved toward Molly. "The one Anders was caught making out with only one week after Casey Conway's death?"

Molly looked at Anders for help, but his eyes were on Selena, silently conveying a message to her that made the woman frown and shake her head in objection. Molly felt a twinge of jealousy over the silent communication they seemed to possess. What was Selena doing here anyway? Anders had said she left town yesterday. Why would he say that if it wasn't true?

Selena let out an audible sigh and then went after the reporter, stepping into her path before she could reach Molly. "That was a big misunderstanding," she said, using her body to block the reporter. "This woman is an employee. She was talking to Anders and accidentally tripped. She's very clumsy and has trouble controlling herself around him."

"Excuse me?" Molly took a defensive step toward her, or tried to, but Sue's arm tightened around her shoulders, holding her back.

Sue whispered in Molly's ear. "Don't make things worse. Selena's trying to cover for you."

The reporter's eyes narrowed on Molly. "And a paparazzo just happened to capture it on camera?"

"That poor excuse for a human being has been stalking Anders since Vegas. He was just waiting for something like that to happen so he could capture it on film and blow it out of proportion."

The reporter raised a manicured eyebrow at Selena, still unconvinced. Then she turned to Anders. "Anything you'd like to say about this, Mr. Ostergaard?"

"No comment." His tone was as disinterested in the topic as his vacant expression.

"Seems to me like there's more to the story and you're holding back. I thought we had an agreement here?"

Selena put her arm around the reporter and escorted her back to where they were standing before Molly interrupted the photoshoot. "Our agreement was to give you an exclusive on the events leading up to Casey's death. That doesn't include anything that's happened here in Key West."

The reporter smirked. "What happens in Key West, stays in Key West?"

Selena laughed as if the reporter had made a hilarious joke.

Anders' bored expression didn't change.

"Let's continue." Selena nodded to the photographer. "I know you all have a plane to catch."

The makeup guy rushed forward with a brush to powder Anders' face.

Sue spoke softly near Molly's ear. "What were you saying about Oscar?"

"Oh, shit. Come on!"

Molly followed her friend to the stairs and then made the mistake of looking back. Anders was removing his shirt, exposing his bronze, chiseled torso in all its glory. It was disconcerting to realize she'd had sex with him less than twelve hours ago and hadn't gotten to weave her fingers in the light brown hair that dusted his pecs or stroke the ridges of his ripped abdomen.

Well, if she had, she couldn't remember it.

Anders leaned back against the waist-high brick railing, using his arms to brace his body on the edge. He stared pensively off to the side as the makeup guy sprayed an oily substance on his chest and shoulders making his skin glimmer with the sheen of fake sweat.

The guy must have said something funny to Anders because his handsome face suddenly lit with a wide smile.

Like a wrecking ball, regret slammed into Molly's chest, hard and heavy. She'd blown any chance of having a friendship with Anders. Or anything else for that matter. Not that she ever stood a chance with him anyway, but last night she'd made certain he'd never look at her like anything else but a woman he'd had drunk sex with once.

"Are you coming?" Sue called from the bottom of the stairs.

"Yeah. Sorry." This time, Molly didn't look back, because she just couldn't bear it.

Animal control was in the process of removing the snake from her Kia Rio when Molly and Sue joined Oscar on the sidewalk. A young white guy with dreadlocks and a pierced eyebrow was reaching into the car with some kind of prong tool. He was dressed for the job in a brown Crocodile Hunter type uniform but no other protective gear.

"Please don't get bit!" Molly cringed with worry, crossing her hands beneath her chin.

"It's cool. It's a scarlet kingsnake." Dreadlocked Steve Irwin used the tip of the prong to grab the reptile by the neck and pulled the creature out of the car. He held it up, using his bare hand to support its four-foot-long body. "Easy, little dude," he said when the snake started to thrash in an attempt to get away.

Molly squeaked and took a giant step back. Sue stepped behind Oscar, who appeared to be more fascinated than concerned. "It won't hurt you. It's not venomous."

"What makes you so sure?" Molly eyeballed the snake with skepticism.

"Didn't you ever hear the rhyme, 'Red touching yellow, kill a fellow. Red touching black, friend of Jack.'" Oscar shrugged and grinned through his goatee. "I was an Eagle Scout when I was a kid."

"You were?" Molly eyed him with disbelief. "How did I not know that?"

"It's true," Sue confirmed. "He doesn't talk about it much."

That wasn't the only thing Oscar Martin didn't talk about. He was also pretty mum about his BFF Anders Ostergaard. Ignoring a little stab of annoyance, she said to the Animal Control guy, "So how did a scarlet kingsnake get in my car?"

Dreadlocked Steve Irwin was putting the snake in the plastic trashcan he'd taken off the truck. "Probably swung down from the tree and came in through the open window. We'll take him out of town and drop him off someplace where he won't get into any more trouble."

"Great," Molly said without enthusiasm, feeling no sympathy for the snake. "Does this sort of thing happen often?"

"Not really." He flipped the lid on the can and then picked it up to load it onto the back of his truck. "Scarlet kingys are native to the area, but encounters are pretty rare. They're shy and tend to stay out of people's way. This little dude was probably just looking for a warm place to take a nap."

"See." Oscar slipped his arm around Molly's shoulders. "You weren't in any real danger after all."

Sue snorted. "If that thing would have come out of its hiding spot while she was driving, she might've crashed her car and been seriously injured or worse."

"Don't scare her, babe. None of that happened."

The Animal Control guy honked his horn as he drove off and they waved back to him.

Molly glanced over at Sue and saw the brooding expression on her face. "What's wrong?"

Sue shook her head in contemplation. "First, you slip on a greasy step and nearly break your neck. Then less than two days later you find a snake in your car. Honey, I don't mean to scare you, but something doesn't smell right about this."

"What do you mean?"

"I mean someone is out to do you intentional harm."

Molly snorted at the ridiculousness of the notion. "What are you saying? Someone's pissed at me because I sold them a book they really hated? Or maybe I butchered their favorite song."

"I'm serious."

"Sue…" There was a warning note in Oscar's voice. "Don't go letting your imagination run away with this. The snake came through the window Molly left open. It was a freak accident."

"Except, I didn't leave the window open," Molly pointed out.

A triumphant smile spread across Sue's face. "See what I mean?"

Oscar shook his head. "Don't go jumping to conclusions. Have you asked Cheyenne if she left the window down? Or maybe you forgot to put it up?"

"He's right." Molly stepped away from them, heading for the passenger side of the car. "There's a perfectly reasonable explanation for this. I mean, why would anyone want to hurt me?" She grabbed her purse from the seat and rolled up the window before locking the car.

When she turned around, Sue was tapping the toe of her combat boot beneath her long floral skirt and rubbing her pursed lips in thought. "Maybe you weren't the target. As potentially dangerous as the incidents were, they do seem like pranks. Is Cheyenne being bullied at school?"

"No, of course not. Well, not since she became friends with April Linus. The mean girls leave her alone."

"Are you sure?"

"Positive. Chey would tell me if she was being bulled," Molly insisted, but suddenly she wasn't so sure. What if the mean girls were starting to bother Chey again? Would they actually try to physically harm her? The thought made the acid in Molly's stomach boil.

"Nobody is trying to hurt Cheyenne or Molly." Oscar stepped between the two women. "You're making a mountain out of a molehill, babe, and you're scaring Molly." He put his arm around Sue and Molly too.

His wife nodded solemnly. "I suppose I am."

He squeezed her gently. "Let's go inside. I'll put on a pot of coffee and we can talk about the wedding."

Sue's face lit up and she gushed, "It was gorgeous, wasn't it?"

"Gorgeous," he agreed and winked at Molly. He knew how to distract his wife.

As they headed up the sidewalk, Molly glanced back at her

car. Could someone have put the snake there intentionally? It wasn't venomous, so it wouldn't have killed her or Cheyenne, but Sue was right. She would've lost control if it had shown itself while she was driving. Anger roiled in Molly's stomach. If those spoiled brats tried to hurt her baby girl… Oscar squeezed Molly's shoulder, reassuring her it was all right.

Molly's fury eased and then abated. She was letting Sue's overactive imagination mess with her head. Oscar was right, it was just a freak accident. Nobody was trying to hurt them.

Oscar was a good man. Smart and sensible and steady as a rock. Sue was lucky to have him.

When they entered Dixie's, Anders was standing next to the bar with the reporter and her crew.

He reached out to shake hands with the photographer. "Thanks a lot for everything."

The reporter was grinning at him as if she'd completely fallen under his spell after one short interview. "It was a pleasure meeting you, Anders. Thank you for inviting us to Key West."

"The pleasure was all mine."

As Molly slid onto a bar stool, she tried not to notice the intimate timbre of his voice, but his tone was like warm salted caramel. It tickled her nerve endings and left her jealous as heck that he wasn't talking to her.

Her purse buzzed as she placed it on the bar. She dug into the front pocket and pulled out her phone. It was a text from Jeff Worth, the IT Specialist with no sense of humor. He was still holding out hope she'd go out with him again and she hadn't had the heart to cut him loose.

Molly, it's Jeff. Did you get the message I left you? Was wondering if you'd like to have dinner Friday night?

She didn't look at Anders because she knew it would be like pitting a tiger against a koala. Poor Jeff wouldn't stand a chance. So, she stared at her phone and weighed her options. She could sit around mooning over her one-night stand with Anders, or she could forget about him and move on. But seeing Jeff again? Wouldn't she just be using him if she went out with him again?

Making up her mind, she typed back, *Jeff, you're a nice guy, but I don't think it's going to work out between us.*

His reply was almost immediate. *I make horrible first impressions. Give me another chance. I'll even let you pick the restaurant this time.*

He wasn't making this easy.

Anders walked the reporter to the door and bent to kiss her cheek. "Absolutely not. I hope I gave you everything you need, Elizabeth."

Molly tried not to hear innuendo in his words and failed. Mentally scolding herself for being immature, she started typing a reply to Jeff. *That's sweet but—*

"Dinner? Tonight?" Elizabeth sounded wary of the offer. "But I'm on my way back to Miami."

Molly paused mid-text and made the mistake of looking up.

Anders was definitely flirting with the reporter. His right arm rested casually on the doorframe as he leaned into her personal space. "I'll fly over then. The benefits of having my own plane. Email me your hotel info and I'll pick you up at eight."

The charming grin Anders gave the woman made Molly's gut burn. She didn't want to be angry or jealous, but both emotions were already threading through her stomach.

Elizabeth looked at Selena who was standing slightly behind Anders. When the publicist gave the reporter an enthusiastic thumbs-up, Elizabeth's suspicious gaze softened and she smiled at Anders. "Okay then. Looking forward to it."

Oscar was in the process of pouring a round of coffee. Sue caught his eye and he shrugged as if to say he had no clue what was going on.

Molly's gut twisted into a painful knot and she hated herself for it. What Anders did with Elizabeth the reporter or anyone else was none of her business. She looked down at her phone, surprised to see it in her hand. That's right, she was texting Jeff. She hit the backspace button, deleting what she'd typed and instead wrote, *Okay, let's try again. Friday sounds great.*

She hit send and immediately regretted it. She was just using Jeff out of spite and it wasn't fair to him. She'd call him and apologize later when she wasn't so sick with jealousy over another man.

Setting the phone on the bar, she glanced over her shoulder and saw with relief that the reporter and her crew had finally left the building. Anders and Selena sat a table talking quietly but intensely about something across the top of Selena's laptop.

Oscar placed a steaming cup of coffee on the bar in front of Molly. "How do you take it?"

Answering for her, Sue said, "Light and sweet." She gave her husband a meaningful look that Molly was about to question, but her phone buzzed again.

This time, it was an incoming call from a number she didn't recognize. If it was Trevor again, she was changing her number.

Bracing herself for another confrontation with her ex, and perversely looking forward to the fight, she barked into the phone, "What?"

There was static on the other end of the line before Cheyenne's voice broke through the noise. "Ma? Can you hear me?"

Molly's irritation faded. "Cheyenne? Is that you? I was wondering when you were gonna call."

"I need you to come and get me."

"Is everything okay? Did you have a good time?"

"Ma, listen—"

"Whose phone are you using? We have a bad connection."

"Ma, I have—" When the squealing spray of static swallowed Cheyenne's reply, Molly frowned. Something was wrong.

Sue must have sensed Molly's apprehension because she

turned around on her stool and her weathered face knitted with concern. She mouthed, "*What's going on?*"

Molly shook her head. "I can barely hear you, Chey. Speak up."

"I can't," Cheyenne said.

"What do you mean you can't? Where are you?"

There was no response as the connection seemed to cut out for a moment.

Molly slid off the stool. "Chey?" Her sudden movement or maybe the note of alarm in her voice drew curious gazes from both Oscar and Anders.

"Ma…"

Molly's grip tightened on the phone. "Can you hear me? Where are you?"

Another long, staticy pause followed the question and then Cheyenne's voice came through the receiver loud and clear. "Jamaica."

CHAPTER EIGHTEEN

"You're where?" Molly's heart stopped. When it started beating again, it was with the hope that Cheyenne was exaggerating or making up some elaborate story to distract her from the real problem. "What's really going on, Chey?"

"I'm serious. I'm—Jamaica—need help." Static muffled her words, but Molly gleaned her meaning.

"Is April with you? Did you put her up to this? Did you try to go to the Bahamas on your own?" Molly didn't mean to shout, but a surge of anger popped her top off. Her daughter had gotten herself into some kind of trouble, and Molly couldn't help unless she understood what was going on.

"No, Ma. She's not here. Listen to me. Someone was shot."

When Cheyenne's voice wavered on the word "shot," Molly's grip tightened on the phone. Cheyenne rarely ever lied. She'd never used to withhold information either, but then she'd contacted her father and invited him to her birthday party without Molly's knowledge. Cheyenne was changing and Molly wasn't certain she could trust her anymore. Though that note of fear in her voice sounded very real.

Molly's hand was sweating. She readjusted the cell phone against her ear and spoke calmly. "Who was shot, Cheyenne?"

Sue slid off her stool and moved closer to Molly. Oscar started around the bar. Anders stood up sharply, his expression grim with concern. He ignored Selena, who was saying something to him. Feeling disconnected and outside of herself, Molly took in all of these things and more—the neon yellow Corona Extra clock on the wall beyond Anders' head, the low-volume chatter from the baseball game on the television above the bar— through a hazy filter as she waited for Cheyenne's reply.

"Poor Mr. Peabody!" Cheyenne's whine snapped Molly out of her fog.

"Tell me what happened."

Cheyenne's voice was high-pitched and unsteady. "April and I went for a swim. And then...then a seaplane landed in her backyard, and I...I saw everything. He shot Mr. Peabody. I didn't know what to do. I hid in the cargo hold and then the man...he flew the plane to Jamaica and, oh my goodness, Ma, I'm in Jamaica."

"Who's Mr. Peabody? Is he dead?"

Sue grabbed Molly's arm. "Someone's dead?"

She waved her off and covered her ear to concentrate on what her daughter was saying. The connection was still wavering in and out and Cheyenne was talking quickly.

"I don't know his real name. He fell into the water. Oh, Ma, the man who shot him is friends with the Jamaican police. I watched them from the plane. Two uniformed officers met him on the dock. They shook hands and were laughing. Then they all went off together somewhere."

"Did anyone see you?"

"I don't think so."

Raising her gaze to meet Sue's worried eyes, Molly gave her a helpless look. Oscar stood beside his wife, his face pinched with concern too.

"Where are you now?"

"In a building next to the marina. The sign on the door says Falmouth, Jamaica."

"Listen to me, Cheyenne. I need you to find a policeman and—"

"Didn't you hear me, Ma? The killer is friends with the police! I have some money. I'll take a taxi to the airport and wait for you there."

"Is there even an airport in Falmouth?"

"Montego Bay," Anders said from across the room, and his cool, confident baritone spread over her jangled nerves like a salve.

She met his steady gaze and held it. "Is that far?"

"Maybe forty minutes by car."

Molly's stomach fell. She turned away from Anders and leaned on the bar because her head was spinning. "Cheyenne, the airport is too far. Stay where you are."

"I can't. Should I call Trevor? He'd come for me."

"No!" Molly said quickly. Trevor absolutely could not find out about this. Molly didn't doubt for an instant he'd use it to prove she was an unfit mother. Encouraging Cheyenne to get into a cab and find her way to the airport alone was the last thing Molly wanted to do, but what choice did she have? "Don't be silly. *I'll* come for you. Go to the airport. But call me again the moment you arrive. I'll book the next flight to Montego Bay and give you my flight information when we talk again." Molly thought she sounded amazingly calm and reasonable. Only her trembling hands belayed the nervous breakdown she was having inside.

"Thanks, Ma."

"Cheyenne, please be careful."

"I will. Hurry, Ma."

When the line went dead, Molly set the phone on the bar and stared at it in complete and utter shock.

"What the hell happened?" Oscar said.

Molly opened her mouth but no words came out. She was still trying to process it. She looked at Oscar and then Sue. "Cheyenne says she witnessed a shooting, hid inside a plane, and somehow ended up in Jamaica with the murderer."

"We have to call the local authorities." Sue picked up Molly's phone.

"No." Molly snatched it back to stop her from dialing. "Cheyenne says the murderer is friendly with the Jamaican police. She could be in even more danger if we notify them."

"Police corruption isn't uncommon there." Anders had moved around the table, still observing from across the room. "Calling the police might alert the wrong people of her presence on the island."

"Do you believe her?" Sue asked Molly. "About the murder?"

"I believe she's in trouble and needs my help. What do I do?" Instinctively, she looked at Anders who stood so calm and solid, like a mountain in the midst of a turbulent sea.

Pursing his lips, he gestured toward her with his chin. "Do what you said you were going to do. Go get her and bring her home."

Molly nodded and squared her shoulders. "I need to speak with April." Turning away, she grabbed her purse and keys from the bar. "April will know something about this. She has to."

"Wait." Sue stepped into Molly's path. "That might be dangerous."

"I'll be fine." Molly started for the door, thought of something, and stopped again. "Can you do me a favor?" She dropped her keys. Bending to pick them up, she dropped them again. She was visibly shaking now. "Can you call the airport and book me on the next flight to Montego Bay?"

"You shouldn't drive. Let Oscar take you."

"Oscar has a job to do. You both do. The bar will be opening in a few hours. I can't take you away from your work."

"This is more important."

"It's all right. I'll be fine." She started for the door again and dropped her keys once more. "Dagnabit!"

"Molly—"

"I can do this on my own."

"But you don't have too."

"Sue, please, just book my flight—" Eyes on her friend, she squatted to pick up her keys and landed on a sneaker instead. Anders stood over her, dangling her keys. She rose to her feet with as much dignity as she could muster. Holding out her hand, she said, "Thank you."

The expression on his handsome face was unreadable. His big hand swallowed the dangling keys and then he reached down and shoved them into the skintight front pocket of his jeans.

"What are you doing?"

"We're taking my car."

He turned away from Molly and exited the building. She stood staring after him.

Selena slammed her laptop closed with a loud plastic crack. "He won't listen to me." She rose to her feet and came around the table with her arms folded across her slender torso. "I advised him to stay out of it. If you don't want to be the cause of the complete and utter destruction of his career, I suggest you talk some sense into him. Maybe he'll actually listen to *you*."

Anders knew he could be a stubborn SOB when he wanted to be. Molly stood beside his car trying to convince him she didn't need his help, but she was shaking like a corn kernel about ready to pop.

Opening the passenger side door and holding it for her, he waited for her to come to her senses and climb in. "Every moment you waste arguing with me is a moment you lose trying to figure out what happened to your daughter."

Molly shot him a scathing look and got into the car.

He closed the door behind her, walked around to the driver's side, and slid into the seat. Pressing the ignition button to start the car, he gestured with his chin. "Tell the GPS the address."

"Fancy." Her sarcastic tone wounded his pride a little.

The Bugatti was more than "fancy," it was the greatest piece of car engineering since the creation of the automobile. A brand-new million-dollar machine. The interior still had that new car smell, a heady blend of oil-rubbed leather and gunmetal. It was his dream car.

He kept his hurt feeling to himself though and thought of Molly and what she was going through. She was remarkably calm except for the slight tremble that gave her anxiety away. If anything like this ever happened to Obie, Anders would be bouncing off the walls with worry. Resisting the urge to reach over and hold her hand, he pulled the car away from the curb and started up Green Street, heading north.

"Do you believe your daughter actually witnessed a murder?"

"I don't know. It's possible, but I think it's also possible she's lying to me so I go easier on her."

"But what if she isn't lying? Don't you reckon you should call the police?"

"No," Molly said quickly. "No police."

"But—"

"Please don't make me regret getting in this car."

"Okay. Relax. No police."

As they drove in silence, a light vanilla fragrance drifted toward him from the passenger seat, triggering a barrage of provocative images from the night before. Damn, but he'd sworn to himself he wasn't gonna go there. Last night was a mistake. He was only helping Molly now because her daughter was in trouble and he liked the kid. He had to remember that.

In other circumstances, he likely never would've spoken to Molly again.

Anders drove past the quirky and colorful architecture unique to Key West, watching the late-Victorian era homes with their gingerbread accents and the simple cigar maker's cottages give way to modern shopping centers, gas stations, chain hotels, and fast food restaurants on the eastern side of the island.

"Thank you," Molly said, drawing his gaze. She was staring out the window. "First the tumble down the stairs, then the snake, and now this. No wonder my nerves are shot. If anything happened to Cheyenne, I don't know what I'd do."

"Back up a minute. What snake?"

Molly told him about the reptile in her backseat, and how she thought she'd been bit only to discover the snake wasn't venomous. A knot formed in the pit of his stomach. Molly MacBain was having a string of bad luck lately. Something about that didn't smell right, but he kept his thoughts to himself because she didn't need anything else to worry about. "Why wouldn't April call you if something happened to Cheyenne?"

"Maybe she doesn't know?" Molly's head came up suddenly and her lips pressed together in a grim line. "Or she's in on it."

"Have you tried calling her?"

"No. Everything happened so fast and I'm not thinking straight."

"Call her. See what she says."

April didn't answer the phone, so Molly left a message asking the girl to call back as soon as she got the message. Still gripping the phone, Molly rested her hand in her lap. "Chey wanted to go to the Bahamas to look for some mythical buried treasure. When she told me she was in Jamaica, my first thought was that she tried to go to the Bahamas on her own and messed up somehow."

"Would she do that? Could she be making up the murder just to cover her butt?"

"If you would've asked me that question a year ago, I

would've said no and felt confident about my answer, but now I'm not so sure. My pride wants to believe my daughter would never lie to me, but she hasn't been acting like herself lately. She's been secretive and...and making choices I don't agree with behind my back."

Molly's phone buzzed in her hand. "It's a text from Sue. 'No flights to Montego Bay until 7 a.m. tomorrow. Plane change in Miami. Cheapest flight is $650 per person.' What? Cheyenne!"

"What's wrong?"

Molly shook her head and looked away, staring pensively out the window. "It's nothing. It's just, Cheyenne knows I don't have $1,300 lying around."

"I can loan you the money."

"No!" Molly said quickly, her pretty violet eyes going as round as plums. "Thank you, but I can't borrow money from you. I'll ask Sophie."

"Sophie and Jimmy are in Greece. Why bother them on their honeymoon when I can help you?"

"Turn here." Molly pointed to the driveway as it came up quickly.

The long, winding private drive was shrouded in tropical foliage. Anders took it slow. There were no news vans hovering on the outskirts of the crime scene, no police presence in the driveway. If a murder had happened here, no one knew about it yet.

Molly turned in her seat to study him. "Why *are* you helping me? I hope you aren't feeling obligated in some way because we slept together."

The point-blank reminder of the previous night made Anders choke on air. "That had nothing to do with it. I'm helping you because you're a friend of my brother's and your daughter is friends with my son."

"Be careful, a girl might misinterpret that as a proposal."

He chuckled, liking the way she busted his chops. Rolling to a stop in front of the Linus' sprawling Spanish-style mansion,

Anders put the car in park. A smile still tugged at the corner of his mouth as he admired Molly's profile. The high cheekbones. The pert nose. Big violet eyes. Her full, giving mouth and pointed chin. She had a quiet beauty, the kind that crept up on you with time and proximity. The kind you didn't see coming until it dazzled you.

Molly scoffed as she reached for the door handle. "At least I know you're not helping me just because the sex was great."

"What do you mean?"

"It was a disaster and you know it."

"It wasn't."

She shot him a look that said cut the crap and climbed out of the car.

Anders pushed his door open too and then spoke to her across the Bugatti's sleek silver roof. "Okay, maybe it wasn't great. But I enjoyed being with you, Molly."

She stared at him, her violet gaze a little wary, as if she was trying to decide if he was being sincere. He was. Admitting it surprised him, too.

Forcing himself to look away from her, he took in the white stucco structure with its white marble columned portico, terra-cotta roof tiles, and ornate ironwork. "Nice."

Molly squinted up at the mansion and frowned. "Pretentious. Let's go."

As they stood in front of the oversized arched French doors waiting for someone to answer the bell, Anders thought of something that might create a whole new set of problems. "Does Cheyenne have a passport?"

Molly looked at him blankly. "No. I don't have one either. Do I need one?"

"If you want to fly to Jamaica, you do."

Her smooth brow furrowed with concern. "I—"

The door opened and a middle-aged Hispanic woman dressed in an elaborate maid's uniform greeted them with a politeness that didn't match the disinterested expression on her face. "May I help you?"

"I'm Cheyenne's mother. Is April at home? I need to speak with her."

"Miss April is not available at the moment. I suggest calling before you come next time."

As she started to shut the door, Molly said, "Wait! It's important that I—"

The door closed firmly in her face.

She looked up at Anders a bit stunned. His chest swelled with indignation on her behalf and he nudged her aside. After pounding on the door, he hit the doorbell several times to get their attention.

The maid opened the door again. This time, she made no effort to hide her feelings. "Keep that up and I'll call the police."

"Good. You do that," Molly said, stepping in front of Anders. She was several inches shorter than the maid, but that didn't deter her from confronting the woman. "Maybe the police can bring April to the door because I've been trying to get in touch with her. It isn't like her not to call me back. In fact, if you don't produce April within the next five minutes, I'll call the police myself."

The maid huffed with exasperation. "Wait here." She shut the door in Molly's face again.

Molly pivoted, craning her neck to look up at Anders. When she'd jumped in front of him, he never stepped back, and he wasn't compelled to do so now. He liked standing close to her.

"Maybe we'll get somewhere now," she grumbled.

"Or she's calling the cops. We can't force April to come to the door, you know."

"Maybe one of us should look around before they kick us off the property. Cheyenne mentioned she and April were going for a late-night swim."

He nodded. "I'll do it. You wait here."

"Thank you. And Anders?"

He started to step away but stopped when she said his name. He really didn't want to acknowledge the way her sultry voice made his belly hum. "Yeah?"

Their gazes met and something akin to static electricity crackled between them. Her lips parted slightly with a quick indrawn breath. "Be careful."

Itching to touch her, he kept his hands at his sides and nodded instead. "I will."

He took the stairs two at a time and headed around back. A pair of security cameras affixed to the corner of the house caught his eye. There were others on the perimeter of the property attached to strategically placed poles and he'd bet there were a dozen more just like them. If someone was killed on Linus' estate, wouldn't those cameras have spotted it? Taking out his phone, he flicked through his contacts until he found the number he was looking for and put the phone to his ear.

Mitch Thompson answered on the second ring. "Hey, Anders. What's up?"

A retired Navy SEAL and Jimmy's former CO, Thompson funded his treasure-hunting ventures by taking odd jobs and occasionally hiring himself out as a mercenary. He knew how to get things and didn't have a problem skirting the law. Anders had never had a reason to seek out anyone with that particular set of skills, but Thompson had offered his number with the insistence Anders reach out to him if he ever needed anything. He'd had no idea he'd be taking him up on the offer so soon. Anders wouldn't normally trust a person he barely knew with something this sensitive, but Thompson was Jimmy's father-in-law now, which meant he and Anders were family.

"Any chance you'd be able to get me a couple of US passports?"

"For yourself?"

"No, I have mine. For Molly and Cheyenne MacBain."

"Sure. Something wrong?"

The fenced pool sat back about a hundred feet from the house and was surrounded by dense tropical foliage. As Anders went toward it, he noted more cameras pointed in various directions. Overkill for a mansion this size, in his opinion. He'd seen less security at the White House when he sang at the president's birthday bash last summer. No doubt he was being watched by Philip Linus' people right now. How long would it be before they came after him? He walked a little faster. "I can't go into it just now, but I need the passports as soon as possible."

"Sure thing. It'll cost a little more, but I can put a rush on it and have them to you in a few hours."

"Do it. The price doesn't matter."

"Text me a couple of photos. I'll meet you at Dixie's when the documents are ready."

"Sounds good. Thanks, Mitch." Anders hit end on the phone before he lifted the gate latch. The pool area and open Tiki bar were empty, and there was no indication anyone had been there recently. He headed for the palm-thatched building.

Opening the door, he stuck his head inside. "Anyone here?"

When silence greeted him, he walked deeper into the pool house. He moved a curtain aside and peeked behind it. A discarded dress lay in a pile on the floor. He bent down with the intention of picking it up but stopped when something cold and metallic pressed against his temple. He went very still as a prickle of apprehension skipped down his back. Then he slowly lifted his hands in supplication.

"I don't want any trouble." His deceptively calm voice belied his pounding heart.

"You're trespassing," the man on the other end of the gun said in a low, gravelly rasp that raised the hairs on Anders' arms.

"I was looking for April."

"Why?" The barrel of the gun pressed against Anders' head.

He swallowed hard and tried to keep his breathing steady.

"Molly MacBain needs to talk to her. The maid isn't cooperating. I thought I'd have a look around."

"She isn't here."

"Where is she?" Anders started to turn around, but the gun barrel pressed back, reminding him he was one wrong move away from death. Closing his eyes, he struggled to resist the ice-cold shards of fear that scraped his spine.

When the thug didn't reply, Anders expelled a deep breath. "Look. Molly is worried about April. She isn't returning her calls. Can you tell me why that is?"

"Linus took the girl to Paris last night. Said it was an early birthday present."

"She went by herself?"

"Just her and Linus."

"Molly's daughter was here last night. Cheyenne MacBain. April just ditched her?"

"A servant was told to take her home."

"You work for Philip Linus then?"

The gun disappeared as the thug stepped back. Anders turned around slowly so as not to startle the guy into doing something stupid. Dressed all in black from the top of his closely cropped head to the boots on his feet, the thug stared at Anders with obsidian eyes. Eyes Anders knew as well as his own. He gaped in disbelief. "Jonas?"

"Hello, brother."

CHAPTER NINETEEN

A tidal wave of conflicting emotions smashed against Anders like it always did when he saw his baby brother. Affection. Anger. Tenderness for the little boy who'd suffered at the hands of their bastard father. Frustration that he'd turned out just like him. Disgust. Hatred. Love.

Anders unconsciously took a step forward. "What are you—"

The gun was in Jonas' hand again and pointed at Anders' heart faster than he could whistle. Anders clenched his jaw as he stepped back with his hands raised in front of him. "I see some things never change."

Jonas didn't respond.

"How come you're not still in jail?"

Nothing. Not even a flicker of emotion on his stone-cold face.

His little brother was bad news, always had been, but he'd never pointed a gun at him before and that just pissed him off. "Put that thing down before I take it from you and shove it up your—"

"Careful, brother," Jonas said softly. "I'm the one with the gun."

Anders stopped talking, but his annoyance spiked another octave higher. He gritted his teeth. "What are you doing here, Jonas?"

"Maybe I've gone respectable."

Anders snorted derisively. "So? What? You're working ground security for Philip Linus now?"

Jonas shrugged.

"Who took Cheyenne home last night and what time did they leave?"

"No idea. Why?"

Anders didn't answer. If Cheyenne was telling the truth and she had witnessed a murder on the estate then he had to assume someone was trying to conceal it. Linus himself, or more likely someone working for him. Anders' gaze narrowed on Jonas. Was his brother involved in this and trying to cover his tracks to avoid going back to prison? It was possible. The last Anders had heard, Jonas was doing time in the Alabama State Penn for felony assault charges.

"Anders?" Molly's voice drifted toward them from the pool area.

Jonas' black gaze shifted, but otherwise, he stood eerily still.

Anders took an impulsive step forward. "Don't hurt her."

His brother surprised him by lowering the gun. "You should leave the premises."

Moving carefully at first, Anders walked past him and stuck his head out the cracked door. "I'm here. I'll be right out." He glanced back at Jonas, but he was gone.

Anders was fairly certain the building didn't have a rear exit, but somehow, Jonas had managed to evaporate into thin air.

"Fucking ninja bastard," he muttered under his breath. Opening the door to exit, he nearly bulldozed Molly. When he caught her arms to steady her, the unexpected contact sizzled through his fingers like an electric shock. He let go of her abruptly, stepped around her, and headed for the gate. "Let's get out of here. I found some things out."

"Me too." She jogged to catch up with him.

"You first." He slowed his stride so she could keep pace with him easier.

"April's stepmother came to the door. Courtney said April's father took her on a surprise birthday trip to Paris last night. She was going have a servant drive Cheyenne home, but the staff couldn't find her. Courtney assumed Chey had called a cab and left on her own."

"I found out pretty much the same."

"From who?" Molly looked back at the pool house with curiosity.

Anders grabbed her elbow to keep her moving forward. "I bumped into a security guard. He didn't know anything else. Did you tell the stepmother Cheyenne is missing?" He lifted the latch on the gate and held it open for Molly.

"I wanted to. I wanted to give the woman a piece of my mind. I mean, what fourteen-year-old girl calls a cab to get a ride home from a friend's house at ten o'clock at night? But Courtney's young. She can't be more than twenty-two or twenty-three and so pregnant she's about to pop. She said that's the only reason she didn't go with them to Paris." Molly bit her bottom lip as her eyes narrowed in thought. "I think she was telling the truth about Cheyenne. She seemed genuinely clueless about it all. I told her I have a family emergency back in Oklahoma and have to go out of town. I wanted to talk to April about managing the shop for me while I was away."

"Do you reckon Cheyenne and April planned to go to the Bahamas together, but April's father threw a wrench in their plans with the surprise trip?"

"So, Cheyenne went by herself?"

Anders nodded.

Molly's mouth hung open as she grappled with this new

possibility. "I honestly don't know if she would do something like that."

When they reached the car, Anders walked with Molly to the passenger side. "Ain't it odd Linus would jet to Paris for an impromptu vacation with his daughter when his wife's due to have a baby at any moment?"

Molly shrugged. "Half the things rich people do don't make any sense to me. I guess when you've got enough money to do whatever you want, whenever you want, it makes you silly."

"Now that's the truth." He opened the door for her and waited for her to climb in.

She turned back to him so suddenly she almost bumped into his chest. "Sorry. I'm dissing rich people and I totally forgot you're one of them."

The corner of his mouth quirked into a smile. "Don't worry about it. I was too silly to notice."

He was still chuckling to himself when he made his way around the car.

"What am I going to do about passports?" Molly said as Anders slid into the driver's seat. "Will the government issue emergency ones?"

He shook his head. "They'll still take a couple of weeks to process."

"I don't have a couple weeks."

"It's okay. I made a call. I just need a photo of you and Cheyenne and we'll have the passports in an hour."

"Will they be legal?"

"What do you think?" He cocked an eyebrow, giving her a look that said *come on now,* and started the car.

As he drove down the long, foliage-shrouded driveway, he felt Molly's eyes on him. When he glanced her way, a smile blossomed on her pretty face, lighting it from within. Her eyes glistened with moisture. "I always knew you were a good man, but I had no idea how good. I'm terrified right now, but you're keeping me steady. I appreciate that so much and I appreciate the offer of a loan. I hate having to ask anyone for money, but for Cheyenne, I'll swallow my pride. I promise to pay back every penny."

"About that. I've been thinking. You need to get to Jamaica as soon as possible. You don't need to fly commercial. I have a plane. I only have to file a flight plan and—"

She leaned forward and kissed his cheek. It was a chaste kiss, not more than a peck, but it had the same impact as a spark touching a powder keg. His grip tightened on the steering wheel as fire blazed through his body. He dared a glance at her. She was sitting on her legs with her heart shining in her eyes. His chest tightened.

"Thank you," she said thickly. "Just…thank you."

Dagnabit. He muttered in his head and belatedly realized he'd used Molly's word, but hell, it summed up exactly what he was feeling. If he was going to help her, he needed to put some distance between them because he didn't want to hurt her. This, whatever it was, wasn't going anywhere except maybe back to bed and he really didn't want to take advantage of her like that. Molly was good people. She just wasn't for him. He thought about creating some distance between them by intentionally pissing her off, but he'd be a total ass if he picked a fight with her while she was so worried about her daughter, and he honestly didn't want her to hate him. She needed his help and he fully intended to give it. He just needed something that would force the two of them to cool their jets while they focused on getting Cheyenne back home safety.

And, suddenly, he knew just the thing.

After retrieving her snake-free car from outside the bar, Molly drove home to pack a sling style backpack for herself and a duffle bag for Cheyenne. Then she called a cab to take her back to

Dixie's because she wasn't sure how long she was going to be gone and didn't want to leave her car in the street again. She beat Anders back to the bar and was scarfing down a fish sandwich when he strolled in with Obie.

"Howdy, cowboy," Molly said when he ran into Dixie's ahead of his father. She slid off her bar stool and caught him up in a hug.

The place was hopping for mid-afternoon on a Sunday. Most of the seats were full, but the bar stool next to hers was open. As Anders headed toward it, several heads turned and one woman spontaneously rose to her feet, drawing curious looks from the other folks at her table. Anders seemed oblivious. His expression was impassive as he slid onto the empty stool and looked down at his son who was squeezing her like she was a tube of toothpaste.

"Take it easy there, Obie." Anders touched his arm to urge him to let up.

"It's all right." Molly laughed, hugging the little boy back. "I really needed a hug like this."

Anders turned away to catch the attention of the bartender.

Ashley, a young, pretty brunette not immune to Anders' undeniable charisma, stopped what she was doing and came to see what he needed. "What can I do for ya, Mr. Ostergaard?"

"Did Mitch Thompson drop anything off for me?"

"Not that I know of. I haven't seen him around."

Obie climbed up on the stool Molly had vacated and she took the one on the other side of him so the boy now sat between her and Anders.

Ashley's gaze drifted past him to the person who approached him from behind. A shapely middle-aged woman with big eighties hair and too much makeup stepped between father and son, giving her back to Obie and Molly. A cloud of cheap perfume wafted toward them, making Obie sneeze.

"You're Anders Ostergaard, ain't ya?" she said in a voice hoarse from smoking too many cigarettes.

"I might be." Anders turned on his stool to face the woman.

"I knew it!" She cackled. "My friends didn't believe me so I just had to come right over here and prove it to them." She had a strong Appalachian accent and a laugh that sounded more like a cough.

"Where you from, darlin'?" he said, his accent thickening to match hers.

"Oh, my Lord, he called me darlin'." She fanned herself with a hand. "Hiawassee, Georgia."

"I've been up that way. It's a real pretty area. I played at the Georgia Mountain Fairgrounds in '07."

Obie gazed up at Molly with a flat expression on his face. He must be used to strangers gushing over his parents when they were out in public. His mother was probably just as famous as Anders if not more so. Molly pushed her plate toward the boy, offering him the untouched half of her sandwich. He met her eyes with uncertainty. When she nodded, he gave her a small smile and then reached for the food.

"Me and my sister Peggy Ann saw you in concert," the woman was saying to Anders.

"Did you now?"

"Can I get a picture and an autograph? Peggy Ann's gonna die with envy. I'm Darlene, by the way."

"Sure. Nice to meet you, Darlene."

"I can take the picture," Molly offered, holding out a hand for Darlene's phone.

"Why, thank you, sugar. Let me get on the left. That's my best side."

While Anders autographed a napkin, taking care to spell the woman's name right, something dawned on Molly. The gracious, polite man who was charming the leopard-skin leotards off Darlene wasn't the same man Molly had gotten to know over the past few days. He had his game face on, a mask of sorts he put on when he was working. He'd made the transition so seamlessly

Molly hadn't seen the shift. There was some distance protecting the man he was with the person fans wanted him to be. He'd let his guard down around Molly at some point. He must have if she could note the difference.

Obie reached for her Coke and took a long sip to wash the sandwich down. Molly smiled and rubbed his back affectionately.

Mitch Thompson arrived while Anders was taking a quick selfie with two more fans who'd waited their turn to meet him. Molly hoped off her stool and helped Obie down before she stooped to gather her luggage. A big warm hand touched her back. She straightened to find Anders standing startlingly close to her. He bent his head and his warm breath tickled the sensitive inner shell of her ear as he spoke softly. "Mitch and I need to have a private chat. Grab your stuff, take Obie, and meet me outside."

Then he turned away and followed Mitch to the office.

Pulling her gaze away from Anders' fine backside, she looked down at Obie and flushed with guilt. The boy was gazing up at her with his father's slanted blue eyes. He couldn't know what she was looking at or why she was embarrassed, so she brushed it off and gestured for Obie to go in front of her. "Come on. Let's get out of here."

She placed a twenty on the bar to pay for her meal and waved to Ashley before following him outside.

Molly couldn't believe she was actually going to leave the country with a bogus ID. It would serve her right if they didn't let her back in. She'd worry about that later. The most important thing was finding Cheyenne before she got herself into real trouble. The thought of something bad happening to her baby girl made her ill.

Anders didn't keep her waiting long. When he pushed open the glass door, he squinted against the bright Florida sunshine and stopped to slide on the pair of dark sunglasses he produced from his pocket.

"Is everything all set? Did Mitch have any trouble with the…you know?"

"The passports? Nope. Got them right here." He patted the breast pocket of his white button-down shirt. He wore it untucked and unbuttoned, low enough to reveal the navy tank top beneath. He hadn't changed the clothes he'd worn from the photoshoot, he'd only added the shirt.

He took the duffel bag from her and walked to the corner. She and Obie followed. "Where's your car?"

"I didn't want to leave it at the airport, so I called an Uber."

"I don't understand. Why would you need to do that? It's not like you're going with me."

The Uber stopped at the curb. It was a black SUV with tinted windows. Anders refused the driver's offer of help with the luggage and opened the rear passenger side door for Molly. Obie climbed in first while Molly stood on the curb baffled but adamant about one thing. "Anders, you're *not* coming with me."

"Have to," he said, tossing the duffel into the backseat. "I'm the pilot."

CHAPTER TWENTY

Cheyenne used the bathroom in the dockside office to change her clothes and brush her teeth. Worried someone would come back and discover her, she moved quickly. The bathroom was tiny and white-walled with just a toilet and sink. There was no mirror and only one small window high in the wall. It was open, letting in the warm sea breeze, which carried the scent of salt water and fish. Her stomach grumbled at the thought of a fried fish sandwich. She had money in her wallet. She just needed to find a place that sold food. She'd seen a cruise ship docked not too far away. Where there were cruise ships and tourists, there had to be restaurants. She'd go that way and get a cab to the airport from there.

She was proud of herself for how calm and logical she was being. Deep down, she wanted to curl up in a ball and cry, but she wasn't thinking about that right now. Right now, she had to stuff her bathing suit and swim shorts back into her backpack and find her wallet. She had eighty-five dollars and some change. She'd been hoping to use the money for the sci-fi convention in Miami, but that totally wasn't happening now. When Molly got done with her, she was going to be grounded until she was fifty.

At least the money would buy her something to eat and get her a cab ride to the airport. She hoped.

Realizing she should've found her wallet by now, her heart began to sink. She flipped the bag and dumped the entire contents onto the floor. The clothes she'd just changed out of, a hairbrush, toothpaste and toothbrush, deodorant, the mystery novel she was reading, a couple of pens, and the nearly empty bag of Twizzlers. The wallet was missing.

"Oh, my goodness," she whispered. She shook the empty backpack as hard as she could as if that would make her wallet magically appear. It must have dropped out when she went through her stuff on the plane. Voices drifted through the open window.

She shoved everything back into the backpack. With a racing heartbeat, she stood up and double-checked to make sure she had everything before she hurried into the main room of the sparse office. Through the giant windows that overlooked the marina, she could see two men standing on one of the piers talking to a third man who was on a fishing boat. They were in the opposite direction of the seaplane and not looking her way. She dreaded going back to look for her wallet, but she'd never make it to the airport without money.

The men appeared to be deep in conversation. Taking advantage of that, she slipped out the door and made her way around the building as casually as possible. Once she was out of their direct view, she dashed to the farthest pier and made her way down the long, skinny boardwalk, passing a bunch of docked sailboats and motorboats. She was pretty certain the man called Wade hadn't come back. He would have had to pass by the office and she was sure she would have heard him. She could only hope he'd stay away a little longer.

He'd left the plane's door open and that was how she'd gotten out. She'd been afraid to open the cargo hold's hatch. With no windows, she couldn't know what or who she'd find on the other side, so she'd made her way up the staircase, peeked out the window, and fled when she saw the coast was clear. Somewhere along the way, she'd lost her wallet, but she was pretty certain she'd dropped it in her hiding spot between the two crates.

She hated the idea of going back inside that plane. If Wade came back while she was in the cargo hold, she'd be trapped. With a gut full of lead, she reached for the railing and climbed the steps. The plane dipped slightly under her weight as she entered the fuselage. It was quiet. The smell of exhaust fumes was heavy in the air. She started down the aisle toward the back of the plane when the door leading from the cargo hold opened. Cheyenne's heart stopped when Wade stepped out. Still wearing a fancy three-piece suit, the dark-skinned man was distracted by something in his hand. Cheyenne wanted to run but she was so scared she couldn't convince her body to move. Wade glanced up from the object and did a double take. His nostrils flared slightly and then he turned the object around for Cheyenne to see.

It was her Key West High School ID.

"I believe this belongs to you," he said mildly in a heavy Jamaican accent.

Cheyenne gasped and took a step back. He slowly stalked toward her.

"Looks like I had a stowaway. Were you a witness too?" His expression changed. Darkened. Looked fit to kill. And then, quick as a snap, he came after her.

Cheyenne spun around and flew out the open doorway. Leaping from the top step, she landed squarely on the dock and then ran down the long pier. When she dared to glance back, she saw Wade stumbling down the steps of the rocking plane. He was coming. She had to go now. Heart pounding, Cheyenne rounded the corner of the whitewashed office building and nearly plowed into a bicycle that hadn't been there before. A young Jamaican man was sitting behind the counter, talking on the phone. He didn't spare her a glance. Guilt trickled through her as she eyed the bike. She couldn't believe she was even hesitating. Her life depended on this. When he turned away, she grabbed the bike and hopped on. The rear wheel skidded in the sandy dirt as she got her bearings and began to pedal as fast as she could.

"Hey!" the man in the office shouted, but she didn't look back until her wheels hit the blacktop.

Wade rounded the corner of the building, pushed the younger guy out of the way, and kept coming after her. Cheyenne's heart leapt. She took off across the parking lot and shot out onto the empty street. Older than Anders and definitely not as fit, Wade ran out of steam before she made it to the end of the block. She hung a left and didn't slow down until a half dozen blocks separated her from the marina.

The streets were pot-holed and narrow and sidewalks were absent or too dilapidated to use, so she stayed close to the stucco-sided buildings. She got off the main road as soon as she could and headed down a back alley. The tightly packed dirt was actually less rutted than the blacktop and made it easier to pedal. She kept an eye on the twin smokestacks poking out over the rusted rooftops as she weaved her way toward the cruise terminal.

Children ran around the dusty, garbage-ridden neighborhood, playing in the street. A group of senior citizens sat on plastic chairs next to a burned-out car. A man pushed a grocery cart full of junk across the road. No one paid attention to Cheyenne as she whirred passed them on her bicycle, but she was still on edge in the unfamiliar place. And Wade was looking for her. She could feel it.

How was she going to take a cab to the airport with no money?

Tears sprang to her eyes as she peddled down another small alley, this one tucked between a row of tiny square houses and a tall wooden fence struggling to hold back the irrepressible jungle. She came upon a pack of dogs and four children playing with a ball. The kids moved aside to let her pass, but one of the dogs broke free of the pack and ran after her bike, barking. Cheyenne liked dogs, but this one was snarling and nipping at her feet. She yelled at it to go away, but it didn't back off until she reached the end of the alley. She hung another right, came out onto a much wider street, and saw the parking lot for the cruise ship terminal just ahead.

As she flew past the old-timey "Welcome to Historic Falmouth Jamaica" sign, her bike wheels bounced over the pristine red cobblestones and her teeth bumped together. She hit the brakes and jumped off the bike, then parked it beside the black wrought iron fence that surrounded the port entrance. No one stopped her as she entered the complex through the main gate and blended in with a group of tourists who were disembarking from a trolley. They were all heading toward the cruise ship, which was still some distance away. The sound of happy steel drum music greeted her as she entered the craft market.

The cruise ship terminal was nothing like the real Falmouth. This version looked like something out of a Disney theme park. Cheyenne had done all the parks for free a few years ago when her mom performed with some other country artists at the American Gardens Theater at Epcot.

Just like the theme park pavilions, the craft market crawled with more American and European tourists than actual Jamaicans. The covered kiosks in the center of the plaza sold things like T-shirts, hats and purses, painted coconuts, and handcrafted wood items, while the red brick buildings around the exterior housed familiar American restaurants like DQ, Quiznos, and Nathan's. Cheyenne's stomach grumbled as the scent of boiling hotdogs wafted toward her. She wet her dry lips and swallowed hard.

A family of seven sat at the picnic table in front of her, enjoying their lunch. The oldest kid, a girl about her own age, barely touched her food. She was too busy listening to music on her iPhone. One of the younger children, a little blonde-haired girl of maybe six, waved when she caught Cheyenne staring.

Cheyenne gave her a weak smile and waved back before she turned to go. Her gaze landed on a police officer standing maybe ten feet away. She had no money to take a cab to the airport. She couldn't even buy a hotdog, but approaching the police still didn't feel like a good idea. The stern-looking officer was scouring the crowd as if he was looking for someone. Her? Possibly. The officer removed the walkie-talkie from his belt and put his mouth to the receiver. Her instincts screamed at her to run. Her heart rate escalated and her palms began to sweat as she took one step back and then another. She bumped into a pillar and caught it to keep herself from falling over. For a brief moment, the warmth of the sunbaked stone soothed her nerves. She followed the wide, solid structure around and hid behind it, removing herself from the officer's line of sight.

Wade knew her name and her general description from her student ID. If the police were on his side, the whole force could be looking for her. She stayed behind the pillar listening for any indication that she'd been spotted. Had Wade somehow followed her here? She was hot, tired, hungry, and trembling in her Keds, but she was ready to run if she had to. Where would she go? She needed to find another phone. Maybe the teenager from that big family would let Cheyenne borrow hers?

A deafening horn blast made Cheyenne nearly jump out of her socks. Tourists started moving toward the ship. Her instincts once again screamed at her to move. Bracing herself, she ducked behind a heavyset man and followed closely behind him, keeping her head down. The policeman was still there. Still watchful, but he didn't look her way.

The sign to the next area said "Arrival Plaza." It contained more red brick shops with their yellow barn doors spread open for business, more cobblestones, strategically placed palm trees and an ornate fountain in the center. All that was missing was a life-size Mickey Mouse in swim trunks and dark sunglasses.

The cruise terminal sat at the point of a triangle-shaped port resembling The White House. Or maybe a fancy bank with pillars and a vestibule. When the electric doors parted, she welcomed the refreshing blast of cool air, but she could've done without the live reggae band jamming on the stage. They were so loud she could barely hear herself think.

Maybe someone from the cruise ship company could help her. She couldn't see much beyond the line of tourists standing directly in front of her and the ceiling fans circulating to the beat of the music. As the dreadlocked singer sang the chorus to Bob Marley's 'Don't Worry About A Thing,' Cheyenne rose up on tip-toe scanning the crowd for someone who looked like an employee.

Deciding she needed to get closer to the boarding area, she sidled past two women who were talking animatedly and juggling a bunch of shopping bags. When she made it past them, she looked up and locked eyes with the police officer from the plaza. He was standing maybe twenty feet away. He nudged the man next to him and pointed to her. The man was Wade.

Cheyenne's stomach sank. Spinning around, she shoved past the women again, this time knocking the bags out of their hands. They shrieked and grabbed for her but she slipped away, crouching down as she weaved her way through the crowd away from Wade and the police.

When she stopped to catch her breath and get her bearings, she discovered she was only tenth in line from the security check-point. The passengers heading back to the cruise ship filtered through this one spot where they stopped to run their belongings through the x-ray machine and walk through the metal detector. If she could just reach a cruise ship employee and beg them for help, she might have a chance of getting away. But the line was moving at a snail's pace, making her more anxious by the moment. What if no one wanted to help her? What if they turned her into the Jamaican authorities? She was probably making a huge mistake, but she didn't know what else to do. She looked over her shoulder again, half expecting the crowd to part and let Wade and the police officer through.

"Hi!" The little girl standing in front of her said.

Cheyenne tore her gaze away from the sea of unfamiliar faces and looked down at the girl. She was the blonde-haired six-year-old from the craft market.

"Hi," Cheyenne said back.

"I like your backpack." The girl pointed to the collage of colorful cartoon horses covering the canvas. Cheyenne had had the bag since she was ten and only used it for traveling and overnight trips.

The little girl was American and her accent was similar to Ma's. Cheyenne's own accent wasn't as pronounced, probably because she'd moved around so much as a kid.

Remembering her manners, Cheyenne forced a smile. "Thanks. Do you like horses?"

The little girl's face lit up. "They're my favorite."

The line moved forward. Cheyenne and the little girl followed the other kids in front of them.

"My name's Abilene. What's yours?"

"Cheyenne." She smiled again, but this time it wasn't fake. "We're both named after cities."

The little girl beamed. "I'm named after a city in West Texas. All my brothers and sisters are named after places my parents like to visit."

"Cool." Cheyenne glanced over her shoulder, feeling Wade's presence bearing down on her.

"Cheyenne is the capital of Wyoming," Abilene declared.

"That's right." Cheyenne bent her knees to make herself shorter.

The line moved forward again. A bored cruise ship employee

on the other side of the x-ray machine pointed to the conveyer belt when Cheyenne didn't automatically drop her bag.

In a droning voice, the pimple-faced man shouted to the passengers over the music. He was British. "Packages, purses, wallets, watches, anything metal, anything not attached to your person other than the clothes you are wearing... Goes on the belt."

This was Cheyenne's chance to speak up and ask for help, but the music was so loud and the man looked less ambitious than a dumb jock the day before spring break.

"Keep it moving, girls," he barked and Cheyenne lost her nerve.

Not knowing what else to do, she dropped her bag onto the conveyer belt and tried not to look too conspicuous. Smiling at Abilene, she avoided eye contact with the employee. "How many brothers and sisters do you have?"

"Five plus me." Abilene pointed to the teenager with the headphones who stood directly behind her parents and the boy next to her. "Juneau's my oldest sister. She's sixteen and Austin's thirteen. Vail is ten." She poked the little girl in front of her who turned around to tell her to stop it. "The babies are Minnie and Paul. They're twins."

"Wow, you have a big family."

"Do you have any brothers and sisters?" Abilene asked.

"No."

"You're nicer than Juneau. You can be my sister if you'd like?" Abilene's hand slipped into hers.

"I'm Vail," the ten-year-old said. "You're pretty."

"Nice to meet you both."

Vail grinned. "Are you coming on the cruise ship?"

Glancing over her shoulder again, Cheyenne thought about it. "Yeah. Can I hang out with you?"

Both girls nodded and smiled and then started talking excitedly about their plans to go to the pool with two sliding boards.

Cheyenne kept her head down when she took her turn walking through the metal detector. She picked up her bag, slid it onto her back, and then planted herself between Abilene and Vail.

Their parents were juggling the toddler twins and the purchases they'd made today.

"Here, I can help." Cheyenne took one of the shopping bags from Abilene's mother.

The frazzled woman smiled. "Thank you, honey. Juneau, take this other bag." Juneau took it without enthusiasm, and the boy, Austin, caught the bag his father shoved at him. The parents flashed the stack of boarding passes at the crewmember standing at the bottom of the ramp. Tall and British, with a kind, smiling face, the young man greeted the family warmly and scanned the parents' tickets.

When he waved Abilene's family through, Cheyenne hesitated. Should she step out of line and ask him for help? He seemed friendly enough, but what if she was wrong? What if when he realized she wasn't a passenger, he turned her into the police? Their eyes met and she held her breath. Her heartbeat pounded in her ears as his gaze moved over her face and then bypassed her for the couple standing next in line.

Abilene tugged Cheyenne's hand and then she was walking up the ramp with the family.

No one asked her for ID or questioned her presence. She was just another kid. Harmless and therefore invisible to the ship's crew.

At the top of the ramp, she looked back toward the security checkpoint and spotted Wade. Her stomach tightened into a knot as she watched him arguing with the friendly crewmember who wasn't letting him pass. If he got through, it would be game over. There was nowhere left to go except over the side of the ship and, yeah, that wasn't happening.

When two large security guards moved in to give the ship

employee backup, Cheyenne relaxed a fraction and let out the breath she'd been holding. She was still trembling when she faced forward and followed the family to the elevators. When they stopped to wait in line, the parents turned around and eyed Cheyenne with curiosity.

Abilene's father readjusted baby Paul on his hip and said to his wife, "Did we have another child and I somehow missed it?"

Cheyenne dropped Abilene's hand and stepped toward the girl's parents. In a desperate whisper, she said, "I need help."

CHAPTER TWENTY-ONE

Flying shotgun on a bumpy, four-seat propeller plane was not on Molly's bucket list, but she'd always wanted to visit Jamaica. Just not under these circumstances when her daughter was in danger. To make this twisted nightmare even more surreal, Molly was sitting in the passenger seat of the cockpit beside Anders Ostergaard who was flying the pea-sized aircraft.

This had to be some kind of divine punishment for not attending church regularly since she was sixteen or for all of those illicit daydreams she'd had about the man beside her. The saying "be careful what you wish for" never rang so true.

Obie sat behind his father reading a comic book. The plush bucket seats and high-curved ceiling made the interior feel roomier than it actually was, but the width from door to door was narrower than her Kia Rio. She could've reached out and touched the pilot's door if she wanted to. She'd always been a confident flyer, but that was because she'd always sat in coach, sipping overpriced Bloody Marys and listening to her iPod, completely oblivious to what was happening inside the cockpit.

Every time Anders moved his hand to fiddle with the knobs

and switches on the control panel, he bumped her arm. It couldn't be helped, but the inadvertent contact made her nerve endings crackle. She tried to put sensation out of her mind. Tried to forget about the dull headache that was a constant reminder of the night of dissipation they'd shared. Tried to ignore the heady cologne that kept wafting toward her and the rich timbre of his voice in the headset as he rattled off numbers and such to ground control. He sounded like a professional pilot and it was sexy as hell.

They hit turbulence not long after take-off—a pop-up storm with high winds. All the while, Anders remained as loose as a goose. Nothing fazed him and that quiet confidence, real or not, reassured Molly better than any empty promises he could have made.

Now that they'd left the storm behind, Molly sat staring out the window at the wispy clouds streaming past and the blue sky beyond. There was nothing but turquoise Caribbean Sea beneath them, but she didn't want to think about being out over the water in a tiny aircraft with no land in sight so she focused on Cheyenne.

It should've taken her less than two hours to reach the Montego Bay airport, but she never called Molly to say she'd made it. When a third hour had passed, Molly had a minor melt-down because she knew something had gone terribly wrong. They'd been at the Key West airport getting ready to board the plane. Anders suggested she call Mitch Thompson, who'd offered to help in any way that he could.

Mitch had a contact in Jamaica—someone reliable who knew how to find things—and he assured them that a young, Caucasian American girl traveling alone wouldn't be that difficult to locate. Sabato Banton had a network of discrete associates throughout the island who would contact them the moment Cheyenne was spotted. That didn't reassure Molly as much as she wished it did, because if Mr. Banton could find Cheyenne easily enough, so could the man who committed the murder… If he was real. Molly still had doubts about that.

She didn't want to consider the possibility Cheyenne was telling the truth about witnessing a murder. Molly's heart thumped hard against her rib cage. Was she a terrible mother for not believing her daughter? But they'd checked out the Linus estate and nothing seemed to be amiss. Would Philip Linus leave his very pregnant wife home alone if someone had been killed on his premises the night before? Absolutely not. And with all the security cameras around the estate and his private security team on alert, Molly doubted much got past the man. No, as much as it pained her to admit it, Cheyenne had to be lying. An attempt to cover her butt in the hopes Molly would go lighter on her punishment.

If she survived, the little voice in the back of her mind whispered and Molly's chest burned. She had raised Cheyenne to be an intelligent young woman with common sense, but she'd never been on her own like this before. What if her lack of experience with people led her down the wrong path and she trusted the wrong person? Things could go bad very quickly.

"Hey," Anders' voice came through the headset.

She swiped a tear from her cheek and looked over at him.

His slanted eyes narrowed with concern. "Let's talk about something. Get your mind off Cheyenne for a bit. I know you're worried about her but stewing over it isn't going to do you or your daughter any good."

"You're right. I just feel so helpless."

"You're doing everything you possibly can right now. We'll get her back. I promise."

We'll. The pronoun wasn't lost on Molly. It felt good knowing she wasn't alone in this. She would've figured something out on her own if she had to, she always did, but for once in her life, it was nice to know a man had her back. Even if it was the last man on earth she ever would've expected to be there for her when she needed it the most.

"Thank you, Anders. Everything you've done for Cheyenne and me… We appreciate it so much."

"I know you do and I'm just happy I can help."

They sat in silence for a moment. Anders cleared his throat. It sounded like static as it came through the headphones. "So, what's your favorite song?"

Molly knew he meant well, but she wasn't really in the mood for small talk. She glanced down and shook her head.

"Come on now. And don't suck up to me by telling me it's one of mine because I won't buy it."

She smiled. She couldn't help herself. The twinkle in his eye was hard to resist. Tentatively, she said, "Do I have to pick just one?"

"Yep. If you had to pick just one song to listen to for the rest of your life, what would it be?"

"If I answer this. I expect you to do the same."

"Of course. Now let's have it. You only get one minute to decide."

"No pressure or anything." Smiling to herself, she turned her head away to stare out the window. The light had begun to shift with the setting sun and the pure blue ocean was a deeper indigo.

"What's the first song that comes to your mind? I got mine already."

Narrowing her eyes, she gave him a sideways look. "You've played this game before."

"Maybe." He winked at her and then faced forward again grinning. "Forty-five seconds."

"'Crazy Love.'"

"By Van Morrison?"

"Yep."

He pursed his lips and nodded, clearly impressed. "Can't go wrong with Van," he said, and then began to sing the song a cappella. His rich, decadent baritone came through the headset, crooning to her about the woman he always runs back to because he's crazy about the way she loves him. Molly forgot about her problems, forgot about the plane that was way too tiny and the reason they were flying to Jamaica, and grinned at Anders as he hit the chorus. When he dug into the song with a growly "love, love, love, love," the notes vibrated through her body and made her belly hum. Gazing at him through glassy eyes, she was dazzled by the sheer pleasure of hearing him sing just for her, as if the song was about her—

No. She didn't want that. Not for real. She sat back in her seat and fought the pressure building behind her eyes. She wanted to go back to one week ago when he was some untouchable celebrity and she was just a fan. Things had gotten complicated and messy very fast. Still, how could she ignore the voice serenading her through the headset? Oh, my goodness, how could she not have it bad for him when he sang with his heart and soul... For her.

When he ended on a note she felt deep in her loins, she sat quietly for a moment, pulling herself together. When her emotions were back in check, she gave him a benign smile. "That was beautiful. Thank you."

"I like that song a lot. I might need to add it to my repertoire on tour. I like to do a cover or two in each set."

She didn't want to think about him singing that song to thousands of other women, so she said, "Your turn. What's your favorite song?"

"'Simple Man' by Lynyrd Skynyrd."

"I thought Garth Brooks was your hero."

"One of 'em, but as far as songs go, 'Simple Man' is my anthem."

"Why?"

He shrugged. "I grew up poor. I know what it's like to be hungry. To not have a pair of shoes that fits because you outgrew your last pair too quickly. To have a hole in the roof of your double wide during the rainy season and a father who's too drunk to care. Whenever I start getting too big for my britches, I put on that song and remember. Sometimes it's painful to go back there, even in my mind, but I feel like I owe it to my momma and my roots and my son to be a better man. A simple man."

Touched that he was sharing something so personal with her, Molly blinked back the moisture in her eyes and looked at Obie. The boy was staring at the back of his father's seat, his comic book forgotten in his lap. She wondered what the little boy was thinking and whether if, at nine, he was old enough to understand what his father's childhood had been like.

On impulse, Molly touched Anders' forearm. He glanced down at her hand. She was about to pull it away and apologize for the presumption when he took Molly's hand in his. Entwining their fingers and pressing their palms together, he rested their joined hands in his lap.

How long had it been since she let a man hold her hand? Since she'd felt the leashed power of a broad palm and large, lean fingers cradling her fragile bones so gently. Felt safe and protected by the strong, capable man claiming her with the connection. Like she was one half of something whole.

She settled back into the leather bucket seat, realizing only then she'd been sitting so stiffly her muscles were starting to ache. The soft sound of humming came through the headset. A refrain of 'Crazy Love.' Anders' eyes were on the horizon as he maneuvered the yoke, steering the aircraft into a wide turn while his thumb unconsciously tapped the rhythm of the song against her hand.

They approached Sangster International Airport at twilight. Anders released her hand to fiddle with switches and knobs on the complicated control panel while he did more of his sexy pilot talk with the control tower. The crystal-clear waters surrounding the airstrip shimmered purple in the afterglow of the sunset as he brought the plane lower and lined up the runway. It was a smooth landing despite the gusty sea breezes trying to blow them off course. When they taxied past a row of commercial airplanes, which looked like giants in comparison to their little propeller plane, Molly felt a little queasy. They'd just flown nearly 600 miles across nothing but ocean in what was essentially a smart car with wings. If Cheyenne was okay, and Molly prayed that she was, the girl was going to be dead meat for putting her through all of this.

"Welcome to Jamaica." A jovial airport employee greeted them outside the plane. "MoBay is honored to have you as our guest, Mr. Ostergaard. My wife and I are big fans of your music."

Even in Jamaica, Molly thought with an amused smile as she helped Obie climb out of the plane. Anders was retrieving her bags from the small cargo area behind the backseats. He chatted with the employee in the friendly, genial way he chatted with anyone who said they were a fan of his.

"You can put that one back." Molly pointed to the duffel bag she'd packed for Cheyenne. It wouldn't be needed until they found her and there was no sense lugging it around until then. She slid on her backpack as Anders and Obie slid on theirs.

A customs agent met them inside the building in the VIP lounge. She was a heavyset middle-aged woman with a thick Jamaican accent who recognized Anders too. Taking advantage of the situation, he ramped up the charm so the woman wouldn't look too closely at Molly's fake passport. In the midst of thanking him for the selfie, the woman glanced down at the passports, studying all three of them closely. Molly held her breath as the customs agent looked more closely at her passport. When the agent brought her stamp down hard on the book, Molly jumped.

The woman handed the passport back. "Welcome to Jamaica, Ms. MacBain."

"Thank you." Molly took the passport and quickly tucked it away inside her bag next to Cheyenne's. She had a terrible poker face and wasn't sure how much longer she was going to be able to keep a bland expression on her face without cracking.

"Do you have a signal yet?" Anders asked as they waited for Obie to use the bathroom.

Molly took out her phone and looked at the screen. "Oh, I do!" She called her voicemail.

"Well?"

Molly shook her head. "No messages. From Cheyenne or anyone else."

"Maybe she couldn't find a phone."

"Maybe," Molly said, but a knot of worry started to form in her stomach.

When Obie returned, they started for the door that led to the terminal.

"Hang on a sec." Anders stopped to reach into his bag. He pulled out a black baseball cap with a gold New Orleans Saints fleur-de-lis logo and a pair of Gucci sunglasses that probably cost more than Molly made in a week. He donned them both. "There are a lot of American tourists out there. Our search of the airport will go a lot faster if people don't recognize me."

Molly nodded and looked down at Obie. "Ready?" She met the boy's questioning gaze with a soft smile. "What's the matter?"

"I hope nothing bad happened to Cheyenne."

"I hope so too, cowboy." She squeezed his shoulders. "We're here now. We'll find her."

"I'm going to help you look." He put his comic book away, folding it into his backpack.

Touched by the little boy's thoughtfulness, Molly hid her smile and matched his grave expression. "Thank you, Obie. We could use another set of eyes."

"Stay close to us." Anders' tone was harsher than necessary. "Don't go wandering off."

Obie stiffened and looked up at him with wide, wary eyes.

Molly observed the exchange with curiosity. Father and son

barely spoke to each other, but when they did, their obvious disharmony was painful to watch. As a father, Anders was uncharacteristically awkward and unsure of himself and Obie was clearly intimidated by Anders, the big, scary stranger whom he was told to call Dad. Anders was a good man. Even-tempered and caring. Well respected by his peers and fans alike. Molly would bet her favorite guitar and last dollar he didn't have it in him to intentionally hurt another human being, especially a child, but Obie didn't know that. Time and proximity would teach them both they had nothing to fear.

Taking Obie's hand, she gave it a reassuring squeeze and tugged him along. Because of their VIP status, they were able to bypass the long lines at the immigration checkpoint and enter baggage claim through the private lounge. They checked the arrivals hall first in case Cheyenne was waiting for them there. Finding no trace of her, they went outside and walked around to the departures area, which was on the ground floor at the opposite end of the building.

The bland white walls, the rows of gray bench seats, and the big windows overlooking the concourse combined with the Burger King across from the International check-in counter didn't distinguish Sangster International Airport from any other in the world. Molly's stomach grumbled as the scent of flame-broiled hamburgers wafted toward her. She'd eaten half a sandwich at Dixie's, hardly enough to fill her up. She hoped wherever Cheyenne was, she'd found some food.

"There's no sign of her here either." Anders had removed his sunglass and his eyes looked strained and weary as he scanned the crowd again. "I reckon we should grab something to eat while we wait for her and figure out what we're gonna do next."

Feeling exhausted from stress, travel, and the remnants of her hangover as well as hungry and disheartened, Molly couldn't do more than nod and follow him to the fast-food restaurant.

"We should try to get in contact with Sabato Banton, Mitch's contact," Anders said between bites of his Big Fish Sandwich. He'd abandoned his disguise when he removed his hat to eat, but so far no one had recognized him.

His wavy locks stuck out in wild tangles and there was a smudge of ketchup on his whiskered cheek. A wave of tenderness washed over Molly and suddenly her throat was thick with emotion. Anders could've been anywhere else in the world right now, anywhere at all, but he was here with her, helping her search for her daughter. Molly wanted to thank him properly. She wanted to smooth his messy hair with her fingers, and lick the condiment off his cheek before tasting his mouth…

"Molly?"

"Huh?" Realizing he'd been speaking to her and she hadn't heard a word he was saying, her face flamed with heat. "Sorry. What was that?"

Anders' tense expression softened and a small smile tugged at the corner of his mouth. "I know you're tired. I was just saying I reckon we should check out the marinas in Falmouth too."

"That's a good idea." Molly picked up her forgotten hamburger. "I'll be fine. I just need coffee."

"Please excuse the interruption." A tall, impeccably dressed Jamaican man stood between Molly and Obie.

"Hi there," Anders said, wiping his face with a napkin.

Dismissing the guy as just another fan looking for an autograph, Molly took a bite of her burger.

"Are you Molly MacBain?"

Her heart leapt as her chin snapped up. She spoke around the food in her mouth. "I am. How do you know my name?"

"May I join you?"

"Sure." Glancing at Anders' unreadable expression, she chewed her food quickly and washed it down with her Diet Coke as the Jamaican walked around the table to sit across from her.

Dressed in a three-piece suit, the man was clean-shaven with closely cropped hair. He spoke proper English with a soft, melodic accent. "I understand you are looking for your daughter."

"Are you Sabato Banton?"

Anders reached for Molly's hand. Covering it with his own, he squeezed it with a gentle warning and glared at her to *be quiet*.

He was right. She shouldn't jump to conclusions or toss Banton's name around until she knew who exactly they were talking to.

"I'm a friend." The man said and his warm smile made Molly relax a fraction. "Your daughter was spotted in Falmouth."

Molly sat up straighter and her stomach tightened with hope. "Do you know where she is?"

Anders squeezed her hand again and turned to the Jamaican. "Can you tell us something we don't already know?"

"I was hoping you could tell me what you know. To help us in the search."

"Like what?" Anders eyed him skeptically.

Molly didn't understand his hesitation to trust this man. No one else knew she was in Jamaica, so he had to be working for Sabato Banton. The man had kind eyes too, not to mention a flare for fashion. His Hugo Boss wool silk suit was sharp. Molly wanted to trust him, especially if it would help her find Cheyenne faster.

"Does your daughter have any contacts in Jamaica or any other Caribbean Island for that matter? Anyone she could turn to or try to contact if she was in trouble?"

Molly shook her head. "No. No one. She's never been out of the country before and I don't know anyone who lives in the Caribbean."

"Is there any particular reason she wouldn't contact the authorities and seek their assistance?"

Unsure how to answer that question without giving too much away, Molly looked at Anders for help.

He squeezed her hand again and then his hard, blue gaze

studied the man. "She's scared. She's in a foreign country. She doesn't know the culture." Anders shrugged. "You know how kids are."

"Indeed. I have two daughters of my own. I can't imagine what you're going through, Ms. MacBain."

"Thank you," she said faintly.

The man stood and pulled a business card from his pocket. He offered it to Molly. "If you hear from your daughter, please don't hesitate to call. I'd be glad to pick her up and bring her to you. Good evening."

Molly looked at the business card. The white cardstock was blank except for a phone number.

"Wait!" she said as the man started to turn away. "Your name? Who do I ask for?"

"It's a direct line. But forgive my lack of manors. Winston Wade at your service." He bowed slightly before he retreated, leaving Molly to stare after him bemused and disappointed.

If Banton's people couldn't find Cheyenne, where the heck was she?

CHAPTER TWENTY-TWO

Anders caught his second wind after they stopped for a Grande-size cup of coffee from Starbucks. The drive along the coast from Montego Bay took about forty-five minutes. Despite the forecast on the radio predicting rain, it was a clear, starry night and traffic was light. Molly was quiet, sipping her Café Mocha and texting with Sue back in Key West, while Anders contemplated their encounter with Winston Wade. There was something about that slick suit and polished accent he just didn't trust.

At the first boatyard they came to in Falmouth, Anders struck up a conversation with a local fisherman and learned there were three public marinas in the area. There was no sign of Cheyenne or the seaplane among the mishmash of dilapidated buildings and boats at the first two stops. The third was located off a dirt road near a poor residential area, but the marina itself was in surprisingly good condition. The single building on the premises looked like new construction. A squat, square office with a white-washed exterior and a large picture window overlooking the parking lot. The place wasn't far from the cruise ship terminal. Maybe a mile, which explained the higher caliber of clientele docked in the small marina. It was just a short jaunt by taxi for boaters wanting to visit Royal Caribbean's custom-built "historic" port.

The office was dark and locked up tight for the night. Anders checked the door while Molly and Obie walked around the far side of the building. A couple street lamps from the parking lot lit the vessels docked closest to shore while the full moon cast the rest in a silvery glow. Most of the boats were dark, but music came from a radio somewhere off to the right.

Anders followed Molly and Obie to the farthest dock.

"Watch your step," Anders said when Molly slipped on some loose gravel.

Obie caught her around the waist and she draped her arm across his narrow shoulders to steady herself.

"I'm okay. Let's keep going."

Even with the caffeine boost, she had to be exhausted. And probably still hung over from the wedding too. He'd drank a lot of water today, but a dull throb caused by too little sleep mixed with too much alcohol still pulsed against the backs of his eyeballs. He was going to need a good workout, a hot shower, and comfy bed before he felt like himself again. Except, he wouldn't be able to relax until they found Cheyenne.

The wooden boards creaked under his sneakers as he followed Molly and Obie down the narrow dock past a half dozen sailboats and motorboats. Obie carried a small flashlight, which he used to scan each slip they passed. Just beyond a yacht the size of his tour bus, Molly stopped short and Obie nearly plowed into her.

"What's wrong?" Anders' heart thumped against his ribcage with hope.

But Molly's voice was subdued. "The last slot at the end of the pier."

In the farthest corner of the marina, maybe twenty feet away, a red and white seaplane sat dark and innocuous in the water.

Molly started for the plane at a brisk pace.

"Wait." Dodging around Obie, Anders grabbed Molly's arm when she wouldn't slow down. "Let's think this through."

She spun on him. "Let go of me!"

He didn't. Leaning closer, he hissed, "Keep your voice down. If Cheyenne was telling the truth, we don't know what we could be walking into."

Molly's face was tilted upward and the moonlight caught the flash of anger in her lavender eyes. Standing on tiptoe, she lashed back at him. "And if she was lying, we're wasting time being cautious for no reason." For a moment, anguish pinched her face. "She's out there somewhere, scared and alone."

Her pain rippled through him in a way he didn't want to examine too closely. He loosened his grip on her arm. "Molly, something doesn't feel right about this." There was an odd tension in the air. It covered his skin with gooseflesh and made the back of his neck tingle. "I reckon it's just the anticipation because we obviously found the right place. Cheyenne must have phoned you from that building." He gestured toward the marina office with his chin.

Molly glanced at the building and then gazed up at him with worried eyes. The sea breeze ruffled the loose curls around her face. "Check the plane, but please be careful."

"Wait here."

Molly nodded and took Obie's hand.

Thunder rumbled in the night sky as the moon dipped behind a billowing gray cloud. Anders paused, giving his eyes time to adjust to the darkness. It was a hell of a time for the weather forecasters to be right for once.

The plane appeared to be empty, but the occupants could be sleeping. Or, if Cheyenne was on board, possibly incapacitated and sitting in the dark. He sure as hell hoped not. When Jonas was three, their father had tied him up, duct taped his mouth closed, and stuck him in a closet for six hours while Anders and Jimmy were at school. The poor kid pissed all over himself and screamed his throat raw. He was terrified of the dark for years after that and claustrophobic too. Anders didn't wish that kind of terror on nobody, especially not a sweet innocent teenage girl like Cheyenne.

He stopped in front of the plane and stood listening for signs of life, but the wind gusting off the water made it impossible to hear anything subtle.

The only way he could be certain that no one was inside was to try the door. From his experience as a pilot, he knew owners of small aircraft rarely locked them. The damage a crowbar could do to the structure of a plane cost a heck of a lot more to repair than any equipment that might be stolen. If the aircraft was locked, that would be a good indication the pilot had something valuable to hide. Good thing Anders had learned how to pick locks in his misspent youth.

He glanced back at Molly. She and Obie were two inky figures in the night with their backs to an empty boat slip. She took a step toward him. He held up a hand, motioning for her to wait.

Facing the seaplane again, he carefully lifted the pull-up handle. A strange ticking noise came from the door, like the sound of a failing car battery trying to make a spark.

Reacting on pure instinct, he dropped the handle and ran.

He was diving for Obie and Molly when his brain registered what he was running from.

Bomb.

His right arm curled around Obie as he tackled Molly in the chest, shoving them both backward over the side of the dock. The seaplane exploded in a massive red-orange ball of flames as they splashed into the water.

He lost his hold on Obie when they hit. Reaching through the dark water for the boy, he found nothing but empty space. Molly was beneath him, struggling to reach the surface. He pulled her up and reached out again. Nothing. Anders' heart pounded in his ears as his hand made a wide arc and then made contact with a thin, spindly arm. He pulled the boy close and all three of them reached the surface at the same time.

When the boy blinked at him through large, wet eyeglasses, Anders chuckled hoarsely. "You didn't lose your specs."

Molly let out a heart-breaking wail and he realized she thought Cheyenne had been inside the plane. Crying, Molly tried to climb onto the dock, but her arms were too weak to pull her up. She shrieked in frustration.

"Molly. Please, honey. You're gonna hurt yourself."

Obie pulled back, treading water in front of him. "I'm okay, Dad. I know how to swim."

Anders looked at his son's small, pale face in the water. Saw his bravery and determination and nodded with pride. "Stay close." He kissed him on the head and then swam to Molly.

Sliding an arm around her waist from behind, he pulled her back against his chest. She fought him at first, struggling to get away from him, but he held her tighter until she finally gave up and sank against him, sobbing.

"Hush. Hush now. We don't know for certain Cheyenne was in there." He prayed he was right, but his gut told him no one was inside that plane.

"She was telling the truth and I didn't believe her."

"There was good reason to doubt her story, but it's okay. We'll find her."

Molly turned in his arms. The water was warm, but she was shivering. Waves lapped against their shoulders as they floated face to face, their limbs entwined.

She chewed on her bottom lip. "Do you really think she's alive?"

"I do."

When Molly reached up to wipe her tears away, she accidentally splashed him in the face. "Then where is she? Cheyenne never made it to the airport. Never called me again to let me know where she was. Someone must know we're looking for her because they tried to blow us up!"

"I don't think we were the target."

Molly frowned. "If that wasn't meant for us, who was it for?"

"Maybe whoever set the bomb up was hoping Cheyenne would come back to the plane. And if that's the case, then she's still alive."

Molly squeezed her eyes shut, trying not to cry.

Not the reaction he was expecting. "What is it? Talk to me."

"This just proves Cheyenne is in more danger than we realized. Someone is trying to kill her. I'll never forgive myself for not believing her—"

"Dad, someone's coming," Obie whispered from the shadows.

"Come here." Anders opened his arm and the three of them took cover under the dock.

The footsteps weren't the frantic response from someone who'd witnessed an explosion. They were the slow, methodical tread of someone who wasn't the least bit surprised to see an aircraft spontaneously explode in the marina. Pieces of metal and wood still burned on the water's surface all around them. The end of the dock had been completely taken out. Only the pillars remained and maybe seven feet of pier beyond their hiding spot.

The steps stopped just above their heads. Anders put a finger over his mouth, gesturing for quiet. The boy nodded. Molly pressed her lips together tightly, and a fat tear leaked out of her left eye. He pressed a kiss to her forehead.

"It's done," Mr. Slow-tread said. "I doubt the girl will speak to anyone else. Not when she thinks her mother is coming for her. Once I find the girl, there will be no witnesses left to tie us to the scientist's death."

Molly tensed. Anders gave her a reassuring squeeze.

There was something about Slow-tread's voice that made the back of Anders' neck prickle. Proper. Articulate. Rhythmic. Anders' musical ear was too well trained for him not to recognize where he'd heard it before. They'd met the owner of that voice only a few short hours ago at the airport.

Winston Wade.

Who the hell was Wade talking to? Sabato Banton? Or someone else?

"Yes, sir. I understand. I take full respons—" Wade's icy coolness evaporated as whoever was on the other end of the line laid into him. Sounding stiff and strained, he placated the guy in charge. "Yes, sir. I understand I can't afford any more mistakes. I promise you, there won't be any."

Obie sneezed. It was quick and low, but loud enough to possibly be heard above. The boy opened his mouth to say something, but Molly covered it.

Wade was listening.

No one moved a muscle as Wade came to stand by the edge of the dock. His shadow reflected on the water, which meant the moon had re-emerged from the clouds.

Another soft growl of thunder rumbled in the sky and then fat pellets of rain began to pelt the water. Wade turned on his heels and jogged up the pier toward the mainland. The moon sank behind a stout, dark gray cloud as the storm kicked into high gear.

"Stay here," Anders shouted over the deluge. "I'm gonna make sure he's gone."

Molly grabbed his shoulder. "Be careful."

"I will."

Gripping the edge of the pier, he hoisted himself up out of the water and knelt on the sodden wooden planks. He ducked down as headlights swung around in the parking lot. Wade was leaving in a hurry.

Things didn't move quickly in Jamaica, but the local authorities would be along sooner or later. It would be better for them if they weren't around when the cops showed up.

Dropping down on his stomach, Anders poked his head over

the side of the dock. "Coast is clear. I reckon we should get the hell out of here."

He pulled Obie up first and plopped him down on the dock before reaching for Molly. When she hesitated, he said, "What's wrong?"

"Isn't there a ladder I can climb?"

"No. It was blown to bits. Come on now. Give me your arms."

"But I'm too heavy."

"Darlin', I can deadlift twice my own body weight. I'm pretty sure I weigh more than you but if you want me to do the math, you'll have to tell me how much you weigh."

"That's not happening." She glared at him but moved closer, offering her arms.

He caught her and lifted her up. She was heavier than he was prepared for, but only because she was wiggling like a tarpon trying to break away from a line. She landed on top of him, thigh between his legs, breasts pillowed against his chest. A solid, compact little weight that was distracting enough to make him forget about the rain blowing up his nose and stinging his face.

Molly looked up at him with a bemused expression. "She's alive."

"Told you so."

Rather than climbing off him, she climbed up him until they were face to face. She cupped his cheek, beaming at him. "Thank you, Anders."

"For what?"

"For bringing me here. For saving my life. For calming me down when I started to lose it."

He shrugged. "Sometimes you just gotta blow off a little steam."

"You're right." She bent her head and kissed him.

The kiss was sweet and firm and way too short, but it sent an electrical current zigging through his bloodstream. His hand slipped under her mass of soaked hair and cupped the back of her head, pulling her back for more.

"Uh, Dad. Someone's here."

Shit! He'd totally forgotten about the kid. Pulling away from Molly, he sat up fast, flipping her over as he positioned himself in front of her and Obie.

An elderly Jamaican man holding up a broken umbrella came toward them on the dock. "Mek haste, mon," he said, motioning them to hurry. "You no want to be here when dey police come."

"No. We don't," Anders said matter-of-factly. "Come on. Let's get outta here."

Ducking to shield themselves from the rain, they followed the old man around the whitewashed building.

When they reached the partial cover of the short awning, the old man stopped and turned around. "The girl who come off de iron bird dis morning, she flee on a bicycle."

"You saw my daughter?" Molly stepped closer to the man. "Was the girl tall and thin with dark brown hair?"

"Yes. Yes. Yer girl flee toward de port. Go now before dey come."

"Thank you, sir. Thank you so much!" Molly grabbed the man and hugged him.

The old man pushed her away with a deep, husky laugh. "Mek haste now."

"Thank you." Anders waved as he ushered Molly and Obie to their rental car. Only one of two vehicles in the parking lot. The other was an old pickup truck with a rusted hood. Their sedan was clearly a shiny new tourist mobile. Wade had probably followed them from the airport to make sure his trap worked.

Anders turned on the heat as he sped out of the parking lot, heading in the direction of the port. The temperature outside was too warm to catch a chill but being soaked to the bone was no picnic.

"You okay back there, Cowboy?" He glanced over his

shoulder at Obie, who looked like a half-drowned owl, blinking at him through those ridiculously large specs.

The boy nodded and his glasses slid down the bridge of his nose. He pushed them back up. "Just wet."

A smile tugged at the corner of Anders' mouth. "You've got clothes in your backpack. You can change back there if you want?"

"I'm okay."

"He's tougher than he looks," Molly observed with an affectionate smile for the boy. She sat in the passenger seat, untangling her hair. "I can't believe that man tried to trick us into giving him information at the airport."

Anders glanced at her. "You picked up on that too?"

"Wade has a distinct voice. I'm so stupid for wanting to trust him." She spoke through chattering teeth. "And he tried to kill us!"

Anders cranked the heat up to full blast.

"Thanks."

"You were just desperate. Don't be so hard on yourself. We'll figure this out." Spotting a sign for the cruise ship port, Anders hung a left.

She glanced at him suspiciously. "Why aren't you telling me to call the police? We were almost blown up back there."

Anders gripped the steering wheel tighter and squinted against the glare of the rain-soaked windshield. The wipers were crap. "Because I reckon Cheyenne was right. She'll be in more danger if we contact the police. We don't know who Wade was talking to on that phone."

Molly wrapped her arms around herself and sat back against the seat. "There's probably a lot of American tourists hanging around the cruise ship terminal. Maybe she went there looking for help."

"Maybe she got on a cruise ship." This suggestion came from the back of the car. Obie sat forward between the seats.

Anders caught his son's image in the rearview mirror. The kid had been so brave earlier. Strong and steady in the hands of danger. He might be small and timid on the surface, but deep down where it counted, he had his mama's brass and his father's grit. Anders' heart swelled with pride. "Put your seatbelt on, son, and sit back."

Molly smiled at Anders with a tenderness that made his heart thump against his chest. He wasn't sure why she was looking at him like that, but he liked it too damn much.

She shifted sideways to look over the seat at Obie, who'd put his seatbelt on. "I don't think they'd let Cheyenne on the ship without a ticket and passport."

"She might've snuck on," Obie suggested.

Anders glanced over his shoulder. "Like a stowaway?"

"Yeah."

He gazed at Molly, trying to gauge her thoughts. She stared back at him with a question in her eyes.

Then she shrugged and sat forward again. "At this point, anything is possible." Tucking her long, wet hair behind her ear, she reached for her backpack on the floor between her knees. "I'll check to see if any cruise ships left port today." She pulled her phone from the bag.

"Good thing you left your cell in the car, mine's toast."

Looking down at the screen, she stiffened and pulled it closer. Grabbing his forearm, she exclaimed, "There's a text from Cheyenne. A video message."

Anders slowed the car down so he could glance at the phone while she held it up and pressed play.

Cheyenne was seated at a table in what looked like a Mexican restaurant between two little girls who were giggling and leaning into the shot. The teenager looked happy, healthy, and safe. She waved to the camera. "Hi, Ma! I'm okay. I'm on a cruise. The Templeton family rescued me from Falmouth. They're letting me stay in a cabin with their daughters."

"Hi, Mrs. MacBain!" The youngest girl waved into the camera before bursting into more giggles.

"This is Mr. and Mrs. Templeton." She turned the phone around, panning past a table full of at least a half dozen kids and landing on an attractive middle-aged couple with kind faces.

"I'm Karen and this is my husband, Alan. Cheyenne told us she was lost so we invited her to stay with us. We're on our way to the Bahamas and due in port Tuesday morning at eight a.m. We'll keep her safe and fed until we can hand her back over to you."

The phone whipped back around to Cheyenne. "Please don't worry, Ma. I'm okay. Really. I'm actually having fun. Oh, and the Templetons are from Oklahoma, so they're practically family. Love you, bye!"

The tension that had been cramping Anders' shoulders since the explosion eased from his body. "Well, that's a relief."

Molly nodded and stared at the phone in her lap. "They look like good people. Do you think they're good people?"

"Cheyenne seems to think so. You can hear it in her voice. She sounds relaxed."

"She said she's okay."

"Trust her. She's a big girl."

Molly swiped at her eyes and nodded.

"What's the matter?"

She shook her head. "Nothing. I'm fine. Just relieved she's alive and healthy." She smiled at him, but then her smiled faltered and she put her face in her hands. "I'm a terrible mother."

"No, you're not."

"My daughter's life was in danger and I didn't believe her."

Anders reached over and threaded his fingers through her mass of damp red curls. Rubbing the back of her neck, he said, "You're here, ain't ya? You came when she needed you, despite your doubts. You've put your own life at risk to save hers. If that don't make you a good mama, I don't know what would."

Pulling the car off to the side of the road, he waited for another car to pass then he made a wide turn and headed in the opposite direction.

"Where are you going?" She pushed her hair away from her tear-stained face.

"Back to Montego Bay. No sense getting a hotel here. I reckon we could all use a good night's sleep before we head on over to the Bahamas."

"What about Wade?"

"The way I see it, he thinks we're dead. And he either doesn't know where Cheyenne is or, he does know, and he can't get to her. We just need to beat him to that port on Tuesday morning and be there waiting for her when the ship arrives."

Molly shook her head with frustration. "What if Wade gives us trouble? He tried to kill us! I can't ask you to put yourself or your son in any more danger than you already have."

His knee-jerk reaction was to say it was no trouble at all, but he wasn't free-styling it up Everest alone, he was putting other people's lives at risk. A good climber calculated his routes and recognized his limits. Anders was man enough to admit he couldn't handle this situation on his own. "I'll call Mitch Thompson. See if he can help us deal with Wade."

"*I'd* like to deal with Wade," Molly grumbled. "Five minutes in a locked room with him is all I need." She punched the car door with the bottom of her fist for emphasis.

"Easy there, mama bear. We'll get your cub back. And one way or another, Wade will get what's coming to him."

CHAPTER TWENTY-THREE

"We're not staying here," Molly announced when Anders turned into the parking lot of the beachfront resort. Water surrounded the high rise on three sides. A modern oasis plunked down in the middle of a tropical paradise, it appeared ritzy and expensive even in the darkness. By daylight, it would look like one of those fairytale places in travel magazines that made you wonder who the heck could afford to vacation there.

"What's wrong with this place? It's the best hotel in town."

She couldn't swing a dinner at a five-star restaurant let alone a stay at a five-star hotel. She bent to read the sign. "The Crystal Blue Resort and Spa. Yeah, the motel up the road is good enough for me. You can drop me there."

Anders cocked an eyebrow at her as if he was questioning her sanity.

She bowed her head and exhaled heavily. "I can't afford this place, Anders."

"Good thing you don't have to pay for it then."

"You've already done enough for me. I don't know how I'm going to repay you for the flight, let alone everything else."

"Just so you know, I accept neck massages as currency."

A laugh bubbled up Molly's throat but it came out in a cough. Was he intentionally flirting with her or just trying to be cute to distract her from the point she was trying to make? "I'm being serious."

"So am I." The rain had stopped but the moon was still playing peekaboo between the clouds as he drove under the hotel portico and parked the car. He rubbed the back of his neck. "I think I pulled something when I dove in the water earlier."

The valet attendant crossed in front of the car to come around to the driver's side.

Molly sniffed. "Good thing this is a spa because I'm not giving you a massage."

He looked dejected. "I reckon you wouldn't. But can't blame a guy for trying."

"The hotel is just too—"

"I'll get a suite and if it makes you feel better, you can sleep on the couch." He didn't wait for her response but got out of the car and handed his keys to the attendant. "The bags are in the back seat. Just two. The woman will carry her own. She's not really staying here."

"He's hilarious," Molly muttered to herself. She turned in her seat to talk to Obie. "Your father can be a stubborn—" She stopped when she realized the boy was sound asleep. She hated the idea of owing Anders for the hotel too, but what was a few hundred more dollars? The thought of all that money made her nauseous, but Obie needed to go to bed and she was honestly too exhausted to fight with Anders about where they stayed the night.

Molly waited with Obie while Anders checked into the hotel. When he returned, she climbed out of the car. "You're going to have to carry Obie."

"We could wake him?"

"If you make him walk to the room, he might not go back to sleep. Cheyenne was like that at his age."

Anders looked down at Obie in the back seat. It was almost eleven o'clock at night. He'd been asleep for at least thirty minutes. Probably longer. He nodded. "Hold the door for me."

She held it open as far as it would go while Anders leaned into the car. In his papa's arms, Obie looked much younger than his age. When Anders settled the sleeping boy against his chest and a little arm curled around his throat, a deep and primitive longing stabbed Molly in the gut.

She wanted another baby.

His baby, a little voice in her head whispered, and her heart squeezed at the thought.

She snorted softly. *Keep dreaming, little voice. Keep dreaming.*

They followed a bellman through the hotel lobby's gorgeous atrium over white marble flooring, past dancing fountains and potted palm trees. The place was several steps higher than the fanciest hotel she'd ever stayed at. When they got into the elevator, Molly stepped back against the glass wall. Obie was curled around his father, fast asleep, his cheek smooshed against a broad shoulder. He really needed a shower. They all did. They smelled like the human equivalent of wet dog. Maybe they'd have to wake him after all.

As the elevator started to rise, Anders turned to look at Molly. She smiled as their gazes lingered. His thick wavy hair was rumpled and still damp. He had a roguish five o'clock shadow and a twinkle in this eye that suggested he was smiling back at her even though his mouth was set in a firm line.

Something passed between them. A physical awareness. The look in his eyes changed. Heat replaced the humor. His gaze dropped to her chest and she realized her damp T-shirt was clinging to her breasts. Her nipples tightened under his blatant interest. Heat climbed up her neck and flushed her face, but she didn't shy away from him or try to cover herself. If he wanted to play, she knew how to play. She leaned against the cool glass and turned her gaze away, pretending to be interested in something in the atrium while gently arching her back.

His soft, low chuckle made her belly quiver, and she suddenly felt as awkward as a teenager with her first crush. Okay, maybe she was a little out of her league.

The hotel room was over the top. Ultra-modern decor, white marble walls, floors, and accents, and a private balcony with a breathtaking view of the starry sky and moonlit bay below. A giant four-poster bed sat in the center of the space, facing the open pocket doors.

As Anders tipped the bellman, Molly walked farther into the room, afraid to touch anything. She turned when Anders came into the room.

"Help me change him out of these clothes." Anders set Obie on his feet because he was waking up.

The little boy rubbed his eyes sleepily. "I'm itchy and wet."

"Maybe he should take a shower before he puts on his PJs," Molly suggested.

Anders wrinkled his nose and nodded. "Good idea. Do you want help?"

Obie shook his head. "Where's my backpack?"

"By the door." Anders poked his head into the bathroom and turned on the light. "There's soap and shampoo on the counter."

"Got it."

When Obie shut the door, Molly eyed the king bed, wondering if Anders intended for the three of them to share it. They'd fit, but it would be a little weird, not to mention presumptuous. "So, where's that couch you promised me?"

He glanced at the bed as if noticing it for the first time though it was the largest piece of furniture in the room. "Sorry to disappoint you, but it's not a couch. It's all they had without a reservation." He produced a keycard from his pocket, touched it to a small white dome on the wall, and the pocket door next to it slid open. "I was thinking you and Obie could share the two queens in the connecting room and I'd take the king. If that's all right with you? I need the extra legroom."

"Of course, I don't mind sharing. I was serious about the couch though." She started for her bedroom, but he caught her arm. When she looked up at him, his grip softened but he didn't let go.

"I know you were. Don't worry about it, Molly. I've got more money than I know what to do with. I offered to help you because I want to. No strings attached. The important thing here is that we get Cheyenne back safe and sound. That's all that matters to me."

Her heart squeezed with gratitude and she tried not to cry again. She'd been doing too much of that lately, but it was difficult not to when he was being so kind. She knew of Anders' reputation. Knew that the people he worked with couldn't say enough nice things about his big heart and his humble and generous nature, but reading the stories and witnessing his goodness firsthand were two different things. She couldn't help but be dazzled and so incredibly thankful.

Swallowing hard, she blinked back her tears and let out a watery laugh. "If you weren't as tall as a redwood, I'd kiss you right now."

A smile tugged the corner of his mouth. He bent at the waist and offered his cheek.

She could've given him a chaste peck and been done with it, but that wouldn't have done her gratitude justice. Leaning toward him, she shifted to the right and kissed his lips.

Startled, he pulled back slightly.

"I'm sorry. I didn't mean to..." Her voice trailed off.

His warm, slanted eyes were so close. A pure sky blue inside a turbulent expression that churned with surprise, confusion, and a little bit of irritation. Her heart sank. What had she done? She shouldn't have kissed him. She was taking advantage of his generous nature and using it as an excuse to get closer to him. Not to mention, Obie was in the next room taking a shower. The water had been running for a few minutes now. He'd be out shortly. The little boy already had to suffer through watching her accost his father at the marina, he didn't need to see it again. But even if Obie hadn't been there, she had no right to touch Anders.

Moistening her dry lips, she opened her mouth to try again. "I shouldn't have done that. I—"

He kissed her.

Her stomach dipped and spun like a tilt-a-whirl at the state fair as he cupped her face and molded his lips to hers. The sweet contact ended when he pulled back abruptly. Slightly breathless, he gazed at her with blue eyes that were as dark and tumultuous as a storm-tossed sea.

"You're trembling." His hand stroked up her bare arm, leaving more goose bumps in its wake. "Do you want me to close the balcony doors?"

The ocean breeze brought cooler air with it likely carried in by the rain, but that wasn't why she was shivering. "It's not that. I'm just nervous."

"Nervous?" His head tilted to the side as he studied her curiously.

Molly snorted. "As a long-tailed cat in a room full of rocking chairs."

A short, barking laugh escaped his throat. "But you kissed me."

"I shouldn't have. For starters, Obie—"

"Is still in the shower." Anders slid his hands around her back. "My God, I've never met anybody like you, Molly MacBain."

He kissed her again, but this time she met him halfway. With a soft groan, he pulled her against his chest and deepened the kiss. And just like that, she was back at the fair, soaring through the sky on the flying swings, alive and free. Her nerve endings sang as she relished the taste of him, his scent, and the strength of his body. The possessive touch of his hands as he cupped her bottom and pulled her pelvis against his rapidly increasing hardness.

A bang against the door broke them apart. Molly spun away from Anders and stood trembling worse than before. The doorknob rattled as if someone was trying to get into the room. Anders motioned her back and then cautiously approached the door to peer through the peephole.

Molly's pounding heart tripped then picked itself up again and started racing for an entirely different reason. "Who is it?" she whispered and suddenly remembered why they were in Jamaica and what almost happened to them less than two hours ago. Was it Wade? Had he found them?

When Anders didn't reply, Molly ducked into her room looking for something she could use as a weapon. She settled on the stainless-steel ice bucket because it had some weight to it.

When she peeked around the corner, she discovered Anders had flattened himself against the wall.

He shouted through the door. "Can I help you?"

The rattling stopped and then a puzzled male voice said, "Vanesa?"

"You've got the wrong room, buddy."

Another pause. "Oh, shit. Wrong floor. Sorry."

Anders didn't move.

Molly held her breath.

He leaned toward the peephole again and peered through it. "He's gone." Turning away from the door, he stopped short when he saw Molly. "What were you planning to do with that? Offer him a drink?"

She gripped the ice bucket beneath her chin like a fiddle. "No." Slightly embarrassed, she came into the room and placed the bucket on the dresser. "If it was Wade, I was going to hurl it at his head."

Anders pressed his lips together and nodded with approval. "Great idea."

As they stared at each other, a current passed between them as if he too was recalling what they'd been up to before the interruption. The shower had stopped. Obie would be opening the bathroom door at any moment. But even if that weren't the case, they couldn't do that again simply because it was pointless. A fling between the two of them couldn't lead to anything but heartache. Conflicting feelings of longing and regret tumbled in her chest like a pair of old sneakers in a clothes dryer. Molly swallowed hard and realized Anders was trying his damnedest not to bust a gut. She squinted at him suspiciously. "Are you laughing at me?"

"No," he said and then ruined it by laughing.

She picked up the ice bucket, but instead of hurling it at his head, she tucked it under her arm. "I'm going to take a shower and go to bed. I'm keeping this with me in case I need it."

His laughter followed her into the other room, and he was still chuckling when she closed the bathroom door and turned on the shower. She should've been annoyed, but he had a great laugh. The sound of it filled her with lightness. They were forming a friendship of sorts and she didn't want to ruin it by sleeping with him again. Thank goodness for Obie. Not a lot could happen with him there.

Having sex with Anders again would be amazing if they did it right, but it would also be a disaster. He'd never see her as a friend and she really wanted to keep him in her life. So, no more flirting. No more kisses. And definitely no more touching. Fate, in its twisted way, had blessed her with a second chance and she wasn't going to blow it. From here on out, she was keeping her hands to herself.

Anders jerked awake, breathing heavy and sweating despite the cool breeze blowing in through the open balcony. He'd been having a nightmare, but the details were already fuzzy and fading from his mind. He breathed deeply and smelled the sea.

Blinking to clear his eyes, he lifted his head off the pillow and took in his surroundings. He was sprawled in the middle of a massive bed. Beyond the open doors at his feet, the rising sun glittered off the surface of an aqua blue sea. Molly leaned against the railing, admiring the view. Her gloriously messy red-gold curls spilled down her back, dancing in the breeze. There was a light dusting of freckles on her bared shoulder. She had them on the bridge of her nose too and the apples of her cheeks, but they were so pale he hadn't really noticed them until last night. Recalling the hot kiss they'd shared, his loins began to quicken.

"Molly?" His voice was husky with sleep.

She turned around. There was a dreamy expression on her face that faded when she met his eyes. "I'm sorry. I didn't mean to wake you. We don't have a balcony in our room."

"Come here." He held out his hand. When she didn't move toward him, he propped himself up on an elbow. "Molly?"

"I can't."

"Why can't you? Are you worried about Cheyenne?"

She shook her head and glanced away. "Yes, but that's not it. Kissing you last night… It was a mistake."

"Well, how about you come over here and we'll see if we can get it right this time?"

When Molly didn't move, he realized she wasn't playing coy or hard to get. He sat up in bed. Tucking the sheet around his waist, he left his chest bare as he settled back against the headboard. "How was it a mistake?"

"I just… I don't want to be another notch on your bedpost." Her gaze darted away and then back again. "As the saying goes."

Her shapely bare legs stuck out from beneath a rumpled, oversized blue T-shirt. The wide neckline hung off one slender, freckled shoulder. Fiery curls tumbled to her elbows in wild disarray. And even though her eyes were strained, and she was fidgeting like she had ants in her pants, she was the most adorable thing he'd ever laid eyes on. God, how he wanted her. "Darlin', you'd never be a notch on anyone's bedpost. You'd be more like a gouge, etched so deeply it ain't never coming out."

"What's that supposed to mean?"

He shrugged and wiggled his feet beneath the sheet. "It means I reckon you're kinda unforgettable."

There was no sassy comeback. No twist of humor on her luscious mouth. The look on her face was troubled and a little uncertain.

His smile faded as he realized he meant what he'd said. Molly really was something special. He didn't want to hurt her, and if they hooked up, she was gonna get hurt. She knew it too. That was why she was pulling back.

Molly cleared her throat and came into the room. Sitting primly on the edge of the bed near his feet, she said, "Obie seems to be warming up to you."

"You reckon so?" He tugged the sheet up, making half an effort to cover his chest, and he raised a knee to hide his erection. His body wasn't on board yet with the decision to cool their jets.

"Yeah, I do." She smiled and her gorgeous dimples popped him in the gut like a pair of champagne corks. "I think he likes spending time with you. Cheyenne's like that. She's always excited to do mother-daughter stuff with me. Sometimes I worry she enjoys it too much and I have to push her to spend time with kids her own age, but she's an old soul. She's always connected with adults better than other children."

Anders plucked at the bedsheet. "I can see that in Obie. But what sorta stuff can I do with him? What do we have in common?"

"Take him out to dinner. Just the two of you. Go watch the sunset together. Ride bikes. Teach him how to play an instrument." In her enthusiasm, she grabbed his foot and forgot to let go. "There's so much you can do together. So much you can teach him."

He enjoyed the way she expressed herself. She was a passionate woman. Whether she was singing a song, drinking a cup of coffee, or kissing a man she was hot for, she was all-in every time. He nudged her hand with his toe. "You give good advice, you know that?"

She glanced down. When she realized where her hand was, she let go of him and stood up. Smiling a little too brightly, she shrugged. "That's what friends are for."

CHAPTER TWENTY-FOUR

"... And Mrs. Templeton took us for manicures and pedicures, and tonight after dinner, we're going to see a Broadway musical revue," Cheyenne finished enthusiastically.

Molly smiled into the phone. She was sitting inside the airport terminal in a small room reserved for private plane passengers. "I don't know how I'm ever going to repay Mr. and Mrs. Templeton for everything they've done for you, and I mean that literally. You have to start politely telling them no when they offer to buy you stuff." She got up and strolled to the slanted floor-to-ceiling window to watch Anders who was walking around the plane doing his pre-flight check.

A few feet away from her, Obie sat on the floor playing on the new iPad Anders had picked up for him at the airport.

"Don't worry, Ma. The musical is free, and so is dinner. No one on the ship noticed the Templetons picked up another kid in Jamaica and they aren't mentioning it to anyone."

"That's very kind of them, but the other stuff—"

"The mani-pedis were a gift from the Templetons. I tried to

tell them no thank you, but they insisted. They said I deserved it after what I'd been through."

"I'm so proud of you, baby girl. And I'm so sorry for thinking you disobeyed me and tried to go to the Bahamas on your own."

"You don't have to keep apologizing, Ma."

"I'm just so relieved that you're safe. I love you, Chey."

"I love you too."

"I'll see you tomorrow morning. Anders and I will be waiting for you when the ship docks."

"'Anders and I?'" Cheyenne said with a teasing note to her voice. "Sounds like you're a couple or something."

"Hardly," Molly scoffed but heat flushed her face.

On the ground, Anders reappeared from the far side of the plane. His eyes were hidden behind his Gucci sunglasses. A gust of wind caught his hair and toyed with the shaggy blond locks.

Molly scratched an itch on the tip of her nose and turned away from the window. Driving her fingers through her hair, she fluffed the wild curls. "You know, I always knew he was a great person, but he's been amazing. Flying us all over tarnation and saving our butts when Wade tried to blow us up."

"I still can't believe you were almost blown up."

"It's all right, baby girl. Anders called Mitch last night. If anyone can deal with Wade, he can. I have faith in him. And Anders too. He's not going to let anything bad happen to us."

"You've really got it bad, Ma."

Molly flushed. "I do not."

"Yeah, you do."

Anders looked up at the window and smiled when he saw her watching him. She caught her own reflection in the glass. Dressed in a flowy, sleeveless bohemian-style V-neck top with red floral print, a pair of well-worn jean shorts, and her backup pair of Keds, she realized she'd chosen the outfit because it flattered her figure. She could deny it until the cows came home, but she wanted to look good for him.

"We're just friends," Molly insisted.

The door opened behind her and a tall, thin Jamaican man dressed in a suit entered the room. Molly took a step back and bumped into the window before she realized it wasn't Winston Wade. Another man followed behind the Jamaican.

"Mitch," Molly exclaimed, nearly dropping the phone in her surprise. "I have to go. Have fun tonight. Thanks for calling."

"Okay, Ma. See you tomorrow."

Molly dropped her phone into her backpack as she beamed at Mitch. "What are you doing here?"

Mitch grinned through his thick handlebar mustache and opened his arms wide as he came toward her. "Is that how you greet the cavalry? Come here, red."

Molly hugged him with enthusiasm. Tall, lean, and fit, he might look like an aging long-haired hippie, but Sophie's father was a retired Navy SEAL and still as wily as they came. "It's so great to see you. Anders is outside getting the plane ready."

"We made it just in time then. I want you to meet my friend Sabato Banton."

When Molly looked past Mitch to say hello, her smile faded. Mitch's friend was standing by the door, but he wasn't alone.

"What is she doing here?" The words were out of Molly's mouth before she could stop them. She couldn't help herself. Anders' publicist was dressed in a short-sleeved navy jumpsuit looking sleek, professional, and overdressed for Jamaica.

"That's a good question." Anders stood at the top of the stairs leading down to the tarmac, his hand bracing the open door.

"Your label sent me." Selena crossed her arms. "They're concerned about your welfare."

"They're only concerned about their bank account. How did they know where I was?"

"There's a paparazzo following you. He's already published pictures of you walking through the airport with Molly yesterday along with more accusations about an affair."

Oh, no. Guilt stabbed Molly in the stomach. The only thing worse than having an actual fling with Anders and losing his friendship would be *not* having one and ruining his reputation anyway.

"Damn it!" Anders' curse twisted the knife handle impaling her a little deeper.

"I'm so sorry," she whispered.

Selena went on as if Molly hadn't spoken. "And you blew off Elizabeth Warwick. So our plan to romance her into going easy on you is finished."

Their plan? Molly frowned. He'd flirted with the reporter so she wouldn't write a bad story about him? Molly didn't know if she was relieved to hear the full story or disappointed he'd go along with something like that.

A muscle worked in his jaw as he glanced away. "I'll call her tomorrow and explain."

"Forget it. You have bigger problems with that paparazzo on your trail."

"Not to worry." Sabato Banton stepped away from the wall. "I'll find out where the photographer is staying. When he steps out of his room, I'll have my nephew Romario remove his equipment from the premises."

"I'd appreciate that." Anders shut the door behind him and came into the room to shake Mitch's hand. "Glad to see you. Thanks for coming on such short notice."

"No thanks needed. We're family now, aren't we?" Patting Anders on the shoulder, Mitch turned back to his friend. "Sabato's got some information on Cheyenne."

"My connections spotted your girl boarding the Goddess of the Seas yesterday afternoon. The ship is on its way to Nassau."

"Yes, we've heard from Cheyenne," Molly said. "She's safe for now. We're on her way to meet her."

"That's good news." Mitch grinned at Molly. "Can I talk you into calling the local Bahamanian authorities?"

Molly pressed her lips together grimly and shook her head. "No, I want to keep this quiet."

Sabato's gaze flickered to Mitch before returning to Molly. "There's a man after her. His name is Winston Wade. He used to be a high-ranking member of the Jamaican special forces. Now he freelances for the underworld. He's extremely dangerous."

Molly folded her arms and squared her shoulders. "I know. We met Mr. Wade. He tried to blow us up last night."

"What?" Selena pushed past Sabato to get to Anders. "Are you all right? You weren't hurt, were you?" She squeezed his forearm. "This has gone too far. You're risking your life for someone you hardly know. It doesn't make any sense."

Molly flinched but couldn't argue with the woman. What she was saying was true. All of it.

Anders drove his fingers through his hair. "Don't start, Selena. Please."

"Just listen to reason for a moment. That's all I ask."

"For what it's worth." Mitch bent closer to Molly. "I'm in. I'll help you get your daughter back, and I'll deal with Wade when the time comes."

Molly was so grateful for Mitch. Now that he was here, she technically didn't need Anders. She didn't have to put him in any more danger than she already had. But that meant saying goodbye to him much sooner than she expected. Disappointment mushroomed inside her chest. Ruthlessly ignoring it, she did what she had to do. "They're right." She turned to Anders. "You've done all that you can for me and Cheyenne. You can go home."

Yanking his arm away from Selena, he stalked toward Molly and loomed over her frowning. "You still need me. How are you going to get to Jamaica or back to the U.S. without my help?"

Mitch leaned into the conversation. "You aren't the only pilot in town. I can take it from here."

Though he was replying to Mitch, Anders' gaze remained

fixed on Molly. The intense expression on his face was as formidable and unyielding as his body. "I appreciate your help, Mitch, but I'm not going anywhere."

Molly's heart leapt and then started to fill with hope. If Anders left, she could get through this without him but having his steady confidence by her side would make her feel so much better. She was afraid. So many things could go wrong between now and tomorrow. If wanting him to stay made her selfish then so be it.

"The label is not going to approve," Selena insisted. "They won't even let you ride a bicycle without a helmet. You're worth millions to them."

"And I'm insured."

"You're more valuable to them alive."

"Too bad." He started to turn away from her.

"You have no idea the kind of spot you're putting me in here."

Anders rounded on Selena and bellowed, "*No one asked you to come.*"

Everyone in the room grew quiet.

Selena stared at him bug-eyed and bewildered. Fidgeting awkwardly, she closed her gaping mouth as an afterthought.

Molly, stiffly observing from the sidelines, almost felt sorry for the woman even though she'd poked the bear and brought this on herself. But Selena seemed genuinely taken aback by Anders' outburst. Probably because he was usually so calm and easygoing.

He was anything but at the moment. Tension tightened his shoulders and radiated off his body in waves. Big and muscular, he was pissed off in a way that would've intimidated the soup out of her if she hadn't known him better.

Anders strode away from them, heading for the small continental breakfast buffet that had been set out for them and helped himself to a bottle of water.

Mitch snorted and said to Selena, "I told you coming here was a bad idea, but you wouldn't listen."

Molly got the sense Selena wanted to say something, but she wisely kept her mouth shut.

Anders leaned back against the counter. His anger seemed to deflate as he exhaled heavily and opened the water bottle. "Look, Molly and I can use all the support we can get. I'd like you to stay, but you're going to have to get with the program. We're going to the Bahamas to meet Cheyenne. Things could get dicey if Winston Wade finds out where she's heading. You have a decision to make. Either come with us willingly and keep your opinions to yourself or head back to Key West and wait for me there."

Selena stared at him, contemplating her response.

"About that..." Mitch hedged, bending forward slightly. Then he nodded toward Sabato, before pivoting to look at him. "You wanna tell them?"

The Jamaican puckered his lips and nodded sagely. "Winston Wade left Montego Bay this morning." He paused, his gaze flickering to Molly. "On a flight bound for Nassau."

Even though Mitch assured Molly they'd stop Winston Wade before he got within a hundred yards of the cruise ship, she had her doubts about how a treasure hunter, a famous country singer, and a worried mother were going to stop a professional killer. Mitch's SEAL training was their ace in the hole though and evened the odds considerably. Parting with him in Montego Bay made Molly nervous, but he promised he'd meet up with them again in Nassau after he took care of some business in Jamaica.

Molly needed to use the restroom before they boarded the plane, so she hadn't stuck around to find out what Selena decided. When Molly exited the airport and met Anders outside, she was relieved to see the publicist had left with Mitch. Anders was talking to a member of the ground crew while Obie climbed into his seat. The boy pulled the door closed before Molly could offer to help him. Not wanting to interrupt Anders' conversation, she walked around to the far side of the plane to the front passenger seat. The doors opened out like a car but were higher off the ground. It was sorta like climbing up into a monster truck. She reached for the handle and yanked the door open.

Selena was sitting in Molly's seat, typing on her phone. She didn't glance up from the screen as she said in a bland tone, "Can I help you?"

Confused and mildly irritated, Molly frowned. "You're in my seat."

"Get over yourself, honey. This will never be your seat."

"Excuse me?" Molly's brows rose and her ire jumped a few more notches.

Anders called to Molly. "Ready to go?"

She shut her mouth and stepped back. Fuming, she opened the rear passenger door and climbed in next to Obie, who watched her with a concerned expression. She gave him a bright smile. "Come on, let's get you buckled."

The pilot's door opened and Anders climbed in. Settling in his seat, he looked over at Selena, then shifted to look back at Molly. The expression on his face clearly said, *What gives?*

Molly shrugged and sat back with her arms folded, making her unhappiness with the seating arrangements clear.

A grin tugged at the corners of his mouth. He shot her an intimate wink.

She felt it low in her belly. Clenching her thighs, she shifted uncomfortably.

His grin widened.

She stuck out her tongue.

He chuckled and faced forward again, flicking switches on the control panel.

The private wink almost made Molly feel better about being

evicted from her seat. If Selena was paying attention, she might have seen it. Hoping she had, Molly smiled smugly. It was clear the woman didn't like her, but she didn't have to be so rude about it. Anders would be back in Nashville soon enough, and Selena wouldn't need to worry about Molly ruining his reputation, getting him blown up, or seducing him into bed. Nope. That last one was definitely not going to happen anyhow, but it didn't hurt to make Selena squirm.

Molly glanced at Obie and did a double take when she found the boy grinning at her. Questioning the silly smile, she puckered her brow. In an impressive imitation of his father, Obie winked at her. A bubble of laughter escaped her throat. She rubbed the top of his blond head, messing his hair. He giggled and pulled away from her, returning to the game on his iPad.

The Ostergaard men were determined to make her feel better and it was working.

CHAPTER TWENTY-FIVE

Flying had always been a form of therapy for Anders. The flight from Jamaica to the Bahamas had given him time to clear his head and think about what he wanted out of life. At twenty, he'd wanted to be somebody. He wanted a way to meet women and get laid as often as possible. And he wanted money and success. Not fame. He'd never wanted fame, but that had been part of the package when he decided to pursue a career in country music. At thirty, he'd wanted his freedom. He wanted out of his marriage. He wanted another platinum record and he wanted to be the biggest country music superstar the world had ever known. He'd achieved those goals and then some.

Now, at thirty-eight, his priorities were changing again. He hadn't taken the time to acknowledge that, which was more than likely why he'd been so restless lately. As they crossed the Windward Passage between Cuba and Hispaniola, he reached some conclusions and set some new goals.

For starters, he wanted to help Obie get over his shyness, and the only way to accomplish that would be to keep the kid with him from here on out. Greer was just going to have to deal with it. Honesty, he didn't expect her to put up much of a fight. These days, she was too focused on her career to waste her time antago- nizing him. Secondly, as soon as he got back to the States, he was going to hire the best PI in the business to find out the truth about Casey Conway's death. He'd left it in the hands of the Vegas police for long enough and the only thing they'd turned up was a sketchy suspect with a dubious motive. Anders wouldn't be able to make peace with what happened to Casey until her killer was brought to justice. Lastly, he was going to take the rest of the year off and stick around Key West. Maybe work on a new record or audition a few acts for the indie label he'd been thinking about starting. His good pal Jimmy Buffet had a full-blown recording studio in town and he'd offered to rent it out to Anders any time he wanted.

Anders' reason for wanting to stay in Key West a little while longer had nothing to do with a certain feisty redhead, he told himself. He had enough on his plate as it was and he couldn't promise her more than a few great months. A little voice in the back of his head said *maybe that would be enough*. But, some- how, he didn't reckon it would be and that concerned him.

"Did they just say there's a hurricane heading this way?" Sele- na's voice came through the headset.

Anders turned the radio up to listen to the air traffic controller repeat the severe weather advisory. "Attention all aircrafts, Nassau tower. Flight conditions expected to deteriorate over next twenty-four hours. Cat.1 hurricane on course for NAS. Wind shear already affecting east runway. Standby for instructions."

"A baby hurricane." Anders made light of it, hoping to ease some of the panic he'd heard in her voice. He also didn't want to frighten Obie, who was listening on his own headset. "If we're still on the island when it makes landfall tomorrow afternoon, it'll blow right over us."

"As long as Cheyenne's ship arrives safely ahead of the storm." Molly's husky drawl, sexy as hell, came through the headset, making the base of his spine tingle. "I'd gladly ride out the storm in Nassau as long as my baby girl is safe in my arms."

Selena's voice seemed abrasive in comparison. "You do what you want, but Anders and I are leaving for the States as soon that ship arrives. He has a press conference in Miami on Tuesday."

"Since when?" Anders balked. "You never mentioned anything to me about a press conference."

Selena's eyes were on her phone. She turned the screen toward him. "I just found out myself. Your record label set it up. They cc'd me on the email they sent you. They want you to make a public statement about Casey Conway's death and dispel the negative rumors that you were involved because she found out you were cheating on her with a groupie. They wrote the statement for you."

"Damn it," he muttered under his breath. "Write them back and tell them to move the press conference to Key West and make it Thursday. And copy me."

"Fine," Selena said, not sounding fine about it at all, but typed back a reply.

"I am not a groupie," Molly grumbled in the headset. "When are they gonna let that go?"

"I'm sorry about all this, darlin'." Anders truly regretted getting her mixed up in his problems. The only thing she was guilty of was bad timing. She didn't deserve to be persecuted by the media for something that had nothing to do with her. "I'm going to do that press conference just so I can set the record straight."

"The label will expect you to read what they wrote," Selena insisted.

"I'll say what I want to say and nobody is going to stop me." Anders' grip tightened on the yoke.

Selena turned off her cell phone and neatly tucked it away in her purse. She was a tough cookie, but she had her limits. Anders realized she was only trying to do her job. "Look. I know you worry about me, but Molly did nothing wrong here and everyone keeps trying to somehow blame her for what happened to Casey."

Selena sat stiffly in her seat. "I know she had nothing to do with that."

"Then cut Molly some slack and help me set the record straight. I need to know you're on my side, Fry."

Warmed by his intentional use of the nickname he'd given her, Selena smiled at him. "I'm always on your side. You know that. The only reason I'm here is to look out for you." She tucked a limp strand of dark brown hair behind her ear. "I'll see what I can do."

The air traffic controller from NAS broke into his headset, giving Anders his approach instructions, and the conversation inside the airplane died away while he concentrated on landing.

Molly was shoved aside by the small stampede of fans who rushed Anders the moment he entered the airport terminal. His temporary anonymity was gone, but he took it all in stride, smiling amicably for the dozens of photographs snapped in his face. He bent down for selfies and scribbled his autograph on everything from plane tickets to a pretty young women's Hard Rock Nassau, Bahamas T-shirt, which she was currently wearing.

Selena announced that she'd be back with security and marched off somewhere while Molly held tightly to Obie's hand and found a safe place to stand on the outskirts of the madness. The publicist was back in minutes with four uniformed airport security guards who shoved their way into the mob. Then Anders was on the move, stopping just long enough to invite Molly and Obie to join him in the circle of bodyguards who ushered him toward the black SUV that was waiting for them.

The mob dispersed when they realized Anders wasn't stopping for any more autographs, but the security officers stayed with him. They were passing one of the baggage claim carousels when something made Anders stop abruptly. Not expecting his change of direction, everyone in the group kept moving toward the exit. Molly was the first to realize Anders was making a beeline toward a tattooed man dressed in black.

She fleetingly wondered if he was a musician. Maybe a drummer or something from a metal band whom Anders had met in the music industry. But the hostile looks the two men exchanged suggested the guy was something more than a passing acquaintance.

"What are you doing here?" Anders growled.

"None of your business." The other man's voice was gravelly and low.

The airport security officers caught up to Anders. They were ready to step in, but he lifted a hand communicating that he didn't need assistance and they backed off, giving him space. Missing the whole thing, Selena stood just outside the doors to the terminal, talking on her cell phone.

"First, you turn up at Linus' house and now you're here. Is there something you want to tell me about Winston Wade?"

The man said nothing but stared at Anders with a face made of granite.

"*Answer me,*" Anders hissed, and his rage was so palpable both Molly and Obie jumped. She tightened her grip on the boy's shoulders.

The man in black didn't even twitch.

Anders stepped forward aggressively, sticking his nose in the other man's face. Mindful of the onlookers, he kept his voice low despite his fury. "If you have anything to do with Winston Wade or the man he killed, I will personally escort your ass back to prison."

The man in black's eyes flickered with a look that dared him to try it, but the rest of his face remained passive.

Anders cursed under his breath, turned on his heels, and

stalked away. When he came even with Molly, he gave her a look that said *let's go.*

She grabbed Obie's hand and walked faster to keep up. "Who was that?"

Anders' jaw tightened. His turbulent gaze remained fastened on the direction he was moving as he spoke through gritted teeth. "My brother."

CHAPTER TWENTY-SIX

When Molly stretched out in bed that night, staring at the rotating ceiling fan, she found herself thinking about the encounter with Anders' brother at the airport. On the drive to their B&B, the only thing he said about his brother was that his name was Jonas and he should be in prison. Then he changed the subject and Molly felt uncomfortable bringing it up again. She wondered if Jonas was the reason Anders didn't talk publically about his past. Was he embarrassed by his brother's criminal record or trying to hide the truth about his sketchy family from the media? Jimmy Panama might be a former Navy SEAL, but he was no saint. He'd done his fair share of dabbling in questionable activities.

In the public eye, Anders had a reputation for being a squeaky clean, salt-of-the-earth, all-around good guy with a sweet, affable disposition. Casey Conway's shocking death had certainly put a dent in the world's perception of him. And Molly was discovering things about him she never would've guessed. Like the fact that he was an unsure parent and had been an apathetic husband in his marriage. He intensely disliked his youngest brother. And he could be as stubborn as a steel pole in a windstorm.

She still liked him too damn much.

The rain had woken Molly from a light sleep when it came down in a deluge, pounding against her bedroom windows. Mitch had made good on his promise to meet them in Nassau and arrived in time for dinner. He said the outer bands of the hurricane were nothing to worry about, but Molly had lived in Florida long enough to know what a tropical storm felt like and this was different. The short bursts of intense rain were just a taste of what was coming.

A sense of impending doom hung in the air, but that had more to do with Wade, who was out there somewhere waiting for Cheyenne. Her ship was still scheduled to arrive at 8 a.m. ahead of the eyewall, which wasn't expected to make landfall until mid-afternoon, but Molly worried the forward momentum of the storm was stirring up the water and causing high seas. She couldn't do anything about it but pray the ship would make it safely to Nassau.

Mitch had arranged lodging for them at a secluded bed and breakfast near Love Beach on the northwest side of New Providence Island. When they arrived at the inn, Selena went inside with Obie to get their rooms situated while Molly helped Anders with the bags. She wanted to speak with him privately about their game plan in the morning, but he wanted to wait until Mitch arrived to talk about it. Anders was still in a pissy mood and walked off before their conversation was over.

Ms. Vivian, their good-natured hostess, lived in the attic of the old, three-story Victorian farmhouse and rented out the other rooms. A young, athletic-looking couple from the UK occupied one of the four units on the second floor, so someone had to stay in the small room off the kitchen on the first floor and Selena made certain it was Molly. But she didn't mind. The bed was comfortable and it was probably a lot cooler sleeping on the first floor of an old house with no central air conditioning. She hoped Selena was nestled in her bed and sweating like a pig trying to pass a peach pit.

Molly rolled onto her side and admonished herself. Maybe she was being a bit harsh, but the woman just rubbed her the wrong way with her contemptuous looks and subtly disparaging comments. *This will never be your seat.* Did she treat all of Anders female friends that way? Did he know how Selena acted behind his back? Probably not. But it wasn't Molly's place to enlighten him. He'd figure it out someday and kick the woman to the curb.

Or at least a girl can hope.

Fluffing the pillow, Molly turned away from the window to stare at the old wooden door and its ancient brass knob. A light flicked on in the kitchen, filtering through the one-inch gap at the bottom of the door. It had to be after midnight because she'd managed to sleep for at least an hour or two before the heavy rain band blew in and woke her up. The sound of running water from the sink made her sit up in bed. She rubbed the sleep from her eyes before sliding her bare legs out from under the bedsheet. She padded barefoot to the door, cracked it open a few inches, and peeked out.

Anders was standing in profile in front of the farmhouse sink, a glass of water forgotten in hand as he stared out the rain-soaked window. He wore a black muscle shirt and loose black boxers. His dirty blond hair was sleep-tousled and a day's growth of beard shadowed his jaw. He looked so gorgeous and disreputable he made her palms sweat.

He must still be angry about the run-in with his brother. Not only could she see the tension in his shoulders, she could feel the hostility simmering inside him like a pot ready to boil.

She never knew Jimmy had a younger brother. Jonas didn't have the look of an Ostergaard. Was he a half-brother then? Or adopted? Did Jimmy have an issue with him too? Whatever the circumstances, it was clear Anders and his youngest brother did not get along.

Anders had been mostly introspective on the plane ride to Nassau, but he'd been flat out brooding since the airport. After disappearing into his room, he'd gone out for a run while Molly played a game of Monopoly with Obie. Ms. Vivian served dinner at six and Mitch had arrived just in time to join Molly, Selena, and Obie for a meal that would've been tense and awkward without his presence. After dinner, Mitch went off to find Anders, and Molly took Obie to the beach to watch a spectacular sunset. They had to dodge a rain band on the way back to the house, but it had been worth it.

Molly went to bed around ten and fell asleep listening to music on her phone, but she was wide awake now and feeling restless. She crossed her arms and leaned against the doorframe. "Wanna talk about it?"

He took a sip of water before he set the glass down and stared at it. "No."

She probably should've left well enough alone and gone back to bed. "What's the deal with your brother? Jimmy has never mentioned him."

Anders snorted softly. "Let's just say he's the black sheep of the family."

Molly cracked a smile. "Well, I know a little something about that—"

Anders slammed his hand down on the counter so hard the glass jumped. "You know nothing about it."

Molly stiffened. She knew he was just redirecting his anger at her, but it still got her hackles up. Instead of fighting with him though, she stepped back and shut the door firmly.

As she stood frowning at the rustic wood panel, her irritation grew. Where did he get off shouting at her and saying she didn't know anything?

She reached for the brass knob, yanked open the door, and

nearly walked into Anders who was standing on the other side preparing to knock.

She gasped and took a half step back.

The expression on his face was unreadable, but there was a storm brewing in his somber blue eyes. Quietly, he said, "The deal is he's a dangerous ex-con. I tried to fix him once, but he's broken beyond repair. Jimmy and I wrote him off years ago."

She was surprised by his sudden willingness to open up to her and glad he thought he could, but she was still angry. "So, you've got family baggage. We all do. It doesn't mean you get to dump on people because you're still moping about what went wrong. Your brother is a grown man. He's made his own choices. But you have a choice too. You can choose to stop letting something you can't control have so much power over you. You've been sulking around here like a slug in a salt factory and now you're biting my head off? No, sir. I think you owe me an apology."

He nodded and looked down at his feet. "You're right. I'm sorry."

"See, I—"

He tugged her forward and kissed her. Surprised by the unexpected assault, her fingers dug into his shoulders and she groaned with approval. He tilted his head and pushed his tongue inside her mouth and her body went up in flames. Goose bumps rose on her skin as his left hand slid under the hem of her long T-shirt and over her panty-clad ass. Without breaking the kiss, he lifted her off the floor, took a few steps inside her room, and shoved the door shut behind them.

As he kissed her deeply, her brain melted and she couldn't think of anything beyond the taste of him and the feel of big hands cupping her bottom. Her blood hummed and her stomach tightened.

He emitted a low, primal growl before he tumbled her back onto the bed. She sank into the plush mattress and spread her legs for him as he settled between her thighs.

He was hard and eager beneath his silky black boxers and her body wanted him as much as he wanted her. But her brain reminded her she didn't want this. *Friends.* She just wanted to be friends. She turned her head to the side, and he took it as an invitation to explore the tender spot behind her ear.

"Anders…" She gave his broad shoulders a gentle shove.

"Hmm," he mumbled as he found a particularly sensitive spot behind her ear and concentrated on it.

She let out a sound halfway between a grunt and a purr, but she didn't let the tingly sensations he was making her feel deter her. "Anders, stop. Please."

His head came up. His blue eyes were dark and glazed with passion. The skin across his cheekbones was tight and rosy with desire. He smelled of soap and the woodsy, masculine scent that was uniquely his. Heat radiated off of him, another symptom of his need for her.

Molly cleared her throat before she spoke, but her voice was still low and gravelly and didn't sound like hers at all. "What are you doing?"

"I reckon it's kinda obvious, ain't it?" His voice was low, too. The husky tones brushed over her skin like sandpaper, making goose bumps rise in their wake.

"I mean, what are your intentions?"

The corner of his mouth quirked into a sexy smile. "I intend to have my way with you. If you'll let me."

Molly's heart leapt like a cheerleader at a pep rally. While it was doing high kicks and backflips, making her blood pound, her brain blew the whistle on all the fun. "This is a bad idea."

"Why?"

"Because I'm not a groupie."

He rose up on his elbows and his heavy erection inadvertently pressed against the juncture of her thighs. Or maybe the move was intentional. Either way, Molly was all too aware of the fact only two thin scraps of fabric separated her from the heat pulsating against her tender skin.

"I know you're not a groupie. I never thought you were. Look." furrowing his brow, he shook his head slightly. "I can't promise you anything beyond this moment. I just know I want you and I need this."

Molly frowned. So, he was using her after all. She snorted softly. "Now *that* makes more sense. This sudden hankering for me. You're just looking for a warm body to fuck out your frustrations. Go to hell!" She shoved him away and started to sit up, but he caught her by the waist and flipped her back down.

Hovering over her, pressed belly to belly, his eyes glittered in the dim light. "There's nothing sudden about my desire for you."

"Move out of my way."

He growled in frustration and flopped back on the bed beside her. In his sudden absence, Molly felt shockingly bereft. Sexual longing hummed through her veins despite the fury making her tremble. She took a deep, steadying breath. "Do you want to sleep with me because your brother got your hackles up and you need an outlet?"

When he said nothing, she turned her head. He was trembling too and his erection was tenting his satin boxers obscenely. Her traitorous body tightened in response.

She needed to come to terms with the fact she wasn't going to have her world rocked tonight. Pressing a hand to her stomach, she tried to hush the dancing butterflies, but when Anders spoke again, the deep rumble of his voice stirred the tiny flutters.

"You're right about me being frustrated." He met her gaze. "But it's not about my brother. Molly, I reckon I've wanted you since the moment you doused me in hot coffee and landed in my lap at Dixie's."

The butterflies leapt and swarmed. Molly swallowed the sudden thickness in her throat and smiled faintly. "I was just trying to get you to take your shirt off."

He snorted. "Figured as much." A smile tugged at the corner of his mouth.

As they stared into each other's eyes, the sounds from the room crept into their intimate space. The rain had slowed to a trickle, at least for the moment. The fan blades whirred softly, spinning around and around, in no hurry to get anywhere. The old-fashioned clock on the nightstand audibly ticked away the seconds.

Molly let out a shaky breath. "Is that true?"

Anders shifted, turning toward her, and the old bedsprings groaned and squeaked beneath his weight. His eyes gleamed in the dim light from the lamp on the bedside table. His voice was like a caress. "Yeah. It's true."

"Dagnabit," she muttered softly.

He shifted a little closer and his warm, faintly minty breath touched her cheek. "Is wanting you such a terrible thing?"

"I'd be lying if I said it was, but—"

"Molly, I want you so badly it's making me half nuts, but I don't do long-term relationships. Not anymore. What happens next is up to you, but I want you to go into this with no expectations."

This was exactly what she didn't want, but the offer was so tempting. She wasn't sure if she had the strength to refuse. Saying yes to no-strings-attached sex with Anders Ostergaard would be so easy, while preserving her dignity and their friendship by saying no thank you would be anything but. She had to do it, though. If only to protect her heart.

"I—" The words stuck in her throat.

Anders rolled onto his back to stare up at the ceiling fan again. The soft patter of rain outside suddenly intensified, pounding against the bedroom windows in a deluge.

"I shouldn't have asked that of you." He drove his fingers through his hair, mussing it up more before he tucked his hand behind his head. "I'm sorry. It was wrong. It's just, you're unlike any woman I've ever met and it's twisting me up inside."

The sincerity in his voice tugged at something deep in the core of her being and made her ache for him.

She sat up and turned to face him. He looked so big and sexy laying in her bed, her good intentions didn't stand a chance. She grabbed the hem of her oversized T-shirt and lifted it over her head. The scrunchie in her hair went next. Her mass of long, red curls tumbled down around her bare shoulders as she sat before Anders, naked except for a pair of skimpy cotton panties.

Though he stayed very still, watching her with heavy-lidded eyes, his chest rose and fell like he was in the midst of running a marathon.

Molly slid her panties off, scooted forward, and hooked a leg over his hips to straddle him. Only the thin layer of his satin boxers separated her from his hardness. At the contact, waves of electricity shot through her body. She groaned and braced herself on his torso. His hands settled on her waist.

"Are you sure?" he whispered huskily.

"Yes." She nodded. "Yeah, absolutely."

A slow grin spread across his handsome face. Her lower belly clenched and the slow pulse between her legs began to beat double-time.

She pushed his shirt up and helped him remove it, then she bent down to kiss his chest. His pecs were rock solid, the bronze skin hot and salty. The buzzing in her ears grew louder as she kissed her way up his neck and found his mouth.

Their tongues tangoed in a hot, wet, luscious dance. The hair on his chest scraped the tender skin of her breasts as they pillowed against his hot flesh. Anders stretched their joined hands over his head and rested them against his pillow.

She undulated against him and whimpered.

He sucked in a harsh breath and muttered against her lips, "Fuck."

"I'm trembling."

"Are you cold?"

That was like the match asking the flame if she needed a coat. Molly shook her head. "No, I've just…never felt like this."

"Your heart is going a mile a minute. I can feel it against my chest."

"Yours too." She smiled and nuzzled his jaw.

Outside, the rain surged against the windows as short flashes of lightning illuminated the room.

He kissed her again and the world spun as he rolled them over. When he removed his boxers and came back to her, she was ready for him. He gripped her hips and buried himself deep with one hard thrust.

They both gasped and went very still.

Molly clung to him, quivering with relief and desperation. His skin was shockingly hot against her over-sensitized flesh. The pulse between her thighs thumped against the hard steel pinning her to the mattress. Her body clenched and rippled with anticipation. She arched to take him deeper and saw stars. Crying out, she grabbed his ass and bucked against him.

"Oh, God," he groaned and started to move inside of her.

Wild for him, Molly demanded more, urging him deeper. The ancient bedsprings screamed in protest, squeaking obscenely, rivaling the storm outside. Shifting the angle, Anders came into her faster and harder, driving her up the bed until she had to reach for the slats of the headboard to keep her head from knocking into it.

The bed squeaked.

The wooden headboard thumped against the wall.

The rain blew and the wind howled.

But Molly only noticed these things abstractly.

Every nerve ending in her body was attuned to the rising tension bringing her closer to the edge. His mouth was on her breast, suckling the nipple almost too roughly. The pleasant pain shot straight to her groin. She let go of the headboard and grabbed his ass again. Arching beneath him, she wrapped her legs around his waist and met his urgent thrusts.

Anders cursed and she contracted.

A white light exploded behind her eyelids as her body was anointed in a surge of euphoric sensation.

"Molly. Sweet Molly. Oh, God," Anders muttered against her ear as he kept thrusting, almost desperately now.

Responding to his delirious pleas, she wrapped her arms around his neck and bit his shoulder.

Suddenly, he stopped and looked down at her. His eyes were black and glossy with the madness of desire. His flushed face was tight with strain.

"You're beautiful," he whispered fiercely, and her heart soared.

Thrusting again, he groaned into her mouth as he started to come apart. Then he shouted as his climax overtook him and he shattered in her arms.

He collapsed on top of her, burying his face in the crook of her neck with a sigh.

Molly stroked his back, savoring the weight of him pressing her into the mattress. She took a deep breath and sighed too. Tomorrow she might mourn her decision to be with him, but right now, with her body still thrumming and her heart swollen with joy and love, she had no regrets. How could she when—

Something thumped against the bedroom door and shattered.

Startled, she looked toward the door, half expecting someone to come barging in on them.

Anders hadn't seemed to hear the noise. Drained from the intensity of his release, his body rested heavily on top of hers, not moving.

"Anders? What was that?"

He didn't respond.

"Wake up. Something broke."

"Huh?" he muttered against her shoulder. "It's just the storm."

She tried to shove him off, but she would've had better luck lifting a truck off her chest.

"I think someone's out there."

His head came up and he looked at her with bleary, hooded eyes.

"An intruder?" he murmured.

"I don't know. Possibly. They broke something." By now, Winston Wade had to know they were still alive. What if he found them? Molly tensed and grabbed Anders' shoulders. "Obie's upstairs alone? What if it's Wade?"

"Mitch sent me a text about an hour ago saying he's in downtown Nassau tailing Wade. And besides, he assured me Wade doesn't know about Ms. Vivian's place. He's not connected in the Bahamas like he is in Jamaica, but I'll check it out." Moving slowly, Anders pulled away from Molly and sat on the edge of the bed.

"Anders!"

"I'm going. I'm going."

"Please be careful." She pulled the bed sheet over her body as he slid on his boxers. "Take a weapon."

He gave her a sardonic look. "I'm telling you, there's nothing to worry about. It was probably just the wind."

The storm was pretty intense. The rain was blowing so hard now, it looked like a hose spraying a steady stream of water against the window. Maybe he was right and something had hit the side of the house, but she would've sworn the noise came from inside.

Anders opened the door and stopped short, looking down at the ground.

"What is it?"

"Nothing. Just broken glass."

She climbed out of bed wrapped in the sheet and joined him at the door.

"Careful," he said, holding her back.

The glass of water Anders had left on the counter was now scattered in a thousand pieces across the kitchen floor. "How did that happen?"

Anders shrugged. "Maybe I left it too close to the counter and it rolled off?"

"That doesn't make a lick of sense."

Caught by the wind, one side of the old casement windows above the sink yawned open and then slammed back against the frame.

"Mystery solved." Anders nodded toward the window. "The wind blew the glass off the counter."

"But I definitely heard something hit the door." Bending to check for damage, she was disappointed when she didn't find anything.

"That old door is made of solid wood." Anders touched her arm. "A bighorn sheep could ram its head into it, and I doubt you'd notice any damage. You probably heard the glass hitting the floor and your guilt made you think otherwise."

"Guilt?" She stood up and frowned at him.

His arms slid around her sheet-clad waist and hauled her closer. "Guilt. For stealing my heart."

Molly rolled her eyes. "Now don't go getting cheesy on me just because we had sex."

"It's not cheese, it's charm."

"That's what you call it?" She snorted and pulled away from him to hunt down a pair of shoes and her nightshirt.

"Where you going?"

"To clean up the glass. Stay where you are. I don't want you to get cut." She slid the shirt over her head and slipped a pair of Keds on her feet.

"You don't have to do that," he said, watching her make her

way around the worst of the glass to get to the pantry closet on the other side of the kitchen.

"Since I'm the only one here with shoes, I do." She paused in front of the kitchen sink. An odd feeling came over her. Something didn't make sense about this. She knew what she'd heard. The glass wouldn't have fallen on the floor and shattered into a million pieces like that, but what other explanation could there be? After shoving the window closed, she flipped the old-fashioned hook latch back into place. "You know, this window wasn't open earlier."

"It might have been shut but not latched."

"I guess." She eyed it with doubt and then continued on to the pantry where she found a broom and dustpan behind the door. "Go on back to bed and keep it warm. This won't take long."

Anders stayed where he was, leaning against the doorframe watching her sweep up the glass. "You reckon we need to talk about the elephant in the room?"

"If you're referring to my ass then no."

As she was bending over in front of him with her can up in the air, she thought it might be a possibility.

"No." He chuckled. "I'm talking about the fact that we didn't use a condom."

Molly's stomach did a little flip and she almost tripped over the broom. Catching herself, she stood up and looked at him. "If you're wondering if I'm on the pill, I am." She carried the dustpan to the trashcan to dispose of the broken glass. "And I haven't had sex in a very long time so I know I'm disease free. Do I need to be worried about you?" She shook the glass into the can and steeled herself for his answer. She really didn't want to hear about his sexual exploits, but she needed to know.

"I always use protection."

She raised a skeptical eyebrow at him.

He shifted uncomfortably. "Well, except for tonight. I'm not usually so careless. I even remembered to use one that night I was skunk drunk after the wedding."

She was well aware of that because she'd found the used condom in the wastebasket next to her bed when she was freaking out the morning after. She scrunched her nose at the memory.

"But tonight…" He shrugged helplessly. "It never crossed my mind."

Molly's hand trembled. She reached for the broom and went back to sweeping up the last remnants of broken glass. "And other women haven't made you forget like that."

"Never."

Their eyes met. The current that was always present between them hummed.

He shifted again and straightened away from the doorframe. "You almost done?"

"Almost."

"I'm clean," he said. "I get a checkup every six months, and I've only been with one other woman in that time."

"Just one?"

"Yeah. Casey. And, yes, we used protection. Every time."

"Oh," Molly said flatly and dumped the last bits of glass into the trashcan. Of course, now, she couldn't *not* picture them together. The beautiful blonde starlet and the hunky country star. She really didn't want to feel jealous of a dead girl, but the bitter stab got her right between the ribs. She returned the broom and dustpan to the closet. "I think I got it all."

"What's the matter?" he said when she met him at the door.

"Nothing. I'm really tired and we have to be up early to meet the ship. Are you staying or going back to your room?"

Not waiting for his answer, she tried to slide past him. He caught her waist. "What Casey and I had… It was nothing. Just a few days of meaningless sex. This is different."

"Different how?"

"Well, for starters, I like you. We're friends. Maybe more than that. I don't know what this thing is between us, or what's gonna happen tomorrow, but I want you to know that I didn't make love to you tonight just because I'm crazy hot for you. I did it because I wanted to be close to you. I care for you, Molly."

She swallowed the lump in her throat and blinked back the moisture pooling behind her eyes. He had her at *We're friends.* Maybe she hadn't screwed everything up by sleeping with him after all. Maybe they could be something more. He cared for her and she cared for him and that was a start—not an ending—in her song book.

She went up on tiptoe and tugged him down so she could reach his mouth. When their lips met, she kissed him sweetly. He picked her up, arms beneath her legs, cradling her against his chest as he carried her into the room. Divesting her of her nightshirt, he removed his boxers and followed her down onto the bed. They made love tenderly and further explored the indescribable thing that crackled between them, and her heart soared a little higher.

CHAPTER TWENTY-SEVEN

Anders slipped out of Molly's bedroom just before dawn. He showered in his own room and dressed for the day in a pair of jeans and a V-neck T-shirt that matched his eyes. He could be vain sometimes, he'd admit. But having a job that required him to look a certain way made him more conscious of his appearance. He wanted to look good for Molly. He wanted her approval. He wanted...

Hell, he didn't know what he wanted. He studied his reflection in the mirror above the sink. His toothbrush poked out of his mouth. His finger-combed hair was still damp. He needed a shave but ladies seemed to like the light beard. They said it made him look more ruggedly handsome. He wanted to look ruggedly handsome for Molly.

He wanted to see her eyes dilate with interest when he walked into the room. Wanted to feel the spark that zinged between them whenever their gazes met. He wanted to take her again like he had just an hour ago, right before he left her bed. He'd entered her while she was still soft and dewy with sleep. Rode her gently until she was wide awake and urging him on. Hell, he was half hard just thinking about being inside her again.

Reaching into the front of his jeans to readjust himself, he thought about rubbing one out to take the edge off. Testing the idea, he fisted his rapidly expanding erection and closed his eyes. Letting his head fall forward, he imagined Molly astride him naked and gasped when he saw stars. The damn woman and her tight little body were making him hornier than a teenager.

Someone pounded on the bathroom door.

The toothbrush fell from his mouth.

He dropped his cock and spun around half expecting whomever it was to barge in and catch him with his hand down his pants. Grabbing a bath towel to cover the bulge in the front of his jeans, he said, "Yeah?" When his voice croaked on the word, he cleared his throat and tried again. "What is it?"

"Anders?" It was Selena. *What the hell?* She must have let herself into his bedroom. "Mitch called the B&B. He's been trying to reach you on your cell. You forgot to give him your new number." Anders had picked up a new phone in Montego Bay to replace the one that took a swim with him in the marina.

"Did he tell you what he wanted?" He picked up his toothbrush and stuck it back in his mouth so he could finish brushing his teeth.

"The cruise ship came in early to beat the storm."

He froze. "How early?"

"Around 5 a.m."

He spat toothpaste and rinsed his mouth out with a scoop of water. "Please tell me Mitch has Cheyenne."

Anders' ears prickled with dread. He opened the bathroom door and found Selena sitting primly on his unmade bed. Surprise derailed him for a moment. How long had she been there? Had she'd heard him jerking off in the bathroom? The notion made him queasy. Annoyed she thought it was okay to let herself into his room in the first place, he growled, "What did he say?"

"The family who was looking after Cheyenne said a man

fitting Wade's description approached them in the cruise ship terminal. They were distracted for a moment and when they turned back, Cheyenne was gone."

Anders' clenched his fists in frustration. "God damn it! I thought Mitch was on his tail. Does Molly know?"

"No, I came straight to you, but I'll tell her about Wade." Selena stood up and headed for the door. "Maybe now she'll notify the authorities and let them handle this."

Anders shook his head. "Wait. I'll talk to Molly. I told you before, we're not getting the police involved. I trust Mitch. I want to see how he wants to handle this."

Selena turned around in the open doorway, her brow knit with concern. "That woman almost got your son blown up. How are you going to protect him and yourself when bullets start flying? You're not Superman."

"You're right." Anders' chest tightened with guilt. He'd brought Obie along for selfish reasons. He thought having the kid around would help put some distance between him and Molly, but that plan had not only crashed and burned, he'd put his son in grave danger. "Can you do something for me? Can you take Obie back to Key West? Sue and Oscar will look after him until I get back."

"No!" The shout came from Obie who stood outside in the hall in Spiderman PJs. He pushed past Selena and came into the room. His hair was tousled from sleep and he wasn't wearing his glasses. "I don't want to go."

Unsure of how to handle this, he looked at Selena for help.

She shrugged. "I'll see if I can still get a flight off the island. It's not like there's a hurricane bearing down on us or anything."

"Thanks, Fry."

For a moment, she looked as if she wanted to say more, but she pressed her lips together and turned to go. "Don't forget the press conference. I managed to get it moved to Thursday in Key West. You better be there."

"I will. I promise."

When he and Obie were alone, Anders sat on the edge of the bed and met the boy's steady blue gaze. Anders swallowed hard, trying to think of how to send his son away when all he wanted to do was to keep him close. It wasn't safe for him though, Selena was right about that.

Obie put his hand on Anders' shoulder. "I don't want to go home, Dad. I want to stay with you."

The words squeezed Anders' heart. "I'm not sending you home, cowboy. Just back to Key West. It's too dangerous here with the storm and all."

"But you said it was a baby hurricane. Please, I want to help."

"You can help by going with Fry and being good for Ms. Sue." He hadn't planned on bringing this up now. Time was of the essence and he needed to break the news to Molly and get in touch with Mitch ASAP, but the troubled expression on Obie's face got him in the gut. "I've been thinking, what if I didn't send you back to California at the end of the summer? What if you stayed with me permanently from here on out?"

Obie's expression was unreadable. "In Key West?"

"Well, no." He patted the spot on the bed next to him. Obie stayed where he was. Anders rubbed his whiskered jaw then drove his fingers through his hair and exhaled heavily. "I don't live in Key West, son, but I reckon we could stay at least through the New Year. What do you think about that?"

"I like Key West."

Anders nodded. "Key West is pretty."

"And nice."

"Yeah, real nice."

Obie launched himself into Anders' arms and squeezed him tightly. As he held his son, joy washed over him like a tsunami, subtle but mighty, and he knew he'd made the right decision.

"Thanks, Dad." Obie pulled back. "Promise you'll bring Cheyenne home safe?"

Anders swallowed the lump in his throat. "I promise." He kissed Obie's head then watched him dash out of the room.

Wiping moisture from his eye, he stood up and pressed his lips together grimly. He was not looking forward to telling Molly about her daughter.

Cheyenne lay shivering on the cold, gritty warehouse floor, watching Wade pace back and forth on the other side of a large office window. He was on the phone. She curled her legs into her chest and buried her face in her knees. Her hands were zip-tied behind her back and her head hurt. Wade had hit her from behind just before he'd shoved her into the backseat of a car. The lump behind her right ear throbbed like it had a pulse. If she thought about it too much, she was going to be sick again.

A tremor rolled through her body, and she squeezed her eyes shut, trying not to cry. She was going to die. She'd heard Wade talking about it in the car when he thought she was unconscious. He was worried about someone named Albatross figuring out how much he'd screwed up. The guy on speakerphone told him Ma and Anders had survived the trap he set for them in Jamaica and that Anders was a famous celebrity. Wade let out a string of cuss words and almost lost control of the car. His friend suggested he ransom Cheyenne for money, but Wade hadn't liked that idea. Ominously, he said, "Albatross won't be pleased. He's going to come for me. If I don't make this problem disappear, I'm a dead man."

A chill had settled into Cheyenne's bones and she couldn't stop shaking. She didn't know who Albatross was, but the dude sounded scarier than Wade.

A boom of thunder made Cheyenne jump and she winced as the plastic cuffs bit into her flesh.

Outside, the wind howled and the rain splashed against the

roaring surf. They weren't far from where Wade had snatched her from the cruise ship terminal. He'd taken her to an industrial area by the water. The abandoned warehouse smelled of fish and moldy wood from the old crates rotting in the corner. There were four windows. Tall and narrow, they sat a good eight feet off the ground. Two of the windows were boarded up, and two were open and missing glass, but it didn't matter. Even if she could get her hands free, there was no way she could reach the windows without a ladder.

They hadn't been there long, maybe ten minutes. Wade had dragged her into the warehouse and ordered her to stay while he made a phone call. Cheyenne's teeth were chattering too hard to argue, and her legs felt like Jell-O, so she wasn't going anywhere anyway.

Why hadn't she listened to Mrs. Templeton and called Ma last night to let her know the ship was arriving in Nassau early? She'd said she would, but then she started talking to the other girls and completely forgot. If she would've remembered to call, maybe Wade wouldn't have gotten to her first and—

Wade opened the door and came out of the office. Dressed in a navy three-piece suit, he looked like a groomsman in a fancy wedding, not a murderous kidnapper. "Give me your mother's phone number."

A sliver of fear skittered down her back, but she fought against it. She hated feeling afraid. Raising her head, she glared at him. "Go to hell."

Wade chuckled. "Those are brave words from a little girl. Give me her number."

"Why?" She didn't trust anything he said, but she had to ask.

"So we can tell her where you are."

Cheyenne's stomach twisted into a tight knot. "You mean, so you can kill her too."

Wade's expression was impassive and his lyrical voice was

calm. "You have a very big imagination. Who is the man traveling with your mother?"

Cheyenne swallowed hard. "Man?"

"Yes. Tall, blond, athletic build." Wade bit out the words, growing more agitated. "What is his name?"

If Wade didn't recognize him, she wasn't going to help him out. "I-I don't know."

"Stop lying. He's a celebrity of some sort. Who is he? I will find out, even if you don't tell me."

Cheyenne clamped her mouth shut and shook her head. She didn't want to die, but she didn't want Wade to hurt Ma or Anders either. And he would hurt them. It didn't matter that Anders was famous, Wade would kill him too before he disappeared. Cheyenne's stomach lurched, and bile climbed up her throat. She breathed raggedly through her nose.

"Your mother hasn't gone to the police. Why?"

Cheyenne shook her head again.

"Don't lie to me again." He grabbed the front of her shirt and lifted her clear off the ground.

She gasped and squeezed her eyes closed as she turned her head away. "I don't know. I swear."

He let go of her and she landed hard against the concrete floor, whacking the tender spot on the back of her head. The stab of pain brought fresh tears to her eyes. She curled into a ball and watched Wade take out his phone. He swiped the screen, searching for something. When he found it, he turned the phone around and showed it to Cheyenne. "And the little boy in the photograph? Who is he?"

Blood pounded in her ears as she stared at a picture of Obie eating Burger King. "Leave him alone," Cheyenne blurted before she could stop herself.

"Is he your brother?"

"He's only, uh, six," she lied, hoping the boy's small size and baby face would save him. "He doesn't understand what's going on. D-don't hurt him. Please!"

"I have no interest in the child. Give me the number."

She stared at him, dizzy with relief that he wasn't planning to go after Obie too.

Suddenly, Wade lunged forward, growling, "Give me the number or I'll change my mind about your brother."

Cheyenne gave him the number.

He moved away from her and called Molly.

Nausea churned in Cheyenne's stomach again. She used her shoulder to wipe away the tears streaming down her face and sniffled loudly.

Wade's voice was soft and pleasant. "Ms. MacBain? Sorry to wake you. Your daughter's ship arrived early." He paused. "Yes. Yes. An hour ago." Another pause. "Forgive me, it's Winston Wade."

Molly shouted through the phone. Cheyenne's heart leapt at the sound of her mother's voice even though she couldn't make out what she was saying.

Wade clenched his teeth and scowled, but his polite tone stayed the same. "Your daughter is fine. I'll let you speak to her in a moment, but first, I have a proposition for you."

Anders was closing his bedroom door when he received a text from Selena confirming she'd booked two first class tickets on the last flight out of Nassau. She and Obie would be in Miami before lunchtime. With one less thing to worry about, he jogged down the stairs as quickly as he could, heading for Molly's room. He was two steps from the bottom when the front door opened and Mitch blew in with a squall of rain and leaves.

"Hey." He pointed with his thumb. "I thought that was you in the taxi. I was just gonna call you."

"What taxi?" Anders met him in the hall.

"The one that just pulled out of here like a bat out of hell." Mitch was looking back over his shoulder. His head snapped around. "Where's Molly?"

Anders didn't understand his concern. She wouldn't take off without him. Even though he was certain of it, he started for the kitchen. "She's in her room. I was just coming down to tell her about Cheyenne."

Mitch followed him. "I don't think she's in her room."

Anders flipped on the light switch as he passed through the kitchen and didn't stop to knock on her door. Shoving it open, he stopped just inside the room and took in the unmade bed, the dark ensuite bathroom, and the Keds missing from the floor. The knot in his stomach sank to his feet. "She's gone," he said, half stunned.

Mitch was on the move, heading for the front door.

Anders jogged to keep up with him. "How are we going to find her?"

"There are only two yellow cab companies on the island. We'll call them and figure out where she's heading."

They dashed into the rain, running for Mitch's rented black SUV.

Anders climbed into the passenger seat. "You think she's going to try to get Cheyenne back on her own?"

"Looks that way."

As they sped off in the direction Molly had gone. Anders put his phone to his ear and waited for the first cab company to pick up. "She's gonna get herself killed."

Mitch bent forward, squinting to see out the windshield. The wipers were going a mile a minute. "Then we better find her before she finds Wade."

CHAPTER TWENTY-EIGHT

Molly sat in the back of the speeding taxi cab, debating if she should call the police. They would have a ton of questions like, for starters, how come she hadn't called them sooner? How could she admit the truth? That she'd rather gamble with her daughter's life than risk losing a custody battle to her selfish bastard of an ex-husband?

On the phone, Wade had claimed he was interested in striking a bargain. He would deliver Cheyenne safely back to Molly in return for their silence. It sounded like a fair deal, but she couldn't help feeling like a canary flying into a trap set by a big, fat, sly cat. Wade said Molly should bring her man along but tell no one else. Molly didn't want Anders to risk his life again for her. If she'd told him about Wade's proposition, the stubborn man never would've let her go alone, and she had to do this. Every second Cheyenne was with Wade her life was in danger. If Molly came alone, he wouldn't expect a fight from her, but she was prepared to do whatever she had to do to save her daughter.

What would Anders think when he discovered she was gone? A lump of regret formed in her throat and she swallowed hard. What did it matter? If the price of one blissful night with him turned out to be her daughter's life then—no, she wouldn't go there. She should've planted herself at the cruise terminal the moment she arrived in Nassau and waited there all night. Instead, she'd been out souvenir shopping and watching sunsets. Screwing a fantasy man who would never love her the way she wanted him to love her.

The cab stopped in front of a boarded-up grocery store. She swiped a stray tear from her cheek and squared her shoulders. She could do this. She had to for Cheyenne.

The American expat taxi driver turned around in his seat. In his mid-sixties, he was deeply tanned from spending too much time in the sun. "You sure this is where you want to be dropped off? The hurricane is only a few hours from making landfall and she's already tossing debris like rice at a wedding."

"I'll be careful." Molly fumbled with the door handle. "Damn it."

"Lift the latch. That's it." The driver leaned on the steering wheel. "This part of town is mostly boarded up because it's so close to the waterfront, but just a few blocks west, The Old Wharf Bar is open for business, even at this hour of the morning. They're having a hurricane party."

"Thanks for the info." Molly forced a smile as she handed him some cash and opened the door.

As she slid across the seat, her hand went to the pocket knife duct taped to her inner thigh, making sure it was still there even though the six-inch piece of metal was pressing into her soft flesh like a cookie mold. She'd found the makeshift weapon in a kitchen drawer along with the tape. She might be bringing a knife to a gun fight, but at least she wasn't coming empty handed.

Molly had borrowed the raincoat she was wearing from Ms. Vivian's hall closet. She pulled the hood up and tightened the belt around her waist before she dashed across the empty street and made her way to the arched entrance of the city dock.

It was just past 7 a.m. on a Tuesday morning, but except for the occasional motorist speeding past, the town was deserted. No one was stupid enough to be out roaming the streets in a hurricane. The sky was an odd purplish-gray with patches of yellow and orange where the sun was trying to break through the clouds. Squinting against the gusting wind, Molly stood with her back to a bumper-sticker covered stone column. It wasn't raining just now, but the dark gray band coming her way suggested it would be very soon.

A car turned the corner, an innocuous brown sedan. It stopped at the curb, ten feet away from her, and the passenger side window went down. Winston Wade sat in the driver seat. "You came alone? Where's your man?"

"I didn't tell him where I was going." She folded her arms across her chest and bent to look into the car. "Where's Cheyenne?"

"You'll see her soon enough. Take off your jacket and leave it there."

"But it's cold." It wasn't that cold, but it would be once the rain started again.

"Do it. Or I'll drive away right now and you'll never see your daughter again."

Bile climbed up Molly's throat. She clenched her teeth and nodded tightly. "Fine."

Keeping her eyes on Wade, she untied the jacket and dropped it on the ground by her feet. She was wearing a pair of green cargo shorts and a loose white T-shirt. The shorts were just baggy enough to hide the knife taped to her inner thigh, or so she hoped.

"Lift your shirt."

"No." The tension building up inside of Molly snapped and she lunged for the car, slamming her hands against the side of it. "Go to hell, you son of a bitch. We had a deal. Take me to my daughter."

"Do it."

Trembling with anger, Molly stepped back and raised the T-shirt, bearing her mid-section. She turned around in a circle before he told her to.

"Get in the car."

Molly climbed into the passenger seat and sat facing forward with her hands in her lap. Glancing at Wade, she took in his black turtleneck, pants, and boots. There was a gun in the leather holster strapped across his chest. The sight of the gun flashing silver in a sliver of daylight made her ill. Maybe she was in way over her head.

It was too late though. The car pulled away from the curb and made a U-turn. Wade stuck out his hand. "Give me your cell phone."

"Oh!" Molly gasped and turned around, looking back at the raincoat lying in a pile on the sidewalk. "It was in my coat pocket."

"Good." He kept driving.

"Is Cheyenne hurt?" Molly steeled herself for his answer.

"She's alive."

Panic fluttered in her breast. "That's not what I asked. Is she *hurt*?"

"I've had no reason to harm your daughter."

This eased Molly's worry, but only slightly. The unspoken word "yet" hung in the air like a heavy, gray thunderhead.

Less than a quarter of a mile up the road, they passed The Warf Bar. The place the cab driver had mentioned. The two-story concrete building had boarded up its windows, but a big painted sign beside the door said: "We're open...until the building blows away." Island music blared through the open door though there was no sign of anyone going in or out of the building. A block past the bar, Wade turned into a district of warehouses situated on the waterfront beside a marina.

The buildings were maybe twenty feet wide by forty feet deep and in various stages of dilapidation. One looked like it had been burned out fairly recently.

Molly cleared her voice before speaking, but it still sounded strained and scratchy. "How is this going to go? You're just going to give Cheyenne to me and let us leave in return for our promise that we'll forget about what happened?" If she hadn't been so distraught earlier, she might have realized how ridiculous that sounded.

"That's right."

Molly raised a skeptical eyebrow at him. "You're just going to take our word for it that we won't talk?"

Wade's smile was pleasant and unconcerned. He shrugged. "Thanks to the information in Cheyenne's wallet, I know where you live and I also know you're the owner of a bookstore in Key West. The Ever After Book Shoppe. How quaint that sounds. If you should decide to speak to anyone about me, I will hear of it. I have connections in Florida. It will only take a phone call to destroy everything you hold dear, including your daughter."

Molly shivered and rubbed her bare arms.

"Do we have an understanding?"

She nodded because she couldn't bring herself to speak just now.

Wade drove to the very end of the row and then turned down an alley that was barely wider than the car. He turned again and couldn't go any farther because they'd reached the water. The warehouse's entrance was steps from the passenger side door. Molly grabbed the handle and started to get out of the car.

"Wait. Stay where you are while I come around."

A heavy padlock secured the metal barn doors. As Molly watched Wade fiddle with the rusty lock, the rain started again, fierce and heavy, like a hose nozzle had suddenly turned on full blast. She'd only have one chance to use the knife, so she needed to pick the right moment. Wade was a good head taller and fifty pounds heavier than she was. She had to go for a kidney or maybe his crotch. One would kill him. The other would just slow him down long enough for her and Cheyenne to get away. While Wade's back was turned, she thought about taking advantage of the moment. But she hesitated a fraction too long.

The door opened and he shoved her inside.

Cheyenne was sitting on the ground, her wrists tied together and her arms linked around one of the steel posts that ran from the ceiling to the floor. Her face brightened when she saw Molly. "Ma!"

Molly pressed a fist to her chest and struggled against the overwhelming urge to cry. She started toward Cheyenne. "My sweet baby girl, I—" She was cut off when Wade yanked her back by the hair.

He dragged her toward another post and threw her down. She landed hard on the filthy concrete floor and saw stars when she banged her bruised thigh. "Stop. What are you doing?"

"Shut up." A knee came down on her back, pinning her to the floor.

"But we had a deal."

"There's been a change of plans." He twisted her arms behind her back and dragged her across the rough ground toward a steel pole.

"Stop it! You're hurting her!" Cheyenne wailed and the fear in her voice broke Molly's heart.

"You lied to me just to lure me here," Molly hissed. "You had your chance to get away. If you hurt us, nothing will stop Anders and Mitch from finding you and killing you."

"Brave words for a woman who's stupid enough to think I would simply let her go."

Molly prided herself on being street savvy. On being able to read people. Her gut told her not to trust Wade and she'd done it anyhow. Now Cheyenne was paying the price for her mistake. "Let my daughter go. Please."

"Stop talking and be still or I'll tape your mouth shut," he said, duct taping Molly's wrists together behind her back so her arms were locked around the pole. He tossed the tape aside as he headed for the door. "I'll be back."

"Where are you going?"

"To get the boat ready. We're going for a little ride."

In a hurricane? He was insane. She started to tell him that but he was already on the other side of the door, engaging the padlock.

"Ma, where's Mitch and Anders? Did they follow you? How are they going to break the lock?"

Ignoring the guilt that sat heavily on her chest, Molly climbed to her feet awkwardly. "They aren't here. I came alone."

"What? Why?"

"I can't explain right now. We don't have much time, but don't worry. I got this." One of the benefits of knowing a former Navy SEAL was that they taught you things you hoped you'd never have to use, like survival skills and self-defense tactics. A few months ago, Jimmy decided to teach Sophie how to use a knife and escape from different scenarios, and Molly had sat in on the lesson. Now here she was, in a real life-or-death situation with a knife strapped to her thigh and her wrists bound behind her back.

Planting her butt back against the post, she fisted her hands and lifted her arms as far as she could raise them. Then, she slammed her bound wrist down on the pole. She winced as shards of pain darted up her forearms.

"What are you doing, Ma?"

"Hush." Arms stinging like a firecracker, Molly bent at the knees again and raised her hands once more. This time, she made sure she pulled her wrists apart when they hit the pole. The tape snapped, and she fell forward, landing hard on her shoulder.

"Damn, Ma. How'd you do that?"

"I told you, I got this." Molly reached under the leg of her cargo shorts, ripped the knife from her thigh and then used it to cut Cheyenne free.

The girl flew into Molly's arms and squeezed the oxygen out of her lungs. "I never thought I was going to see you again."

"I was afraid too, but we're together now. Let's get out of here."

"How?"

Molly stood up and eyed the sketchy pile of crates in the corner of the room as she tucked the knife into her pocket. The window above them was open, but it was at least seven or eight feet off the ground. "I think those crates will hold together long enough for us to climb. We'll have to hurry though."

Molly picked the best-looking crate of the bunch and tried to drag it over to the window. It was heavier than it looked. "Get on the other side and help me push."

Together, they muscled the three-foot-square wooden box to the wall. Molly already knew she wasn't going to be strong enough to pull herself up into the open window. "Stack some of those loose boards on top."

They grabbed the pieces of rotten wood and made a pile.

"That's good enough," Cheyenne said, already climbing up onto the crate. "Let's go."

The teenager had at least five inches on Molly and she was lithe, lean, and agile. Despite her lack of athletic ability, Cheyenne managed to pull herself up into the window fairly easily. It was a narrow fit, but she straddled the ledge sideways.

"Come on, Ma!"

Grunting, Molly climbed up onto the crate not nearly as gracefully as her daughter had. "What's down below?"

Cheyenne leaned out to investigate. "About five feet of dock. It looks slippery, but I think if I hang down, the drop won't be too bad."

Molly caught the ledge and tested out the wobbly pile of wood. It had stayed in place for Cheyenne, but Molly was wary of it. She needed the extra boost though if she was going to make it onto the ledge. This wasn't going to be pretty. "You go ahead, I'll be right behind you."

"No, I'm not leaving you." Cheyenne's brow furrowed and, for a moment, she was six again, frightened and distressed after a bad dream.

"You have to move out of the window for me to climb up there."

The padlock on the door rattled.

Wade was back.

There was no more time.

Molly's heart climbed into her throat. She shoved at Cheyenne's foot. "Go. Hurry. Don't wait for me. I want you to find your way out of here. There's a bar about a block from the entrance to this place. It's open. You'll hear the music. Go there, find a phone, and call Anders."

"But, Ma! I can't do it by myself."

"You can and you must! Please, baby girl. You got this far on your own. I was wrong for not trusting you. You are smart and brave, and you're a survivor just like me. I love you, and I'm so proud of you."

Cheyenne's face crinkled with anguish. "I won't let you down. I love you."

Witnessing her daughter's pain revitalized Molly. She wasn't going down without a fight. Girding herself for what she needed to do, she gave Cheyenne Anders' phone number and then climbed off the crate. If Cheyenne was going to get away, Molly needed to distract Wade or stop him altogether. Dashing across the room, she planted herself behind the door and took out her knife. She had one chance to take him by surprise.

The metal door blew open, missing her by inches as it slammed back against the wall. Wade rushed into the warehouse then stopped short when he realized Molly and Cheyenne weren't where he'd left them.

Molly aimed for his kidney. The blade bounced off bone, pricking him in the back but not doing any serious damage.

He shouted and swung around, knocking her sideways into a crate. She was too stunned to feel the pain as the rotting wood disintegrated beneath her.

"Where's the girl?" he shouted, stalking toward her. He grabbed her by the hair and dragged her forward. "Tell me or I'll burn this place down with you in it."

Molly had lost the knife when she missed her target, but she still had her fists. She swung her arm around and smashed Wade's nose. He howled and let go of her. She scrambled to her feet and made it through the door. Plunging into the blowing rain, she made it past the car before he caught up with her.

Grabbing her from behind, he put her in a headlock and squeezed her throat until she was choking for air.

"Where is she?"

Molly shook her head or tried to. She couldn't move, couldn't breathe. She could suddenly feel again though and her body was throbbing like a toothache from being tossed around like a rag doll.

"Is this a trick? Is she hiding in the office? If I have to search for her, I'll shoot you where you stand, and then I'll shoot your daughter when I find her. And I will find her."

Trembling from head to toe with a mixture of fear and fury, Molly tried to tell him to go to hell, but the words were garbled in her throat. She pulled at his arm, urging him to let up. When he eased his grip, she sucked in a deep gulp of air. "Cheyenne is no threat to you. She's a teenage girl with a big imagination. No one will believe her story, even if she tries to tell it. Even I didn't believe her at first." That still pained Molly to admit, but it was the truth.

"I was going to make your deaths look like an unfortunate boating accident, but now you've left me no choice." He withdrew his gun from its holster and shoved it against Molly's head.

A deep quake rippled through her body, and her knees threatened to crumble. "No. No, please."

Grabbing her arm, he shoved her forward, bypassing the car as he headed toward the side of the building where Cheyenne had jumped out the window. If she was still there waiting for Molly, it would be over for the both of them.

Just before they reached the corner, Molly tripped on purpose and stumbled. Wade nearly pulled her arm out of its socket, dragging her to her feet.

"Keep moving," he said, forcing her to step down onto the wooden dock that ran the length of the building.

Cheyenne was nowhere in sight.

Leading Molly to the small motorboat tied to the dock, Wade told her to get in. The boat was rising and falling on the rough surf, making it impossible for her to step into the vessel without falling. She tumbled forward, landing hard on the wet, slick surface. Wade produced more tape and bound her arms behind her back before he slapped a piece across her mouth.

This was it. She was minutes away from death. At least Cheyenne had gotten away. Molly could go to her grave knowing Cheyenne was safe. Even if she ended up with Trevor, she was a good kid. She'd be okay. And Anders... Wade would've killed him too if Molly had brought him along. Maybe she'd done the right thing after all. She loved him. She was so grateful for last night, for being able to show him just how much he meant to her. She could die with no regrets. Fate was a funny thing. From the first time she'd heard Anders' voice on the radio to the moment she spilled hot coffee on his lap—all of it had been leading to that one cataclysmic moment when the stars aligned and, for the space of a few hours, fantasy became reality and he was hers.

Wade untied the boat and pushed away from the dock before returning to the wheel. Molly leaned against the rear bench seat, bound and gagged, exhausted and defeated.

Providence had a cruel sense of humor.

Forcing herself to get up and climb to her feet, she only made it to her knees on the slippery surface. With Wade's back turned, she tried to free herself from the tape like she had in the warehouse, but gathering the momentum while kneeling on the topsy-turvy deck was a thousand times more difficult. She lost her balance and fell hard against the seat.

Glancing back at her, Wade shouted, "Stay down."

She ignored him and struggled to her knees again.

The boat rocked wildly.

The wind howled.

And Molly raised her bound arms up and slammed them down against her thighs. It didn't work. Wade turned around and kicked her sideways. She flew backward against the seat, and one of her hands slipped free of the soggy duct tape.

Hope fluttered in her chest. She ripped the strip off her mouth and ignored the sting as she desperately scanned the deck for something she could use as a weapon. Her gaze settled on the oar attached to the inside of the boat in case of an emergency.

They were only twenty feet from shore because the wind and surf kept pushing them back.

It was now or never.

$$\text{\textinterrobang}$$

"Molly!" Anders shouted from the dock, but his voice was carried away by the wind.

She lunged for something. Wade turned around. Molly picked up an oar and swung for his head.

Anders clenched his fists as Wade deflected the blow and knocked Molly backward. She sprawled on the deck and Wade raised his gun.

No. No. No.

A single shot rang out.

Anders tensed and jerked as if he'd taken the bullet himself. His chest exploded with pain and his knees threatened to buckle. *Molly, no...*

Wade staggered back a step then crumpled to the ground.

The shot hadn't come from the boat. It had come from above Anders' head.

Mitch ran around the corner of the warehouse with his gun drawn. "What the hell happened? We heard a shot."

Cheyenne was behind him, bedraggled and pale. "Where's Ma? What happened to Ma?"

Before Anders could reply, a rogue wave caught the motorboat and picked it up sideways. "Molly!" The word tore from his throat as the little boat capsized.

"Ma!"

Anders kicked off his shoes.

"Wait!" Mitch said. "It's too dangerous."

Anders ignored the warning and dove cleanly into the churning water. Swimming toward the boat with strong, powerful strokes, he pushed through the waves that smacked him in the face and resisted the current sucking at his legs, trying to pull him under. The boat was nose up and sinking fast when he reached it. Wade's body floated face down in the water beside the oar and other debris.

"Molly!" Anders shouted again and got slapped in the face with a mouthful of salt water.

A head popped out of the water. Gasping, Molly shoved her sopping wet hair out of her face.

Anders' chest swelled with emotion, and he laughed. She was okay. The damn woman was alive. He grabbed her and pulled her close, supporting her as she struggled to tread water in the rough surf.

"I was trapped," she shouted over the howling wind.

"You done good." With one arm locked around her waist, he started swimming awkwardly toward the dock.

"Wade's dead," she shouted again. "Someone shot him."

Anders had almost forgotten about that. Scanning the warehouse's roof, he saw a masked figure stand up holding a rifle. The man had been lying flat against the roof, blending in so seamlessly he would have remained invisible if he hadn't given himself away. He was dressed in some sort of black military gear.

"On the roof," Molly shouted the warning to Mitch.

Mitch spun around and pointed his gun.

The figure carefully set the rifle down and put his hands up in supplication. He bent just as slowly and placed his hands on the edge of the roof. Tucking into a ball, he rolled forward over the edge, executing the feat with graceful control. Then he hung down the fourteen-foot wall, stretching his long body out before he let go and dropped the remaining four feet to the ground.

Mitch was tense and ready to fire if necessary.

Only a few feet away from the dock now, Anders held back, keeping Molly behind him.

The mystery man cautiously reached up and removed his mask.

Staring in disbelief at his brother, Anders' chest tightened and he whispered, "Jonas."

Mitch lowered his gun and put it away.

"Help them." Cheyenne tugged on Mitch's arm.

Mitch pulled Molly up while Anders gave her a boost from behind. Cheyenne flew into her mother's arms while Mitch crouched beside them, shielding them from the wind and rain. Anders climbed out of the water himself without assistance.

Jonas stood a few feet away, silently observing the scene.

Anders was torn between wanting to rail at his brother for killing a man and wanting to thank him for saving Molly's life. If Jonas hadn't shot first, she'd be dead. When Anders gained his feet, he faced his brother. "What are you doing here?"

"Linus sent me after Wade." Jonas' low, gravelly voice was

barely audible over the snapping wind. "Told me to take care of the situation."

Anders frowned. "So you shot him dead?"

Jonas' face remained impassive as he lifted his shoulder in a shrug. "Not the plan but this was easier."

The total lack of emotion in his voice chilled Anders to the bone. This was what his baby brother had become? A monster capable of taking a human life with the proficiency and callousness of a professional killer?

Anders eyed the military-grade uniform. Recalled the insane acrobatic skills and high-powered rifle that looked like something out of a sci-fi war movie, and suddenly he wasn't so sure what he was looking at. What if Jonas wasn't just an uneducated, mentally damaged ex-con doing grunt work for a paranoid millionaire? What if he was something more?

Molly wrapped her arms around Anders' waist, pulling him away from his thoughts. Smiling at Jonas, she said, "Thank you for saving my life."

Jonas nodded once then glanced away.

Giving Anders a squeeze, she said, "You too. How did you find me?"

"We tracked you to the city docks." He cupped her upturned face. "We found your raincoat in a puddle. Your phone's toast."

"Dagnabit."

"Hey, let's get out of the storm," Mitch suggested and led them to the shelter of the open warehouse.

Jonas didn't follow. Anders noticed this with some irritation, but there was nothing he could do about it now. The conversation wasn't over. He'd figure out what was really going on.

Inside the relative warmth and safety of the warehouse, Mitch picked up the story. "We were about two blocks from The Warf Bar when Anders realized Cheyenne had left a message on his phone. We walked in there and found the kid sitting on a bar stool sipping a hot toddy like she was Ingrid Bergman in Casablanca."

"It was tea!" the teenager insisted, laughing. "I left the message for Anders and was just waiting for him to call me back or come and get me."

Anders had walked through the door not expecting to find her there. When she'd flown off the stool and into his arms, he caught her and squeezed her so tight she squeaked. He was just so happy and relieved to know she was safe. His elation had faded when Cheyenne babbled out the story of how she'd gotten away from Wade but Molly hadn't.

Anders cleared his throat, attempting to dislodge the lump that had set up residence there. "Chey led us back to the warehouse. She was a rock star."

Molly gave Anders a watery smile and stepped into his arms again. "Thank you for jumping into the water and saving me from drowning."

Hugging her back, he kissed the top of her head because he was too choked up to speak. Molly was safe and sound, but he was still shaking from the adrenaline rush that had pumped through his veins when he'd spotted her on the boat. Growing up with an abusive father, Anders often hadn't known where his next meal was gonna come from, if their poor excuse for a home would survive the next tropical storm, or if he was gonna get a whooping for no good reason. It had been absolutely terrifying at times, but none of those dread-filled moments from his childhood compared to how he'd felt when he thought Molly was dead.

And that, more than anything, scared the God-forsaken crap out of him.

CHAPTER TWENTY-NINE

Molly was relieved they were able to make it back to the B&B before the worst winds hit the island. The eye made landfall on Eleuthera, a small Bahamian island east of Nassau, before the hurricane made a sharp right turn and headed north, aiming for the Carolina coast. Molly rode out the worst of the storm in bed curled up with Cheyenne, talking about everything that had happened to them since the wedding. Well, almost everything. She didn't tell Cheyenne about the night she spent with Anders. She didn't need to know about that. So happy to be able to hold her little girl in her arms again, Molly barely noticed when the power went out and the storm shutters rattled, threatening to tear off their hinges. Eventually, she took a nap and Cheyenne went in search of Mitch. When Molly woke up, the power was back on, and Ms. Vivian had dinner on the table. A simple meal of homemade vegetable soup and fresh crusty bread.

The men sat at opposite ends of the table while Cheyenne sat across from Molly, chattering about the day's events in an almost manic way. Molly didn't know what to make of it. When they were alone in the room earlier, Chey had seemed fine. Now she was too animated, too excited, as she recounted once again how Molly had let herself be captured just so she could rescue Cheyenne. That hadn't been Molly's plan exactly, but thank God and Jonas Ostergaard, it had all turned out okay in the end.

Anders was quiet through the meal. Molly suspected he was brooding over his brother's unexpected appearance. Jonas was an odd character. Anders said he was an ex-con, but Molly was having a hard time believing it now that she'd witnessed him in action. He had military training. There was no doubt about it in her mind. Not many people could hit a moving target on a pitching boat in the middle of a hurricane, let alone nail their target square in the head. The memory of it still made her queasy. The bullet had gone in but it hadn't come out the other side. Wade's face had gone blank just before he crumpled to the deck like a marionette.

Jonas hadn't stuck around long after showing himself. He vanished when they left the dock to take temporary shelter in the warehouse.

Mitch wiped his mouth with his napkin and then set it aside. "I think we should high-tail it out of Nassau as soon as it's safe to fly just in case Wade's body turns up and the police launch a manhunt for his killer."

Somehow, Molly didn't think Jonas would let that happen. He seemed too professional. Too efficient. He'd probably already erased any evidence of Wade's death.

She was more than ready to go home, but there was one thing that still bothered her. "Wade was talking to someone on the phone in Jamaica. How do we know the person he was talking to won't come after Cheyenne?"

Mitch and Anders shared an inscrutable look. Then Anders glanced down at his soup. "We don't."

Leaning back in his chair, Mitch shook his head. "I doubt she's in any more danger. With Wade dead, there's no one to prosecute."

What he said made sense, but Molly wished she could know for certain it was over.

"I'll be okay, Ma." Cheyenne stood from the table and picked up her empty bowl of soup. "Mitch suggested I take some self-defense courses when we get home, so next time I'll be ready. He also recommended a fascinating book about Navy SEAL mental toughness. I've already started reading it."

Next time? Molly's nerves couldn't take another escapade like this.

"It's mind over matter, little McB. Mind over matter." Mitch held out his fist.

Cheyenne steadied her bowl in her right hand so she could bump his fist with her left. They finished with an exploding hand thing.

Bemused, Molly watched her daughter practically skip from the room. "Should I be worried about that?"

Chuckling, Mitch leaned forward on his elbows. "Nah. What you got there is an adrenaline junkie."

"A what?"

"The kid reminds me a lot of myself at her age. Too curious about the world. Too smart for her own good. And too eager for a challenge that's really going to test her mettle. It's why I became a Navy SEAL. It's also why I hunt treasure. She got her first taste of adventure and now she's never gonna quit."

If Mitch was right about Cheyenne then Molly supposed it was better than the alternative. A teenager who withdrew farther into her shell, scarred for life over being kidnapped and almost killed by a psychopath.

Anders pushed his seat back and stood.

"Where are you going?"

He looked at her as if surprised she'd spoken to him. "The kitchen?"

Heat crept up Molly's face. "I thought we were gonna discuss when we're heading home."

Picking up his empty bowl and a half-drank bottle of beer, he said, "I've already looked into getting out of here tonight, but Key West International is backed up with flights because of the storm. We can fly into Miami though. I reckon it might be easier to slide through customs in a bigger airport."

"That's fine by me. I'm tired after the day we had, but I'll sleep better tonight knowing I'm back on American soil."

Mitch nodded. "I have a stop I need to make before I head back to the States." He smoothed his handlebar mustache. "Can I meet up with you in Miami tomorrow morning?"

"Sure." Molly reached for her glass of iced tea. "Are you coming back to Key West with us?"

"Nah, I have a business meeting I need to get to, but I wanted to give something to Cheyenne before I disappear for a little while."

"Whatever it is, I'm sure she'll love it. Thank you for being so kind to her, Mitch."

"She's a good kid."

Anders was still standing beside the table. "Anything else?"

"No, that's it." Molly sipped her iced tea and gazed at him over the rim of her glass.

He shrugged. "There you go then."

As she surreptitiously watched him head for the kitchen, the soup she'd eaten congealed into a glob of goo in her stomach.

This wasn't just about Jonas. Something else was wrong. Anders was shutting down. Withdrawing from the easy camaraderie that they'd developed over the past few days. He'd said they were friends. Maybe more. He said he cared for her. Had he been lying? No, she hadn't thought so at the time and still didn't.

It had been an incredibly stressful day for all of them and it still wasn't over. Maybe after they got back to Key West and had a good night's rest, things would be back to normal.

Whatever normal was.

The sensation that Molly's adventure was over grew with every passing minute they were in the air. The evening flight from Nassau to Miami was quiet and uneventful. Cheyenne was absorbed in the book Mitch had given her, and Molly kept to small talk because Anders wouldn't have it any other way. He barely made eye contact with her. It was frustrating and a little heartbreaking but there was nothing she could do about it. She couldn't shake the feeling she was being propelled toward an ending she wasn't ready to face.

The benefit of traveling with a famous celebrity on a private plane was that the customs officer didn't look too closely at their passports. Molly didn't know if that was a good thing or a scary thing, but she was glad to be back on American soil. When Anders booked them a pair of rooms in a nice beachfront hotel, she wasn't thrilled about taking yet another handout from him, but she didn't have much of a choice. They were all too exhausted to continue on to Key West.

Molly woke early, refreshed from a good night's sleep and eager to get back home. A part of her was also eager to speak with Anders again. She was certain they could work out whatever was bothering him because that was what friends did.

She was sitting on her bed, combing out the knots in her damp hair and watching Cheyenne attempt to do push-ups when someone knocked on their door. Molly got up, pointing to Cheyenne with her comb. "That's probably Anders. Get your stuff together."

"In a minute. I'm not done."

Molly peeked out the peephole. When she saw it was Mitch, she opened the door with a wide smile. "You made it."

His long brown hair was pulled back into a ponytail. He was looking right at home in Miami Beach, wearing a Margaritaville

T-shirt, flip-flops, and a pair of board shorts. "Yeah. I'm glad I caught you. Where's McB?"

"You mean Wonder Woman? She's over there doing push-ups."

"Right on." He laughed and came into the room.

"Hey, Mitch." Cheyenne gave up on the training and got up to give him a hug.

"Remember that book I told you about? The one written by Emory Constantinople, that old guy in Bimini who knew Hemingway?"

"Yeah. It's out of print."

Mitched reached for the hardback book sticking out of the back of his shorts and handed it to her. "Lookie what I got."

"Where did you get it?" Cheyenne's face lit up and she caressed the old, dusty book like it was the treasure itself.

"From good ol' Emory. I made a pit stop in Alice Town on the way here."

Molly sat on the bed and crossed her legs, uncertain how she felt about this budding friendship between her teenage daughter and the seasoned treasure hunter. She narrowed her eyes. "So that's what you were up to last night?"

"I figured I was in the neighborhood, it wouldn't hurt to drop by and see if he had any extra copies of the book lying around."

Cheyenne grabbed his arm and tugged his attention back to her. "Could he tell you anything about the Firefly Emerald? Or if Hemingway knew anyone named Alice?"

"He said he saw the emerald once just after Hem won it in a card game in Cuba. He showed it to him. Said he was going to bury it, but Emory thought he was joking."

"So it's real." Cheyenne's wide eyes glittered with amazement.

Molly was intrigued now too. "And Alice? What about her?"

Mitch crossed his arms as he leaned back on the dresser. "Emory said when he was a boy, he used to feed a bunch of stray cats in town. Hem was fond of one particular queen Emory had hand-raised from birth. She was all white except for a thin black stripe on her nose. She was a big cat with an even bigger attitude to match. Hem got a kick out of her, so Emory gave him the cat as a gift. Hem took her back to Key West and named her Alice."

Molly shivered with goose bumps. She didn't understand Cheyenne's frown.

Squeezing the book to her chest, she scrunched her nose in confusion. "So Alice was a cat?"

"Just check out Chapter Six." Mitch chuckled. "Hey, I've got somewhere to get too. I just wanted to drop that by." He turned to Molly. "I bumped into Anders in the lobby. He wanted me to tell you, he's got a limo waiting for you downstairs to take you back to Key West whenever you're ready."

"A limo?" In the midst of picking a knot out of one of her curls, Molly frowned, confused. "He never said anything to me about a limo. I thought we were flying the rest of the way home? Where's Anders now?"

Mitch shrugged. "On his way to the airport, I imagine. He said he had to hustle back to Key West for a business meeting and didn't want to wake you, if you were sleeping in."

Blood roared in Molly's ears. She couldn't hear the rest of what Mitch said to Cheyenne or their goodbyes at the door. Anders had left her. He'd just walked out of her life and left her in Miami like he had absolutely no obligation to see her the rest of the way home.

He had no obligation though. Not to her or Cheyenne. He'd brought them safely back to the States, put them up in a nice hotel, and made arrangements for their ride home. That was a hell of a lot more than Trevor had ever done for them. Molly had always been the one covering *his* rent and making *his* car payments. But still, she couldn't help but draw comparisons and expect more from Anders. Why would he think Molly would rather drive three and a half hours to Key West when she could've just gotten up a little earlier and flown home in an hour? He could have asked her what she wanted to do, but he'd made the choice for her and the reason for that was kind of obvious. He was done with her.

When Trevor had left, Molly had been mad and hurt, but down deep, she was relieved. She'd only known Anders for a few days, and they'd made no promises to each other. They weren't even actually a couple. But this, this felt a hundred times worse because she loved him. Really loved him. Her palms were sweating, and her heart was palpitating, and she felt like throwing up.

She loved him. And he'd abandoned her.

When Cheyenne came back into the room, talking excitedly about her treasure hunt, Molly put on a brave face. She didn't want her daughter to know there was a giant bloody wound where her heart used to be or that she was inches away from crumbling into a pile of dust.

Molly wanted to refuse the limo and rent her own car, but she wasn't in the right state of mind to drive three and a half hours in traffic on a two-lane road. So, she accepted Anders' last bit of charity with resignation and climbed into the back of the car with Cheyenne.

The closer they got to the island, the more her feeling of despair morphed into anger. She was royally pissed at Anders for ditching her in Miami without so much as a goodbye. There was absolutely no excuse for his behavior. They might not have a future, but they'd survived a dangerous adventure and risked their lives together. And besides having sex, they'd bonded as friends. She deserved his respect. She deserved an explanation. When she realized how hard she was trembling with contained fury, she forced herself to calm down. Taking a deep breath, she gazed at Cheyenne.

She was deeply involved in her book and only spoke to Molly when she wanted to show her one of the pictures scattered between the text. Instead of going straight to Chapter Six, her methodical child had started on page one and read her way through. By the time she finally reached the section, she didn't seem too impressed.

"This chapter is talking about Hemingway's wife, Pauline, and her obsession with spending money on their house." She turned the page and then pulled the book closer to study one of the photographs. Turning the book to Molly, she said, "Look! It's a picture of Alice."

The cat was lounging wantonly across the tiled base of the infamous fountain in the backyard of Hemingway's Key West estate. "So?"

"So? So I need to talk to April as soon as we get back to Key West. I called her from the hotel while you were in the shower this morning. She said she's going to Dixie's for Anders' press conference."

Molly was staring out the window again, but her head whipped around at the mention of Anders. "Anders is having a press conference today?"

"Yeah. Didn't he mention it?"

He had, but Molly had forgotten it was today. It still didn't let him off the hook for leaving the way he did. "I guess that was the business meeting Mitch was talking about."

"Can we go?"

Molly's gut burned. She knew she should probably go home and stay home, at least until she cooled down and could think more clearly, but she didn't always do the smart thing. "Yeah. We can go."

Dixie's was packed with press who took up the first few rows of tables and curious onlookers who stood behind the cameras and flashing bulbs, gawking. The stage had been turned into a dais for the long, white cloth-covered table that was set up for the press conference. Anders sat behind the table with another man Molly didn't know. Chubby and balding with a neatly trimmed brown beard and a gold stud winking from this left ear, he might have been Anders' manager or a representative from his music label.

When she spotted Anders, her foolish, hopeless heart skipped a beat. But a beat was all it took for her to remember she was furious at him for abandoning her in Miami. She might have understood if only he'd stopped by to explain.

Someone bumped into Molly and she realized she was blocking the door. Cheyenne was already pushing her way through the crowd, following the wall of tinted windows toward the stage.

The chubby man with the earring said something funny in response to a reporter's question, and Anders grinned. He was back to his charming, good-natured self, looking handsome as the dickens in a white button-down shirt with his hair combed back from his face.

Anders leaned into the mic and his deep, amplified voice danced along Molly's nerve endings. "Uh, I believe that would be a question for Fry." He looked off to the side of the stage where Selena was standing by. She shook her head emphatically, and the crowd chuckled.

A reporter in the front row raised her hand. "What can you tell us about Miss Conway's death?"

"I spoke with the Las Vegas police department this morning," Anders' tone sobered to match the question. "While they've arrested Casey's stalker, Albert Everett Mooney, for his involvement in the murder, they haven't gotten any relevant information out of him regarding the woman who paid him to put the strychnine in Casey's food."

As Molly made her way through the crowd to Cheyenne, she found herself feeling sorry for Casey. Strychnine was awful stuff. Cheyenne wrote a report on it for extra credit once after she read the Agatha Christie novel *The Mysterious Affair at Styles*. Chey always gave Molly her school papers to proofread even though she rarely made a mistake. The poison caused wild uncontrollable spasms, frothing at the mouth, and eventual asphyxiation. It wasn't a pleasant way to die.

"Is it true you missed Miss Conway's funeral because you've been on holiday in Jamaica these past few days?" A British reporter asked.

Molly didn't want to hear his answer. She turned to go, but Cheyenne stopped her. "Ma? What's wrong?"

People were packed in all around them. There was no easy escape. Molly shook her head at Cheyenne's concerned expression and stayed where she was.

There was a slight edge to Anders' voice. "I was helping a friend with a personal problem. That's all I'm going to say about it."

"Was this friend the woman you've been photographed with lately? The redhead."

Molly backed up a step and bumped into the woman behind her.

"Hey."

"Sorry." Molly pushed her hair off her forehead. She was sweating and having trouble catching her breath. It was way too hot in here. She needed air.

Anders looked at the man sitting beside him. "My manager can answer this. Tuck?"

Tuck nodded and leaned toward his microphone. "Mr. Ostergaard paid his respects to the Conway family via a private telephone call. He's also made a large donation in Casey's honor to the children's charity she supported. The Conway family has expressed their extreme gratitude for his generosity and appreciated his decision to let them grieve in peace." Tuck covered the mic and whispered something in Anders' ear. Receiving a nod, Tuck said to the press, "As for the woman in those photos, Mr. Ostergaard wants to make it clear the woman is nobody to him. Those pictures were manipulated by

a hungry paparazzo out to capitalize on a blatant misunderstanding."

The woman is nobody to him. Cringing at the words, Molly
burned with embarrassment. The world knew she meant nothing
to Anders. She was just some woman who caused him bad press.
That was why he'd left her in Miami. He'd lied. He never cared
about her. She was just there for his temporary amusement.

The British reporter pressed. "So, you're not in a
relationship?"

"Mr. Ostergaard is—"

Anders touched Tuck's arm and leaned toward his own
microphone. "For the record, I'm single and plan to remain that
way for the foreseeable future. Thanks for coming." He stood and
made his way toward Selena. More questions were flung at him,
but he ignored them as he hopped off the stage and disappeared
into Jimmy's office.

"Wow." Cheyenne's eyes widened as she tucked a strand of
her dark brown hair behind her ear. "Why is the press harassing
him so much? You and Anders a couple?" She snorted, clutching
the Hemingway book to her chest. "How nuts would that be?"

"Nuttier than a five-pound fruitcake." Molly forced a smile,
but the corners of her mouth refused to turn up. Tears burned
the back of her eyes. "I have to go. Look, there's April by the bar.
She's waving. I'll see you at home later."

"Yeah." Cheyenne frowned with concern, but Molly
pretended not to notice.

She didn't wait to greet April. She had to get out of there
before she did something stupid, like grab a reporter and tell her
side of the story. But what would that accomplish besides pissing
Anders off and making an even bigger fool of herself? It wouldn't
change anything.

Molly pushed her way outside and didn't stop until she
reached the street corner. Taking a deep breath, she squinted
against the glare of the sun. The air was so thick with humidity

you could almost drink it, but it still offered some relief. Just being away from Anders helped clear her head. She waited for a pair of mopeds to whiz by before she crossed the street. She needed to stop pining over a relationship that was never meant to be. It was time to move on and get back to real life.

CHAPTER THIRTY

Loud, bluesy music spilled out of Sloppy Jo's Bar as Cheyenne and April turned the street corner and headed up Duval. Cheyenne had suggested they walk to the Hemingway House. It was hot enough to cook eggs on the asphalt, but the sticky breeze coming off the ocean made it more bearable. It felt good to be home again. She wasn't eager to do a repeat of the past few days. Not yet. She realized she had a lot to learn before she ventured out in the world on her own again. She was going to be prepared the next time adventure came calling because she knew it would. Mitch said it was in her blood.

"I'm glad you're back." April gave Cheyenne a sideways hug as they waited to cross the street. "I want to apologize again for bailing on you. Like I told you on the phone, my dad surprised me with a trip to Paris. He said it was an early birthday present and the jet was waiting for us at the airport. He didn't even let me pack or change out of my bathing suit. Our maid threw some things into a bag for me and I got dressed on the jet." April stopped and squeezed Cheyenne's arm. "He actually went with me. Just the two of us. We haven't spent time alone together like that in years. It was amazing." The traffic light changed and they stepped into the crosswalk. "You still haven't told me how you ended up going to Jamaica with Anders Ostergaard."

Cheyenne scratched an itch on her cheek and narrowed her eyes. "Remember that seaplane that landed in your backyard?"

"Yeah. What about it?"

The mild curiosity on April's serene face made Cheyenne pause. Did she really not know anything about the guy who was murdered? April was always talking about how her father was too busy to spend time with her, and yet he decided to take her on a last-minute vacation to Paris the very night a man was shot dead in her backyard? It seemed suspicious, but Cheyenne didn't want to make any accusations without having all the facts first.

Tucking the book that she was carrying under her chin, Cheyenne gathered her hair and tied it back into a low ponytail. She didn't like lying to her friend so she twisted the truth. "I got to fly on a plane smaller than that. Anders took my mom and me on a trip."

"So, what he said about your mom meaning nothing to him wasn't true?"

"Yes and no. They aren't together or anything. But they're friends." At least, Cheyenne thought they were. Maybe not. Now that they were back in the real world, maybe Anders didn't want to hang out with them anymore. The thought hurt more than Cheyenne expected it to. Pushing the pang of regret aside, she said, "I figured out the riddle."

"You did?" April scooted in her high heels, trying to keep up with Cheyenne's brisk pace.

She couldn't keep her excitement from growing as they turned down Oliver Street to cut over to Whitehead. "Come on, I want to show you something."

"Why are we going to Hemingway's house?"

Cheyenne gave her a sly smile. "You'll see."

They stopped at the little booth next to the front gate to buy a ticket. It was off-season, so there wasn't a line. Cheyenne grabbed April's hand and made a dash around to the back of the house, passing at least a dozen curious cats along the way. April tried to keep up, but her ultra-mini skirt and heels slowed them down on the rutted concrete. A lawn maintenance crew was working on the west side of the property. When April's heel caught on something and she stumbled, one of the gardeners stopped raking and looked at them with a curious frown. Cheyenne slowed down and tried to walk the rest of the way with more restraint.

She led April to the small fountain in the backyard and let go of her hand, and they both stood staring at the odd piece of recycled art.

April frowned. "What are we doing here? And why are we staring at a cat fountain? You know that's just a urinal from the men's bathroom at the old Sloppy Joe's."

"I know." Cheyenne's grin widened. She was bursting with the urge to share her secret, but she held it together as she offered April the book she'd been clutching for dear life ever since she made the discovery. "Open it and read the caption on the photo."

April opened to the page, moved the horse-shaped bookmark aside, and read the caption out loud. "A gift from a friend in Bimini. Alice the cat sunning herself in the gardens at Hemingway's home in Key West."

Cheyenne quietly recited the riddle. "How I long for those halcyon days, Alice basking upon my chaise. Money came and money went, but time with me was well spent. The Devil's light, so near and yet so far—"

"It rests beneath my baja mar," April finished, slamming the book shut and turning to Cheyenne. "Baja mar. Shallow sea. You're a genius!"

Cheyenne grabbed April's arm. "The entire chapter was about how his wife spent a ridiculous amount of money on this house, while he spent his time fishing and getting drunk in the local bars. And where do you spend time after you drink?"

They both looked down at the fountain and scrunched their noses in disgust.

"So, the riddle was written from the point of view of a urinal." April handed the book back. "Gross, but brilliant. Is the timing right?"

Cheyenne nodded. "Yes. According to the book, Hemingway made several trips between Cuba and Key West while he lived here. It's possible he either used the urinal to cover up the hole he dug or temporarily removed the urinal to bury the emerald beneath it, but either way, it's down there."

They stood for several moments, shoulder to shoulder, staring at the fountain and contemplating their discovery.

April shook her head. "Wow. Should we tell someone?"

Cheyenne's gut tightened, rejecting the idea. "I don't know."

"You might get a finder's fee?"

April was right, but Cheyenne wasn't sure exactly why she was hesitating. She'd been so exhilarated when she solved the riddle— as excited as she'd been when she dug up her father on Facebook and he responded to her private message—but, like then, the feeling of triumph was fading fast.

Maybe some things weren't meant to be excavated. Cheyenne had tried to connect with her father, but so far, nothing good had come of it. Mitch said Navy SEALs listen to their intuition and trust their gut. Cheyenne put her hand on her stomach, covering the spot that felt heavy and a little nauseous.

She turned to her friend. "No. This doesn't feel right. Hemingway buried The Firefly Emerald where he thought no one would find it. Just because we figured out where it is, doesn't mean we have to do anything about it. Just knowing that it's not a myth, that it really exists, is enough for me."

"I get it." April slid her arm around Cheyenne's shoulder. "Some secrets are better left untold." An odd, vulnerable expression crossed April's face for a moment, but then she glanced away and it was gone.

One of the cats rubbed against Cheyenne's leg. It was a white cat with a black stripe on its nose. Not Alice—she was long buried in the property's pet cemetery—but one of her descendants maybe.

"Looks like you made a friend," a male voice said behind them.

April dropped her arm, and they both turned around. "Damian Rios," she said.

"Hi, April."

Damian was boy band cute with melty dark brown eyes and a smile that did something funny to Cheyenne's insides. She knew him from school, but he didn't know her. He'd transferred away earlier in the school year and had gone to live with his aunt in Tampa, but the rest of his family still lived in town. April never talked about him, but Cheyenne knew she used to have a crush on him too. She'd heard a rumor that April's father caught them making out and was so angry he made Mr. Rios send Damian away.

"What are you doing here?" April whispered, glancing around nervously.

Maybe the rumor was true.

His uniform shirt was tied around his waist so his tank top showed off the lean muscle in his arms. Resting his hands on his narrow hips, he grinned. "I came home for my little sister's *quinceañera*. Turning fifteen is a big deal in my family."

"Valentina is in my homeroom class." Cheyenne regretted speaking the instant Damian's hooded gaze turned her way. "Our birthdays are only a few days apart. She's nice," she finished lamely. Valentina was the person who'd told Cheyenne about where Damian had gone. And why he was sent away.

"This is my friend, Cheyenne." April introduced them almost as an afterthought as she crossed her arms, uncrossed them, and then crossed them again all while looking over her shoulder.

Damian grinned. "Looks like the company you're keeping these days has improved. It's a pleasure to meet you, Cheyenne."

April frowned slightly. "I'm still friends with Greenlee."

"That's too bad."

Dropping her arms, April ground her heels into the rutted pavement. "If my father finds out you're in town, he's going to take away your scholarship to Stanford."

"Relax. I'm only here until Tuesday. I'm keeping a low profile."

April sniffed. "It doesn't look like you're trying very hard."

"I'm just helping my father out today. One of his workers called out sick." His eyes danced with humor, and then his head tilted to the side. "It's great to see you, April."

She nodded and admitted reluctantly, "It's good to see you too."

"You're looking gorgeous as always."

April's posture changed. Drawing her shoulders back, she lowered her chin and looked up at him coquettishly. "I am?"

"I'd almost forgotten how the sparkle in your blue eyes reminds me of the sun glinting off the sea."

Cheyenne snorted but resisted the urge to roll her eyes. Did girls actually fall for that corny crap? She doubted it.

"You're so sweet," April said, toying with her necklace.

April Linus had graduated high school with honors and was the valedictorian at her commencement. She was one of the smartest and most level-headed girls Cheyenne knew. A few pretty compliments from this smooth-talking Casanova, and she was losing her flipping mind. "While I'm enjoying watching this impending train wreck, we were kind of in the middle of something here."

April fidgeted uncomfortably and said to Cheyenne, "You don't know what's going on."

"Don't I? He's flirting with you at great risk to his college career, and you're encouraging him despite the fact you know deep down it's a very, very bad idea."

"The kid's got grit." Damian chuckled. "I've got to get back to work. Call me later? My number is still the same."

"I'll think about it."

"Don't think too hard." He winked and strolled away, rejoining the rest of the lawn maintenance crew who were trimming the shrubs around the cat cemetery.

"Don't think too hard," Cheyenne mimicked Damian once he was out of earshot. "Of all the sexist things a boy could say, that wins first place. Why girls have any desire to date boys is beyond me. I'm joining a nunnery."

April chuckled. "You say that now, but just wait until you have a crush on somebody. Crushes don't make sense. It's like falling in love. You have no control over how or when it's going to happen."

"You're not in love with him, are you?" Cheyenne was horrified by the thought.

"No, absolutely not." April smiled as she crouched down to pet the little brown tabby cat that was rubbing her leg for attention. "I'm just repeating something my mother told me. She used to give me all sorts of advice. It was like she knew she wasn't going to be around to tell me this stuff when I was older. Sometimes I think she knew she was sick for a lot longer than we did."

"Are you going to meet Damian later?"

April shrugged and scratched a spot under the cat's chin. "I don't know. I have to think about it."

CHAPTER THIRTY-ONE

The evening after Molly returned from her Caribbean adventure, she found herself driving to The Boneyard to meet Jeff Worth. When he'd called to confirm their dinner date, she almost canceled, but then she reminded herself she was moving on. And moving on meant not sitting home alone on a Friday night feeling sorry for herself. She needed to get out and have some fun, so she'd gone shopping that afternoon and splurged on a tight red mini dress and four-inch spiked heels. The outfit was for her and her self-confidence, not for her date.

Jeff was waiting for her in front of the restaurant, dressed more casually this time in a green Hawaiian shirt with yellow and red parrots and a pair of khaki pants. His brown eyes nearly bugged out of his head when he saw her, and Molly couldn't help but grin. She knew she looked good and that made her feel good.

"You… That dress… Wow."

"Thanks. I'll take wow." She slipped her hand into the crook of his elbow. "Shall we?"

The Boneyard restaurant was overpriced and campy, but Molly loved its quirky atmosphere. The bar and guest seating area were situated in the backyard of an old Victorian style house that, at one time or another, had been a seamstress shop, a Jazz Age tattoo parlor, a speakeasy, a gambling den, and most notoriously, a bordello. The entrance was through a white picket fence covered in ivy and down a winding sandstone path shrouded in tropical foliage.

At the hostess stand, Molly's smile faded when she spotted Anders seated at a table near the stage with a group of people. Wishing she could sink into the mossy patches between the pavers, she took a step back and lost her balance when her heel caught a rut. She wobbled and had to clutch Jeff's arm to keep from going over.

His eyebrows lifted with a questioning look. "Are you okay?"

"I'm fine. Just my shoe." She smoothed her hair nervously.

Sue had mentioned Anders' bandmates were coming into town, but Molly never would've expected them to pick The Boneyard for their reunion dinner, especially when there were so many restaurants in town to choose from... Unless Sue had suggested it knowing Molly was going to be there on her date. She wasn't sure what her friend was hoping to accomplish, but she'd only succeeded in putting Molly in a very awkward spot. Sue was going to get an earful the next time Molly saw her.

The animated group looked like they were having a great time and weren't going anywhere soon. Anders' manager Tuck was on his right and Selena Fry was on his left. At least five musicians Molly recognized from the band and three women—girlfriends or wives maybe—filled the rest of the seats at the table.

"Let's go someplace else," Molly blurted before she could stop herself.

"What? Why? You picked this place."

"I know, I just..." Her voice trailed off when her mind went blank and she couldn't think of one legitimate reason to leave.

The Boneyard was one of her favorite restaurants in Key West, especially on a Friday night with live steel drum music playing, frozen drink specials flowing, and a light breeze stirring the evening air beneath the soft orange glow of string lights. What was she doing? She had as much right to be there as Anders did. The best thing to do was ignore him and try to have a good time too.

Molly kept her gaze averted as they followed the hostess past Anders' table, but she knew the exact moment he spotted her. She felt his gaze like a lightning bolt, charged and caustic. Goose bumps rose on her skin and heat flushed her face. Fury roiled inside of her as she treaded carefully on the uneven, pebbled ground. Falling on her ass right now was exactly the last thing she wanted to do. What right did he have to be angry at her? He probably thought she was stalking him or something ridiculous like that.

Their table was located in one of the worst spots in the outdoor restaurant. Near the kitchen door and farthest from the stage. At least they'd gotten a table on short notice. Even in the off-season, weekend reservations at The Boneyard were tough to get unless you were someone special like Anders Ostergaard.

The waiter stopped to take their drink order and drop off two glasses of water. Molly ordered a margarita and Jeff ordered white wine. When the waiter was gone, Molly tore open her straw and stuck it in her glass. She was so thirsty, she finished off two-thirds of the water before she realized Jeff was staring at her.

"Sorry." She sat back and picked up the straw wrapper. "I was thirsty."

"Interesting place."

Molly took a deep breath and shoved Anders out of her thoughts. Forcing herself to focus on making polite conversation with her date, she said lightly, "You've never been here before?"

He shook his head. "No. The livestock is interesting though. You'd think that would be considered a health hazard."

He was referring to the red cockerel that was pecking the ground beside their table. The roosters, hens, and chicks that roamed the outdoor dining area were considered part of the kitschy atmosphere along with the mismatched yard-sale quality tables, plates, and glassware.

Molly shrugged. "Not really. It's part of the ambiance."

"That's one name for it." He snorted softly, picking up his glass of water.

The band finished the song they were playing and announced they were taking a short break. A recorded version of Don McLean's 'American Pie' took over the speakers as they left the stage.

Molly's gaze drifted toward Anders. His face was crinkled with humor as he put an arm around his manager's shoulders and said something that must have been pretty funny because a bubble of laughter erupted from the table.

She was such a fool. She'd slept with him against her better judgment and the jackass lied to her and said he cared about her. Damn him and his gorgeous smile. This was why they said you should never meet your heroes. *You know what else you shouldn't do with them? You shouldn't fu*—

"Frozen margarita?" The waiter set the cocktail on the table in front of Molly. She faced forward, twisting her straw wrapper into a tight little rope, strangling it until it broke in half. The waiter took their food order and then dashed off again.

Jeff sat across from Molly, staring at his glass of white wine. Here they were again. Why had she agreed to a second date? To get out of the house and have a nice evening. That was why, she reminded herself. She really needed to try a little harder.

She took a long sip of her margarita and then pasted on a smile she wasn't feeling.

"So, uh, how was your week?" Jeff's hand trembled as he reached for his glass. He held the stem but didn't pick it up.

Was he getting nervous again? She sniffed the air discreetly, hoping she wouldn't smell stress sweat. She didn't. She took another long sip of her margarita and started to feel a buzz. She hadn't eaten since breakfast when she'd nibbled on an English muffin. "Cheyenne and I went out of town for a few days. We did a brief tour of the Caribbean and came home."

"Wow. Business must be booming at the bookstore." He chuckled and finally took a sip of wine.

Molly sat straighter, fighting a frown. "We do okay. How about you? How was your week?"

"I played golf. When I wasn't working, of course."

"You golf?" She stirred the slush in her drink. "You didn't mention it in your Couples.com profile."

"I find it puts some women off. But, yes, I golf every free moment I get."

"So, you're a weekend golfer?" She sipped her drink, half listening.

"Weekend. Weekdays. Sometimes I go before and after work."

Molly finished off her drink, sucking the straw until the grating sound of air bubbles drew a look from Jeff that suggested he didn't approve.

She didn't really care. "That must be an expensive hobby, golf-ing." If this had been a first date, she would've started peeking at her watch and scrambling for a reason to move the date along so she could get out of there.

Jeff shrugged. "It's my passion. It's worth it to me to cut corners in other aspects of my life. I live modestly so I can support my hobby."

Molly understood passion. Her passion was music, and she'd cut corners in her own life and raised her daughter on the road just so she could keep playing. Performing at Dixie's was enough to pacify her craving, but some days she missed being out on tour.

"You know what?" Molly pushed her glass away and leaned back in her chair. "Good for you. I personally loathe golfing, but if it makes you happy then keep doing it for as long as you can. Maybe you should lead with that on your Couples.com profile though. I bet there's a single gal out there who loves golf just as much as you do."

Jeff picked up his glass, but it never made it to his mouth. "Does that mean you, uh, aren't going to go out with me again?"

"No," she said truthfully, and the brutal honesty felt good. "But it doesn't mean we can't have a nice dinner and share each other's company for a couple of hours."

"I suppose, but wow. I never saw this coming." He had the expression of someone who had been blindsided by a hockey puck. "I appreciate your candor. It's just…wow."

Molly's cell phone buzzed in her clutch purse. She'd told Cheyenne to call if she needed her. Chey was meeting her father for dinner at Captain Tony's Saloon. Molly had offered to go along to introduce them, but Cheyenne had wanted to meet Trevor by herself. It was going to take some getting used to, but Molly realized her little girl was growing up. As much as it bit her butt that Cheyenne was having dinner with her father at that very moment, Molly knew she had to step back and let Cheyenne make some of her own decisions. And mistakes.

"Sorry, it's a text from my daughter. She says she's just checking in, but I want to call her to see if she's all right and use the restroom while I'm up. It might take a few minutes, but I'll be back. Will you stay?"

Jeff's bemused expression cleared and he nodded. "I have a steak coming and another glass of wine on the way. I'll stay."

When Molly stood up, the world popped into ultra-high definition and she realized her buzz was stronger than she thought. She stopped to smooth the front of her snug-fitting dress. Tossing her long mass of red curls over her shoulder, she patted Jeff's arm and started for the bathroom, carefully making her way across the scattered stone walkway. She phoned Cheyenne on the way and got her voicemail.

The narrow path followed the far side of the house between a tall, ivy-covered fence and past the discretely hidden staircase, which led to the former bordello on the second floor. A gate marked "emergency exit only" stood at the end of the path. She turned into the alcove that separated the men's room from the ladies and ducked into the bathroom.

After she used the facilities, she checked herself in the mirror. Her buzz was still going strong, and it felt damn nice. Fluffing her hair, she decided she looked smoking hot tonight. The top of her breasts bulged provocatively above the neckline of her dress. The hemline was a lot shorter than she was used to wearing, making a good portion of her thighs feel exposed and vulnerable. The silk panties beneath were so negligible that she might as well be bare. She hadn't intended to see Anders tonight, but she hoped he'd noticed what he was missing.

Exiting the alcove, she turned the corner and stopped short as her traitorous heart thumped against her chest. Anders stood in the path beside the bordello stairs with a brooding expression on his face.

The butterflies in her stomach stood up and did the wave.

Molly squared her shoulders and was reminded how her breasts strained again the tight bodice. He noticed too. His gaze grew hot and his nostrils flared. She moved toward him on legs that felt like pudding and somehow managed to look him in the eye. "Let me pass."

"No." He didn't move.

Her lower belly tightened. "What do you want?"

He cleared his throat, and his eyes flicked to her face. "Who's the guy?"

"Are you serious? Why do you care?" Heat climbed up her throat. "You ditched me in Miami and you've ignored me since we've been back. No, you don't get to inquire about my love life." Trembling with indignation, she reached out to steady herself on the wooden banister.

He gritted his teeth, and a muscle flexed in his jaw. "I needed some time."

"Time for what?"

"I just didn't think you'd move on so fast. Christ, Molly, you were in my bed two nights ago."

Outrage sputtered through her body like a burning fuse. "If I was a foot taller, I'd slap your mouth sideways." She started up the steps, intending to go around him, but he grabbed her waist and spun her to face him. Standing on the second step, she was almost eye level with him. "Dagnabit. Let go of me."

"What am I supposed to think seeing you dressed like that, clearly on a date with another man?"

"You don't get a say in who I spend time with. I'm nothing, remember?"

He frowned. "What the hell are you talking about?"

"The press conference— Never mind." She tried to pull away from him, but he wouldn't let go.

"I care because we're friends."

Molly let out a bitter laugh. "Friends? Friends call and check in when they've just been through a traumatic event. You abandoned us in Miami, Anders."

"I hired a limo."

"I didn't want a fucking limo. I wanted you." Tears flared behind Molly's eyes and she scrunched her face to keep them from falling. She looked down for a moment and sniffled. Then she took a deep breath and pulled herself together. "At first, I just wanted to be your friend. Because after getting to know you, I couldn't imagine not having you in my life. But there was something else between us. Chemistry maybe. I don't know. I-I fell in love with you. I didn't mean to or want to, but I did." Her stomach was still in knots, but at least her heart felt lighter. She was turning into a regular Honest Abe. The truth was liberating, even if it didn't change a thing.

There was pain in Anders' expression and something else. Regret maybe? He let go of her and rested his hands on his hips.

She could have run away then, but she stayed where she was, too curious to hear what he was going to say.

"When I saw Wade point that gun at you..." Anders shook his head as if he was trying to get the image out of his mind.

Molly recalled the moment with a shudder. "Yes?" she prompted when he looked like he was having difficulty getting past it.

Anders drove his fingers through his hair, carelessly tossing the dirty blond waves. "I can buy anything I want. Travel anywhere in the world. I could never work another damn day in my life and still live like a rich man for the rest of it. But none of that mattered." He squeezed his eyes shut. When he looked at her again, there was moisture on his eyelashes. "None of that could help me save you and I just..." His voice trailed off and he shook his head.

The remnants of Molly's anger evaporated, leaving behind an intense ache that made her feel raw and vulnerable. "What are you saying?"

He cleared his throat. "I'm sorry I didn't call to check up on you."

She waited for more, but when he just stood there staring at the ground, she shook her head in exasperation. "That's it? I tell you I love you and your response is to apologize for not calling?"

His head snapped up, and he leaned forward aggressively. "If you love me then why are you out with another man?"

"Are we seriously back to that?" Molly stomped her foot in frustration. "You sound like a jealous idiot." She shoved his chest as hard as she could to move him out of the way, but he barely budged.

"Because I *am* a jealous idiot," he shouted.

They both stopped and stared at each other, panting heavily.

Molly's stomach leapt, but she refused to let it sway her. If he wasn't going to admit to himself why he was jealous, she wasn't going to wait around for him to figure it out. This needed to end now. For her own sanity. "I can't do this."

"Wait. Stop." He grabbed her waist when she turned to go. "I have feelings for you, Molly, but—"

"But what? 'You're single and plan to remain so for the fore-seeable future'," she quoted from the press conference. When he didn't correct her, a chunk of her heart broke off and floated away. "So, this really is goodbye?"

"No. Yes. Yes, Molly, it is. I'm sorry."

Her chest was jam-packed with so many emotions she could barely breathe. Along with sadness and disappointment there was anger and frustration. And love. She still loved him so damn much her heart hurt. If this was truly the end, she wanted to say goodbye to him properly on her own terms. "Come upstairs."

CHAPTER THIRTY-TWO

Anders followed Molly up the stairs without question, because frankly, he'd follow her anywhere. From the balcony, she opened one of the French doors and let herself inside, tugging him along behind her. He was still trembling with adrenaline from their argument. Still nauseous from rehashing Nassau.

Watching Molly defend herself on that boat had triggered memories from childhood. His drunken father throwing his poor, fragile mother to the ground and kicking the crap out of her while she was pregnant with Jonas. The feeling of helplessness, because if Anders tried to interfere, Jimmy would take the brunt of the punishment. Anders had woken from patchy nightmares these last two nights with his mother's screams still echoing in his soul. Watching her be put in the ground before her thirty-fourth birthday was the hardest thing he'd ever had to face. He couldn't go through that pain again. He couldn't let himself love someone so deeply that his next breath depended on hers.

He wasn't ready to say goodbye to Molly. Not yet. But he couldn't give her what she wanted—what she deserved—because he was a coward.

His cowboy boots scuffed the faded hardwood floors as she led him into the room. It had a slightly musty mothball smell. Two antique sofas sat facing each other in the center of the space. A couple of old paintings on the wall depicted nudes posing in sexually provocative positions. One particularly spicy piece of art made Anders stop for a closer look. A randy, naked man stood behind a voluptuous Victorian-era woman who was bent over a table with her skirt hiked over her waist and her plump bare ass in the air, waiting to be taken from behind.

Molly tugged his hand, encouraging him to keep moving. His gaze shifted to her tight, round ass accentuated by her clingy red dress. Her thighs were bare, showing off a pair of legs that seemed disproportionately long for someone so short. She shot him a look over her shoulder that made the sleeping cicadas in his stomach start to hum.

The second room was a twin to the first, taking up the whole west side of the second floor. Several boxes and a few pieces of dusty antique furniture that had seen better days were stacked in the corner. At the back of the room, there were three doorways, closets maybe, covered with gaudy red velvet drapes.

"What is this place?" he finally asked.

She gave him an impish smile. "Just a storage space now, but back in the early 1900s it was a bordello. There are stalls behind those curtains where the girls used to take their gentleman callers. And for an extra fee, you could watch while you were waiting your turn." Dropping his hand, she demonstrated how the little strip of wood on the wall swung up on a hinge to reveal a rectangle-shaped hole that would be about eye level for someone seated in a chair. All three stalls had the same peepshow feature.

"Why are you showing me this?" he said cautiously.

"Because." She held the curtain aside and peeked into the stall. "I think you owe me a proper goodbye." Looking back at him, she shrugged. "Unless you'd rather just shake my hand so I can get back to my date?"

Anders frowned as a primal feeling clawed at his gut. He gritted his teeth and fought the urge to march downstairs and punch the guy in the face.

"Your choice," she said, and then disappeared inside the stall.

The cicadas in his stomach chattered louder. He was suddenly sweating like it was the hottest, stickiest summer night in Southern Alabama and lightheaded with an erection that was threatening to pop the zipper off his jeans. He reached for the curtain and followed her inside.

The three-by-four stall wasn't big enough for a cot. Instead, there was just a sturdy, counter high oak bench to the left. Molly perched on top of it with her legs crossed demurely. A whore she was not, but that didn't mean he wasn't willing to take her like one if that was what she wanted. On the wall behind her, a frosted window let in the moonlight and the glow of string lights from the restaurant below. The band had started playing again, and a steel drum rendition of Bellefonte's 'Jamaica Farewell' vibrated against the glass.

The bench was the perfect height for a customer to step right up and be served in perfect view of the peephole. There was a wide narrow stool in the corner of the small space, possibly intended for a lady to kneel upon while performing fellatio. Unable to handle the provocative images that thought called to mind, he shoved them aside and faced Molly with a mixture of anticipation, uncertainty, and rapidly escalating need.

"Good call." She grinned and unfolded her legs.

When she reached for him, he stepped between her spread thighs and kissed her with the desperation of a man struggling for his next breath. He was drowning and she held him under, her fingers in his hair, her breasts pillowed against his chest, her nipples hard as marbles. He tilted his head, his tongue delving deeper, scraping against hers as he pressed his erection against her soft, wet warmth. When she dug her fingernails into his shoulders and groaned, he melted like a candle in an inferno. Undulating his hips with the frantic need to be inside her, he felt the pressure building at the base of his spine and yanked back, putting some space between them to slow himself down.

Struggling to catch his breath, he rested his forehead against hers and cupped her face. "You sure you want to do this here? In a whorehouse?"

"A former whorehouse. And, hell yeah. Doesn't it turn you on a little bit?"

"You turn me on."

She kissed him again. A slow, deep kiss that left his head spinning and his heart pounding against his chest like it was trying to break free. He was seeing spots before his eyes and knew that was because every ounce of blood in his head had pooled into his groin. He reached down to pop the button on his fly and lower the zipper to ease some of the pressure.

"I need you." Molly's blue-gray eyes were dark as storm clouds and her face was soft with passion. "I need this. Before we say goodbye, take me like you mean it."

"Yes." He nodded, half delirious, and stepped back. Hooking his foot around the low stool in the corner, he dragged it over so it rested just below Molly's dangling feet. He pulled her down from her perch and placed her on the stool. "Turn around." While she obliged his husky command, he shoved his jeans and underwear down to his thighs.

She leaned forward over the bench, arching her back to present herself to him. Encased in the tight, clingy red fabric, her firm round ass was displayed to its best advantage. Unfastening his cuffs and a few buttons on his dress shirt, he pulled the sweaty garment over his head and tossed it aside. When he touched the backs of Molly's thighs, she gasped softly. He stepped closer, stroking the satiny smooth skin upward until he reached the hem of the obscenely short dress and slid his hands underneath to palm her ass. He was trembling with the urge to take her hard and fast, but it would be over too quickly and he didn't want that. He wanted to make it good for her. *Before we say goodbye.* Her words pinched a spot in the vicinity of his heart.

Using his thumb, he rubbed the damp crotch of her satin panties. She was ready for him. *Him.* Not the other guy. Her date could take a long hike off a short pier. Anders placed just a bit of pressure on the spot he knew would make her squirm. She groaned and pushed back on his hand.

"Please, Anders." Her husky voice was sexy as fuck. "I can't wait any longer."

His ass and thighs tightened in response and his erection lurched. Hooking his fingers around her panties, he lowered them until they pooled around her five-inch stilettos. She stepped out of the scrap of satin and kicked it to the side before arching her ass toward him again and encouraging him to continue.

He slipped his hands back under the hem of her dress and slid them over the luscious globes of her ass to grip her waist. When his erection bumped her opening, they both gasped, and Molly tensed beneath him, panting hard in breathy little wisps. He eased into her slick silky heat, reveling in the throaty groan she made as he slowly buried himself to the hilt. Taking just a moment to savor the way her tight body contracted around him, he withdrew and came back into her hard. When she whimpered, he came into her again and repeated the motion until he was pounding into her with mindless aggression. Molly braced her left hand on the bench and her right on the wall for stability as she drove back on him, matching his thrusts with a violence of her own, all the while mindlessly chanting, "Yes, yes, Oh, God, don't stop…"

He stopped as a sudden thought occurred to him. Buried deep inside her body, he rasped, "That bozo downstairs…"

Tossing her glorious red-gold mane over her shoulder, she looked back at him. "Why are you stopping?" She ground into him, trying to scratch her itch.

A surge of anger pounded in his temples. He grabbed her

hair, fisting the mass just shy of truly hurting her, to hold her still. "The one you're having dinner with, are you going to see him again?"

"What if I said yes?" She bit her bottom lip, taunting him with a raised eyebrow.

His gut lurched and jealousy ignited inside him like wildfire. He tightened his grip and thrust into her just once but so hard she grunted and gasped.

A dreamy smile spread across her face, and a dimple winked at him. "Why don't you try a little harder to make me forget him?"

Releasing her hair, he shifted his hands to her breasts and yanked the fabric down, tearing a seam. The full mounds spilled into his hands as he started moving inside her again. With his gut still burning with jealousy, he pounded into her with a madness that blinded him. Molly braced both hands on the frosted window, begging him not to stop.

She was his, damn it. *His.*

"Say my name." He rolled her swollen nipples between his fingers.

"Oh…"

"Say my name," he demanded, rubbing the hard nubs and enjoying the way they strained against his palms.

"Anders. Oh, God…"

His name on her lips tickled down his spine like a fingernail. His lower back tightened and his balls swelled. Molly was a live wire, writhing beneath him, electrified and hot to the touch. Reaching under her right arm, he braced her across the chest and pumped into her faster. Skin slapped against skin in an erotic echo of the bordello's past life. He was close. So close. She moaned and began to shatter in his arms, milking him and coercing him to follow. His own release gathered at the base of his spine and shot up his shaft. His muscles went weak and pure feral instinct took over until he was bumping and grinding against her, wringing out every last ounce of euphoric sensation.

Anders opened his eyes. A rectangle-shaped sliver of light was cast on the wall above his head. He thought nothing of it until it suddenly disappeared with a small click. The peephole. Had someone been watching them? Her date maybe? Had he come looking for her and gotten an eyeful? As twisted as the notion was, it gave Anders a smug sense of satisfaction. He wasn't proud of it, but there it was. He bumped his hips against Molly one last time and then reluctantly withdrew from her.

He stepped back as she straightened and took a moment to tuck her boobs back into her bodice. She pulled the hem of her skirt down last, and he was disappointed to lose the view. He pulled his jeans up and refastened them.

Still panting slightly from the exertion, she turned around on the stool. Her skin was flushed and dewy with sweat. She reached up to cup his cheek. "Thank you for everything, Anders. Take care of yourself." Her thumb stroked the healed scar on his right cheekbone and her eyes suddenly glistened with moisture.

Her touch made him feel powerful and weak at the same time. He wanted to dissolve into it. He wanted to run away from it. Before he could do either, she dropped her hand and stepped off the stool. She picked up her discarded pair of panties and slipped them on.

"Molly…"

"Please don't make this more difficult than it has to be." She grabbed her clutch purse from the floor and paused at the curtain. "Goodbye, Anders."

Molly wasn't dead. She was vibrant and beautiful and very much alive, but as Anders watched her go, he forgot to keep breathing. When the ache in his lungs became too unbearable, he gasped and leaned heavily on the bench, clutching his chest and shaking.

A good fifteen minutes passed before he was able to make his way back downstairs. Molly and her date were gone. The bus boy was cleaning their table. His bandmates looked like they were in no hurry to wrap up the evening. They were celebrating Tuck's birthday belatedly since they hadn't been together in May when he turned forty-nine. The party had been Anders' idea, but he was no longer in the mood to socialize. He stopped by the table to say his goodbyes.

"You sure you don't want the limo to give you a ride back?" Tuck said after ribbing him for going soft with old age when it came to partying.

"I'll walk. It's only a few blocks."

"You want to give Selena her cell back? She left it on the table." Tuck handed the phone to Anders.

"Where'd she go?"

Tuck shrugged. "Clarissa saw her leave."

Anders frowned. It wasn't like Selena to take off without her phone. "When?"

"Maybe twenty minutes ago." Clarissa sat beside her husband Ray, sipping a martini while he lounged in the seat beside her, absently tugging a lock of her long blonde hair. Clarissa glanced at him for verification. "That sound right?"

Ray shrugged. His eyes were hidden behind a pair of lightly tinted sunglasses. "Don't know. Don't care."

"It's all right. I'm sure I'll see her tomorrow. If she comes back for her phone tell her I have it."

"You still blowing us off for that kid's birthday party?" Ray asked. Besides being the band's drummer, he was also in charge of scheduling rehearsals. It was the reason they'd shown up in Key West. The band was eager to get back out on the road.

"I promised my boy I'd take him." Anders' gut tightened as he thought of Molly. She would be there. They'd see each other again. He wasn't leaving town yet. He hadn't told the guys he was thinking of postponing the tour until January, but he had to do it soon.

He had an appointment in the morning with a real estate agent to purchase a house just a couple blocks west of Duval Street in Old Town. A two-story traditional Old Key West style home, yellow with white trim and wrap-around porches on both floors. What sold him on the property had been the pool house, which the current owner, an opera singer, had renovated into a rehearsal space. The soundproof room could easily be converted into a recording studio and the two-bedroom apartment on the second floor used for guests.

The main house was built in 1936, but it had been renovated with modern, high-end finishes. Four bedrooms, four baths with an open floor plan. It was big but not too big. Perfect for a family of four with room to grow. Anders could afford something nicer, something on the water like the Linus' sprawling Spanish-style mansion, but he didn't need all of that to make him happy. And neither did Obie. Plus, Jimmy and Sophie lived in the neighborhood. He and Obie would enjoy having them close by.

He was buying the house to give his son a home.

That was the only reason.

CHAPTER THIRTY-THREE

"The party's in the backyard."

Molly conjured up a smile and followed the uniformed maid through the house toward the sound of music and laughter. If the number of cars packing the long driveway were any indication, half of Key West was at Casa Linus on that sunny, Saturday afternoon. It was kind of April to share her nineteenth birthday party with Cheyenne whose actual birthday was on Sunday. Just because Molly wanted to crawl into her PJs and sulk, she couldn't let either girl down by not making an appearance.

She was heartsick over the whole mess with Anders. She never meant to fall in love with him, but she had. He had feelings for her too, strong feelings, but for some reason he didn't want to acknowledge them. Maybe he was just afraid. She'd been scared of risking her heart again too, but telling Anders how she felt had been liberating. Now she could move forward with no regrets from her end, but she was still sad. Still wondering what might have been if he'd given them a chance. He might've eventually gotten past whatever was holding him back, but there were no guarantees. She needed some sofa time with a pint of Chunky Monkey and a cozy blanket to come to terms with the things that were beyond her control.

The maid led Molly to the large lanai where four dozen white-covered tables were decorated with multi-colored daisy centerpieces and dozens of matching balloons. A catering crew was prepping the dinner buffet. In the center of the room, between two gift tables, a gorgeous sheet cake large enough to feed a football team said *Happy Birthday, Cheyenne and April!*

Party guests milled about, both inside and out by the pool, faces Molly didn't recognize and doubted Cheyenne knew either. Trevor was there somewhere, and Molly was girding herself for the reunion. Sue and Oscar were coming by later, but Sophie and Jimmy were still on their honeymoon. Molly had seen the pictures Sophie posted on her Facebook page. Greece was stunning, and they were having a blast. Despite Cheyenne's lack of friends and family at the party, there was a table full of gifts addressed to her.

Molly tried not to tear up, but she was so moved by April's thoughtfulness. Putting Cheyenne's name first on the cake. Making sure she got just as many gifts as April did. Cheyenne had gotten used to not expecting much fuss for her birthday. Their celebrations were modest. Sometimes it was just the two of them and a cupcake because that was all Molly could afford. Her family didn't do gifts. There were just too many children and grandchildren for it to make sense. What April had done for Chey today was beyond special.

"Ma?" Cheyenne called as she dashed around a waiter to get to Molly. "You made it!"

"Oh, my goodness, this is incredible. I feel underdressed." Molly tugged on the T-shirt she wore with a pair of jean shorts as she glanced at a young woman walking by in black mini dress. "I thought the invitation said: 'casual pool party'."

"You're fine. You look great." Cheyenne glanced over her shoulder nervously and her long, skinny legs shifted from one navy blue Ked to the other. "Ma, um, Trevor's here."

Molly's smile faded. "I know. Where is he?"

"Hello, Molly."

At the sound of her name, her stomach took a dive. Trevor Schaffer was standing behind her holding a blue plastic cup. The last fourteen years had been good to him. His dark brown hair, the same shade as Cheyenne's, only had a few strands of gray. He was shorter than she recalled, but at 5'10", he still towered over her. He was still whip lean. Still boyishly handsome though the corners of his eyes had a few extra wrinkles. He wore a light blue dress shirt opened at the collar, no tie, and navy slacks with brown loafers. He wasn't smiling, but he wasn't frowning either.

"Trevor." She nodded, folding her arms across her chest and wishing she'd worn heels instead of sandals. "Glad you could make it."

He snorted softly. "You're a terrible liar."

"I'm trying to be polite." She glanced at Cheyenne, saw she was as tense as a mouse in a cat house, and squeezed her arm reassuringly. "Cheyenne tells me you're heading back to LA tonight." She and Molly hadn't had much of a chance to talk about how the reunion had gone, but Cheyenne had mentioned he didn't plan to stay the entire weekend.

"I have to attend a wedding in Sacramento with my wife, but I've invited Cheyenne to come and stay with us for a couple of months. We have a very prestigious prep school twenty minutes from our house. I think she would excel there if she gave it a try." He handed his cup to a passing waiter.

Molly focused on breathing in and out through her nose as her blood pressure spiked. "And what did she say?"

"She said she had to ask you."

Molly's gaze flickered to Cheyenne in surprise. A week ago,

Chey would've jumped at an opportunity like this, and Molly be damned. Was Cheyenne using her as an excuse to blow off her dad? The teenager was staring at a spot between them, her expression guarded.

Molly moistened her lips. "Well, then—"

"Before you bring custody into this," Trevor began, the tops of his ears turning red just like Cheyenne's did whenever she lost her temper. "Let me assure you, I consulted with one of the best family attorneys in the country. She advised me of my rights as Cheyenne's father. If I took you to court, there is a very strong chance you would lose."

It took every ounce of self-control Molly possessed not to launch herself at the self-righteous son-of-a-bitch. Not involving the police when Cheyenne had ended up in Jamaica might have been risky and dangerous, but Molly felt more certain than ever she'd made the right call. Trevor would've jumped at the opportunity to use the incident against her in court. Molly could have lost custody of Cheyenne altogether.

Trying hard not to cause a scene, Molly leaned forward and kept her voice low. "Is this why you came here? To ruin my daughter's birthday?"

"Our daughter," he corrected, not even attempting to be quiet. "You are so selfish, you know that? Did you ever stop to ask her what she wants? She contacted me, remember."

Cheyenne had bowed her head, but Molly could see her face was red.

She'd just been through a huge ordeal where she'd proven she was capable of using her brains and her instincts to survive on her own. But instead of being more confident and determined to spend time with Trevor, she was being remarkably quiet. Well, it looked like she was learning a valuable lesson. Put your fingers in the fire and you're gonna get burnt. Cheyenne had lit this match. She could put it out.

"You know what?" Molly rocked back on her heels, resting her hand on her hips. "I trust Cheyenne to do what's best for herself. If she wants to spend time with you, I'll support that. And if she wants to go to some fancy prep school, I'll support that too as long as you pay for it."

Trevor looked like he was getting ready to argue, but Molly had stolen his thunder. His eyes narrowed with suspicion. "What's the catch?"

"No catch. Cheyenne, you don't have to decide right this minute. You can let him know on Monday."

Cheyenne raised her chin and regarded Molly with wide, wary eyes.

"She'll be in touch with you, Trevor. Like I said, it's up to her."

Finally noticing the party guests who avidly watched the drama, he lowered his voice. "How will I know you won't tell her what to do?"

"Because she means it." Cheyenne turned to face her father, standing on Molly's side of the invisible line. "It's my decision. I've actually been thinking about your offer since you mentioned it last night, Trevor. It sounds great, but I like my school. As for visiting you, I think I'd like to take things slow and see what happens."

Trevor's expression was inscrutable. He nodded, glanced around the room, and sighed. "I just—I don't understand. It's a great school."

"She's made her decision, Trevor." Molly gave Cheyenne's shoulder a reassuring squeeze. "Trust her. I do." They exchanged smiles and Molly knew they were going to be all right.

Trevor's gaze was bleak. "I guess that's it then."

"The party's not over." Cheyenne touched his arm tentatively. "I'd like to introduce you to my friend, April. This is her house."

Molly held her breath, half wanting Trevor to be the cold,

self-centered jerk who'd walked out on her fourteen years ago and half wanting him to man up and accept the gift of a second chance Cheyenne was offering him.

His gaze flicked from Cheyenne's hand on his arm to Molly's face. She raised her eyebrows, daring him to make a choice.

He swallowed hard and then nodded slightly. "Sure. I'd be glad to meet her." He took Cheyenne's hand and they both looked at Molly.

"Ma?"

"Go on. I'll be fine." And she meant it.

The closing took a little longer than Anders expected because the real estate agent had brought the wrong keys. They had to wait for another agent to drop them off, but now the keys were in his hands and the house was his. After he saw both agents out, he sat on the plush chenille sofa, taking in his new living room. When his gaze landed on the forty-eight-inch flat screen, he decided that was the first thing that had to go. The couch was okay, but he was upgrading the TV.

When he married Greer, they'd lived in her house, a Malibu mansion on the beach, but this was Anders first home. He took a moment to savor that notion and liked the warm fuzzy feeling that settled in his belly. Obie was going to like it here. *Molly would like it too.* He ignored the little voice that whispered in the back of his brain and reached for his phone.

After shooting a quick text to Greenlee to let her know he was running late and would meet her and Obie at the party, he got up to close and lock the French doors that opened to the backyard.

The doorbell rang, drawing his head around. He wasn't expecting visitors. Slipping his phone back into its leather holster, he headed to the front of the house thinking one of the real estate agents had left something behind.

Selena was standing on his doorstep, which was odd because he hadn't mentioned the house to her. "What are you doing here, Fry?"

"Looking for you. I heard you have my phone."

"Yeah, but it's back at the condo."

"I'll get it later. We need to talk. Are you going to invite me in?" Dressed in black slacks and a dove gray blouse, she looked like her sharp, efficient self, but something was wrong. There was a slightly shell-shocked look in her eyes.

"Uh. Yeah. Come in." He stood back and let her pass. "Everything okay?"

When they reached the living room, she spun around. "When were you going to tell me about the house?"

Anders frowned. "Last time I checked, I didn't have to report to you."

She dropped her purse on the end table. "Does your manager know?"

"What's gotten into you lately?" Anders rested his hands on his hips, not liking Selena's audacity one bit. He'd always written off her presumptuousness as just a quirky personality trait, but she was really crossing the line coming to his home and demanding answers about something that was absolutely none of her business.

"Did you tell the band?" Not one iota of emotion flickered in her eyes. Her jaw was set and her shoulders were rigid.

Anders squeezed his fists in frustration. The woman was impossible. "I just closed on the house fifteen minutes ago. I haven't gotten around to mentioning it yet. And it doesn't matter, I'm still gonna finish the tour."

"How about Molly. Does she know?" Selena's voice wavered on Molly's name.

Anders' gut clenched. "What did you want to talk to me about, Fry?"

She reached into her purse and pulled out a magazine. "Can you read this article and let me know if you'd be willing to do a follow-up interview with the journalist. It will only take a few minutes."

"I reckon I can." Anders sighed. "But I need to be quick about it, Obie's waiting for me. Let me see it."

When Selena placed the open magazine on the coffee table, her hand trembled slightly. The woman was normally tense, but today she was as jumpy as a jackrabbit. A sad smile tugged at his lips because the silly metaphor made him think of Molly. God, he hoped she was still at the party. He wanted to see her and talk to her, if only for a few minutes. He missed the woman too damn much.

He forced himself to focus on the article. It was nothing new. Just more trash about his relationship with Casey Conway. He'd only gotten to the second paragraph when a metallic clicking noise crackled to life a foot from his left ear. His head came up, and he caught his reflection in the darkened television screen. Selena was standing close to him, holding something that looked like an oversized remote control. She shoved it against his neck.

Agonizing pain darted through his body. His muscles tensed and he lost control, jerking violently. He fell forward and landed hard on the floor between the coffee table and the couch an instant before everything went black.

Molly stopped a maid who was hustling past her with a dustpan and broom. "The line to the bathroom is ridiculous. Is there another one I could use?"

The frazzled woman pointed. "In the library. Through the living room and down the hall. The second door on the right."

"Thanks."

Molly was careful not to bump into anything as she cut through the living room. Everything was white from the marble furniture and the leather sofas to the accents and knickknacks. If it was her living room, that area rug would've been spotted with Merlot or spaghetti sauce within the first week. The house was gorgeous, but it was too big and pretentious for Molly's taste. She liked to wear high fashion not sit on it.

She found the door to the library and went inside.

"Wow," she whispered, tilting her head back to take in the room, which was open in the middle to the second floor. "Cheyenne would just die."

Packed with books, the white shelves on all four walls stretched to the ceiling. On the main floor, two white leather chairs with footrests sat at an angle facing an electric fireplace. The bathroom was to Molly's left next to a spiral staircase leading to a catwalk that wrapped around the room's perimeter mid-way up.

She had to get a picture of this for Cheyenne. After using the toilet, Molly snapped a few shots with her phone. Deciding she needed to get an aerial view too, she climbed the spiral staircase and made her way around the narrow walkway to find the best angle.

She'd taken two pictures when footsteps below made her freeze. How embarrassing would it be to get caught nosing around April's house like a poor relation? Molly stepped back, flattening herself against the wall.

Jonas came into the room. He was the last person Molly was expecting to see. Clad in black, he wore a holstered gun strapped across his chest. He carried a book under his arm. As he crossed the room to return the thick hardback to its place on the shelf, his tattoos peeked out of the back of his shirt collar. He didn't look like a reader, but he seemed even less like the type to go around tidying up after other people.

"You're back." April came into the room and closed the door.

Jonas turned around. The stony expression on his face slipped for a moment, displaying his surprise.

Molly stretched on her toes to peek at April. She wore a hot pink satin slip dress that clung loosely to her slender, curvy frame and a pair of matching platform heels. Her long, white-blonde hair was piled on top of her head in a sexy, careless up-do.

She stopped a few feet away from him. "I haven't seen you around the house since before I went to Paris."

He frowned. "Are you following me?"

The edge to his low, raspy voice made alarm bells go off in Molly's head.

"I was looking for my cat." April made a half-hearted effort to check the room. "He sneaks in here sometimes. My stepmom has a fit because he uses the books as scratching posts."

"He isn't here." Jonas started for the door, but she stepped into his path making him pull up short.

When they stared at each other a few seconds too long, Molly's heart stopped. *What are you doing, April?* Talk about putting your fingers in the fire. Jonas might be an ex-con or he might be a crazy special forces ninja. That didn't mean he wasn't dangerous. The last time Molly saw him, he'd killed a man. Seeing April and Jonas together was like watching a fluffy white kitten toy with a snarling wolf. At any moment, the beast was going to snap.

"You have a habit of disappearing on me." April twirled an escaped strand of blonde hair around her finger.

"Maybe you should take the hint."

Yes, please take the hint, April. Molly wanted to shout, but she forced herself to keep quiet. It wasn't her place to interfere. She glanced to her left and nearly jumped out of her skin when she saw a pair of blue eyes staring at her from the bookshelf near her head. A fat orange tabby cat was squeezed into a tight space. Removing her hand from her pounding heart, Molly gestured to the cat to be quiet. It blinked at her with disinterest, then put its head down and went back to sleep.

"I saw you return a book to the shelf." April gestured with her chin. "What were you reading?"

He ignored the question and started around her again.

"Wait." She grabbed his arm.

The touch was like a spark igniting an explosion. Jonas spun her around and slammed her up against the bookshelf hard enough to make some of the books on the higher shelves fall.

Molly's heart dropped and she started around the catwalk, intent on rescuing April. The next words out of the girl's mouth stopped her momentum.

"If you're going to manhandle me, you better be prepared to kiss me." A wry smile twisted April's lips. Pressed back against the bookshelf, she didn't appear the least bit frightened of the scowling assassin who pinned her arms, holding her immobile. She arched provocatively, offering her healthy, heaving bosom to his face.

Molly held her breath, waiting for the rabid dog to take the bait. Again, April and Jonas stared at each other a shade too long. Something crackled in the atmosphere around them. The tiny hairs on the back of Molly's arms stood on end and she shivered.

Jonas let go of April so abruptly she teetered sideways on her high heels before catching herself on the bookshelf. He left the room without looking back.

April stared after him, a disappointed frown wrinkling her brow. Then she sighed and followed him out the door.

Molly relaxed and finally remembered to breathe again.

Wow.

It wasn't Molly's place to give April Linus advice. The teenager was Molly's employee and her daughter's friend but, oh my goodness, somebody had to do it. April's stepmother certainly didn't set the best example for the girl. After all, she was the person to thank for the teenager's enormous breast implants.

Molly had never said anything about it out loud, even to Cheyenne, but Molly thought April's "birthday gift" from her stepmother had been wildly inappropriate for an eighteen-year-old girl. April was lovely. She didn't need cosmetic improvements to make her sexier or womanlier or whatever the motivation had been behind the boob job. April needed some unsolicited advice from a responsible adult about Jonas, and Molly was going to give it to her.

What would Anders think of this? She wanted to tell him what'd she'd just seen, but they didn't have that kind of relationship anymore. For all she knew, he was already halfway back to Nashville right now. She fought off a wave of sadness and made her way back down to the first floor.

Checking that the coast was clear, she slunk out of the library. She cut through the living room just as Philip Linus himself was coming down the open staircase.

"Miss MacBain, wonderful to see you. May I have a word before we join the party?" He met her in the foyer. Linus was a short, slender man of about fifty. Not handsome, but not ugly either. His dark brown hair was as neat and precise as the custom-fit gray business suit he wore. An invisible cloud of expensive cologne hovered around him.

"Uh, sure." She hated to admit, she was slightly intimidated by the real estate tycoon and surprised he knew her name.

He guided her back into the living room. "The incident that happened here a week ago. I know your daughter witnessed it. I wanted a chance to explain."

Alarm flickered in Molly's chest. She looked over her shoulder to make sure Trevor wasn't lingering within earshot. She lowered her voice, hoping Linus would follow suit. "You do?"

Linus nodded and his voice lowered a fraction. "The man who was killed—Richard Vanlith—he was a dear friend." Linus looked down as if his friend's death still pained him, but when he looked up again, his dark, wily eyes were clear. "Richard had stopped by that night unannounced, not an uncommon thing for him to do, but I had to cut the visit short because I was taking April on a surprise birthday trip to Paris. Because of the nature of Richard's business, he had enemies and Wade was hired to eliminate him. Unfortunately, your daughter witnessed the hit."

Something didn't ring true about his story. "I'm, uh, sorry for your loss."

"I thought you might be curious as to why the incident hasn't been publicized."

"I did wonder why I haven't heard anything about it in the news."

"That's because I asked the local police to keep the investigation quiet. I assume you didn't report your daughter's disappearance because you found her yourself and didn't want her involved in any more trouble?"

Molly looked over her shoulder again, nervously smoothing the front of her top. A small group of people chatted in the dining room on the other side of the entryway, but Trevor was nowhere in sight. "Yes, that was the reason. I'd still like to keep her out of it if that's all right with you?"

"I understand your concern. As a parent, I would do everything in my power to protect April and do what's best for her."

"I'm concerned about the people who hired the hitman. Do you think Cheyenne is still in danger?"

Linus shook his head negligently. "She's safe. Wade was trying to clean up after himself, but now it doesn't matter because he's dead." Molly must have appeared skeptical because he leaned closer and lowered his voice a bit more. "Look, I'm acquainted with the person who employed Wade for the hit, Ms. MacBain. He assured me he has no interest in hurting innocent children who pose no threat to his organization."

Was the word of a criminal even worth anything? She wasn't so sure, but she and Cheyenne couldn't live their lives looking over their shoulders. Molly felt queasy and relieved at the same time. "Have you told the police about all this?"

"It's not necessary. They've closed their case file on the investigation since the actual killer is dead. I sent one of my men to track Wade down and bring him back to the States so justice could be served, but there was a standoff in the Bahamas and my man was forced to shoot Wade in self-defense."

Did he really not know what went down in Nassau? Or was this just the version he'd told the police? Molly swallowed the lump in her throat as Linus took her hand and patted the back of it.

"I'm relieved you got your daughter back safely. Cheyenne is a lovely little girl and a good influence on my daughter. I approve of their friendship immensely."

Molly's cell phone chirped and vibrated in her purse with an incoming text message. She ignored it. "Thank you. For everything you've done, Mr. Linus. As long as my daughter is safe, I'm willing to follow your lead on this and put this whole mess behind us. And Cheyenne will do the same. I'll ask her not to mention anything to April about what happened."

Molly still sensed something off about Linus' story. Would the police really keep something like this on the down-low just because a rich guy asked them to? She guessed when you had enough money, you could do what you wanted however you wanted, and people didn't ask too many questions.

He squeezed her hand and then let it go. "I would appreciate that. I don't want to upset April. Richard was a dear friend to her mother as well." Linus' cell phone rang. He reached into the breast pocket of his coat to retrieve it. "I have to take this. Please excuse me and enjoy the party."

A little taken aback by his abrupt departure, Molly watched him head in the direction of the library. Then she remembered her own phone and the text message that had come in while they were talking. She pulled it out of her bag and swiped the screen.

The text was from Anders.

Her stomach lurched. Why was he texting her? She tapped on the message to open it and then grew impatient while it took a moment to load. It said: *Hey, Molly, closed on the house. How about you skip out on the party and help me christen the place like we did last night? ;) -A*

What the hell was he talking about? What house? Molly frowned. Did he buy a house? And why was he acting like everything was fine between them when that couldn't be farther from the truth?

She texted him back. *Where are you?*

The doorbell rang, and Molly only half noticed the maid who rushed to answer it. Greenlee Fiori, Obie's nanny, came through the door holding Obie's hand. Molly's heart thumped against her chest. So, Anders was still in town. Her relief was replaced by confusion. What kind of game was he playing? And why was he buying houses in Key West if he was supposed to be leaving town?

Obie's eyes widened behind his glasses when he saw her. "Molly," he shouted and ran into her arms, almost knocking her down.

"Hey, there, cowboy. I'm so glad to see you." She gave him a squeeze.

Her phone vibrated again. She glanced at it. A street address in Old Town. Nothing else.

"Hey, is your dad coming to the party?" She brushed the little boy's silky blond hair from his eyes. His bangs were getting too long.

Obie tilted his head back to look up at her. "He said he was. After his meeting."

Greenlee tucked the two birthday cards she was carrying under her arm. "He texted me a little while ago and said he was running late."

An uneasy feeling settled over Molly. Something was wrong. "Where is he now?"

Greenlee ignored her and leaned into the hall mirror to check her makeup.

Molly's chest tightened with impatience. She turned the phone around to show the girl the last text she received. "Is he here?"

Greenlee straightened away from the mirror and looked down at the phone. "How'd you get that address? He didn't want anyone to know."

"How long ago did he text you?"

Greenlee shrugged. "I don't know. Maybe a half hour ago."

Molly crossed her arms and nodded toward the Greenlee's phone. "Do me a favor and call him."

Obie must have sensed the tension in Molly because his brows knit with concern. Greenlee opened her mouth to argue but changed her mind when she saw the expression on the boy's face. She raised her phone and swiped the screen to light it up. "What do you want me to say if he answers?"

"See if he's all right and find out when he's coming to the party."

Greenlee dialed Anders' phone.

There was no answer.

Molly's stomach knotted. "Text him. Ask him to call you. Tell him it's an emergency. He knows you're with Obie, right?"

Greenlee looked at her like she was crazy. "You're trying to get me fired."

"This isn't about you. Please text him. Or give me your phone and let me do it."

"Have at it. I'm out." The teenager handed the phone to Molly.

There's an emergency with Obie, please call right away. She sent the text and waited. As the seconds ticked by, anticipation tightened the knots in her stomach until they were almost unbearable. She held both phones, her own phone in her right hand and Greenlee's in her left. Her focus was on Greenlee's phone.

The phone in her right hand buzzed.

Molly swiped the screen to read the message.

It was a text from Anders. *Hope you're on your way ;)*

CHAPTER THIRTY-FOUR

Molly flew across town in her old Kia Rio, grateful for the off-season and the noticeable lack of traffic. Her anxiety increased the closer she got to Old Town as she pieced the recent events together. Casey Conway was murdered in Anders' hotel room after a fake story about their engagement was leaked to the tabloids. Then, the night after Molly's supposed affair became tabloid fodder, Molly's stair step was greased and she almost broke her neck. That was no freak accident, and the snake had been suspicious too. Sue had been right about that though Molly hadn't wanted to believe it at the time. It was still too surreal to process, but the only conclusion she could come to was that she was being targeted by a psychopath obsessed with Anders.

Those texts weren't from him. She knew that in her gut. Someone must have stolen Anders' phone and they were trying to lure her to his new house.

Molly parked a block away and sat wondering if she should call the police. What would she say though? That she thought a stalker had broken into a house she didn't own? They'd probably hang up on her. She decided to check it out first but keep her phone ready to dial 911.

As she made her way around the corner, she stayed close to the line of six-foot-tall shrubbery that bordered the neighboring house. Her heart stopped when she saw Anders' car parked in the driveway. Was he in there? Was he in danger? An invisible rope linked to the knot in her chest tugged her toward the potential danger without thought to her own safety. She started for the house, determined to save him.

She was at the end of the neighbor's tree line when the front door opened and Selena came out. Molly ducked back, wedging herself between two fat shrubs. Anders' publicist crossed the street and climbed into the driver seat of a black sedan with tinted windows. The car looked familiar, but Molly was almost certain she hadn't seen Selena's rental before today. What was Selena doing there? Maybe Molly was wrong about everything and Anders wasn't in danger. Maybe he really was waiting for Molly to show up for a booty call.

No, that didn't feel right.

A moment later, Selena jerked the car away from the curb, squealing tires, as she drove up the street way too fast. Suddenly, Molly remembered where she'd seen the car before. The night of the wedding when Molly had been talking to Anders in front of Dixie's. The car had peeled away from the curb before the driver turned the corner like a madman. It was odd because Molly had felt like the driver had been watching them.

Had it been Selena that night? Was she the stalker? She'd made her dislike of Molly clear from the start, and she was in town when the incidents started. She'd also showed up uninvited in Jamaica and refused to leave town even after Anders told her to go. Could someone from Anders' trusted inner circle be Casey Conway's killer?

Molly's first impulse was to dash across the lawn and charge through the front door, but dread kept her feet rooted to the spot. What if this was a trap? What if Selena wasn't working alone? Molly really needed a peek inside the house. Making a decision, she sprinted across the lawn and crouched down beneath a window on the side of the house. The blinds on the first two windows were closed. She made her way down to the next window and peered through a two-inch opening into an office. There was no movement or noises coming from the house. A tiny flutter of panic compelled her to get on with it. She needed to stop wasting time and check the inside. There was no telling how long Selena would be gone. And if Anders was hurt—

No. Molly wouldn't think of that right now. He was fine. He had to be fine. Molly was Selena's target.

The front door was unlocked. After quietly letting herself in, she closed the door carefully and stood in the hall, listening to the sounds of the house. The soft hum of a refrigerator. The chatter of kids playing up the street. A lone dog barking in the neighborhood. Treading lightly on the rustic pine floor, she made her way down the center hall. She was almost to the living room when she heard a muffled groan. She froze, as her pulse leapt and her ears prickled, listening for the sound again.

Peeking around the corner, she saw the couch had been knocked crooked and the coffee table was shoved askew. Between the two, an unconscious man lay hog-tied with rope and a gag in his mouth.

"Oh, my God. Anders!" Molly ran to him and dropped to her knees. She set her cell phone on the floor so she could cup his face with both hands. He was breathing, but there was a nasty burn mark on his neck. *Christ, was Selena torturing him?* Molly tried untying his gag but ended up just pulling it over his head. "Anders. Wake up, honey. Please. Oh, God. Oh, God. Just wake up."

He moaned and then his beautiful, slanted blue eyes flickered open. "Molly?" he whispered, slightly dazed.

She smiled through her tears, and her heart soared with relief.

"I'm right here. Thank God, you're awake. What happened to you? What did she do to you?"

At first, Anders seemed bewildered by the question, but then something clicked and his eyes flared. "Selena! You've got to get out of here, Molly. I woke up once. Before she zapped me again with that fucking stun gun, she told me she sent you a text to get you here. It was Selena all along. She murdered Casey. She says you're next. She saw us having sex at the restaurant. I think it pushed her over the edge."

Fear tickled Molly's nerve endings, but the rage boiling in her blood was the stronger emotion. "The bitch can try to kill me, but I'm not going down without a fight. I saw her leave. Where do you think she went?"

"I don't know, but please, Molly. You have to get out of here and go for help. I can't lose you. Please go." He struggled to sit up, but hog-tied, his bound arms and legs pulled him back.

"Stay here," she said as if he had any other choice. She dashed into the kitchen, which was separated from the family room by a breakfast bar, and started opening drawers. Trembling with panic, she searched for something to cut him free. She was just taking a five-inch serrated utility knife from the drawer when the front door opened.

Selena was back.

Molly reached for her cell phone in her back pocket and realized she'd left it on the floor beside Anders. It was too late to go for it. Spotting the phone on the wall, she carefully closed the drawer and grabbed the receiver.

She dialed 911 as Selena's sensible pumps thumped against the hardwood floor, moving toward the living room. "Good news, I found my phone. It was on your nightstand. I also packed a bag for you for our trip."

"911. What's your emergency?"

Ducking behind the wall beside the breakfast bar, Molly tensed, praying Selena hadn't heard the operator's voice.

"What's this?" She came into the living room. "Do we have a visitor?"

Molly carefully placed the cordless phone receiver face up in a bowl of fake fruit on the breakfast bar.

Selena hadn't spotted her yet, but she knew Molly was in the house. "Took you long enough to get here. Maybe the sex wasn't as good as it looked."

Disgust festered in Molly's belly. She trembled with the urge to launch herself over the counter and choke the horrible woman.

"Leave her alone, Selena," Anders shouted. "You're not going to get away with this."

"I already am."

A strange sort of resolve spread through Molly's limbs like a good shot of whisky, steadying her nerves and clearing her mind. Jimmy's lecture on survival popped into her head. *When your life is threatened you should always high-tail it out of there, but if escape is impossible and death is imminent, you should fight. Find something in your surroundings to use as a weapon and fight.*

Molly readjusted her grip on the knife. Crouching down, she moved to the end of the breakfast bar and then stepped out from behind it and stood up. "He's right, Selena. You're not going to get away with Casey Conway's murder."

"Oh, there you are," Selena said pleasantly. Like she was having Molly over for tea.

Anders thrashed on the carpet, struggling against his bonds. "Molly, please. Don't—"

"Shut up or I'll zap you again." Selena pointed a stun gun at him and flicked it on, making it crackle with menace.

"I won't let you hurt him." Molly took an aggressive step forward, positioning herself in front of Anders. Her gaze was drawn to the pair of counter-height stools in front of the breakfast bar. They didn't look too heavy. She could use them as a weapon, if necessary.

Selena switched the stun gun off. "Bahama Mama." She read Molly's T-shirt. "What's that? A souvenir from your romantic rendezvous in Nassau?" Molly wore the white T-shirt she'd picked up in a tourist shop near Love Beach. Below the frozen drink name was a cartoon image of a redheaded 1940s pinup girl riding a blue marlin. Obie had said the girl looked like Molly so she bought the shirt.

"The wind didn't knock that glass off the counter." Molly's face flared with angry heat. "You threw it against the door."

Selena set her jaw but didn't deny it.

Molly snorted. "What kind of sad life must you have? Creeping around, spying on people, watching them make love like a filthy Peeping Tom?"

"Don't antagonize her, Molly." The warning in Anders' voice reigned Molly in, but it was too late. Selena was already spitting mad.

She switched the weapon back on. "You're going to fry until your insides are crispy."

Molly raised her knife and braced herself. "You made a mistake, Selena. You brought a stun gun to a knife fight."

Selena roared and rushed Molly. Throwing down the knife, Molly picked up a metal barstool and swung it at Selena. It whacked her in the side, throwing her off balance. The stun gun flew from her hand and landed on the couch. Molly didn't wait for Selena to recover. She dove at her waist, tackling her, and together they stumbled into the end table. The glass shell lamp tumbled off and shattered on the ground, scattering sea shells across the floor. Molly straddled Selena's hips and pinned her by the wrists as she struggled to overpower her. "Why did you kill Casey?" Molly shouted.

"Because that trashy whore deserved to die." Selena tried to buck her off, but Molly grabbed her hair and channeled her fury to gather the strength to slam Selena's head against the floor. It didn't knock the woman out, but it made her stop fighting for a moment. Molly shifted, pressing her forearm into Selena's throat.

Selena grabbed a sea shell and stabbed at Molly with the sharp edge. It caught her just above the elbow and pain sliced through her arm. Selena used the opportunity to shove Molly off and scramble for the knife, which had slid into the kitchen and partially wedged itself under the refrigerator.

Molly dove for Selena and caught her feet. She tried to kick Molly off, but she held on. She had to win. Anders was counting on her. Cheyenne and Obie were counting on her too, even though they didn't know it. If Molly didn't stop Selena, two children would lose their parents. And Molly didn't want to think about Anders being killed because she'd failed him. His very life depended on her ability to hold Selena off long enough for the police to arrive. *Where the hell were the police?* "Did you really think eliminating the competition was going to help you win Anders?"

"I had to protect him." Selena lunged forward, gaining an inch, but Molly pressed her body weight down on the woman's legs to hold her back. Selena let out a frustrated growl. "I thought this was going to be another job babysitting a famous, self-absorbed jackass and covering up his blunders with the press, but Anders was different. He deserved better than a fame-grubbing slut who made sure everyone knew she was screwing him. And you, an attention-seeking groupie who used her fire-crotch to lure him to her bed."

Molly ignored the insult and shouted, "You admit you tried to kill me, Selena Fry?"

"Yes," Selena shouted back. "And I'm not done yet."

Keep talking. Molly hoped to God the 911 operator was still listening and taking notes.

"You're worse than Casey because you're nobody. Just a fan. But when he met you, he stopped listening to me. He was so smitten with you he couldn't see what you were really about. I had to protect him from you."

"So, you electrocuted him and tied him up? You realize, he'll never forgive you for this."

"I only did what I had to do. Once you're gone, his eyes will open and he'll be grateful. He'll apologize for telling me to go away. He'll thank me."

Molly almost felt sorry for the delusional woman. *Almost.* "And if he doesn't? What will you do? Will you kill him too?"

"If it comes to that. I'm prepared to protect him from himself if I have to."

"That's what I thought." Letting go of Selena's feet, Molly jumped up and dove for the stun gun, throwing herself onto the couch. She bounced off the cushion and tumbled to the floor.

Seeing her coming, Anders rolled closer to the couch's edge and broke her fall with his body.

"Thanks." She grinned at him.

"You're welcome." He grinned back. "Heads up."

Selena snarled, charging Molly with the knife above her head in striking position. Molly switched the stun gun on and pushed off Anders chest, launching herself forward. She made contact with Selena's stomach before the crazy woman could bring the knife down. Selena screeched and tensed up. The knife slipped from her hand as she vibrated like a jackhammer and collapsed to the ground. She lay there, not unconscious, but lacking the strength to move.

"It's over." Molly sank to her knees, exhausted and relieved it was finally, truly over.

"The police are here," Anders said an instant before chaos erupted and men and women in uniform flooded the house.

CHAPTER THIRTY-FIVE

Anders cradled Molly against his chest on the king-size bed in the master suite of his new home. It was late, well past midnight. She rested against his length, her arm draped across his waist, her head on his bare chest. He'd taken off his shirt to be more comfortable but kept his jeans on. She was still dressed.

The nightmare was finally over. Casey Conway's killer was in police custody and Molly was safe. He still couldn't believe it was Selena. He'd trusted her, let her travel alone with Obie for Christ's sake, and she'd tried to kill the woman he— His throat constricted and moisture burned the back of his eyes. He put his lips to the top of Molly's head and kissed her silky soft hair. Selena couldn't hurt anyone now.

When Molly was attacked and he could do nothing to help her, he'd felt like that powerless twelve-year-old kid again. Terrified and frustrated, he'd struggled against his bonds unable to save another woman he cared about. But Molly was nothing like his mother. She was a fighter. She might be small, but she was sturdy. And scrappy. She'd tackled the crazy bitch like an NFL linebacker. He smiled and snorted softly at the memory. He was safe now because of her. He would always be safe with Molly, and that thought gave him peace.

After Anders gave his statement to the police, he learned Molly had called 911 and left the phone off the hook so most of Selena's confession had been recorded. It was enough to put her away for a very long time, and she could even face the death penalty in the state of Nevada.

The paramedics on the scene had patched up the cut on Molly's arm and assured Anders he shouldn't have any residual effects from being zapped with the stun gun twice. They both declined the offer to be taken to the hospital for observation.

While the three-ring circus was still going on, they called their children, wanting to assure them everything was all right in case they heard something on the news. Cheyenne had already planned to spend the night at April's house, and Sue and Oscar offered to take Obie for the night.

Anders also called Guy Dougherty, the Las Vegas detective who was working the murder case. Dougherty had already been informed of Selena's arrest and had just finished speaking with Albert Everett Mooney, the guy who'd been arrested for stalking and poisoning Casey. When he spotted Selena's picture in the new photographic lineup, he cracked and confessed all. How she tricked him into putting the poison in Casey's food by telling him it was a tranquilizer. The creep thought it would knock Casey unconscious long enough for him to take a few pictures of her naked. He apparently had no idea it was strychnine and insisted he never intended to kill her. As dumb as he was depraved, Mooney would likely get manslaughter and a reduced sentence for cooperating with the police.

A part of Anders had wanted to blame himself for misleading Selena in some way, but Dougherty insisted none of this was Anders' fault. Selena was cracked because of mental illness or a personality disorder or possibly both, not because of anything

Anders had done wrong. He'd just been the unfortunate target of her obsession.

Well into the evening, after the last police cruiser had pulled away from the house, he and Molly had made their way upstairs to the master bedroom. Without putting much thought into it, they'd crawled into bed and collapsed from exhaustion. Anders had slept for a couple of hours, but he was way too wired to stay asleep.

Molly shifted, and he sensed she was waking up. Cupping her hip, he turned to face her as she opened her eyes.

"Hey." She smiled at him sleepily. "How do you feel?"

"Content." He smiled. "How's your cut?"

She looked at her arm as if she'd forgotten about it. "Fine. I didn't get to tell you before, but I'm glad you're okay."

He rested his forehead and against hers, and they laid there for a few minutes just holding each other. At length, he said, "Aren't you curious about the house? I reckon you know by now I bought it."

"I was wondering, but I figured it could wait until tomorrow. Mind if I get more comfortable?" Without waiting for his reply, she sat up and slid out of bed.

He knew he was supposed to look away, but he didn't. When she stepped out of her jean shorts and unhooked her bra, his mouth went dry.

"Do you, uh, mind if I get comfortable too?"

She slid the bra through the sleeve of her T-shirt before she climbed back into bed. "Go for it."

There was nothing sexual in that statement or her tone, but blood rushed to his groin.

He got up and shucked off his jeans. He was slightly aroused when he turned back to face the bed. When her gaze drifted over the crotch of his underwear, she didn't comment, but his erection lurched in response, and his gut tightened with anticipation.

He climbed into bed and opened his arms, inviting her back

for more cuddling. Despite what his body was so obviously craving, he just wanted to hold her. He'd liked waking up with Molly in his arms.

A wary expression came over her face, and she didn't move toward him. "What are we doing here, Anders?"

He didn't want to examine it too closely because if he was forced to put his feelings into words, he wasn't sure he'd be able to keep his shit together. He swallowed hard and gave her a teasing smile. "What comes naturally, I reckon."

"We agreed to go our separate ways—"

"No." The word leapt out of his mouth with the force of a cannonball.

She stared at him, mildly stunned.

He couldn't meet her eyes as he sat up and leaned back against the headboard. "I know what I said, but there was a lot I didn't say."

Molly waited patiently for him to continue.

He wet his lips. "Molly. You were amazing the way you went after Cheyenne in the Caribbean, intent on rescuing her and bringing her home. And earlier tonight, you proved again how brave and fearless you are. You make me laugh. You challenge me. You sing like an angel and you're sexy as hell. And you're beautiful, inside and out. I think I've just been scared of opening my heart to someone and then losing them like I lost my mama, but you're nothing like her and, turns out, walking away from you felt so much worse. I reckon what I'm trying to say is, I love you, Molly. I love you and I wanna marry you."

"Marry me?" Molly's auburn brows lifted in surprise, and then she frowned. "We hardly know each other."

"I don't have to hear a whole song before I know I'm gonna love it until the day I die."

"It's hardly the same."

His heart was on the table for her to do with as she pleased. If she rejected him, he didn't know how he was going to pick it up and move on. He straightened away from the headboard and slid closer to her. "We can have a long engagement if you need time to adjust to the idea of being husband and wife, but I want to move in together. Live in this house with Obie and Cheyenne. I bought it for us. I didn't want to admit that even to myself, but I bought it for the four of us."

For a moment, Molly just sat there looking uncertain and a bit bewildered. Then, she came up on her knees, put her arms around his neck, and kissed him. It was just a sweet and tender token of affection, but he was trembling when she pulled back slightly to cup his face. "Anders, I've loved you in some capacity for fifteen years—right now, part of me is jumping up and down and crying hysterically like a fangirl at her first Beatles concert—but this feels so fast. I don't know what to say."

"Say yes."

She didn't fight him when he guided her back on the bed and came down on top of her. As he settled between her thighs, he dug his fingers into her hair and kissed her the way he'd been longing to since the moment he'd woken from unconsciousness and found her hovering over him with tears in her eyes. Breathless and burning for her, he placed butterfly kisses along her jawline until he reached her ear. "Marry me. I'm gonna keep asking until you say yes."

He needed a shave and his dark blond hair was mussed way beyond its typical mild disarray, but he took Molly's breath away. Anders was hers for the taking if she was brave enough to reach for him. Only a thin bedsheet and a couple of scraps of clothing separated their bodies. He was hard and pulsing against her inner thigh. She nipped at his chin. "Roll over."

A sly smile tugged at the corner of his mouth. "You can't distract me that easily," he said but rolled over anyway.

Molly's head spun with nervous excitement. Was this really happening? A few hours ago, she thought she'd never see him again. Now he was touching her and kissing her. And, oh my Lord, begging to marry her.

Sitting up, she peeled her panties off, while under the sheet, he kicked off his briefs and tossed them aside. She was already wet and throbbing for him when she tugged down the sheet and straddled his hips. When she sank down on his erection, they both gasped and froze. Molly was immobilized as pure, unadulterated pleasure soared through her body. Zapped of her strength, she caught herself on his bare chest.

"Molly, please," he panted, sounding delirious and desperate.

Could it be that he actually felt this exquisite connection between them too? Their bodies seemed to know they were made for each other even if their hearts were slow to get with the program.

Perched on top of him, with his body pulsing deep inside of hers, she reached for the hem of her T-shirt and pulled it up over her head. The air-conditioned room brought goose bumps to her overheated flesh and made her nipples pebble. Her head fell back as she began to move on him, riding him at a smooth easy canter. His hands slid up her torso, over her ribcage, and covered her breasts, squeezing them with appreciation before slipping around to her backside. As she bent to kiss his mouth, her hard nipples skimmed the rough hairs on his chest, creating a whole different kind of friction.

Plunging his fingers into her hair, he broke the kiss but held her face inches from his own. "I love you so much, Molly MacBain. Say yes."

She stared into his slanted blue eyes and her heart constricted. The life and love she'd always wanted were hers if she was brave enough to accept his offer. Closing her eyes, she started moving on him again, riding him harder, demanding he follow.

"Say yes," he begged as he cupped her ass and he drove into her, giving her what she needed.

When his urgent thrusts hit a sweet spot, she saw stars and lost her rhythm. "Oh, God…"

"Say yes, Molly. Say yes…" He was relentless.

Her lower belly fluttered and contracted, and her climax bloomed languidly before it spiraled out of control.

"Molly…"

"Yes. I'll marry you…" she gasped and dissolved into a silent white void.

Sometime later, Molly woke to the sound of an acoustic guitar strumming softly. Anders sat in the window seat, picking a tune. He wore his boxers but nothing else. The whole scenario looked like something her vivid imagination might have dreamed up, but it was real. He was real. And he loved her just as much as she loved him. The notion made her heart swell with happiness.

He must have felt her watching because he stopped playing and looked over at the bed. "Did I wake you?"

She shook her head at first because she was too choked up to speak. Blinking the tears from her eyes, she leaned up on her elbows. "It's okay. What were you playing?"

He got up and carried his guitar to the bed. "I've had this tune floating around in my head for the past few days. I was just putting some words to it."

She held the sheet up as he slid into bed beside her. When he started to put the guitar on the floor, she stopped him. "No, wait. I want to hear it."

"It's a little rough."

"I don't mind. I'd love to hear one of your songs in the early stages. Where did you get the guitar anyhow?"

"It was hanging on the wall in the office. Intended as a decoration, I reckon. It's nothing fancy, but it sounds good. You sure you want to hear the song?"

"Yes."

"All right then. It's called 'Your Smile'." His gaze dropped to her mouth and he bent to kiss her lips.

With tendrils of excitement curling in her tummy, she propped herself up against a couple of pillows and settled in to listen.

The pretty melody was soft and easy. The tempo slow. Anders started in a key that favored his lower register. His voice was deep and pure, with just that hint of heartache that always got her right between the ribs.

I was living life, livin' large
touring with my band
Another Sunday, another sad song
I was a phony, lonely man

I had it all but one fall
threw me around the bend
I was just looking for a good time
but what I found was a friend

And all the while your smile
was right here in front of me
I'd drive for miles, sail the Nile
Fly across the sea…
For your smile

Anders glanced over at her with an intense, almost insecure gaze. Molly ached to launch herself at him and kiss him senseless, but she didn't want him to stop singing. Anders Ostergaard had written a song for her. Dagnabit, there was no backing out of the marriage proposal now, even if she'd wanted to. She was a goner. Head over Louboutins in love with this man.

Sitting up, she pulled the sheet with her to cover her nakedness and curled her arms around her knees. Swiping a tear away from her cheek, she sniffled and grinned at him.

Looking for nothing, looking for something
    Not looking in the right direction
    But you were here standing there
    Pretty damn close to perfection

Your red hair, the way you care
    you sparked a fire in my heart
    I couldn't resist you, had to kiss you
    I shoulda seen it from the start

And all the while your smile
    was right here in front of me
    Had to walk a mile in denial
    And set myself free…
    For your smile

He shifted to face her, and then he was singing the chorus. Growing more passionate in his playing as he dug into the song.

And all the while your smile
    was right here in front of me
    I'd drive for miles, sail the Nile
    Fly across the sea…

For your smile

He paused, playing softer now. He finished quietly.

I'll always come back…
For your smile

"Well? What do you think?" He set the guitar aside and then leaned back on the pillows.

Molly let out a laugh through her tears. "I think that was the most beautiful thing I ever heard in my life."

"It's not finished yet. It could use one more verse, and it'll sound better with a full band behind it. Maybe some—"

"Old school steel guitar?"

"Yeah." He grinned.

She couldn't hold back any longer. She launched herself at him and kissed the sexy column of his throat before she settled on top of him and propped herself up on his chest. Gazing at his face, she toyed with his hair, curling one of the thick wavy locks around her finger. "What are you thinking?"

The deep rumble of his voice made her belly hum. "I was thinking maybe we could write that last verse together."

EPILOGUE

Six weeks later...

The little bell above the shop door rang as a customer came inside, letting in a blast of sweltering August heat. Molly didn't look up from her computer screen. She was just about to place a book order, and the internet was being wonky. "Good morning! Let me know if I can help y'all with anything."

"Actually, I was hoping you could recommend a good book about golf."

Molly was about to tell the guy she didn't sell non-fiction when she dragged her gaze away from the screen to find Jeff, the IT specialist she'd dated back in June, grinning at her.

"Hey, what are you doing here?" she exclaimed with surprise and came around the counter to give him a hug.

"I was walking past the shop and thought I'd stop in to say hello." He was wearing a golf shirt and slacks, looking like he'd just stepped off the course.

"Playing hooky on a school day?"

He smiled a bit shyly. "After our last date, I got to thinking. You followed your passion and found a way to play music even if it wasn't the most sensible career choice."

Molly frowned slightly, unsure of where he was going with this, but she was willing to hear him out.

"I figured if you could do it, why couldn't I? So, I quit my IT job and started working at a country club full time. I've only been there a month, but I've already met someone. She's another golf pro like me."

Molly's chest tightened with genuine happiness for the man. She squeezed his arm. "That's great news, Jeff. Good for you."

"Thanks. If you ever want a lesson, here's my card." He gave it to her and they walked to the front of the store together.

"I'm so glad you came by." She stopped short when she spotted Anders and Obie sitting on the bench seat that Cheyenne usually occupied. Obie was reading a comic book and Anders was sitting beside him. His gaze lifted to Molly's as she came closer.

Jeff seemed oblivious to the fact a celebrity was sitting three feet away from him. Even people who didn't listen to Anders' music, still usually went a little gaga when they recognized him. The golf pro just glanced at Anders and kept going.

"When did you get here?" Molly stood in front of her fiancé when Jeff left the shop.

He quirked an eyebrow. "Should I be worried?"

Molly snorted. "Do you really have to ask? What have you got there, cowboy? A new comic book?" She kissed Obie on the top of his head and draped an arm across his father's broad shoulders.

Anders' big hand settled on her hip and they shared a secret smile.

Obie turned the book around to show Molly. "This one's from Cheyenne's personal collection. She said I could borrow it."

"She must really love you, kid. She won't even let me hold those books, let alone read them."

Obie smiled. "I love her too."

Their little family had been living together in their new home for two weeks now. Molly and Anders had decided to redecorate and remodel the house before they moved in. It barely looked like the same place Selena Fry had invaded, attempting to take them both hostage. Selena was like a bad dream now, fuzzy and less frightening with each passing day because she couldn't hurt them anymore.

"So, what are you two doing here? Aren't you supposed to be producing a record or something?" She rubbed Anders' shoulder, glad to see him in the middle of a workday.

"The boys are banging out a new song right now. I thought I'd stop hovering and let them work it out on their own."

Anders had renovated the soundproof room on the lower level of the pool house and turned it into a state-of-the-art recording studio. He'd already signed his first act. Four talented young men from northern Georgia called The Tallulah Falls Band. They were working on their first album for Anders' new Indie label. In September, he was taking the boys out with him on a two-month tour and was hoping to have at least an EP completed by then.

Anders met Obie's gaze. "You want to tell her or do you want me to tell her?"

The little boy thought about it for a minute. "You tell her."

"Tell me what?" Molly said cautiously, unsure if she should be worried.

"We have news." Anders shifted his leg so she could sit on his lap. The bench was tight, but they all fit. "Greer signed the agreement. I have physical custody of Obie from here on out."

Hootin' with excitement, Molly jumped out of her seat then sat back down again. "Oh, that's wonderful news!" She squeezed Anders neck and kissed his cheek before doing the same to Obie. The little boy had a grin that wouldn't quit. "We need to celebrate. I wish Cheyenne was here. She's gonna be so happy."

Cheyenne had gone with Sophie and Jimmy to Miami to shop for baby stuff. Sophie had been almost four months pregnant on her wedding day. Since she was only just beginning to show, she and Jimmy had decided not to tell anyone the happy news until after they got back from their honeymoon. Their baby was due in November—a little girl they were planning to name Emilie Charlotte Panama after Jimmy's late mama. Sophie had already asked Cheyenne to be the baby's godmother.

"How about dinner tonight?" Anders said, giving his son a squeeze. "Obie's choice."

"Can we have a picnic on Uncle Jimmy's boat?" Obie jumped up from the seat so fast he knocked his glasses crooked. He paused to straighten them.

Anders' expression suddenly grew serious. "That's the other news I had."

Molly would've been worried this time if she hadn't noticed the smile he was fighting. "Go on. Obie looks like he's about to faint from the suspense."

Anders chuckled and kissed Molly on the lips. "I bought a boat."

Obie squealed and ran around in a little circle.

Molly laughed and kissed Anders smack on the lips. "You didn't have to do that." Gazing into his slanted blue eyes, she stroked his soft, bristly cheek tenderly. The enormous diamond on her left ring finger caught the light and sparkled. Her engagement ring was obnoxious and she absolutely loved it. "I adore you, you crazy man. Do you know that?"

"The boat was pocket change."

"You're going to spoil this family."

She squeaked in surprise as he dipped her backward. "It's my family to spoil," he insisted and kissed her again.

The bell above the door chimed.

"We're closed," Anders shouted over his shoulder and then attempted to pick up where they'd left off.

"It's me." April Linus stood just inside the door.

Obie stopped running, staggered a little, and waved at April.

"Let me up." Molly tapped Anders' shoulder and he reluctantly straightened her out. She shook off her slight dizziness as she stood up.

"I know I said I'd be late, but my tummy felt better after I ate something."

"I'm so glad you made it in," Molly said, relieved to see April. "We have to inventory those boxes in the back and I can't be here all night. I have a dinner date with a couple of handsome sailors."

"We're gonna head out." Anders stood and pointed to the comic book, reminding Obie not to forget it. The little boy ran over and picked it up. "See you tonight around five?"

"Four thirty. I'm looking forward to our dinner date."

"Me too." Anders bent down and kissed her quickly, but it still set off a firework in her belly. "Love you."

"Love you too." She wanted to pull him back for another kiss but settled for checking out his butt as he headed for the exit.

"See you, April." Catching Molly looking, he gave her a lascivious wink before he followed Obie out the door.

God, how she loved that man.

Following April to the back of the shop, Molly was still grinning to herself when she slid onto the stool in front of the computer. April stopped on the opposite side of the counter. When Molly glanced up from the screen, April's bright, sunny smile faded. She hadn't been dolling herself up in her hoochie mama clothes lately, and she looked younger than her nineteen years.

Molly wished she could take credit for the change in April, but she'd never gotten around to talking to her about Jonas. It didn't seem necessary now that he was gone. Anders had stopped by Casa Linus the day after the birthday party hoping to talk to his brother and that was when he learned Jonas had left town permanently.

April was dressed conservatively in a boxy peach top, black Capri leggings, and white Keds that Molly was pretty certain belonged to Cheyenne.

"What's wrong, sugar?" Molly retrieved her venti mocha from behind the counter and savored a sip.

April took a deep breath and lifted her chin. "I was wondering if the assistant store manager position is still available?"

"Sure," Molly said carefully. "It's full time though. Are you interested?"

"Yes."

"I've always said the position is yours if you want it, but why the change of heart?"

April looked down at the floor and shrugged. "I've been thinking it's time I learn how to take on more responsibility. I'm a grown woman now."

Molly hid her smile and leaned against the counter. "You don't have to work if you don't want to. You're an heiress."

"Not anymore."

About to take another sip of coffee, Molly changed direction and set her cup down.

April's chin quivered, but she pressed her lips together, battling whatever she was holding inside.

"What happened, April? Did your father throw you out?"

"Not yet, but he's going to. He'll try to send me to Switzerland or something, but I won't go. Key West is my home."

This couldn't be about Jonas. The last time they were together, he spurned April's advances and he'd been gone for weeks since then. Maybe it was the other boy? Damian Rios? Cheyenne had told Molly about his banishment to Tampa. "Is this about that young man your father said you couldn't see? Cheyenne told me you spent some time with him back in June while he was here visiting his family."

"Damian and I are friends."

Molly raised an eyebrow. "Just friends?"

April glanced away and didn't answer.

She was obviously hiding something about the boy.

Molly cared about April. It suddenly occurred to her how she might be able to help. "Do you need a place to live? We were gonna keep the apartment above our pool house open for guests, but I'm sure Anders would let you use it. You'd be within walking distance to work."

April's head came up, and this time happy tears sprung to her eyes. "Do you really mean it?" She grabbed Molly's arm and squeezed it excitedly.

"I mean it, but you have to tell me what's going on. Why do you think your daddy's going to send you away?"

Bowing her head, April nodded as if coming to a decision. She sniffled and scratched the tip of her nose. Then she squared her shoulders and let out a deep breath before meeting Molly's eyes. "I'm pregnant."

THE KEY WEST ESCAPE SERIES CONTINUES WITH PASSION PUNCH AVAILABLE 2019 - PREORDER TODAY!

A NEW TITLE FROM

FIREFLY HILL PRESS

COVER COMING SOON

PASSION PUNCH

When April Linus discovers she's pregnant, the pampered hotel heiress walks away from her trust fund to protect her child and the identity of her baby daddy from her criminal father. But single motherhood isn't easy. Keeping her secrets stowed away tightly, she navigates through some rough seas alone and manages to build a new life for herself. Now, two men from her past are back in Key West wanting to rock the boat...

One wants to rekindle their high school romance.
The other wants to put her father in prison.

Black Ops operative Jonas Ostergaard made a nearly fatal mistake four years ago. He let April distract him from his mission. After working his way into her father's circle of trust, Jonas was yanked off the job by his superiors and reassigned. Now he's back to finish what he started, even if that means having to work up close and personal with the one woman who has the power to bring him to his knees.

When Jonas persuades April to help him stop her father from selling a dangerous new technology to a corrupt foreign government, they end up on the run dodging arms dealers in the steamy Amazon rain forest. They quickly learn that together, they can fight anything except for their smoldering attraction to each other.

But April starts to wonder what kind of relationship she could have with a man who may have more secrets that she has. Jonas disappeared on her once, what's to stop him from doing it again?

One thing she knows for certain, none of it will matter if they don't get out of the jungle alive.

REVIEW REQUEST

Dear Reader,

Reviews are like currency to any author – actually, even better! As they help to get our books noticed by even more readers, we would be so grateful if you would take a moment to review this book on Amazon, Goodreads, iBooks - wherever - and feel free to share it on social media!

We're not asking for any special favors – honest reviews would be perfect. They also don't need to be long or in-depth, just a few of your thoughts would be so appreciated.

Thank you greatly from the bottom of our hearts. For your time, for your support, and for being a part of our reading community. We couldn't do it without you – nor would we want to!

~ Our Firefly Hill Press Family

ACKNOWLEDGMENTS

This book would not have been possible without the support and encouragement of Danielle Modafferi. Thank you for believing in me and my writing. I can't express how grateful I am for the opportunities you've given me.

Thank you to my amazing editor Lola Dodge whose guidance helped shaped this book into something I'm really proud of. I literally could not have written *Bahama Mama* without you.

Thank you to Aileen Latcham for your words of encouragement and for giving me the opportunity to fulfill my dream of being a published author.

Thank you to my friends and family for your constant support and patience, especially when I disappeared into my writing cave for hours on end to work.

And thank you to my friends in the Outlander fandom. The idea for this book was inspired by my own experience as a fangirl to a certain someone, *ahem* (Sam Heughan.) I'd like to add another dedication to you, my fellow fan-girls. Never stop daydreaming...

ABOUT THE AUTHOR

 Tricia Leedom enjoys traveling to exotic destinations and having torrid love affairs with hot, dangerous men... even if it's only in her own mind. When she's not writing romantic adventure novels, she reads voraciously, tweets compulsively, and fangirls over a TV show based on the Outlander book series. She earned her BA in Creative Writing from the The University of Tampa and her MFA in Writing Popular Fiction from Seton Hill University. Tricia enjoys funny hashtags, cheap airfare, and fan-girling over a TV show based on her favorite book series. She lives in Southwest Florida with two very spoiled dogs.

Follow Tricia on Twitter and Instagram @tricialeedom

And keep up to date on all of Tricia's future releases, book bargains, sneak peeks, giveaways, special offers, & so much more by subscribing to our newsletter! Join our Firefly Hill family!

ONE S'MORE SUMMER: BOOK ONE OF THE CAMPFIRE SERIES

Author: Beth Merlin

Genre: Chick Lit/Romance

CHAPTER ONE

Standing at the stop, waiting for the camp bus, I was amazed by just how little had changed in the almost fifteen years since I was a camper. To my left were the kids who couldn't stop crying. To my right, the ones far too cool to stand anywhere near their parents. Then, the most recognizable group of all—the teenage girls who stood sizing each other up to determine who would be their fiercest competition for male attention over the summer. I took a deep breath and pulled out the clipboard listing the campers who would be on my bus. I put the whistle I'd been given at orientation around my neck and pushed my way through the crowd of duffle bags, trunks, and families. I felt a tap on my shoulder. I turned around and found myself face-to-face with a girl younger than me, but definitely older than the surrounding campers.

"Are you the bus counselor?" she asked. I nodded and extended my hand, which she didn't shake. "I'm Tara, your CIT," she said coolly. "CIT? Oh, right, my Counselor in Training. I'm Gigi, head

counselor of the Cedar girls." "You look young to be head counselor. How old are you?"

I looked down at my out t of jeans, Converse sneakers, and a Camp Chinooka T-shirt. No wonder she thought I looked young. I couldn't remember the last time I wasn't in stiletto heels.

"I'm twenty-seven," I answered.

"Wow, you're actually *old*," she said, completely unaware of how rude she was being.

"Excuse me. I'm going to go start rallying the troops now," I said.

I climbed onto one of the trunks and blew my whistle. "My name's Gigi Goldstein. I'm head counselor for the Cedar girls, so hi all," I said, giving a little wave. "We're going to start boarding the buses in just a few minutes, so I need everyone to make sure their bags have been loaded on. If you have any special medications you need for the bus ride, keep those separate, and make sure a parent hands them to me before we leave. I'll be right here checking off names, so start making a line."

The older kids rushed to the front of the line, anxious to board and get their first taste of summer independence. I couldn't believe how much older thirteen looked now than when I was that age. The girls looked like mini versions of my twenty-something friends, decked out in trendy clothes and talking about which boys they were going to hook up with over the summer. When the campers had finished filling the bus, I spotted Tara still on her phone.

"Hey, Tara, we're gonna get going," I said, motioning for her to hang up.

"One sec," she called back to me from the curb. "I'm saying goodbye to my boyfriend. We get, like, no reception up at camp. I don't know when I'll speak to him again."

Though I knew how important that last phone call was to a seventeen-year-old who thought being apart for the summer meant the same thing as being apart forever, I snickered at the dramatics of it. Forever was knowing the one man you'd ever loved was getting married to your best friend in just two months. Now *that* was worth some dramatics.

When Tara finally climbed on the bus and mouthed the words 'thank you' to me, I knew I'd just made an ally, if only for the three-hour trip we had in front of us. I settled into my seat closed my eyes and thought back to my very first summer at Camp Chinooka.

I was nine years old and had never been away from home before. My mother had dropped me off at the bus stop but left soon after to make it to her standing weekly facial appointment. Seeing me alone and upset, a girl wearing a faded Camp Chinooka T-shirt and a pair of cutoff Levi jean shorts had come over and introduced herself. Alicia Scheinman had shiny blonde hair, piercing green eyes, and a small smattering of freckles across her nose so perfectly placed you'd swear each one was individually applied with a tweezer. Based on the number of arriving campers who'd stopped to say hello to her, I could tell immediately she was one of the popular girls and I was grateful she'd decided to take me under her wing. By the time the bus came, I knew I'd made a good friend. By the time that first summer was over, I knew I'd made a lifelong one.

A few hours later and somewhere in the middle of the twenty-fifth round of '99 Bottles of Beer,' we finally passed the sign for the road to Camp Chinooka. Tara, who'd sulked most of the trip, perked up a bit and offered her assistance picking up the trash off the seats. When the last camper was off, I made my way out of the bus and was able to take a good look around.

Camp Chinooka had opened in the early 1900s and it still retained much of its original rustic quality. There were a few sports fields, a swimming pool that had been added about ten years ago, and several different cabins that housed activities like arts and crafts and woodworking. Down a large hill nestled the camp's namesake, Lake Chinooka. It was my favorite place at camp—maybe the whole world. I used to love sitting on the dock right as the sun was going down and the only sounds were the crickets in the trees and the wind hitting the sails of the docked boats. My whole childhood had been spent in New York City, and until I got to Camp Chinooka, I'd never known that kind of quiet even existed.

On the far side of the camp, past the amphitheater was The Canteen. The Canteen was an old barn that had been converted into a recreational center. On the outside was a window where campers would line up to buy snacks and treats out of their summer allowance. On the inside, was a jukebox, old couches, and a crude bar that had been made by the head woodshop counselor sometime in the 1970s. It was a popular nighttime hangout for the counselors, who made good use of the bar...and the couches.

Some of the bunks had fresh coats of paint on them, and everything seemed just a little bit smaller. Really, though, so little had changed that I could have been stepping off the bus fifteen years ago. As I continued to take in the surroundings, a man with the sexiest English accent I'd ever heard called out my name. I assumed he was part of the Camp America program, an organization that provided international staff to summer camps. The foreign counselors usually spent eight weeks at camp, earning money so they could travel around the US when the summer session ended. When I was a camper all the girls developed huge crushes on the British counselors, who were always far more interesting and exotic than their American counterparts. Looking around at how all the girls were gazing at this guy, I could tell little had changed.

"I'm Georgica Goldstein," I answered, trying to raise my voice above the noise. I pushed my way through the crowd toward a twenty-something guy in khaki shorts wearing his Camp Chinooka T-shirt over a long-sleeved shirt. He had dark, curly hair being held back with a bandana and some of the longest eyelashes I'd ever seen. Across his face was the perfect amount of stubble, making me wonder if he was trying to look cool or just couldn't be bothered to shave.

"I'm Perry Gillman," he said, juggling several things in his hand. "Head counselor for the Birch boys. Figured I should introduce myself."

"Great," I said, staring into his big brown eyes. "I'm Georgica, which I guess you already know. Everyone calls me Gigi."

"Nice to meet you," he replied, looking completely unruffled.

"I'm gonna start organizing the Cedar girls into bunks. I guess I'll see you around?"

"Without a doubt," he replied coolly.

As I walked away, I tripped over a pile of trunks and duffles, wiping out on the gravel in front of everyone.

Perry reached down to help me up. I stood up and brushed the dirt off my knees.

"Might want to pay closer attention to where you're going," he said.

"I'll keep that in mind," I muttered.

I hadn't handled the first introduction to my male equivalent for the summer particularly well. I was caught off guard by his looks and being back at camp, not to mention the number of adolescent girls gathering under the Cedar sign.

"Hi, everyone," I said, making my way toward them. "My name's Gigi. I'll be your head counselor this summer."

A few of the girls rolled their eyes and snickered. I tried not to focus on them, but I couldn't stop my hands from shaking. "I have your bunking assignments on this clipboard. Please listen carefully."

I heard one girl in the back of the group say, "Listen carefully," mimicking the sound of my voice. I wiped the sweat from my palms and swallowed hard. During my interview, the camp director had explained that head counselors were required to live in the bunk with the campers. I'd have a co-counselor and a CIT to handle some of the day-to-day stuff, but would be living right there with them, as a way to interact more with the girls.

I read off from the huge list of names organizing the campers, counselors and CIT's into different cabin assignments.

"Okay, last but not least, my bunk, Bunk Fourteen," I said, trying to rev up the remaining girls. "Your counselor is Jordana Singer. "I looked back down at the clipboard and realized that Tara was the only CIT not yet assigned.

"Lucky us, Tara Mann's our CIT," I said, smiling at her. "I need the following campers front and center: Emily Barnes, Hannah Davidson, Madison Gertstein, Alana Grif n, Jessica Jacoby, Lexie Simon, Rachel Stauber, Abby Wexel, and Emily Zegantz."

The girls settled themselves into a line and waited for their next set of instructions.

"Dinner's at six. Go to your bunks, get unpacked, and we'll meet in the Cedar horseshoe for roll call."

The girls took off running to make their claims for the bottom bunks and the best cubbies. I followed behind them with Jordana, who introduced herself as we walked. She was eighteen and going to be a freshman at Brown University in the fall. She'd been a camper at Chinooka and thought it would be fun to work as a counselor before going off to college. She had fair skin and really pretty straight red hair that was held back with a tortoise-shell headband. I could tell immediately we would get along.

"What's your story? Where do you go to school?" she asked as we walked toward the bunk.

"I'm not in college. I'm twenty-seven, actually," I answered. She repeated the number, understandably a little puzzled by it. "I know, a little old to be working here," I said. "Are you a teacher or something, with the summer off?" "No, I worked as a designer for Diane von Furstenberg up until a couple of weeks ago." "Wow," she said. "Don't be too impressed. I was downsized." It was a lie. I hadn't been downsized. I'd been red. In fact,

the minute Human Resource's number had flashed on my desk phone's caller ID, I knew what was coming. I'd been anticipating the moment for months, and when it finally happened, I had to admit I'd felt relieved.

I remember how I'd trudged down the long hallway to HR, and saw my boss waiting for me in one of the large glass-enclosed of offices. I'd offered him a weak smile as I sat down, so he'd know none of this was his fault. The HR rep had sat across from us and poured me a glass of water. She slid a box of tissues toward me and placed a manila folder containing what I was sure was my termination paperwork on the table. My boss spoke first, reciting a well-rehearsed speech about how painful the decision to let me go was. Then, the HR rep had launched into her part, rattling off information about COBRA coverage, applying for unemployment, and rolling over my 401K into a personal IRA. I didn't hear any of it. The voice in my head telling me I was a total failure had completely drowned her out.

Two years ago, I'd done something totally out of character and tried out for a new reality show, *Top Designer*, where fourteen contestants competed for a chance to show their collections during New York Fashion Week. Although I had no formal training, I was convinced I could take the fashion world by storm. While there were certainly far more talented people on the show, I believed I had something special—a sense of style that set my work and me apart. The judges had obviously agreed because I made it all the way to the finale. Although I wasn't the ultimate victor, I did win some money to start my own line and more importantly, Diane von Furstenberg had invited me to join their creative team.

I'd broken the news of my decision to be on *Top Designer* to my parents while we were sitting at Georgica Beach over Memorial Day weekend. Embarrassingly enough, I was actually named for that particular Hamptons beach. I like to tell people I was conceived during a particularly hot summer following a particularly dull display of Fourth of July reworks. The unfortunate truth was that my yuppie parents had hoped they'd one day be able to afford a piece of property in the East Hamptons and thought the name would prove inspiring. My grandfather had never approved of me being named after a Long Island beach (can you blame him?) and immediately started calling me "Gigi." Fortunately, like any good nickname, it had stuck. Thank God I didn't have siblings, or one might have had the misfortune of being named Martha's Vineyard, another of my parents' favorite summer vacation spots.

As predicted, my parents hadn't taken the news of my reality show stardom well. Although they'd offered to pay the entire cost of a law school education, they'd made it very clear they were not at all interested in contributing to what they saw as a "self- indulgent waste of time." So, I did what any headstrong twenty- something does when faced with what they believe is their own do-or-die moment. I moved out of my parents' apartment and in with my best friend, Alicia. I used every scrap of savings I had to cover my expenses while I was on the show and prayed that all of it would prove worthwhile. The day Diane von Furstenberg offered me a position, it seemed as though I was on my way. And the day they red me, everything had changed.

Thankfully, Jordana knew enough not to ask any follow-up questions relating to my former employer, but her next question was even worse.

"Boyfriend?" "No," I answered, without even the smallest

inflection. "You?" "I broke up with him a few weeks ago. I didn't want to be tied

down this summer. Good thing—there are some really cute counselors this year. Have you met Perry?"

"I just met him a few minutes ago—seems nice," I answered. "Not my taste, but definitely cute. Some girl will scoop him up." Before we even walked into the bunk I could already hear the

girls arguing over who got what bed and which cubby. Tara's voice was louder than all of them. I looked at Jordana and said, "Here we go." She nodded and pushed her way into the bunk, no easy task with clothes and trunks covering most of the floor. Finally inside, Jordana immediately went to open up some windows, while I took a good look around.

Five bunk beds lined the far wall with stacks of cubbies between each bed. On the opposite side were the two single beds meant for Jordana and me. I threw my bags down on the bed that had my name on it. I turned on the bathroom light and saw two sinks, two stalls, and another row of cubbies for toiletries and sheets. I'd forgotten there were no showers in the bunks. It was nice to see the camp retained some its original rustic qualities, but walking across the lawn, with nothing between the world and my bare behind but a towel... I shuddered at the thought.

Tara had the bottom bunk right across from us and was complaining about not getting a single to anyone who would listen. While the rest of the girls were settling in, making their beds, and hanging posters, I put my own things away.

First, I made up my bed, then turned the top of the cubby into an improvised nightstand. I set up an alarm clock, small lamp, and took out a framed picture of Alicia and me as campers at about the same age as the girls I was now in charge of. I stared at the two of us standing on the porch of the bunk, our hair pulled back with white bandanas, smiles from ear to ear. When one of the campers interrupted my trip down memory lane, I wiped the tears from my eyes.

"I'm Madison—Maddy," she said. She was a slightly over-weight girl in shorts and a T-shirt that were both a little too small on her.

"What can I do for you?" I asked.

"I don't have enough room to put away all of my things," she answered.

"Did you see the cubbies in the bathroom?" I said, pointing to the back of the bunk. "There should be two assigned to you."

She crossed her arms and spread her legs apart. "I already filled them."

"Well, how much more do you have to unpack? Maybe you can just refold some of it a little smaller?" I suggested.

She pointed toward her bed, which was covered in piles of clothes.

"Give me a few more minutes to finish getting settled, and then I'll come over to see what I can do."

She had stopped listening and picked up the picture frame off my nightstand. "Who are they?" she asked.

"I'm the one on the left, and the girl next to me is my friend, Alicia," I answered.

"No way that's you," she said. "I swear, that's me when I was about your age." "But you were ..." Her voice trailed off. I knew the word she was too polite to blurt out, so I said it for her. "Fat."

"Yeah, you were fat," she mumbled. Her eyes were wide open, and she was still staring at the picture. "Are you still friends with that other girl? She was so pretty. Is she still really pretty?"

"She is."

I took the picture back from Madison and looked at it. Instantly, I thought of how Alicia'd look with her hair elegantly slicked back into her wedding veil in a few weeks. More tears flooded my eyes as I imagined her standing there, alone, in her white dress, her parents delicately lifting up the veil and kissing their daughter on the cheek before escorting her down the aisle to meet Joshua. I wouldn't be there to see it.

I was going to *avoid* being there. What kind of person did that?

"So what about all of my stuff?" Madison whined, snapping me back to reality.

Jordana, seeing the tears rolling down my cheeks, came to my rescue.

"You're Maddy, right?" she asked, climbing over her bed to sit next to me on mine.

"Yeah?" Madison replied.

"Whatever you don't plan on wearing in the next couple of weeks, keep packed in your trunk, okay? Then, in a few weeks, rotate."

"I'll try it," Madison replied reluctantly.

Jordana put her arm around my shoulder. "Homesick already?" "Maybe," I replied.

"Pull it together. You're our fearless leader," she teased, trying to get me to smile.

I went into the bathroom and washed my face. When I came out, Jordana had all the girls sitting in a circle on the floor of the bunk so they could introduce themselves to one another. After I told them a bit about myself, I went outside to the horseshoe for roll call.

Within seconds of yelling "Roll call," almost fifty girls came streaming out from the five Cedar bunks, all of them raring to go. The counselors lined them up by bunk and then counted off.

When each counselor nodded to me that they had the appropriate number of campers, I took my cue to speak. This was my make-it-or-break-it moment. In the next few seconds, they would either see me as their friend, big sister, and mentor, or the person who stood in the way of them having a good time this summer. If it was the latter, their sole mission would be to get me to resign before the summer had even begun. Unfortunately, I knew this from personal experience.

"Before we head off to dinner, I just wanted to take a minute to say a few things. First off, if anyone has any problems or concerns, I want you to first talk to your counselor, but if you feel that what-ever it is isn't being addressed, my door is always open. Second, we're all here for the same reason—to have a good time and take advantage of everything that camp is about. We're here to make friends and memories, so let's try to work together and follow the rules, to ensure we have a great summer."

I was losing them. I sounded like every other patronizing adult I used to hate at their age. I quickly changed my approach. "A little birdie told that the Cedar girls haven't won the Gordy Award in over five years. Well, I don't know about you, but I think that it's our turn."

A few of them perked up. The Gordy Award, aptly named for Gordon Birnbaum, the camp's director for the last thirty-plus years, was given to the group that showed the most involvement and spirit during the summer. The winning group got to choose between a trip to Boston, Washington DC, or New York City and the competition usually got pretty heated. Birch had taken it the last few summers, and from what I'd heard on the bus, were intent on winning again this year. I wasn't about to let that happen.

My years of working in the corporate world had taught me that nothing bonds a group together faster than having a common goal, and even more than that, a common enemy. I'd become close with two colleagues when management hired a manipulative, tyrant-esque VP for our division whom we all hated. Our common disdain for him was the glue that forged our friendship, and getting him red had sealed it.

If I could divert Cedar's attention to Perry and his boys, pitting them as the enemy, I would, if even just by default, become their friend. It was a desperate tactic, but these girls were going to look for every possible way to get me to resign, just as I'd done to all of my head counselors when I was a camper.

At their age, Alicia and I had sneaked into our head counselor Mindy's bunk while she was sleeping, covering her in shaving cream, toothpaste, and whatever else we could and, just like the scene from the movie *The Parent Trap*. We hoped when she woke up, she'd be too preoccupied with the mess to notice that we'd sneaked over to the boys' side of camp.

We'd continued our barrage of practical jokes and torments through the first half of the summer until Mindy was so fed up she quit. In hindsight, I realized how awful and immature we'd acted just to have a few moments alone with the boys, but I was not about to let what happened to her happen to me. "I want to remind you ladies that if we win, we get a three-day trip to DC, Boston, or New York, not to mention bragging rights for the rest of the summer," I added. A few of the girls whispered to one another and I could tell I'd stirred up some excitement.

"So, I ask you, are we gonna win the Gordy this year?" I shouted in their direction. I heard a few girls grumble the word 'yes.' I raised my voice. "I can't hear you. I said, 'Are we gone win the Gordy this year?'"

A few more yelled out the word 'yes.' Jordana made eye contact with me and then nudged some of the quieter girls to speak up.

"Are we gonna kick the Birch boys' asses and take the Gordy?" I screamed out like a maniac.

They yelled the word "yes" at the tops of their lungs.

"Good. So now I want you all to repeat after me: We are Cedar, we couldn't be prouder, and if you can't hear us, we'll shout a little louder. We are Cedar, we couldn't be prouder, and if you can't hear us, we'll shout a little louder."

By the third verse, all the girls had joined in, and I started our march toward the dining hall. When the counselors saw my signal, they prompted the girls to follow. We headed to the Great

Lawn, screaming the chant, and continued cheering all the way into the dining hall. When we walked in, we had the attention of the entire room. Perry's eyes were fixed on me. He looked upset we'd already gotten the upper hand and made a beeline in my direction.

"Throwing your hat in the ring for the Gordy?" The girls were still screaming the cheer behind me. "Maybe?" I said, shrugging my shoulders. "You know Birch has won it for the last three summers," he said very matter-of-factly. "Yeah, I think I heard that somewhere," I replied. "Well, it'll be nice to have a worthy adversary for a change." "I'm guessing you're the one who led them to victory last year?" "Last year and the two years before," he answered. "I'm planning on continuing our streak this summer." "Whatever," I said, feeling a bit argumentative. "There's a new sheriff in town." "Rubbish," he answered. "Or, as you American girls say, *whatever*." "We don't say that. I mean, I just said *whatever*, but it's not a fair generalization." "*Whatever*," he teased. "Stop saying that. If you think Americans are such *rubbish*, why are you here?" "I'm working on my doctorate, so I have my summers off.

Although I have to put in some time on my thesis." Attractive or not, he was a little too self-satis ed. Before I could respond, Gordy made his way up to the microphone stand in the center of the room. I didn't know if it was the Chinooka air or water that preserved him, but he hadn't aged one bit. The entire room quieted, and he started to sing the Camp Chinooka alma mater into the microphone. Within seconds the rest of the room joined in. It was amazing how I remembered every word and every in direction, able to sing it effortlessly. When the song was over, Gordy welcomed us all to the centennial summer and invited everyone to enjoy the meal.

The first dinner at Chinooka was always a banquet, but after that, we'd be served cafeteria style for the rest of the summer. The food was just as inedible as I remembered. I picked at some roasted chicken and some lumpy, gray mashed potatoes before pushing the whole plate aside. After all the tables had been served, Gordy made his way back up to the podium to make other announcements. He talked about the new amenities that had been added over the winter, including the new dock and the inline skating rink. He let everyone know that the camp production would be *Fiddler on the Roof*, and because it was the camp's one-hundredth year, we'd be putting on a special performance of it in the newly built outdoor Lakeside Amphitheater. Then, he introduced some key staff and some of the other head counselors from the younger groups, Maple, Pine, Oak, and Elm.

When he got to Perry, I noticed all of the girls in my group whispering to each other. He was by far the best-looking staff member. When Gordy introduced me, I stood up and did a quick wave and the girls in my group cheered. Had I won them over with my spirit and promises of a Gordy victory? Maybe this wouldn't be so hard after all.

Who was I kidding? This whole thing was crazy. Who walked out of their life and went to work at their childhood sleepaway camp at twenty-seven years old? As Gordy finished introducing the last members of the waterfront staff, that answer became painfully clear—only someone with nothing left to lose.

Made in the USA
Columbia, SC
10 July 2018